Blue Suburban Skies

Lillie Holland

Blue Suburban Skies

Matador
9 De Montfort Mews
Leicester LE1 7FW, UK
Tel: (+44) 1858 468828 / 469898
Email: books@troubador.co.uk
Web: www.troubador.co.uk/matador

ISBN 1 899293 84 1

Typeset in 10pt Hoefler by Troubador Publishing Ltd, Market Harborough, UK

Matador is an imprint of Troubador Publishin

Prologue

Barbara was glad that her husband was away on business when the letter came. She had looked at the postmark on the envelope, mentally registering that she had no connections with that city. The writing was unfamiliar, neat and almost schoolgirlish. A short letter was enclosed, written on cheap notepaper. She walked into her sun-filled, well appointed kitchen to read it. The words seemed to jump out at her as she sat at the breakfast bar. For a few moments she felt unable to cope with the intense emotions which that letter had aroused.

With trembling hands she made a cup of coffee and took it into the drawing room. She read the letter again in that more elegant setting, trying to come to terms with the contents. Dazed with shock, she glanced round the room, as if to gain some comfort and security from the sight of familiar objects. The green and gold colour scheme was restful and charming, there were delicate watercolours hanging on the walls, and the long Georgian windows overlooked a large and well kept garden.

Barbara took a deep breath, inhaling the sweet scent of the Crimson Glory roses in the silver rose bowl, and made a mental note to change the water. Strange how domestic trivia could impinge on such a devastating moment. Suddenly she didn't want the coffee. She glanced through the letter again, as if she had missed something, knowing at the same time that nothing could alter those written words.

She had heard of this sort of thing happening. She had read articles about it, and even watched a television programme dealing with the subject. People nowadays seemed to want everything brought out into the open, and endlessly discussed...

She walked over to the window, staring through at the garden, without any real interest in the bright, beautiful glories of the July flowers. That letter, and how to deal with it, occupied her thoughts completely. She would look at the matter from every angle, and make a cool, sensible decision. While she was thinking this, the telephone rang. She answered it with some trepidation, which turned to relief when she heard the voice of Ruth Travers, a friend and neighbour.

'Hello, everything all right? Lovely morning, isn't it? I know that you're on your own for a couple of weeks, and I thought you might like to come round this afternoon, and we'll sit in the garden. I'm avoiding the town just now, too hot, full of tourists, and the sales are on, too. Unless of course, you have other plans.'

'No, I haven't. Thanks, I'll be round, Ruth. We won't be going on holiday until September, so meanwhile we can make the most of the sunshine we get here.'

After a few more words, Barbara replaced the receiver. She told herself that normality had returned to the day, although she knew that nothing would make it normal. Spending the afternoon with Ruth would help, though. They would chat about all manner of things, including their forthcoming holiday in Sorrento. Their respective husbands were good friends, too, and they were going to Italy as a foursome.

Barbara picked up the letter again. She would deal with it in the best way she could, as a woman in late middle age, she was not prepared to let anything interfere with the smooth running of her well ordered, conventional lifestyle. The past was the past, and it had nothing at all to do with the present, nothing at all. Yet even as Barbara reasoned with herself, she knew that the past had shaped the present, just as the present was now shaping the future. Pondering on this, she considered the changes which had taken place over the years.

Crimes of violence had increased, vandalism flourished, horror videos and drug addiction were commonplace now, and there was Aids. These were some of the bonuses which the years had brought, along with the mixed blessings of computers, the Internet, and mobile phones.

At one time people had smoked and eaten fried food without being made to feel guilty. Fur coats were worn fearlessly, and the hunting fraternity pursued their way of life without opposition. Back in the Sixties the powers-that-be had bulldozed the old terrace houses down, and put people into tower blocks, which the tenants had hated. Eventually a number of these "high rise" flats had been pulled down, many were unsafe, and had fallen into disrepair after a few years. Some enlightened councils had even built terrace houses to re-house the displaced occupants.

There was, of course, that other social problem, an evergrowing problem. It was something that politicians really didn't want to know about, Barbara reflected. When they came face to face with it, they were not too sure which way to jump, if they spoke out, would they stand to lose or gain more votes?

Ethnic minorities, Commonwealth citizens, British West Indians, Asian Communities, immigrants had a variety of gravely dignified names now. The word "coloured" might be used privately, but never by the "media".

People had to be either black or white, or they could be nonwhite, or mixed race. Not coloured, though. For some reason it was not politically correct, and a whole new industry had been built up around political correctness. It was pursued in some quarters with a zeal that bordered on fanaticism, like a sort of quasi-religion. Strange to think that a few politically incorrect words could cost someone their livelihood. How topsy-turvey life was.

She slipped the letter back into its envelope, as though that small act could somehow erase the shock and disbelief she had suffered, knowing all the time that it didn't make any difference. She had read the contents. Why not ignore them, anyway, tear the offending missive to shreds, and carry on as though she had never received it?

The temptation to do that was enormous. Why should she allow this bright summer day to be blighted by a letter? Old sayings and clichés ran through her head... let sleeping dogs lie... some things are better not known...

Yet even as Barbara reasoned with herself, her thoughts went back to that younger world, before the term "permissive society" had been coined. Deeply buried memories of the past came back to her with painful vividness. She sifted through the many layers of the years until she found again that beautiful, spoilt, wilful girl who had once been herself, as surely as she was now a shrewd, mature and cautious woman.

* * *

3

Chapter 1

1961

Of course, she knew that she was doing something quite exceptional and daring, by going along to meet him at all. She, Barbara Granger, was the only girl in the Lower Sixth Form at Parkleigh High School who had the nerve to do anything like this, anyway. She tried to imagine Judith Pringle doing it; Pringle, with her buck teeth and pop eyes. *She* would write her essay with the knowledge gleaned at her local library, no doubt. Well, there wasn't much about Trinidad at Fordham library, Barbara reflected, although there was plenty about the West Indies in general. However, she was also a member of Ruddersleigh Central Library, and she had called in there after school finished at four o'clock. Parkleigh was an old established residential area, located about two miles from the city centre, so it was easy to get a bus into the town from there.

The Central Library was an impressive place, situated within in the great Victorian Town Hall. Barbara managed to borrow a book which looked as if it might be useful. There wasn't time to find out what was in the Reference Library. Anyway, you couldn't take out any of those books on a ticket, you had to sit at one of the huge oaken tables, writing out notes from them.

She boarded a Fordham bus back from the city at a much later time than the usual one she caught outside the school at four fifteen. It was quite full, but she got a seat upstairs, and fished her bus pass out from her pocket. Then she rummaged in her school satchel for the borrowed book, and looked through the pages, frowning slightly. She became so absorbed that it was quite a surprise when they reached the terminus at Fordham, and she was the last to go down the stairs. The passengers inside had all alighted, and Barbara scrambled off the platform, dropping the library book in her haste. The young bus conductor picked it up and handed it to her, glancing at the title and the brightly illustrated jacket as he did so.

'Thank you,' said Barbara, slightly flustered. 'It's a library book, I must be more careful with it.'

'Is Trinidad,' said the conductor, smiling, 'I come from there.'

'Oh.' Barbara was rather surprised. He had an Indian look about him, finely modelled features, black wavy hair, and large dark eyes. But he came from Trinidad...

'I'm writing an essay about it.' Even as she spoke, she wondered why she told him that, instead of just taking the book and going. It was one thing to thank him, it was quite another to stand talking to him at Fordham bus terminus, but something held her there. An idea had flashed into her mind, an idea so startling that her heart began to beat faster with the sheer excitement of it.

While she hesitated, wanting to put the idea into words, but not daring to, young Louis Ramdeen of Bamboo Grove, Trinidad, stood looking at her. Excitement of a different sort rose in him, this lovely English girl with a skin so white, so fair, that he could see the little blue veins at her temples. He looked at the fall of loosely waving auburn hair, and into her eyes, the colour of the sea that rolled round his native island. At last Barbara found her voice, spurred on by the image of Pringle's sarcastic smile.

'I wonder – could you do me a favour?' she asked self-consciously, wondering how she had found the nerve to suggest what she was going to.

'A favour?' The young man looked puzzled.

'Could you tell me things about Trinidad? What it's really like, things I wouldn't find in books – everything about the island? It would help me so much.'

For a moment Louis was silent. Many things went on in Trinidad that were not found in books, and he couldn't see himself telling this English girl "everything about the island". But he could certainly tell her a great deal.

'M-mm, it possible. *Oui*,' he said cautiously. Clearly he was waiting for her to take the initiative, quite natural under the circumstances, but rather unnerving for Barbara.

'Could we arrange to meet somewhere? So I could take notes?'

6

'Well, where we go meet then?'

That was the big problem. Barbara could hardly say that she didn't want to be seen with him, but neither did she want to be alone with him. That was what it amounted to, cold-blooded though it seemed. She did some fast thinking. Away from the city centre of Ruddersleigh there was a tiny park at the back of a Roman Catholic church. There was a cinema nearby, to which she had gone on very rare occasions if the film being shown was particularly good and not on at other cinemas. The park was fairly secluded, but not too far away from the busy streets. Certainly nobody she knew was likely to be there in the evenings. They could sit in the shelter and talk, although early April was rather cold for sitting out of doors. If it rained, well, they would have to think about that at the time.

'Do you know where the church of The Holy Name is?' she asked.

'It near Plaza Cinema?'

'Yes, that's the one. There's a little park at the back. Could you meet me there?'

'Is okay. When do we meet?'

'If you're free in the evenings... Thursday evening at seven thirty?'

'I see you then. *Oui.*'

How strangely he speaks, she thought. So rapidly, and with such an odd inflexion. Aloud, she said that she must go. 'I'll see you Thursday. Goodbye.'

'Goodbye' he said, and his teeth, white and even, showed in another smile. Barbara saw him light a cigarette; she knew the bus always stood for a while in the terminus at Fordham. She hurried along home, her cheeks pink with excitement. She was thinking that if her parents knew they would go stark raving bonkers. Somehow this gave an added thrill to the meeting that lay ahead, for there were times when Barbara resented telling her mother where she was going, and with whom. After all, she was over seventeen, and it annoyed her intensely when her parents treated her as if she were still a child. They were so old fashioned in their thinking, they were living in a bygone age. They had made a big fuss once or twice when she had come home late at night. On one occasion when a boyfriend called to take her to a party, her father had actually told him to bring her home at a reasonable hour! As if she couldn't take care of herself.

She walked past the semi-detached houses of the suburban streets, and turned down by the parade of shops, and into Sycamore Avenue. She pushed open the wrought iron gate of the short drive at number twelve.

'You're late, aren't you?' enquired her mother, as Barbara closed the front door behind her.

'Yes. I went into Ruddersleigh Library to get a book about Trinidad. I had to queue for the bus from there.'

'Well, you would have to. It's getting near the rush hour.'

Barbara dumped her school satchel on the floor, and put her grey gabardine raincoat and maroon beret in the tiny hall cloakroom. The sound of a guitar being strummed came from upstairs. 'Oh, Eddie's home, is he? Not in detention, for once.'

'Your father will be home soon. You could lay the table. Babsy.'

'Oh, all right.' Barbara went into the poky little dining room, described by estate agents as a "dinette".

Like many of the other houses in Fordham, Sycamore Avenue had been built between the wars. In the Thirties, green fields had disappeared, trees had been removed, and brick built semi-detached houses had turned what had once been a village in rural surroundings into a suburb of Ruddersleigh. The names of the avenues and roads hinted at the past, Orchard Mount, Farm Road, Chestnut Avenue. "Superior semis" was the estate agents' description of the houses. They had bay windows at the front, with a sitting room and living room, and separate "dinette." The kitchen wasn't very big, but the back garden was a good size, and sometimes Barbara's parents talked of having an extension added to the kitchen.

'I wouldn't mind having a bit less garden to look after,' her father would say. 'There would still be plenty left, even with an extension.' There were so many other more pressing expenses though that nothing was ever done about it. There were three bedrooms and a bathroom "with separate WC" upstairs, and a useful loft. Whenever there was a house for sale in Sycamore Avenue, Helen, Barbara's mother, liked to read the description of it in the local evening paper. Their house had increased in value, of course, but they were still paying off the mortgage.

Fordham was getting very built up now, a huge council estate had gone up after the war, and private building was still going on. The older residents mourned the loss of the village green and surrounding countryside, but the adjoining suburb of Dudley had suffered even more grievously.

Darcy Foster, the local landowner, had kept the village of Dudley exactly as it was when he was a boy, refusing to sell the land to developers. He lived in Dudley, in a big old stone house enclosed in high stone walls. The village green, the tiny cottages, the woods and fields remained untouched during his lifetime. He owned some of the land in Fordham, too, and sometimes on summer evenings he would be seen walking in the places which he knew were lawfully his. Nobody took much notice of the rather shabbily dressed elderly man who needed a stick to get about. People who had grown up in Fordham knew who it was, though, and would murmur, 'There goes Darcy Foster' to the uncaring younger generation. Throughout the Thirties and mid Forties, children roamed happily in the fields and woods, paddled in streams, fished for tiddlers, and picked bluebells. Their parents took them for picnics, and for long walks on a Sunday. It all ended when the old man died just after the Second World War, and his son joyfully sold off every square foot of land that his father had cherished. The builders moved in then, and transformed the place. The little cottages were bulldozed to the ground to make way for modern houses, hedges were ripped up, fields of buttercups disappeared. With its character gone, Dudley became like Fordham, just another suburb of Ruddersleigh, a sprawl of houses, with shops and a new school, and all "amenities" available to tempt people into the neighbourhood.

Barbara went into the kitchen, where her mother was busy preparing the vegetables. She waved the library book in front of her. 'I think this book might be of some help to me with that essay I told you about.'

'Oh, good... can you make some mint sauce, Babsy? I've got lamb chops in the oven, and there's a bit of mint ready now in the garden. I'll clear a space for you to chop it.' She took down the chopping board from its hook on the wall, and put it on the Formica topped kitchen table.

Helen cooked a dinner every evening, so that she could be sure they all had one good meal every day. She knew George just had sandwiches at lunch time, and Barbara usually opted for anything in the salad line at school. Eddie was no problem, he had second helpings at school if possible, and at home too. The meal was always on the table by six o'clock, which allowed for any later activities that members of the family might have. Helen had been a bit surprised, and secretly rather pleased, when Barbara had mentioned that she was going to enter for the Annitsford essay competition. It was a competition held every year in Ruddersleigh, open to all grammar school boys and girls between the ages of seventeen and eighteen. The prize was only ten pounds worth of books, but a certain amount of local prestige went with it. There was always a photograph of the prize-winning scholar in the *Ruddersleigh Evening Chronicle*.

'Is Shirley going in for it?' she had asked.

'Shirley? Not likely.' Barbara laughed at the idea of her closest friend doing anything so academic. She wasn't going to tell her mother that it was partly Shirley's irritating little giggle from the desk behind her that had goaded her on to enter for it. That, and Miss Pickersgill's rather regretful voice, and of course, Pringle.

'Now girls, it's to be an essay on Trinidad this year. Not less than about two thousand words, I understand, and you have six weeks to do it in. Of course, the results aren't announced until the beginning of the autumn term. It's five years since anyone from this school won the Annitsford essay competition. As Headmistress, I consider that to be absolutely disgraceful for a school of our calibre. It isn't that we haven't got the girls capable of doing it, it's just lack of enthusiasm, and sheer laziness in some cases. I've told the Upper Sixth so, too.'

Her eyes rested on Barbara, and it was then that Shirley gave her stifled laugh. She lived in Dudley, and unlike Barbara, she was a paying pupil. She had managed to pass four O levels at sixteen, and she was going to try for a couple more. As for A levels, she knew, and the teaching staff knew, that her chances of passing any were remote. This didn't worry her, being an only child she was doted on, and her parents were satisfied that she was at a good school.

Parkleigh High School had been built during the last year of Queen Victoria's reign. It was a solid, stone structure with surrounding high walls, set a little way back from the busy main road. When the first pupils were enrolled, it was advertised as a school for young ladies. As it didn't take boarders, the pupils were drawn from the solidly middle class element in Ruddersleigh, with a few girls travelling daily by train. They were the daughters of professional men living in charming villages outside the city, or mill owners' daughters from their elegant mansions in the Dales. They wore plain white blouses and maroon ties, and dark grey skirts and cloaks with maroon tam-o'shanters in winter, and straw boaters in summer. The uniform itself had changed with the changing fashions, but the grey and maroon colours had survived. Inside the building the assembly hall was impressive, the classrooms were spacious, with oak desks and parquet floors, with a beautiful spiral staircase leading to the upper floors. There was a science laboratory, an art room, and a gymnasium which had been discreetly added on in the Twenties. Outside, the girls had a tennis court, and a small, pleasant patch of grassy parkland, where they could stroll or sit in summer. Later generations of girls required a playing field, so arrangements were made to share one with a more modern school.

As soon as Parkleigh was open it was announced that a small number of free places would be available for girls who passed a scholarship examination. Mr Theakstone, a Cambridge graduate, was the first headmaster, installed while the building still smelled of newly cut stone and fresh paint. He scarcely bothered to conceal his disdain of the handful of scholarship girls, an attitude which gradually softened over the years with succeeding headships. Miss Pickersgill knew that in the main, it was the scholarship girls who were more likely to bring academic distinction to the school, and quite a number of them became prefects. No scholarship pupil was ever made Head Girl, though; sixty years after Mr Theakstone, a lingering snobbery remained. Apart from the small matter of appointing head girls, Miss Brenda Pickersgill was remarkably fair minded and forward thinking.

She had a commanding presence which was quite impossible to ignore. Solidly built, broad shouldered, deep bosomed, with no discernable waistline, she spoke in measured tones with authority in every word. When she entered a classroom, the pupils all rose as a mark of respect, which she acknowledged with a brief nod, after which they could be seated again. She was in her early fifties, with short, greying hair drawn severely back from her plump, pink complexioned face. She dressed very plainly, usually in two piece suits, her preferred colour seemed to be brown, Brenda brown, the girls called it, although she sometimes wore navy blue.

Although she found Shirley's amusement annoying, Barbara might have let that pass, but during break Judith Pringle came up to her while she and Shirley were discussing their next tennis date with Roger Leffey and Steven Crowther.

'I suppose you'll be going in for the essay competition, then?' Flat-chested, buck-toothed, spotty and bespectacled, Judith Pringle was the archetypal school swot. She was a scholarship girl, and her O level results had been good, although no better than Barbara's. She had pulled ahead since then, mainly because she put her school work before anything else, having few temptations to do otherwise. Barbara had beauty, though, and the excitement of boyfriends and dates frequently came before her studies.

For a moment, the girls stood looking at each other, the one who could never hope to compete by her charms, the other who wanted dates and male admiration, and to show Pringle that she could still beat her academically if she chose.

'I don't know.' Barbara spoke coolly. 'Are you?'

'Might as well.'

'*You'd* better not bother, then, Babsy,' chipped in Shirley, her brown eyes mischievous in her round, perky face.

'There's no reason at all why I shouldn't bother if I want to.' Barbara still kept her voice cool, although her face was hot. She immediately began to talk about something else, ignoring Pringle, who turned away with an infuriatingly smug air, her mouth pursed in a sarcastic little half smile.

A fierce resolve was suddenly born in Barbara. She would enter for the Annitsford Essay Prize, and enter with the intention of winning it. From books and photographs and from any and every source that presented itself she would find out everything she could about Trinidad. That was why on Thursday evening she was standing beside The Holy Name in Ruddersleigh. She was several minutes early for the planned meeting, and rather than stand around, she ventured into the church. Other people were coming and going all the time, genuflecting in front of the altar, sitting silently with their rosaries held between clasped hands, lighting candles, crossing themselves. Barbara was fascinated by the strange foreign richness of the interior, the statue of the tortured Christ with his crown of thorns, the blue robed Virgin Mary holding Baby Jesus, the many saints, and the smell of incense permeating the whole atmosphere. She knew that there were plenty of people of Irish descent living in the slums of Ruddersleigh, and many immigrants from Europe had settled in the more poverty stricken, undesirable parts of the city. Glancing round, Barbara realised that all the women were wearing hats or head scarves apart from a couple of very old ones who had shawls over their heads. Not only was she bare-headed, but her bright auburn locks seemed somehow shameful in that gathering. Feeling like an impostor she went outside, passing a sad faced young priest on the way.

It was a dull, breezy evening, not really the sort of weather for sitting out of doors. She didn't mind that, though, as long as the bus conductor turned up, and she could get the information she wanted. When she walked round the back of the church, though, he was nowhere in sight. The little park was deserted, just a patch of worn grass, with half a dozen empty seats and a small shelter round it. She paced up and down for a couple of minutes, feeling nervous, disappointed, and yet, half relieved. He won't come, she thought, but the next moment, he did. He was walking towards her quickly, a very handsome young man, neatly dressed in a dark suit and short raincoat. Barbara was reassured immediately, he was still coloured of course, but there was nothing scruffy about him. She smiled, rather shyly.

'Hello – how you keeping? You wait long?' he asked, all in one breath. He was smiling too. Barbara was charmed by his funny little greeting. He pushed his windblown hair back from his forehead, and surveyed the park shelter. 'We best had sit in there,' he said. 'Is very windy.' Barbara got a strong impression that he disliked the wind intensely. She felt rather guilty about it as they sat down, with a gap of about two feet between them. She took out her notebook, and even in the shelter the strong breeze flapped the pages about. Suddenly she was overcome by nervousness.

'Well, what you know about Trinidad?' asked the young man.

'First there were the Arawaks, then the Caribs. It was discovered by Columbus... conquered by the Spanish... colonised by the French... ceded to the English...'

'*Oui?*'

'The Spaniards were very cruel to the Arawaks –' she faltered.

'You get all that out of books,' he said briskly. 'I ain't live then. You wanting to know what goes on now – from me?'

'Well, yes. There are things I would like to know...' There was another pause, then she asked somewhat hesitantly if the sands were really golden.

Louis laughed. 'They yellow in parts, white in parts, almost red in parts, and always shining, with the sea bright blue.' Somehow, in those few words he conjured up a picture in Barbara's mind. She saw the shimmering sands, and the blue of the Caribbean sea.

'Bright bright colour everywhere,' he went on. 'Not dull and grey like this. And smell of the flowers...'

Barbara began to take notes. His English was strange, almost pidgin at times, and he spoke rapidly, missing out words, which was very confusing for her. She thought his grammar was out of this world. Sometimes she could scarcely understand him at all, but didn't like to say so. When he said 'with' he pronounced it "wit", and his "these" and "them" sounded more like "dese" and "dem." Listening to his strange accent, she wondered what his mother tongue was. He used the French "*oui*" especially at the end of a sentence, and a number of American expressions she noticed. He was telling her about public holidays in Trinidad. 'Christmas, New Year's Day, Mardi Gras – that best, two days Carnival, Easter, Whitsun, Corpus Christi, Queen's birthday. Discovery Day, Hallowe'en –'

'Just a minute,' said Barbara desperately. 'Can you speak a bit more slowly, please?'

'You think I go too fast?'

I do t'ink, she thought. 'A little,' she said aloud. 'Are there any more holidays after Hallowe'en?'

He shook his head. 'Nothing till Christmas again.'

'Well, cheer up.' Barbara couldn't help laughing. 'It's not so long to New Year again, and then Carnival.'

'Yes, but I ain't there now for Carnival. We go see it in Port of Spain.'

'Your home is near Port of Spain?'

'About twenty miles away. Is a village called Bamboo Grove.'

'Tell me about the Carnival, will you?'

'All day Sunday we getting ready, then dawn on Monday it Joo-Vay,' he began.

'Joo-Vay?' she interrupted. 'Don't you mean *Jour Overt*?'

'We call it Joo-Vay in Trinidad,' said the young man firmly.

Barbara flushed. 'Do you – er – speak French?' she asked hesitantly. 'I mean, what is your native language?'

He appeared somewhat surprised. 'We speak English,' he said. 'What you think?'

'I didn't know... I thought by the way you spoke... not like an English person, I mean.'

'Well, English spoken different in different places,' said the young man, and there was no denying this.

'You just speak English, then?'

'Some things in French. But not French you would understand. *Patois*.'

So he spoke this odd English and corrupted French. She understood the Joo-Vay now.

'No other language?' she persisted. He hesitated very slightly, then shook his head.

'You are – Indian?' asked Barbara, forgetting that she wanted information about Trinidad, not about him.

'That right, *Oui*.'

'I didn't know there were many Indians in Trinidad,' she said. 'I thought they were mostly black people.'

'Biggest part really. Indian people nearly forty per cent, though. Have you read your book yet?'

'Not yet. I wanted to hear what you had to say first.'

'I expect it tell you why we came. When they abolish slavery, they ask Indians to come and work without pay, and then be given they own bit of land, indentured labour – you find all that in books,' said the young man. Evidently he didn't intend to waste time giving Barbara information she could find in books. He continued to tell her about the Carnival. In spite of his odd English he possessed vivid descriptive powers. He told her of the wonderful costumes, of the steel bands all trying to outdo one another, and of the calypso singers. Barbara was overcome with curiosity again, and asked him if he had dressed up for the Carnival. He laughed and admitted that he had dressed as a pirate.

She thought he must have looked very dashing, although she kept that to herself. As he talked, Barbara heard the excitement in his voice. It conveyed a strange excitement to her, too. This young man was bringing to her something of the irrepressible vitality of Trinidad. She no longer felt the wind or saw the dullness of a little park in a Yorkshire industrial city. She saw the colours and the gaiety of the Carnival. She heard the violent percussive effect of the steel bands, and the strange rhythm of the calypso. For a few vivid moments, she too felt the great primal wave which swept through the island on the Monday, the rapture of the Tuesday, the throbbing, ecstatic climax in the evening, and the end of it all at midnight on Ash Wednesday.

'Everyone – bad head!' said Louis, laughing.

Barbara laughed too, but the excitement lingered. This strange young man, he was vital – vital! He began to tell her about the colourful streets in Port of Spain.

'It have so many different sort of people. East Indians, Syrians, Lebanese.'

Another vivid picture rose in Barbara's mind. She saw Japanese, Chinese, Bengalese, English, Spanish, French and Dutch, rubbing shoulders, uncaring, after centuries of bitter fighting for this island. She saw Portugese, Parsees, and Americans, and most plentiful of all, the dusky descendants of African slaves.

She sat, quite enchanted, taking notes as quickly as she could, until Louis began to tell her about the many religions, and how they kept each others' religious holidays.

'Can you please stop a minute? My head's whirling. I'm getting mixed up,' she said.

Louis laughed. 'Don't be down couraged.'

'Down couraged?' Barbara was puzzled, then she smiled. He meant discouraged. She wondered what his religion was. 'I suppose you're a Hindu, then?'

'No. Christian. Parents converted when they little – when their parents converted. Missionaries very active.'

Barbara pondered on this. So he was a Christian. There was no reason why she should feel pleased about this, and yet she did. She wondered which denomination.

'Perhaps you're a Roman Catholic?' she suggested, knowing that she was being very inquisitive, but too overcome with curiosity to care.

'No. I did use to go to the Methodist Sunday School,' he said. 'That was when I was very little.'

Barbara giggled. 'So did I. I wonder why your family were converted, though.'

'People changing a lot in those days. Changing to what they could get most out of.'

'You mean... which religion could help them most?'

'Which help them most – food – clothes, anything. When people hungry they sure change their religion. *Oui*.'

'But most people who come here from Trinidad and other places in the West Indies seem to be black. If there are so many Indians, why don't more come to England?'

'Indians doing all right where they are,' was the reply, which whetted Barbara's curiosity still further. She would have liked to ask him why he had come to England, but she felt this would be going too far.

'There's a strong American influence in Trinidad, isn't there?'

'M-mm. They got military bases there.' He went on talking, and Barbara continued to take notes, but it was growing increasingly unpleasant sitting in that windy little shelter. She felt chilled right through, and she noticed the young man repress a shiver.

'You would like... coffee?' he asked, suddenly.

For a moment, Barbara was too taken aback to reply. Of course she would have liked a cup of coffee, but she couldn't go anywhere with him! She tried to imagine walking into the Plaza Café with him. It would be just her luck to meet someone she knew. It was out of the question.

17

'I don't really know of anywhere –' she broke off just before she uttered the word 'suitable'.

'It have plenty of places in this lime.' The young man lit a cigarette. He was scrutinising her face very closely. Barbara remembered that there was a coffee-bar not far away. She had never been in it before. The only one in Ruddersleigh that she patronised was called Mumbles. It was very popular with the students from Ruddersleigh University, and she had been there quite often with Roger Leffey. She and Shirley went there too on a Saturday, before they went round the shops together.

Dare she risk going into this other one with the young man? It was not his company she objected to. It was the thought of how embarrassing it would be if anyone she knew happened to see them. Still, if she kept away from Mumbles, she wouldn't be likely to meet any of Roger's student friends.

'There's a coffee-bar not far away,' she said. 'We could go there.'

'Okay.' The young man stood up.

'This way,' said Barbara, but she grew silent as they walked along in the gathering dusk. She wished that she had refused the offer of coffee, thanked the young man, and gone home. She cast furtive glances to right and left, caught his eye, and realised with some embarrassment that the glances were not lost upon him. When they reached the coffee-bar he pushed open the door, and looked inside.

'No,' he said decisively. 'Not nice. Full of limers.'

'Full of what?' asked Barbara.

'You call them – Rockers, I think.' Evidently he was particular where he took her. It seemed to be getting a bit crazily mixed up to Barbara. There were plenty of decent places in the city, but she didn't like to suggest any for fear of bumping into anyone she knew. And it was obvious that the young man had no intention of taking her into any noisy coffee-bar.

'I know of a quiet place,' he said. 'Is a few streets away. Shall we go there?'

'Yes. All right,' agreed Barbara, after some hesitation. As she walked along beside him, she felt increasingly apprehensive. The streets at the back of The Holy Name were anything but inviting, and she knew that it was on the fringe of a somewhat disrep-

utable district called Gantridge. She had never been in this neighbourhood in her life before, and as they passed through rows of
neglected old houses and dirty little shops, she felt far from
happy.

They turned up a side street with a tiny café on the corner.

'In here,' said Louis, opening the door. It was incredibly small
inside, and they were evidently the only customers. They sat
down at one of the four tables, and a man appeared from behind
a curtained doorway. For a moment Barbara was paralysed with
fright. He was coloured!

Oh, heavens, she thought. He's brought me into some dreadful, scruffy place patronised by coloured people. Here she was,
with a strange Indian man sitting in a queer little café in an
unsavoury district. How could she know that she was safe? The
coffee might be doped... She became so nervous that she was
reduced to a state of speechlessness.

'Sugar?' asked Louis, when the coffee arrived. Her hands were
trembling uncontrollably as she stirred it in.

'It all right here,' he said softly. 'I been here often. Is quiet,
nobody see you,' he added with a smile.

Barbara felt both ashamed and reassured. The man who had
served them must have told someone in the back that Louis was
there. A little Indian boy of about four came running out from
behind the curtain.

'Louis! Louis!' he cried, skipping up to their table, and looking shy when he saw Barbara. He pushed his face into Louis'
shoulder, and Barbara was reassured still further. The sight of this
child showing affection for the young man made her realise that
she was quite safe. So that was his name – Louis.

'Why, he should be in bed,' she exclaimed, finding her voice.

'You hear that, Ganesh-Baba?' Louis asked him, slipping a
coin into his hand. The boy peeped through his fingers at Barbara,
and hurried away into the back again. It was warm in the café after
the windy Ruddersleigh streets, and Barbara unfastened her belted camel coat, revealing a blue jersey-wool dress underneath.

'You ain't mind if I smoke in here? I ain't blow the smoke in
your face,' said the young man.

'Of course I don't mind,' said Barbara, but to her surprise he
didn't offer her one. She thought this very remiss of him. It was

not that she smoked, except to have the odd cigarette at parties sometimes, but whether she smoked or not, she thought he should have offered her one. While she was thinking this, she saw the young man glancing at her figure, just for a second. It was an unmistakably appraising glance, although his face was impassive the next moment. It was enough to make Barbara fasten up her coat again, but even as she did so, she felt, as she had felt in the park shelter, a curious excitement rising inside her.

'We talk all night – we ain't know each other name,' said Louis, smiling.

'I know your name is Louis.'

'Louis Ramdeen.' He was evidently waiting to hear hers.

'I'm Barbara... Granger,' she said, just a little reluctantly. She hadn't imagined them exchanging names, somehow.

'You heard all you need about Trinidad, then, Barbara?' It was strange to hear her name on his lips. Strange, but not unpleasant.

'I don't know.' She spoke doubtfully. 'I shall have to write something about politics, I suppose.'

'About election time in Trinidad? Everyone going crazy, and everywhere painted up with white paint, saying things about people. Then other people go wash it off, and putting more things. And calypso made up about politicians – you write about that – *oui?*'

'Er... yes.' She still spoke dubiously. 'I don't think I shall write much about it, though.' They had finished their coffee now. 'I shall have to be going.' She picked up her handbag.

'You ain't go see me again?' asked the young man, after a short silence. 'You know enough about Trinidad?'

Part of her said yes, of course she knew enough now. But another part of her... she sat, hesitating. 'I don't know,' she said finally. 'It depends.'

'Can see you again?' he repeated.

'It's been very kind of you.' She stood up, as he showed no sign of moving. 'I think I know enough about Trinidad now, thank you.'

She saw sudden disappointment in his eyes, hidden almost immediately. But she had seen it. She knew that he had only been in England a few months. Was he lonely? A curious sensation stirred in Barbara, she couldn't analyse it. Did he perhaps feel homesick after talking so much about Trinidad?

He stood up without speaking, and they went out into the dark, chilly street.

'I shan't find out whether I know enough until I start writing the essay,' she said, walking along beside him.

'Perhaps you go see me again?' he persisted.

Barbara could see that he was angling for another meeting, using the essay as an excuse.

'Well... perhaps.'

'When we go meet, then?'

'Just a moment. Let me think.'

'I'm working late every night next week. A week on Monday?' suggested the young man.

'I think that would be all right.' And that, she thought, would be the finish.

'Seven o'clock, same place?' They were getting back into the busier streets now.

'Yes, I think that I can manage that.' She hoped that he didn't intend to walk as far as Marsh Street bus stop with her. And then, when she saw him in the light from the shop windows, the odd pang moved in her again, pulling her towards him.

'That pretty!' he exclaimed suddenly, stopping in front of a shop window to look at a dance dress. It was of red chiffon, beautifully swathed and draped, with fine bead embroidery on the bodice. Barbara looked at it.

'You think it pretty?' he asked.

'Very,' she said smiling. What a funny boy he was! 'But it wouldn't suit me at all, not that colour. I have a green dance dress just as pretty as that. It's new, I've only worn it once.'

He appeared to be considering this remark. 'You go dancing sometimes, then?'

'Quite often, especially in winter. Every week last winter.'

'*Oui papi!*' he exclaimed. 'Every week? Not every week, surely?' He sounded genuinely shocked.

'Why not? Do you go dancing?'

'I ain't been since I lived in England. But I used to go at home.'

'Every week?' asked Barbara. He admitted that he had often gone every week for long stretches at a time.

'Well, then, what's so odd about it?'

21

'But girls don't go dancing every week,' said the young man, rather unhappily.

'What do they do, then?' asked Barbara. Now that they were in the hub of the city she no longer felt in the least nervous, and it was too dark for anyone to stare at them.

'Every two –three week.'

'What do you do for partners, then?'

'Different girls every week.'

'A kind of roster system,' said Barbara. 'How perfectly ridiculous.' She laughed.

'Nice girls don't go dancing every week where I come from,' said Louis, ignoring her laughter.

Suddenly she was piqued. 'This isn't a country village in Trinidad,' she pointed out. 'They go dancing every night in the week, here, if they want.'

'Nice girls?'

'Nice girls,' said Barbara firmly. He walked along without speaking for a minute.

'I ain't been in this country long,' he said, finally.

What a square, Barbara was thinking. He's so square his corners show. But sneaking a look at him sideways, she was touched to see that he looked distinctly relieved.

'Well, I suppose some of our ways must seem strange to you,' she said, smiling. They were nearly at the bus stop now. 'It's been very good of you to tell me so much. I shall start writing out my essay from those notes.'

They stood for a moment. 'Now don't forget, you go see me again,' said Louis.

'I shan't forget.' Still they stood. Suddenly she slipped her gloved hand into his, she didn't know why. Instantly he clasped it, and again the strange excitement rushed through her.

'Good night... Louis,' she said softly.

'Good night, Barbara.'

They parted and she arrived hone in an absolute daze after her exciting and informative evening. In bed, she read through the notes she had taken. They were scrappy enough in parts, and yet they were vivid, alive with a curious vitality. Or was it just the young man speaking which had left this indelible impression?

The bright yellow of the *pouis* tree, the scarlet flamboyant, the crimson immortelle! The way he had talked about public holidays, and how everyone loved a fete, pronouncing it "fet" in the French way. How strange, how romantic it all seemed, so different from reading about it in a book. She turned over the pages of her notes. The wild duck, the egret, the scarlet ibis, which lived in the swamp. Yes, she was one-up on Pringle, all right.

It had been well worth it, not only worth it, but she had enjoyed the evening, apart from the first few minutes in that Indian café.

Gosh, if Mummy knew, she thought. If Roger Leffey knew! She pushed the notebook under her pillow, switched out the bedside lamp, and fell asleep.

Chapter 2

While Barbara slept, Louis lay tossing around in bed, thinking of all the things which he had told her, and of the things which he had not told her. Of his life in the house of his uncle, Roopchand Chittaranjan, and of the bitter quarrel between them, which had led indirectly to his leaving Trinidad.

When only eight years old he had lost both parents in a yellow fever epidemic, and after the manner of the Indian, his uncle had taken him into his own home. Roopchand Chittaranjan was a foolish, weak, drunken man, with a shiftless, ignorant wife, Zilla. She was his second wife, younger than him, his first wife having died without bearing children. Zilla didn't fuss over the boy, as his own mother had done, nevertheless, she took him to her heart and loved him. She already had a year old baby boy, to be followed by several more children. It became a noisy, crowded house, and Louis had to rough it with the rest of the children, but simple and silly though she was, Zilla was no less kind to him, despite her own increasing family. Nor was Chittaranjan ever unkind, in spite of his many threats.

'You is hell self, boy! Oh, God, what I do to have boy like you in my house? You is son of a bitch! I give you licks – I take cutlass to you!' Yet he never ill-treated his sister's son.

Chittaranjan worked in the canefields on the Bamboo Crossing estate, fertilising and thrashing the cane during the rainy season, and cutting it at crop time. In January the reaping would begin, and Louis would watch his uncle sharpening his cutlass on a grinding stone, testing the blade until he was satisfied. Then they would fire the trash in the canefields, and the sky would glow red in the sugar districts on the island. Charred bits of leaves would drift around for miles, and the cane would be left standing, ready to cut. Chittaranjan and the other men would slash at it, soot and sweat streaming down their faces, as their cutlasses glinted in the sun.

Behind them came the women, piling the fallen stalks up so that they could be loaded, and Louis and his playmates would beg for the sweet tasting cane to suck. The smell of burning would hang in the steaming air, while the sun beat down out of cloudless skies. By the end of June the crop was over, and the whole village celebrated, dancing and drinking, with the patient oxen beribboned for the occasion.

Zilla tended her vegetable garden, knowing that she could never be very sure of her husband's money. She kept some chickens, and a goat, which Louis fed on para-grass, and fortunately they never lacked for fruit. Guavas, mangoes and coconuts were theirs for the taking. So Louis grew to adolescence, playing football and cricket on the savannah, swimming, fighting, and singing calypsoes. As he grew out of his childhood, though, he became more and more critical of his uncle's household.

Len Rampasad, Louis' friend, was going to high school, but there was no chance of that for Louis. There was no money for a better education at Chittaranjan's house, but he was an intelligent boy and he felt extremely envious of his friend.

Looking back on the vivid, tender memories of his infancy, he remembered the tranquillity of those days when he had been the adored child of Devannan and Sajoodaye Ramdeen. His father had been a kind, hard-working man, and his mother a sweet-natured, thrifty girl. How she ever came to have a brother like his uncle puzzled Louis very much as he grew older. One thing he did know, though, and that was if his parents had lived he would have been going to high school with Len Rampasad. The boy felt cheated, frustrated and bitter, but there was nothing he could do about it.

When he left the elementary school and started work in the sugar factory, he made up his mind to get Teacher Ramlogan to tutor him. It was quite a common practice and fairly inexpensive to pay a private tutor. For in Louis was a strong desire for better things and a better way of life than his uncle's home could offer him. He hated the way they lived, and realised more and more what a hopeless household it was.

Yet, in spite of this, he was genuinely fond of his exasperating relatives. After all, drunken and ignorant though his uncle was, he had taken an orphaned child into his poverty-stricken home. Louis could never forget this. He was also deeply fond of poor, shiftless Zilla, who had dried his tears of grief long ago, and held him in her arms. He loved his cousins, and they loved him, pulling at him with their sticky fingers, and following him around.

'Louis! Louis! Play with we, sing to we! Louis! Louis!'

And as the boy looked around him with adolescent discontent, Zilla began to throw her burdens upon him. She saw that he was different from his uncle, different from her, different from any of them. She knew that he was deeply conscious of his obligations towards them, and upon this knowledge, Zilla worked.

Louis soon realised that he was going to have to give back in good measure for those years during which they had kept him. For a while he managed to pay Teacher Ramlogan, and he became a clerk in the sugar factory nearby. By nature he was a thrifty boy – at least he had the thrift normal to his race, but completely lacking in his uncle. Chittaranjan and Zilla were eager for every cent they could get out of him. He didn't mind giving to his aunt so much, it was the sight of his uncle spending the money on rum which angered him. Zilla would complain endlessly to the boy about her husband's shortcomings, for ever since Louis could remember, his uncle had come home drunk, and quarrelled with her. When the row reached its height he would threaten to beat her, and although he never actually carried out his threats, it was frightening for the children.

Late one night, when Louis was a well grown seventeen-year-old, he was in bed with his cousins, while in the other room Chittaranjan and Zilla were quarrelling. The older children were listening, wide-eyed, while the younger ones slept. His uncle was swearing in Hindi, and threatening Zilla as usual, but this time she screamed for Louis.

'Oh, God, come quick, Louis man! He go kill me today self!'

Little Gary burst into tears, and seven-year-old Henry cried 'Go quick, Louis, quick – quick!'

But Louis was already at the bedroom door. When he confronted Zilla and Chittaranjan, though, he perceived that things were much the same as usual. True, his uncle had his belt in his hand, but he knew from experience that was no great cause for concern.

'She aggravate me into it, man,' he said when his nephew

26

appeared, and then the boy had to listen to both sides of the quarrel. More and more Zilla and his uncle were relying on him. And once having called for Louis when her husband threatened her, Zilla called for him every time.

He was sure that his uncle had no real intention of harming her, and yet he could never ignore her cry for help. She was a thin, frail looking woman, fortunately much tougher than she appeared, otherwise she would never have survived the years with her demanding young family, and her once handsome Roopchand. For the Chittaranjans were a good looking family, and Louis, although fairer skinned, resembled his uncle strongly, taking from him his fine features and good build. But that was all, fortunately for the harassed Zilla.

She was so foolish and ignorant that Louis despaired of her. On one occasion, after a quarrel with some neighbours over a missing chicken, she borrowed money from him. When she did this he knew that she would never return it, but he didn't mind if the money was spent on his young cousins. This time, though, he found out that she had used it to go to the *obeah*-man, and have magic worked on the woman she suspected had stolen her chicken. He was very angry about this, that Zilla, already in debt, should spend money in such a ridiculous way. He tried to explain to her that it was a lot of nonsense, but it was no use. She believed what the *obeah*-man said. She was not alone in this, a number of people in Bamboo Grove believed in magic, and were fearful of having it worked on them.

'Don't vex with me, Louis, man,' she wailed. 'You is right. I ain't see the *obeah*-man no more.'

But he knew perfectly well that she would promise something without the slightest intention of keeping her word. It was hopeless. He turned away in despair. There were times when he became so disheartened with it all that he would go out and get as drunk on rum as Chittaranjan himself. And yet, in spite of these frustrations, he still had a desire to save. He began to put some money away in a tin, and hide it, after the manner of his race. If he had money on him, he would give it to Zilla when she came whining, for it was not in his nature to refuse. But with the money safely away, he could turn out his pockets to show her he had none.

27

When he had saved a certain sum, he intended to put it in the bank, and all went well with this plan until one day when he found the tin emptied of its contents. For a moment the boy was petrified; the dollars which he had concealed so carefully!

The next moment an anger seized him such as he had never before experienced. He knew well enough who had stolen the money. Somehow his uncle had found it, had taken it and spent it on rum. Although Zilla would borrow from Louis and never pay him back, he knew that she would never deliberately steal from him. But a man with the craving for drink like his uncle would stoop to anything for money with which to buy it.

Chittaranjan was not at home, but when Louis questioned Zilla it was quite obvious that she knew nothing about the theft.

'Oh, God, Louis! That damn silly man not touch your money – he just have joke,' she said. But her eyes were wide with fright, she knew as well as he that her husband had taken it. 'Oh, what trouble that man brings on we!' she cried. Then she remembered the meal she was cooking. 'God, man, the rice boil too soft now. Somebody working *obeah* on me this day!'

Louis was too angry to reply. He waited until Chittaranjan came in, and challenged him immediately. His uncle, half drunk, shouted, lied, denied it. But his guilt was plain, both to Louis and Zilla.

'You one big silly fool,' his wife told him. 'You steal the boy's money to buy rum with.' She hoped to make Louis think that his uncle could be excused his crime, on the grounds that he was such a fool.

'I ain't take your money,' insisted Chittaranjan. 'How do I know where you have it hide?' Then the two men quarrelled violently, oaths in Hindi flew between them.

'You one big thief and one big liar!' shouted Louis contemptuously. Finally, Chittaranjan admitted the theft.

'I take it – so what?' he blustered. 'I keep you years when you little!'

Louis lost all control when he said that. His uncle had thrown in his face his childhood dependency – as if he could help it. He sprang forward and seized Chittaranjan by the throat. Zilla was terrified.

'Louis man!' she screamed:. 'He my husband – he you uncle.'

When Zilla screamed, sanity returned to Louis. He released his uncle, and turned away, sickened. If it had been any other man!

But it was not any other man. It was Chittaranjan, a liar, a drunkard, and a thief. Nevertheless, he had taken a weeping boy into his home, and never once struck that boy, even when the neighbours had complained ceaselessly about his misdeeds.

'It okay. Don't cry, Tanty,' he told Zilla. 'I'm going out for a walk.'

The perspiration ran down his forehead. His violent anger in all that heat had made it stream from him. It soaked his shirt, and made great dark patches under his armpits, but he was oblivious of physical discomforts. He felt that he had endured as much as was humanly possible in that house. He walked and walked, distraught, in that merciless heat, the lumps of crude asphalt on the road soft under his feet. When he became aware of his surroundings again, he realised that he'd walked almost to where the main road to the town began. He was within sight of Teacher Ramlogan's house, he could see the mango tree in the yard. Suddenly he knew what to do. He walked up to the house, and asked to see Teacher Ramlogan. They had a long, private discussion, and then Ramlogan called his wife into the room, and the three of them consulted together.

Louis had always been a favourite of his old tutor. He and his wife were both sorry for the boy, propping up the crazy Chittaranjan household. And when Louis finally left them, a momentous decision had been reached concerning his future. He would sleep under his uncle's roof for the last time that night, and the following day he would collect his belongings and move into Teacher Ramlogan's house.

He was very sorry for Zilla. He knew how much she relied on him, but after all, he was not responsible for her hopeless plight, and viewed objectively, it was no worse than that of a number of women in the village. He knew that his cousins would cry pitifully, and beg him to stay, particularly his favourite, six year-old Pearl.

When he got back, he spoke neither to Zilla nor his uncle. It was plain that there had been a quarrel between them, too. They were not on speaking terms with one another. So, rather oddly, his last night at home was probably one of the quietest ever known, in that noisy, brawling household.

29

The following morning Louis told Zilla that he was leaving, and the uproar that he was expecting took place. His uncle was not at home, but his cousins clung to him, weeping piteously, and Zilla was frantic.

'Don't leave we, Louis-Baba, because you vex with he!' she cried. 'You know he just one damn big silly fool!'

Of course Louis knew that, he had known it for years, but he was determined not to be talked round by Zilla. Desperately she tried another line of reasoning, knowing how much he loved his cousins.

'If you go leave we, that man kill me when he drunk – and children left without a mother!'

That didn't impress him either, whatever Chittaranjan was, drunk or sober, he was not a violent man.

'You in no danger, Tanty,' he told her dryly.

'Oh, what I do to get a man like he?' sobbed his aunt. 'Somebody work *obeah* on me when I get married.'

The extent of Zilla's loss could not have been put into words. She had never been much use at disciplining the children herself, and their father was too absorbed in the problem of getting rum to bother about his offspring unduly, but Louis, as he grew older, had brought some degree of order into his cousins' lives. He was the only one they took any notice of, and Zilla knew it. Again she begged him to stay with them, pleading with him in the more expressive language of Hindi, but his answer was the same. He took his belongings and moved into Teacher Ramlogan's house, with the sound of his cousins' noisy weeping still in his ears. And in spite of everything, there was a lump in Louis' throat.

When his uncle arrived home, he found the house in a state of mourning. 'Louis go leave we!' cried the children tearfully. 'He go leave we, Pa!'

Chittaranjan was speechless for a moment. Like Zilla, he had never imagined anything as awful as this could happen to them. If he could have returned the money he would, but it had all gone on rum. He was in debt, too, and had no hope of repaying it. Louis had gone, and he knew well enough that he was to blame. Zilla knew it too, and had no intention of letting him forget it.

'You one damn big fool,' she told him resentfully. 'Now he go we all suffer.'

'Don't talk to me 'bout that worthless boy!' shouted her husband. 'All these years I keep he – now he go leave we! He ain't caring what happens. Sajoodaye shoulda never took up with them no-good Ramdeens. See how he turn out, no better than he father!'

'He father turn out damn sight better than you, man,' said Zilla tearfully. 'Good man like he go and dead, man like you live to drink rum!' She counted this the blackest day of her life, except of course for the day upon which she became Chittaranjan's bride. It was not just the financial loss, although that in itself was a tragedy. It was the loss of the one sound, sensible, reliable member of that dreadful household. She kept on abusing her husband, and he realised she would throw it in his face for years to come. The thought was more than he could bear.

'Woman!' he bawled. 'If you don't shut up I go make you taste my hand!' He moved threateningly towards her.

'Oh, God, he go kill me!' yelled Zilla, but suddenly she stopped. For years one of her greatest comforts had been to call for Louis when her husband threatened her. Now there was no Louis to call for. It brought home her loss as nothing else would have done. It brought it home to Chittaranjan, too. He liked to hear Zilla call for Louis, it was the exciting climax to their rows, besides, it boosted his self-esteem tremendously. Now there was nobody to agree with him that women were hell self, but to stay his hand this once. There was nobody to comfort Zilla and assure her that he would see she came to no harm. It was too much for both of them. Zilla sank down and wept without restraint. Her husband was too dispirited to threaten any more. He sat down beside her.

'He not leave we, Zilla. He just have joke, he come back in two-three week,' he said miserably. He wanted her to comfort him, and say yes, Louis would come back to them before long. But he got no comfort at all from his wife.

'You one big silly fool!' she sobbed.

Chittaranjan hadn't even the heart to reply. He covered his face with his hands, and sat in silence. After a while, unnoticed by Zilla, a tear forced its way through his fingers, and fell onto the floor.

Chapter 3

There was a good deal of gossip in Bamboo Grove about Chittaranjan's stealing from his nephew, and Louis going to live at Teacher Ramlogan's house. Chittaranjan, whatever his secret thoughts, put on a very tough exterior about the affair. In Supasad's rum shop, drinking with his friends Samsoodeen and Babwah, he talked at great length about Louis' ingratitude.

'All these years I look after him, man, I father to he – it does show you people ain't have no shame, dirtying my name. That boy ain't appreciate what I done for he – now he say I steal! I shoulda take he little tail and fling it out! He think he smartever, going live at Ramlogan's house.'

Samsoodeen and Babwah, who knew perfectly well that he had stolen from Louis, were suitably sympathetic.

'This modern generation have no good in it,' said Samsoodeen. He drank his third glass of rum, and wiped his mouth with the back of his hand.

'It have no gratitude,' agreed Babwah.

'And he do that after he get educate with Ramlogan, too. It show you what education do,' said Chittaranjan. The other two men agreed with him as to the evils of education. Encouraged by their sympathy he began to make threatening remarks about what he would do to Louis if he met him.

'I give him licks, man! I bash him up good, before he time to scratch! He nothing but a damn little piss-in-tail boy.'

Samsoodeen and Babwah made approving noises. 'He playing at being man now, but he just force-ripe mango,' went on Chittaranjan. 'When I get after him with a stick, I mash his arse, he not be able to run fast enough.'

His friends made noises again, and Chittaranjan looked at them suspiciously through his rum-haze. 'Tonight, self, I sharpen cutlass for that son of a bitch! I send him to hospital. *Oui!*' His audience was growing rather tired of listening to these threats against Louis. 'He younger than you, man,' Babwah reminded him.

'Too, besides, he ain't drink so much rum,' added Samsoodeen, downing another glass. 'It have nothing like a clear head, man.'

Chittaranjan belched. 'The son of a bitch,' he muttered feebly.

In the meantime, oblivious of his uncle's threats, Louis was settling down in Teacher Ramlogan's house. In the squalor of the home he had left, he had been accustomed to sharing a bedroom with his boy cousins, while the girls shared the other with his aunt and uncle, but here in Teacher Ramlogan's house there were three bedrooms and water laid on, to mention only two of the many differences. Here he shared a bedroom with Charles, the youngest child and only son.

There was no drunkenness in this house, no violent threats, no shouting quarrels – and no water to be fetched from the standpipe every day. They had a yard-boy, too. Life was a good deal pleasanter for Louis, but this didn't mean that he had forgotten his relatives. At times when his uncle was out, he would visit his aunt and cousins.

As soon as she saw him, Zilla's wail would begin. 'Oh, God, Louis man, it hell self in this house, without you! That man – he get worse!'

'Now what he doing, Tanty?' Louis would ask, with little Pearl climbing on his knee. Then he would be given a long account of Zilla's sufferings, ending with a plea for him to return. But that was the one thing he was determined not to do, for now he was saving again, and this time with no fear of having his money stolen. In fact, he was leading a life much more in keeping with his own ideas, and he should have been content. To his own surprise, he was nothing of the sort.

He was restless, preoccupied, with an urge to go even farther afield, having made the tremendous break with the Chittaranjans. Frequently he visited Port of Spain, from which banana boats were leaving, packed with emigrants. Walking through the bustling streets he felt caught up in something which pulled him away from Bamboo Grove with its straggling little houses, and gossiping inhabitants.

33

New ideas and ambitions stirred inside him, urging him to leave the country of his birth, as long ago his people had left the banks of the Ganges and come to Trinidad as indentured labourers. From the yard of Teacher Ramlogan's house he looked at the hills in the distance, and the green canefields. Cane, cane, always the sugar-cane, harvest after harvest, reaping after reaping; stripped to the waist his forefathers had cut cane under the cruel sun. And it was still the same. The harvest and the reaping, and the sweating, sooty men slashing with their cutlasses. Bitter toil to get the sweetness of the sugar, and although he worked in the factory it was still the harvest from the canefields that brought his livelihood.

Suppose he left the island, and tried his luck abroad? England? He had heard that work was plentiful there, and the country prosperous. It was an exciting thought. After a good deal of consideration, he broached the subject to Teacher Ramlogan, for whose opinion he had great respect. The older man suggested that he might do better to go to Canada, but the idea of emigrating to the mother country had become firmly rooted in Louis' mind. Realising this, Teacher Ramlogan didn't discourage him, but he reminded him that he would be giving up a job to go to England, unlike a number of emigrants. He told him to consider things very carefully before taking such a decisive step.

The young man said he would, as in any case he wanted to save more money before he could carry out any such ambition. But rumours swept through Bamboo Grove, rumours that Louis Ramdeen was going to England. The gossip caused by the quarrel with his uncle had barely died down, now there was a fresh spate of talk.

Zilla heard the rumour, and asked him if it was true the next time he went to see her.

'Matter not fix yet, Tanty,' he told her, but he didn't deny that there was something behind the gossip. He knew that she would take it badly, cherishing as she did the faint hope that he would some day return to live there. By his hesitant manner, Zilla knew that he intended to leave the island altogether, and it added the last drop of bitterness to her brimming cup. She lost no time in telling her husband, who listened with mixed feelings.

He still deeply resented Louis' display of independence in

going to live at another man's house, and now... England! 'That worthless boy,' he shouted, but at the same time he felt a certain pride. Not every man in Bamboo Grove had a nephew going to England, even if that nephew was no longer on speaking terms with him.

'He own home ain't good enough – he own country ain't good enough now,' he told Zilla. 'I hope it good enough for he in England. It have a different thing there, he ain't know what it like there – maybe he think the Queen meet he boat,' he added, with sharp irony.

'What you know 'bout England, man?' enquired Zilla. 'Perhaps Teacher Ramlogan tell he to go there.' Like most people in the village she had great respect for Ramlogan. And although he poured scorn on his nephew, Chittaranjan was deeply impressed. A faint ray of hope stirred in him.

'Maybe he send we money home,' he suggested.

'Send money for you to buy rum with?' asked Zilla. 'You think he fool?' She realised only too well that they had nothing to gain by Louis' going to England. It meant she would lose even the chance of seeing him occasionally, and getting a few dollars out of him.

'The son of a bitch,' said Chittaranjan. 'He ain't caring about we, woman! If he come liming round here again I give him licks – I take a big stick – self I sharpen cutlass –'

'Oh, shut up, man!' cried Zilla, risking his wrath. 'Think he little boy? Think he let you give him licks? If he pass you – you too drunk to see. You shoulda leave the boy's money alone, damn silly fool!'

'Woman!' shouted Chittaranjan, stung by her contempt, 'if you go say any more – I learn you respect! *You* get damn licks – and he ain't here now when you start bawling!'

'And why ain't he?' yelled Zilla recklessly, but she made for the door at the same time. So, in characteristic fashion was the news of Louis' going to England received in his uncle's household. And in Supasad's rum-shop, once more Chittaranjan was the centre of attraction. The fact that his nephew was reputedly going to England gave him a certain prestige with his drinking companions. Samsoodeen and Babwah discussed the matter with him.

'It have a lot from the West Indies in a lime call Birmingham,' said Babwah. 'Or plenty does go to London. Maybe too damn many go. It have the white people fed up, boatloads from the West Indies. They say, is we being invaded? They say, is anybody left in the West Indies now –'

Samsoodeen interrupted him. He rather resented the other man talking as if he knew everything about England and emigration. But before long Babwah was airing his views again.

'Once he go to England he ain't see Trinidad again,' he said. 'Once he prosper in England, it have nothing here for he, man.'

Chittaranan then played his trump card. 'He come back – sure thing – you see! That son of a bitch sorry he ever leave the island, man.'

The other two wanted to know why.

'I been to *obeah*-man and have magic work on him,' announced Chittaranjan. 'It powerful magic. It have he damn sorry he set foot in England. He come back and bring he tail – you see!'

His friends were deeply impressed, not only because he had been to the *obeah*-man, but because he had spent money on something else besides rum.

'Powerful magic,' repeated Chittaranjan, enjoying the sensation which he had caused. 'He back here brisk-brisk, and damn glad to be.'

But in spite of threats and gossip, and Zilla's attempt to dissuade him, Louis went ahead saving and planning, for his mind was quite made up now. And as the months passed, emigrating to England became less of a dream every day, and more of a reality. Teacher Ramlogan gave him much good advice on the ways of the world, before Louis left Trinidad. He warned him of the pitfalls which could lie ahead for a young man in a foreign country, particularly in connection with women. Louis listened as usual, with great respect and attention. He was not, however, quite as innocent as Teacher Ramlogan supposed. Before leaving the island he had several nights out with his various friends, including his boyhood companion, Len Rampasad.

There was much last-minute weeping from Zilla and his cousins, and in spite of the excitement he felt when Trinidad finally became a tiny speck in the distance, Louis felt very much alone. But people were striking up friendships on the boat, and before long he met a talkative young negro named Henry Jackson. He was alone, too, and he attached himself to Louis, saying that he had a brother already in England. He told Louis that his brother had bought a house in a city called Ruddersleigh, and was, apparently, very prosperous.

'It where I'm going to stay man. It good lime – it have plenty of work there, why don't you come to Ruddersleigh with me? It have plenty from Trinidad there, and if Sam got room for me, he make room for you too.'

Louis considered this. He was very much alone, and most of the men going to England seemed to have relatives already there. By the time the banana boat had docked in Liverpool, he had decided to try his luck in Ruddersleigh with Henry. On the train to Yorkshire, Henry talked about life in England.

'They ain't no sun here much,' he said gloomily, and in fact it was a rather dull day in September. 'We ain't drink so much rum here, man,' he continued. 'It costing more.'

'Too, besides, it having cigarettes dearer. I heard about that,' said Louis. 'We have to cut down on we smoking.'

'It going to be hard for we.' Henry spoke thoughtfully. 'It have powerful weather in winter. Sam say it get dark in the afternoon, and go on being dark. He says days go longer and then go shorter. I don't know how come it do that.'

Louis began to feel less optimistic about things. It didn't sound to him as though Sam had been very encouraging about his brother going to England.

'Sam say the wind blow damn well through you sometimes.'

'He ain't seem to be liking it so much in England,' suggested Louis.

'He ain't come back to Trinidad, though,' said Henry.

They arrived in Ruddersleigh, and after fortifying themselves with a drink, they proceeded to Sam's address. He and his wife lived in Gantridge, a part of Ruddersleigh that was once the stronghold of the poorer Jewish population. Now it was crammed with foreigners of every nationality, both white and coloured. Many of the houses were dreadfully ramshackle, and living conditions were appalling in parts.

Two old men walked in front of Henry and Louis, talking animatedly together, but not in English. A dark skinned man and woman passed them, also conversing in a foreign tongue.

'*Oui papi!* It like Port of Spain, this, man,' said Henry, 'I ain't thinking it like this.' It began to drizzle, and they asked an elderly man if he could direct then to Sam's address.

'You vant Victoria Road?' asked the man, speaking in guttural English. With many gesticulations he directed them along a dirty, neglected looking street.

'It funny looking lime, this,' said Louis.

'Well, it England, man. You ain't expect to see mango trees growing.'

Already Louis was beginning to wonder if he had done the right thing in coming to Ruddersleigh with Henry. With growing unease he walked along beside his new friend.

'Number thirty. It Sam's place, this,' said Henry, stopping in front of a dreary looking terraced house. The curtains were filthy, two of the windows were broken, and every vestige of paintwork had peeled off years before.

'It have all the houses joined up,' said Louis, looking around dubiously. The high buildings in the city surprised him, and the houses, built in rows, seemed peculiar. At least, however poor a house in Trinidad, if only a shack, it was detached.

Henry banged on the door, and it was opened by another negro, older than Henry, but just as garrulous. This was Sam, and it was hard to tell if he was pleased to see his brother or not. Louis was not too sure; however, they both followed him inside. The smell was overpowering as they walked along the dark hallway, with grimy wallpaper hanging forlornly at intervals. In the kitchen, surrounded by dirt and disorder, was Sam's wife, Lena. She was a slim, good-looking woman, several years younger than her husband. She had curiously hard, glittering eyes. They rested on Henry with an unloving expression.

'You is come, then, man,' she said, without enthusiasm. Her eyes slid round to Louis, demanding an explanation of his presence. Henry did a lot of talking, and Louis chimed in occasionally, when he got the chance. But Sam was talking too. Lena began to cook a meal.

Louis heard the sound of male voices coming from another part of the house; doors were banging, and men were apparently coming and going all the time. It was quite a big house, three stories high, with an attic and cellar, but every ceiling was cracked, and some of the door hinges broken. In fact the whole place was in a state of decay. A game of rummy was in progress in the next room, judging by the shouts from within. Before long the smell of calaloo stew filled the house and drowned the other smells. Drinks appeared from somewhere, and other negroes began to drift into the kitchen.

Henry was eating, drinking and talking, oblivious of Lena's cool manner. Sam seemed to have warmed up now, he became most hospitable towards both his brother and Louis. More men joined them in the kitchen, and more drinks appeared. It grew stifling in there. Louis lost track of time and place.

'Man, it just like back in Trinidad!' exclaimed Henry happily, the perspiration beginning to gleam on his face. 'Let we fire another – it making a party now, all right.'

A few dusky females appeared, and joined the revelry. Louis remembered paying for drink; he remembered singing calypsoes, laughing and talking, but he became too drunk to know why he was there, or what it was all about. A long time afterwards he was lying on a hard, uncomfortable bed, with Henry snoring somewhere near him. He was vaguely aware of this, although he had no idea where he was. He knew that something tremendous had happened to him, and then he remembered. He was in England.

The darkness seemed to be spinning round the room. He felt as though he was falling, in spite of the fact that he was lying down. Eyes seemed to be staring at him out of the blackness; Zilla's eyes, beseeching, little Pearl's eyes full of tears... he turned over and the bed lurched horribly. Teacher Ramlogan's eyes... Len Rampasad's long-lashed eyes... then he saw Lena's eyes, gleaming, hostile, malicious.

He woke with a start. It was morning, and he could hear the sound of rain beating on the window. His head ached abominably, and his mouth felt as dry as burnt trash after the sugar-cane had been reaped. He and Henry were sharing the attic, and he could hear sounds coming from below. Memories of the previous night began to drift back into his consciousness. He wondered how many men were cramped into that dirty, decrepit, evil-smelling house. It made no difference anyway; he was crammed in too, the only Indian among a crowd of negroes. Sam had said that it was all right for him to stay there, as two men had recently left anyway,

39

after an argument. But Sam had been drunk when he had said that; if not drunk, "sweet". And when a man was sweet, he said things he didn't mean.

While Louis was thinking this, Henry woke up and clasped his head in anguish. 'Oh, God, man! I feeling bad. Was a hell of a thing last night – where is we sleeping?'

'I don't know.' Louis got out of bed and opened the door. There was a flight of grimy stairs below. 'It like we at the top of the house,' he said. 'I ain't see any stairs above, just stairs below.'

'*Oui papi*! How we ever get up them damn stairs?' asked Henry, screwing up his face with the pain his head was causing him.

'I don't remember. Is right across my forehead, man. Is hell self.'

'My whole head feel like it bust open,' said Henry gloomily.

'We best had get up, though,' suggested Louis. 'It have no use lay scratching when we got no work.'

Henry looked at him, and a suspicion entered Louis' mind that Henry was not quite as keen on work as he had given him to understand. This became more than a suspicion in the weeks that followed.

True, Henry got a job. Like Louis he became a bus conductor, but not for long. Having both passed their medical examination they were given a short training period, and then with a three shilling float, ticket machine, money bag and number, they were told to get on with it. Being beginners they had no regular run at first, and had to be on different routes, working different hours every day.

'Oh, God, it hell, this, man,' said Henry. 'I ain't know where the blasted stops is – they giving me this damn silly money all the time. They tell me name of place – how the arse do they expect me to know where it is? Is a lot of balls to me, man.'

The worst route of all was the one which ran through Gantridge. It was known in Mill Street Depot as the "murder run". It didn't matter what time a bus went along that route, every stop had a queue. Where all the people came from was a mystery, they streamed out like rabbits from a warren. Sometimes Louis could hear the jabber of four different languages on the bus when he was on the murder run. It added to his confusion as he barred passengers from the platform, and frantically rang the bell. People who could barely speak English wanted to go to places he had never heard of; the island creolese was thick on his tongue, too, and often passengers were unable to understand him.

Miles of tramlines had been ripped up when Ruddersleigh Transport Department changed to buses. However, the buses still followed what had been the tram routes as much as possible, and the old tram depot became the bus station for local journeys, covering the city centre and the surrounding suburbs. The transport workers still called it "the depot". Gower Street bus station remained as it had always been, for longer journeys.

Accustomed to the "Beewee" dollar, Louis had difficulty with English money at first. A lot of foreign coins were passed on the murder run, rushed and confused he took them, and had them knocked off his pay as shortages. Apart from tackling a strange new job in an unfamiliar country, he was having to endure the discomforts of living at the Jackson residence. The house was dirty, neglected, and unbelievably noisy. Every available inch of room was occupied, men were even sleeping down in the cellar. Doors banged incessantly, voices were always raised, singing, shouting, arguing, and games of rummy went on interminably. The place smelled of dirt, men, drink, and West Indian cooking. In fact Louis could not have analysed all the smells in that house. He wondered what it must be like in warm weather, if they ever got any in England.

He had tried to find other lodgings, but it seemed impossible in Gantridge. The days were growing shorter, and dead leaves swirled about the road on some of the bus routes. Henry was dismissed, or left the job, whichever it was, he was no longer employed by Ruddersleigh Transport. Louis felt increasingly uneasy about the domestic situation at the Jacksons. He felt sure that things were going to come to a head before long.

Chapter 4

A violent quarrel broke out between Lena and Henry when Louis was having a day off. From the attic he heard the sound of angry voices down below. There were hurried footsteps on the stairs, and Henry appeared at the door, followed by Lena.

'Get outa here! Get!' she shouted at Henry. 'Don't mind Sam ain't at home! I is telling you, man, we ain't keeping you here! Haul you tail away!'

Louis was not really surprised. Lena quite obviously didn't like her brother-in-law living with them. A young negro named Tom appeared at the door behind her. He was extremely friendly with her when her husband was not around.

'Yes, haul you tail, man,' he said. Because he was Lena's favoured lodger he was behaving as if he owned the house. This infuriated Henry.

'I know you is screwing she!' he shouted, pointing to Lena. 'I know why you ain't want me around – frighten I see too much! Think other people don't know? Think Louis here don't know you is horning Sam, you worthless bitch?'

It was going to develop into a first-class domestic brawl, and Louis was determined to have nothing to do with it. He didn't care if Lena was horning her husband with every man in that house.

'You get out, too, coolie!' she screamed, suddenly turning on him. 'I ain't want no dirty coolie here!'

'Think I want to live in a house full of stinking niggers?' asked Louis. 'I been looking for somewhere else ever since I came. It hell self in this place.' He didn't owe Lena any money. He began to pack his case in front of her.

'Yes, find another mattress to put your money under tonight,' she cried, sneering at his racial characteristics.

'I ain't see a mattress worth putting money under in this place,' he told her contemptuously. He and Henry slept on anything but comfortable beds, but even so, he had an idea they fared better than Lena's cellar lodgers.

'Aw, haul you tail, coolie,' said her lover.

'You shut up, or you go down the stairs damn sight faster than you came up,' snapped Louis, who was beginning to lose his temper in spite of his resolve not to get involved in any arguments.

'Yes, ain't forget there's two of we, man,' put in Henry, who had enjoyed a temporary respite while Louis had been under fire. Threats and curses spattered the air then, and Henry made a sudden rush for Tom. There was a cry from Lena, and Louis heard the sound of skirmishing down the uncarpeted attic stairs. He went on packing; he felt as though he didn't care what they were doing to one another. He could hear Lena's voice raised in shrill abuse, and the two men shouting and swearing.

After a while things quietened down and Henry came upstairs again looking rather dishevelled. He began to pack too.

'Is a helluva country, this, man,' he said.

Louis made no reply. He could see all too clearly that Henry was no asset to any country. Trinidad's loss was not going to be England's gain in his case. He had an idea that money trouble had sparked off this row, although there were other factors as well. Anyway, he'd had enough of Henry, who had been trying to borrow from him, but without success.

He finished packing, and picked up his belongings.

'I ain't be a minute, man,' said Henry, who seemed determined to stay with him. He followed Louis downstairs. Lena and Tom were standing at the open door, to see them off the premises. A last volley of abuse and curses was exchanged.

'Take you tail away – and you! What you leave Trinidad for, coolie boy? They kick you out?'

Louis ignored it all until Lena shouted a last disgusting insult about Indians and lavatories.

'Is a bottle of disinfectant by my bed,' he told her. 'Is the only one in that damn stinking house – I use it every time I go in your filthy W.C. Take it and pour it over you and your sweetman.'

He was ready for Tom if he got aggressive, but Tom had evidently had enough for one day, having already been down the attic stairs in a scuffle with Henry. He didn't want Louis to start as well. The two young men walked down the road, Henry as talkative as ever.

'It have a lime call Netherby a few miles from here. It have plenty work in the mills, there, man. I got a cousin living there – Sam gave me his address. How 'bout we go to Netherby? I ain't liking this lime much.'

'Well, go take your tail to Netherby, then,' said Louis. 'And *crapaute* smoke your pipe. I've got a job here, and what I want is somewhere to live, and not in a house full of niggers.' He followed that up with some pointed comments about negroes in general, and the Jackson family in particular.

'*Oui papi*! That coolie all right! No gratitude – turn on a man after he help you! I shoulda know better – now you start abusing negroes. You ain't going to pick and choose where you live, man. Is the coloured part of Ruddersleigh here – you go try get lodgings anywhere else in this lime! It have plenty from Trinidad here, but they is all negroes – it have plenty coolies, too, but they is all from Pakistan. You think you go find nice-nice house, full of Trinidad coolies? Man, they ain't such a house in this lime – you left them all back on the island, burying they money. *Oui.*'

Henry paused for breath. He had stated Louis' position with unerring accuracy. He was a West Indian, but an East Indian West Indian. He had nothing against the negroes – it was customary to exchange racial insults during heated arguments – but he was not one of them. The Pakistani Indians at the bus depot were friendly enough, but he was not one of them, either. He was a Trinidadian.

At the end of the road, he and Henry went their separate ways. And although they parted on anything but friendly terms, a sense of utter loneliness swept over Louis. For the first time in his life he felt completely without roots. He thought with nostalgia of Teacher Ramlogan's pleasant, happy-go-lucky household. He thought of his uncle's house, too. Awful though it was, they were his own people.

So he walked along, a Trinidad Indian alone in a grey, uncaring city. But whatever he was, or was not, he was indisputably a young man, and of the Christian faith. Ruddersleigh Y.M.C.A. Hostel sheltered him for the night. And the next day he realised that he would have to stay there for a week or two, at all events. It was certainly not cheap, and working irregular hours made things difficult all round. But at least he had a roof over his head, even though it was draining his resources to keep it there.

44

He was often on the murder run, working early turns, late turns and split turns. In between he worked "bangers" as overtime was called at the depot. Meals were a constant problem. The canteen at the depot was always available, but the food revolted him. Whenever possible he went along to a tiny Indian restaurant, and bought himself a meal.

He was often tired, lonely and miserable, but he grew adept with English money, and the work became easier. People no longer palmed foreign coins onto him. He got to know the fare-dodgers and the argumentative types. He became accustomed to women's shoes rattling down the stairs, and to gloves, umbrellas and handbags being left on the bus. Then the fogs began to close in on Ruddersleigh, and Louis hated it, particularly if he had a coloured driver, for they were all nervous and unhappy under foggy conditions.

And just when the weather was getting really bad, and his morale at a very low ebb, he was given a regular run. It was from Beadnell, a fairly select suburb about four miles out of the city, through Ruddersleigh to Fordham, a similar district about the same distance out on the other side. His driver was a burly, good-natured man of about forty-five, and right from the start they got on well together. Jim Askew felt sorry for the young man, and took an interest in him.

They sat together in the canteen, and encouraged by his sympathetic manner, Louis told him some of the problems he was encountering in England, particularly difficulties regarding lodgings. The older man wondered if he could help him. His sister-in-law who had been widowed the previous year had mentioned that she was thinking of taking in a male lodger. She had a fourteen-year-old son, and a married daughter who often visited her, but she was depressed and nervy. For the time being she felt unable to continue with the part-time work she had been doing.

Jim told Louis about this, and said that he would mention the matter to his sister-in-law. 'I'll put in a word for you, lad, and see if there's anything doing. You don't drink, or owt like that, do you?'

'I might fire one,' said Louis cautiously. 'I don't come in drunk.'

'Well, fair enough. I'm not promising anything, mind.'

Louis sat thinking. Lodgings with a white family? He had not considered this, and he felt rather shy at the idea.

Jim was as good as his word, and went along to see his sister-in-law, who lived only a few streets away from him.

'I've been thinking about what you said last time you and Bob were round at our house, Annie. I know a young chap down at the bus depot who's wanting good lodgings. He's my new conductor, a right nice, quiet lad. He doesn't go drinking or owt like that. Nowt rough about him.'

Mrs Askew paused in the act of pouring him a cup of tea. She was in her late forties, a small, trim looking woman, with a brisk but pleasant manner.

'Where's he living now?' she enquired.

'Y.M.C.A. I feel right sorry for him – he just picks at his food in the canteen. I think he could do with some home cooking.'

Mrs Askew was interested. She finished pouring the tea.

'Well, I wouldn't mind if you say he's all right.'

Her brother-in-law hesitated. 'There's just one snag, Annie.'

'Oh, there would be. What is it?'

'He's coloured.'

'What? You don't think I'm taking coloureds in, do you? Nay, Jim! What is he, anyway?'

'He's an Indian.'

'You mean one of them Pakistanis? I've heard about them, killing chickens in the back yard and goodness knows what. Not likely, not in this house.'

'He's not Pakistani, he's from Trinidad.'

'Is he one of them with a turban wound round his head?' demanded Mrs Askew. 'They reckon they never tek 'em off, no matter what they're doing—'

'He's nothing like that at all,' said Jim, with a grin. 'And he's got no nasty habits—in fact, I happen to know he's a very particular boy. He's from the West Indies, and he's a decent lad—do you think I'm daft and can't weigh folks up, or summat?'

'You're none daft, Jim, but it's easier to weigh up your own than to weigh up a foreigner,' said Mrs Askew shrewdly. 'You know what to expect with an English boy, but with one of them fellows...'

'Well, that's that, then. But you needn't go on like that,

Annie. I might tell you he's a very nice looking lad.'

Mrs Askew pondered for a moment. 'I don't know what the neighbours would think.'

'Hang the neighbours. It's your house.'

'I don't know, though... you say he can't eat canteen food?'

'No, he's right miserable, poor lad.'

'Well, you can bring him round. I'll have a look at him.'

So Louis was brought round. Mrs Askew's son Bob was very interested when he knew the young man came from the West Indies.

'Do you play cricket?' he asked.

'Sure thing,' said Louis, smiling.

'Is he coming to live with us, Mam?' asked Bob eagerly, looking at his mother.

'Well, we don't know yet. We're just getting a few things sorted out.'

Now that she had met Louis, Mrs Askew felt less apprehensive about things He was certainly a nice looking boy, and Bob was obviously eager to have him in the house. She suspected that her prospective lodger was a bit shy, and probably homesick, and there was a certain charm in his soft foreign voice and boyish smile. The Askews' house was old, but it had been modernised to some extent. It was a three story building, with the kitchen altered and extended into the backyard, and divided to accommodate a modern bathroom. There was a living room and sitting room, two bedrooms on the next floor and a roomy attic above. Louis was shown the bedroom which had formerly been Mrs Askew's daughter's.

'This was our Susan's before she got married. Her dad died a few months afterwards... will it be all right for you?' The bedroom furniture was of solid mahogany, complete with dressing table, matching chest of drawers, and double wardrobe. Mrs Askew opened the wardrobe door to reveal a full length mirror on the inside.

'It's old fashioned, I know, it was my grandma's, but our Susan liked it, but of course, the bed doesn't belong to it.'

The single divan bed with a white headboard and pink frilly bedspread looked somewhat incongruous beside the heavy Victorian furniture, but Louis saw nothing to criticise. 'Is okay. Is fine,' he said, looking around.

There were other traces of femininity still in the room. There were pink lace mats on the dressing table, and a runner on the chest of drawers. The curtains were pink too, and the wallpaper was a faded all over pattern of pink and mauve flowers. There were two cheap looking prints on the wall, one of a couple dancing in the moonlight, and the other of a couple silhouetted on a balcony. The carpet was a plain moss green, a quiet contrast to all the pink flamboyance.

'Our Bob has the attic. It's full of his junk, there's hardly room for his bed, but that's the way he likes it, and posters all over the wall. He makes a mess with one thing and another, but I don't say owt, because I know he misses his dad. He's doing a bit better at school now, he went through a very bad phase after his father died. Well, you have to get through these things the best way you can.'

Louis was suitably sympathetic as they descended the stairs, which encouraged Mrs Askew to mention a few more details about her circumstances, and the house.

'My dad had a right good job at the mill, and he rented this house, then he bought it. I had two brothers, but they both died with scarlet fever, so I was the only one. Mam had me late in life, then my father died when Ben and me were courting—he wasn't old, you know. Anyway, Mam said why not get married and live here with her, so we did. She died in nineteen fifty eight, and Ben died last year. After Mam's death, though, we spent some of the insurance money on modernising the house. I've got things the way I want them now, and I wouldn't like to move. People say we've had deaths in the house, and I ought to move, but I say we've had births, as well. I was born here, and our Susan and Bob, too.'

'Are you going to leave all that frilly pink stuff in our Susan's room?' asked Bob, who knew his mother's stories about the house and the births and deaths by heart. 'You'll wake up in the mornings and think you're a lass,' he added, to Louis.

'Don't be silly,' said his mother.

'Well, pink for girls, blue for boys.'

Louis looked mystified. 'Is nothing wrong with the room,' he said.

'I was only joking. My room's better, there's nowt frilly in there. I've got a guitar, though. Me and two of my pals thought of starting a skiffle group, you'll have to come and listen to us—'

'For goodness sake, Bob, give him a chance to settle in! And that din that goes on sometimes in the attic is enough to put anyone off living here.'

'I won't mind,' said Louis. 'I'll do calypso for you.'

'Oh, great! Do you hear that, Mam? He'll be joining in.'

'Make it my bingo night, then,' said his mother, laughing. She knew how sullen and difficult Bob could be, but the arrival of the young stranger from Trinidad had brought a new interest into his life. She asked Louis if he had brothers and sisters, but his sad, brief reply about his parents' deaths stopped her from any further enquiries. The following week Louis moved in, and became a lodger in an English home. Dinningley was a built up area which gradually merged into the city, but where the Askew's lived it was a fairly quiet, respectable working class district. It was hilly, with rows and rows of brick terrace houses grimy with the years of soot from reeking Ruddersleigh chimneys, domestic and industrial.

'Mind you, I wouldn't take any coloured lad in,' said Mrs Askew to her friends and neighbours. 'But my brother-in-law knows him well, so I knew he would be all right.' And as Mrs Askew was known to be a very particular person in Rothwell Road, Louis was accepted as being all right. After a few weeks he was simply accepted.

'Nice lad,' said the neighbours, and thought no more about it, and in the cosiness of that terrace house, Louis experienced his first winter in England. There was a kitchen range in the living room, and a fireplace in the sitting room and both bedrooms.

'I only keep one fire going, but there's a little electric fire in the bedroom, the sort that blows the heat out. You can plug it in for a bit before you go to bed. It'll take the chill off. I have one, so has Bob. Our Susan took a lot of bits and pieces away with her when she got married, but I said I didn't want the place stripping, so she left the fire. Do you smoke in bed? I don't mind as long as you're careful, I can't say owt, because I do it, first thing in the morning with a cup of tea. I'll put an ashtray on the little table by your bed.'

Once Louis was living there, Mrs Askew seemed to accept him as part of the family. She gave him a great deal of useful information about the locality, where the nearest corner shop was for the purchase of cigarettes, where the doctor's surgery was, and where the cinema was situated.

'We used to go there a lot at one time, but now with TV people don't bother so much. Sometimes they get good films there, though.'

Louis was intrigued by the kitchen range, the intricacies of the oven and hob, the boiler, and the damper which could be pushed in and out.

'I know it's old fashioned now, but my mother always used it, and she baked all our bread in there. I don't care what they say, a fire heated oven makes the best bread, not that I ever bake bread, not many people do these days. Of course, we could have had the range taken out after she died, but I decided to keep it. Sometimes if it gets really hot, I might put a few scones in, but I use the gas cooker in the kitchen for most of the time.'

Mrs Askew's somewhat senile tabby cat, Tinker, liked to sit on the warm hob. 'He's all right there if it doesn't get too hot, then he jumps down. He doesn't go out too much now in winter, although sometimes at night he's a long time coming in. He used to be off for days at a time when he was younger, that's the worst of tom cats, and they get into fights. We should have had him done when he was younger, but we never got round to it.'

She left Louis to work out for himself what "done" meant. Before he had been there a fortnight, Mrs Askew noticed something strange about her young lodger. He didn't drink his tea, and he just picked at his food. As she had always been considered a good cook, she found this highly displeasing. On the second Sunday, when Louis never touched his roast beef and Yorkshire pudding, she could no longer contain herself.

'You don't seem to eat much,' she said. 'What's the matter, don't you like my cooking?'

'Is not the cooking,' said Louis.

'Well, what is it, then?'

'Is the food. I don't like English food.'

Mrs Askew looked at him incredulously. 'You don't like Yorkshire pudding?' Louis shook his head.

'Or roast beef?'

'I never tasted it.'

'But if you've never tasted it, how do you know you don't like it?' Louis made no reply. In Chittaranjan's house, although they were no longer Hindu, beef was never eaten, on that point the old faith made its last stand. One mouthful of that beef and Louis' gorge would have risen, but he could hardly tell Mrs Askew so. Bob sat at the table, looking from his mother to Louis, concern in his round blue eyes.

'Well, what *do* you like?' asked his mother.

'Indian food. Rice and split peas, and things you don't cook here, fish, and curried chicken...' He named a few Creole dishes. There was silence in the room.

'Mek him what he wants, then, Mam,' said Bob.

'Don't you drink tea, either?' enquired Mrs Askew.

'No.'

'What do you drink, then?'

'Cocoa mostly. Coffee and milk, too.'

Mrs Askew was speechless. This was something she had not bargained for. And how in the world could anyone prefer rice and split peas to roast beef and Yorkshire pudding? It didn't seem natural, somehow. Fancy Jim landing her with this! Still, split peas, rice and curry powder were all cheap, so was cocoa.

'Well, I'll have a go at cooking what you like,' she said.

'Is very kind of you, Mrs Askew.'

She was suddenly touched. Could it be that she was growing fond of the young man? About a week later, on Louis' day off, she met Jim in the local grocer's shop, where he was buying cigarettes.

'Hello, Annie. What's me laddo doing today?'

'He's mending the coal cellar door for me.'

'How are you getting along with him then?'

'Oh, we're getting on fine,' she told him sarcastically. 'You never let on about him not liking English food! Home cooking, indeed! He's getting home cooking all right—like he got at home in Trinidad, though.'

'What do you mean?'

'He won't eat English food. I'm messing about with split peas, rice and curry till kingdom come.'

'Never! I didn't know that.'

'Well, that's the carry-on in our house now. It isn't all rice, though, he likes his chicken and tinned salmon, too. He's not daft you know.'

51

'Still, rice doesn't cost so much,' grinned her brother-in-law. 'I bet what you loses on the roundabouts you gains upon the swings.'

'I know I'm sneezing all over the place with that blasted red pepper. The cat keeps out of the kitchen now when I'm making owt for Louis. I wonder that lad's inside isn't burnt away.'

'He looks well on it, anyway. I don't think you mind doing it as much as you mek out.'

'Oh, well...' Mrs Askew laughed. 'Our Bob thinks the sun shines out of him, you know. I'll have to get back now, and get the rice and split pea's on. The doctor said to keep my mind occupied—well this little lot's keeping me occupied all right.'

'If you ask me, he's just what the doctor ordered, for you and Bob,' said Jim, laughing.

'Well, you might be right at that,' she agreed, and went off down the road.

Life began to settle into a routine for Louis. Occasionally, he wrote to Len Rampasad and Teacher Ramlogan. From their replies he deduced that things were much the same as usual in the Chittaranjan household. He, Mrs Askew and Bob all liked television, and as the nights grew colder and darker, a good deal of viewing went on at that house. Mrs Askew knitted at the same time, and Louis was fascinated, watching her needles flash.

'I never saw anyone do that before,' he said.

'If you give me the money for some wool, I'll knit you some sweaters and things,' she offered. 'You don't have any jumpers, and your teeth don't half chatter sometimes with the cold.'

Louis gave her the money, and she sat knitting for the young man she had once been reluctant to have in her home. Bob was far less cheeky and difficult to cope with these days she noticed. He had someone with whom to exchange masculine talk now, someone from the West Indies to show off to his school friends.

When Louis wore his first hand knitted sweater, both he and Mrs Askew felt rather proud.

'You look all right, love. Turn round, let's see it from the back,' she said. He smiled rather self-consciously, resplendent in a Fair Isle pullover. By this time it was really cold. He was intrigued when he could see his own breath like white smoke in the freezing air. The Askews' celebrated Christmas in the traditional way, and Louis joined in, as he was clearly expected to. He and Bob put up the coloured paper chains and balloons, and trimmed the Christmas tree, bought from Ruddersleigh market. The Market Buildings had been built at the beginning of the century, and the great covered market on the ground floor bustled with activity. Turkeys, chickens and geese were hung up on stall after stall, while hoarse voiced vendors shouted their wares. At some butchers' stalls a pig's head would be on display, with an orange in its mouth. A crush of humanity surged around everywhere, looking and buying. The schools had broken up, and eager children dragged their mothers to the toy stalls, babies cried, and there seemed to be holly and tinsel as far as the eye could see.

'When I was little I used to think we would never get to the end of the market,' confided Bob.

'I'm thinking that now. Stay close, or we'll lose each other in this crush—you don't want me to have to hold your hand, do you?'

'Ha! Big joke. They sell all sorts of pets at the back of the market, birds, mice, rabbits, hamsters, puppies—'

'We ain't here to buy pets. We want a Christmas tree, and your mother doesn't want a great big one, either, so you can stop looking at that one.'

'It's a good one. It's not too big—'

'How we get it on the damn bus? Your mother said what she wants. Best not to vex her, she's plenty vex now with the butcher. She had a row with him, she tell me about it.'

'She has a row with him every Christmas... I could do with a new football for one of my presents. My Uncle Jim always gives me money for Christmas.'

'You'll be able to get a football with it, then.'

'I was hoping somebody might buy me one.'

'Well, somebody might. You go have to wait till Christmas Day.'

'Aw, you're just having me on. I bet you've got one hidden away. People go creeping about at Christmas, hiding things away. I used to pretend I believed in Santa for ages after I found out about him.'

'This tree looks okay, Bob. Is a good shape, and not too big.' Louis eyed one up appraisingly.

'You think it's big enough?'

'Plenty big. I'll be carrying it, remember. We go get some more of those things to put on it, shall we?'

'Yes, they're selling Christmas tree decorations at that stall over there and Mam said she could do with some more wrapping paper. We have to watch Tinker, though. He nibbles at the tinsel if he gets a chance.'

Louis bought a box of decorations for the tree, and some tinsel.

'I never tasted tinsel. Maybe it okay, we have to try it some time. What sort of chocolates does your mother like best? I'm not buying any here, mind. I go to proper sweet shop for that.'

'Well, she likes milk chocolate. Me, I like any chocolate, plain, milk, full of nuts.'

'It's your mother I'm asking about, *oui*.'

'I heard Mam talking to Auntie Elsie about you, they were on about Christmas.' Elsie was Jim's wife.

'What they say about me?'

'Auntie Elsie said was Mam making you owt special for Christmas dinner, and Mam said you would like turkey, and if you wanted curried rice with it instead of what we had, you could have it. And she said she always meks trifle for them who don't want Christmas pudding. That's me for a start, I hate Christmas pudding and Christmas cake, Mam always gets me a chocolate log from t' cake shop. I like Boxing Day, no Queen's speech to be quiet for, and I can have me mates round and go in the attic. No having to listen to them old people saying what a big boy you're getting, and how like somebody int' family you look.'

Louis laughed. 'It okay if old people bring you presents, though.'

'Yes, that's all right. I don't like having to be kissed, though, as if I'm still a little lad. Some of them want to do that.'

'Me and your Uncle Jim will be doing a few hours work on Boxing Day. We've all had to get our holiday timetables sorted out. We'll be having a day off later.'

'When I start work I'll mek sure I never work Boxing Day. Pooh, what a pong of fish now. If they blindfolded me I'd know I was in Ruddersleigh market, with all the smells.'

The whole place had a sour, earthy atmosphere, occasionally swamped by the fragrance from a flower stall, or the smell of hessian sacks, mingled with the tangy odour of oranges, and the less pleasant one of wet fish. The Christmas trees exhaled their own distinctive perfume, redolent of pines and silent forests, standing as if waiting for their innocent greenery to be bedecked with glittering baubles.

'Eh, look at them big boxes of crackers going cheap—'

'Your mother said to buy a tree—'

'We never have enough crackers, and there's always some duds that don't bang. Let's get one, go on, Buggerlugs.'

'What you go call me? I tell your mother—'

'It's not bad, honest. I call me mates that, and Uncle Jim sometimes calls me that. I do know some bad words, though.'

'So do I. If I get my feet trampled on again, I might be saying some.' Louis bought a big box of crackers and some gaudy wrapping paper.

'Now we get the tree and go home. Right?'

'Right,' said Bob, grinning. A suitable tree was purchased, and they pushed their way out of the crowded, brightly lit market into the cold darkness of a winter afternoon. Outside the market entrance a man was emitting a strange yelping cry, which Louis recognised as being someone selling the *Ruddersleigh Evening Chronicle*. He bought a copy, and stuffed it into Bob's carrier bag. The city was buzzing with activity. People were struggling with shopping bags and parcels, women were pulling whining children along, telling them to shut up, or they wouldn't get anything for Christmas.

Louis and Bob had to wait in the bus queue for half an hour before they got on one, even then they had to stand. Louis managed to dump the tree on the platform, but it was a relief to both of them when they finally arrived back at number seven Rothwell Road. Mrs Askew seemed pleased with the tree, although she shook her head when she saw the big box of crackers.

'I thought we'd got enough crackers. I always seem to get the ones where you pull and pull, and nowt happens. I've been busy all day, so I'll get a bit of tea, now. We'll have beans on toast, Bob, and I'll do some fish for Louis. You'd better put the tree out in the backyard for now.'

'After tea we'll put it in a pot and decorate it,' said Bob.

'Louis might not feel like doing that tonight. He's been work-

55

ing, he was on early turn with your Uncle Jim while you were still in bed, and I know what the buses are like this time of the year. I've shopped local as much as I could this week, everybody will be scrambling around in the city, loaded up with stuff. I'm very grateful to Louis for getting the tree for us, and carting it home. That's something your dad always did.'

'Better on early turn than late turn. Jim says the later it is the worse it gets before Christmas. Was bad this morning, people doing early shopping, but no drunks like they'll get tonight.'

'Some people just mek it an excuse to drink theirselves silly. When I was a lass we went to church on Christmas Day.'

'When you were a lass they hadn't invented electricity—'

'Don't be silly!'

'Well, there was no wireless, never mind telly! The most exciting thing to look at was the bacon slicing machine int' grocer's shop—'

'We had the cinema, we went to the pictures, and we got a wireless—well, I can't remember just when, but we had one when most people did. Instead of standing there cheeking me, you can fill the coal scuttle and bring it in. I'm getting the tea ready. All right, Tinker, shut that row, you can have a bit of fish.'

Mrs Askew disappeared into the kitchen, and Louis sat beside the fire reading the *Ruddersleigh Evening Chronicle*. The following day was Christmas Eve, the year was drawing to a close.

He put down the newspaper, and thoughts of Trinidad filled his mind. When this happened he tried to think of other things, but memories of the island and his exasperating family were more than usually vivid, fuelled by all the "festive season, family occasion" articles in the *Chronicle*.

'Your tea's ready, love,' said Mrs Askew, breaking in on his thoughts. 'Are you all right? Tired, I expect.'

'No, I'm okay. I was a bit cold when we came in. I'm nice and warm now.'

'I might have central heating put in for next winter, Jim's had it done, and our Susan has it. Of course she's in a new house, it was already installed. They say it's going to be a hard winter.'

'I might get a bit of sledging in, then,' remarked Bob, sitting at the tea table and shovelling beans into his mouth. 'You should have been here a couple of years ago, Louis. We med a great slide down Anderson Hill, it was like glass. It lasted for ages.'

'Well, I don't want all that ice about again. Your Auntie Elsie slipped and broke her wrist, people were slipping and brekking all sorts. They were sanding the roads from morning till night, but they didn't bother about the pavements. We could brek us necks for all the council cared.'

'Will it get any colder than this?' enquired Louis.

'Yes, it'll snow, and then the snow will freeze. I can remember when the buses stopped running one winter because the petrol froze, and the snow froze on top of power lines and brought them down, and we were without electric light. People had to use candles, and if you only had an electric cooker you'd had it, nowt to eat.' Bob was clearly enjoying recounting all this to Louis.

'Aye, that's true. Luckily we had the gas cooker, and the kitchen range. I did help a couple of neighbours out that time. But it didn't last long, tek no notice of Bob. I doubt if we'll get one as bad as that again, but the sales will be on in Ruddersleigh as soon as Christmas is over. You want to get yourself a really warm coat.'

'Get a duffle coat. That's what I want, Mam. They've got some good ones at Wainwrights, they'll be selling them off in the New Year.'

Later in the evening Bob brought down the special Christmas tree pot from the attic, and he and Louis put the tree in, and proceeded to put the decorations on.

'Put fairy on top, fairy always goes on top,' said Bob, sorting through the box of old Christmas tree baubles, some of which had lost their glitter. They were rejected in favour of the new ones from the market.

'Mind you put the tinsel near the top, too. I don't know why Tinker always goes to nibble tinsel, he knows he shouldn't, but if he's alone in the room for five minutes he's at it. One year he nearly brought the whole lot down dragging on the tinsel, the fairy lights were on as well. If I hadn't come into the room when I did, he could have set the place on fire. Talking of the lights, don't you touch them Bob, your uncle Jim will fix them up and switch them on. They only get used once a year, and I'm nervous of owt like that, I always think they might explode or summat,' she added to Louis. 'Jim and Elsie and family will be here on Christmas Day, but I expect Jim's told you. We tek it in turns, we went to them last year.'

The house was crowded on Christmas Day. At Mrs Askew's request, Louis had lit the fire in the sitting room quite early in the morning, so there were two rooms in use. He and Bob carried four spare dining room chairs down from the attic.

'We should just about be able to manage with them old chairs, and a couple of stools. The table does extend... I couldn't cope with this more than every other year, I can tell you. When the others come we'll get the telly shifted into the front room. Put them parcels of presents under the tree, Bob, and keep Tinker out of the way, or he'll be after the tinsel.'

Jim and his wife and three daughters arrived mid morning, bringing an elderly, rather confused great aunt with them. The eldest girl, Beverley, was sixteen, and had recently started work, training to be a hairdresser. She was the subject of some discussion in the kitchen, between Mrs Askew and Jim's wife.

'Yes, she's got a boyfriend, Trevor Moreton, that lad who used to deliver papers. Of course, it's not serious at their age, but he's a nice lad, and he's just started an apprenticeship—'

The conversation ended abruptly, as Beverley peeped into the kitchen. She was a plump, fair-haired, pretty girl with features very much like her mother.

'Do you like my new dress, Auntie Annie? I bought it with my own money. I got loads of tips last week, we were rushed off our feet.' She twirled around, showing off a stylish, peach coloured frock. Her thirteen year old sister, Sharon, appeared at the kitchen door.

'She gets everything,' she complained. 'All I get are her old clothes.'

'You won't want this then, will you?' Beverley twirled around again.

'I bought you that dress new last month, and one for Lynne as well,' said their mother to the disgruntled Sharon, who was a thinner plainer version of her sister. 'I've been working part time at the bakery to get you girls things for Christmas.'

'Sharon's more trouble than the other two put together,' said Elsie when the two women were alone again. 'Beverley's a good kid. She loves it at the salon, and that young Trevor seems to think the world of her. Lynne's no bother, but that one—' she shook her head, and continued peeling sprouts.

'Mam, is it time to baste the turkey?' This interruption was from Mrs Askew's daughter, who had also arrived with her husband, Kevin. 'I've cut this bit about cooking the Christmas dinner from the *Radio Times*—.'

'For God's sake Susan, I've been cooking the Christmas dinner for years! The turkey is all right for a bit... well, if that Trevor is a hard working steady sort of lad you won't mind if Beverley does stick with him. I wouldn't like to have to cope with three girls, though. One's enough.'

'How do you mean? What trouble have I ever been?' Susan giggled, sipping a glass of sherry. Clutching a beer mug, her lanky, smiling husband edged his way into the kitchen, and squeezed her waist.

'Come into the front room. Your mam's got enough help in here.' He led her away.

'Doesn't she look bonny in blue? No signs of a family with them two then?' Elsie rinsed the sprouts in cold water.

'No, but there's plenty of time. Buying that new house is costing them a bit, but they're both working. Susan says she'd like a baby, but not yet.'

Jim appeared at the kitchen door. 'You two ladies fancy a drink?' he asked.

'Oh, well, go on, then,' said his wife. 'Just a sherry, mind, until we get the dinner on the table. You're going to have one, aren't you, Annie?'

'Aye, just a little one. Remember when I had a drop too much to cook the dinner, Jim? I left everything and went to lay down.'

'I remember.' Jim chuckled, and supplied them both with sherry after which Mrs Askew's face took on a deeper shade of pink.

'I'm going to open the oven door in a minute to look at the roast parsnips and potatoes, they might need turning over.' She prepared a space on the kitchen table.

'I'll get the sprouts on, they're all ready. Now what do you want?' asked Elsie. Sharon had pushed her way into the kitchen again.

'Bob threw a mandarin orange at me.'

'Well, I won't say throw one back.' Her mother finished the last of her glass of sherry. 'Tek no notice of Bob. Me and your Auntie Annie are busy getting the dinner.'

Mrs Askew, by now very flushed with the sherry, opened the oven door to face a blast of hot air. 'He only does it because you make such a fuss, Sharon,' she said, depositing a sizzling meat tin on the table. 'Tell him your dad will give him a clout if he does it again. What's Lynne doing?'

'She's playing Happy Families with Beverley and Dad and Louis. Why does everyone mek a fuss of our Lynne? That Louis pets her up—'

'Well, nobody's going to pet you up with a miserable face like that,' said Elsie briskly. 'You're one big moan, Sharon. I've told you before, we're busy. The men have nowt else to do except smoke and drink and gab at Christmas. Anyway, there's a special present for you at home.'

'Special? I thought I'd had all my presents.'

'Well, seeing Beverley's got that new dress, I bought you that party dress you were looking at in Hudsons, you'll be going to Linda Dewhurst's party next month. Does that cheer you up?'

'Oh, Mam, yes!' A sudden smile transformed Sharon's childishly plain face, and hinted at the blossoming to come. 'Will it fit me, though?'

'If it's the wrong size, they'll change it. Now stop being such a misery, and let me and Auntie Annie get on with things.'

Looking considerably brighter, Sharon left the two women to their cooking.

'I don't half miss Ben when we have a family get together at Christmas. It's not the same without him. I know Bob still misses his dad, but Jim's very good with him. He's lucky to have him for an uncle.'

'Jim thinks the world of him. He always says he's the boy we never had. Mind you, looking at some of the lads today, perhaps it's as well.'

'Bob went very funny for a long time after his dad died, I was right worried about him, on top of everything else. He's settled down more now, and he gets on well with Louis. I wasn't too sure about having him for a lodger at first. I'm glad I did now, even if he is a bit fussy over food. He can be quite helpful, you know, things that men do...'

'Aye, like fetching coal in, and tekking tops off sauce bottles and jam jars.'

They both laughed. 'Well, he got the Christmas tree from the market, something Ben always used to do, and he lit the fire int' front room for me this morning. He talks to Bob, and teks an interest in his model planes and things like that. I'd better open the window, steam in here is awful.'

'He seems a quiet young chap, do you know owt about him?'

'Not much. He doesn't seem to have any family, and he doesn't talk about things like that, so I don't ask questions. People tell you what they want you to know.'

'Well, I know Jim thinks highly of him. Of course, men aren't bothered about family stuff and things like women. They like to keep off them topics, leave coping with illnesses and relations and all that to the women. They can always talk about football, and where they were in the war.'

'Anyway, we're well on with the dinner, now, and if we can get it on the table in about half an hour, we should just about have finished eating when Queen comes on. It's quieter in the kitchen than anywhere in the house now, what with telly, and the kids... I'm going to have a cig, anyway.'

'Do you think smoking helps keep your weight down? You keep fairly trim. I've never smoked, and I've put on a lot of weight this year. I'll be looking out for some new corsets when the sales start.'

'Don't start smoking! I wish I never had. When I had my bad back I went to the Spirella lady and got fixed up. You pay a bit more, but it's worth it. Our Susan wears Playtex, all the young ones seem to these days.'

'Well, I'll have to do summat about losing weight in the new year. I might join one of them slimming clubs.'

'It's best not thought about until after Christmas... talking of food, Susan was supposed to lay the table. She shoulda done it by now.'

'Last time I looked she'd done it right nicely, with all the glasses ready, and the crackers laid out. There's Bob here now.'

'Will dinner be much longer, Mam? I'm starving.'

'Starving! You've been stuffing yourself with one thing and another ever since you got up! Anyway, it's nearly ready. Tell your Uncle Jim he'll be carving the turkey soon... there's someone at the door. It'll be your Auntie Mavis and Uncle Terry. They've got a car now, and they said they'd drive over from Netherby for the day unless the weather was too bad. Mavis is my cousin,' she added to Elsie. 'The children call her Auntie. I don't think you've met her before. It's just the two of them. They never had a family. I'll get the turkey out of the oven now. I had a do with the butcher, you know, the turkey was delivered in the van, but he hadn't put the giblets in, then he said he had! I told him off in the shop, and it was full, too! I said how do you think I'm going to mek gravy with no giblets? He soon said it had been a mistake.'

'That's Anderson, isn't it? He knows how to charge, doesn't he? I stopped dealing with him a long time ago. It looks as if things are just about ready, Annie. Happen we can tek us aprons off for a few hours.'

'Aye, it will only be for a few hours, too. They'll be yelling for their tea at six o'clock, the kids will, anyway.'

Aprons were removed, and Mrs Askew went to greet her cousin. Eventually the dinner was served, drinks were poured, the crackers were pulled, the jokes read out, and paper hats were donned by all.

'Eh, don't ram it on like that, you'll spoil my hair,' complained Susan, as her husband put a paper crown on her head rather too enthusiastically.

'Doesn't Bob get to look like his dad?' That was from Mavis. The great aunt, whose name was Florence, peered round the table. She pointed an arthritic finger at Louis, trying to find some family resemblance.

'I don't know him,' she croaked. 'I don't know who he looks like.'

'Gunga Din,' suggested Bob, a remark which earned him a clip on the head from Jim, who was sitting beside him.

'Of course, he could be Nancy's,' went on the great aunt, undeterred. 'Does anyone remember Nancy?' She looked enquiringly around the table, but nobody remembered Nancy.

'She had a right dark baby. They said the father was a foreigner or summat. She wasn't married. She took the baby away somewhere, it was during the war, of course.'

'Which war?' from Bob.

'Are you putting beer into his pop?' asked his mother, addressing Jim. 'Louis works with Jim, he's lodging with us,' she added to Florence, but her wandering mind had already lost interest in family matters.

'I like goose better than turkey,' she announced. 'More flavour. It's greasy, but the dripping from it does your chest good...'

'I've only topped up his pop with a drop of beer. It's Christmas after all, our Beverley's had a drink of wine. Let the kids enjoy themselves. Annie.'

'I don't know. If I try not to spoil him other people do,' said Mrs Askew, shaking her head. 'Are you all right, love?' she asked Louis.

'Yes, everything okay.'

'Me and Louis' going to play that new card game, and blow football when we have enough puff to do it.'

'Don't talk with your mouth full, Bob,' his mother admonished him, not wanting him to make too big a pig of himself in company, even though they were all relatives sitting at the table.

'It's always full,' put in Sharon spitefully.

'Don't you start off fratching with Bob again,' said her father, with some authority in his voice. 'What his mam says to him is nowt to do with you.'

Sharon went red in the face, and looked about to cry, but as nobody was taking much notice of her she changed her mind and got on with eating her dinner. Mrs Askew's cousin remarked that there was always some new game on sale every Christmas.

'I don't mind any new game, or anyone getting a new game for our Bob. I just thank God he's too old for that John Bull printing set. Every year somebody got him that, that messy ink everywhere, and letters all over the floor. The first set he got he did it on the wall, so you can tell how young he was. I used to dread the sight of that box every Christmas. He'd unwrap his presents, and I'd say to Ben, my God, another of them John Bull things, bits under your feet kicking around for months—'

'Jig-saw puzzles are nearly as bad,' said Elsie. 'The kids lose patience and Beverley once threw the whole thing on the floor because she couldn't find one piece.'

'I never,' from Beverley.

'Yes you did, you ask your father.'

After the Queen's speech, the big clearing away and washing up began.

'Tinker's been sick, Mam!' shouted Susan from the kitchen.

'I'm not surprised,' said her mother with resignation. 'The

way he gobbled up that turkey giblet... I'll get some newspaper to clear it up, and Tinker can go into the backyard for a bit. He'll get no more to eat today. '

'Uncle Jim and Kevin said they would wash up, Mam. I'll help out. Uncle Jim said you and Auntie Elsie should both have a rest in the front room. '

'All right. It's not just the washing up, though, it's the putting away of things, and all the bits and pieces to keep for tomorrow.'

Protesting slightly, Mrs Askew went out of the kitchen and back into the crowded front room, followed by Elsie. Mavis was sitting in an armchair, and Florence was falling asleep in the other. Louis and Terry took cards and board games into the living room, followed by Bob, Sharon and Beverley. Mrs Askew and Elsie sat on the recently vacated sofa, while Lynne sat on the carpet, nursing a new doll and leaning against her mother's legs.

'Doesn't she want to go in the other room with the others?' asked Mavis. Elsie shook her head. 'Jim and Louis amused her a lot this morning. She's tired, she wouldn't go to sleep until late last night, and she was awake early this morning, of course.'

'She's very blonde, isn't she?' remarked Mavis.

'Yes, I expect it'll darken a bit as she gets older. The girls all tek after my colouring.' She stooped and kissed Lynne's flaxen poll. 'I was a blonde when Jim met me, slim, too. Slimmer than our Beverley.'

'Jim's well built, though, like Ben was. Our Susan's going to be like me, I think, she's very slim. I don't know about Bob, he's busy growing now. Look, we've got a bottle of port here, and some clean glasses. I'll switch the telly off, and we'll have a bit of peace and quiet. Florence is asleep.'

'Whose aunt is she?' asked Mavis. 'I'm rather mixed up.'

'She's Jim's,' said Elsie. 'She was widowed years ago—no family of her own. She was always good to my children before she went a bit funny.'

'She was good to mine, too. Ben was fond of her, he wouldn't want us to neglect her now she's very old.' Mrs Askew supplied the three of them with glasses of port, and lit a cigarette, having switched the television off.

'It'll be on enough later on. It's like moving wallpaper when our Bob's home in the holidays.'

'Where's Susan?' asked Elsie.

'She's helping her uncle and Kevin in the kitchen, although it's a bit crowded with the three of them in there.'

As she spoke there was a crash from the direction of the kitchen. Susan poked her head round the door. 'It's only that old vegetable dish, Mam. It's not part of the dinner service. It was nobody's fault, really. It just slipped.'

'Aye, it just slipped.' Mrs Askew shook her head and laughed, enjoying her port. 'If the wiping up cloths get too wet, you know where I keep clean ones.'

Susan withdrew, but appeared again before long. 'Tinker's crying like mad at the back door. Shall I let him in?'

'Oh, go on then, let him in. Don't give him owt to eat, though. He'll go in his basket in the other room, and tell them in there not to pick him up or owt. Our Bob won't, but Beverley or Sharon might try to.'

Before long, Sharon opened the door. 'Bob's cheating at that new card game,' she whined.

'Well, cheat back,' said Elsie wearily. 'If you can find owt to moan about, you will.'

'You never listen to me, and you always tek other people's part.' Sharon went away, closing the door behind her with some force.

'Is she all right? She seems very upset.' Mavis looked concerned.

'She's just a little madam, and if it wasn't Christmas I'd deal with her properly.' Elsie tightened her lips and shook her head.

'Well, I've never had a family. I don't think I could have coped, anyway. They're such a responsibility. Did everybody walk here this morning, by the way?'

'Well, we just live a few streets away,' said Elsie. 'Auntie Florence is in the Eventide Home, but we thought we'd have her with us for Christmas. She had a taxi to our house yesterday, but she did walk here this morning with us. It's cold, but dry, thank goodness. She'll go back to the home after Boxing Day.'

'Susan and Kevin walked from that new estate, the Burnside. It's a good walk here from there, but it doesn't bother the youngsters.' Mrs Askew lit another cigarette.

'I was going to say me and Terry could run everyone home before we set off for Netherby.'

'Are you sure? It would mean more than one journey. Terry might not be too keen.'

'It was Terry who suggested it to me. We're not bothered what time we get to Netherby. '

'Well, that's kind of you. We won't be late home, Jim's working tomorrow, anyway.'

'Yes, and Louis. They mek a bit extra, of course.' Mrs Askew drew pensively on her cigarette, and remarked that she was trying to give up smoking.

'Annie, you've been saying that for years!' Mavis laughed, and her cousin joined in, and the slight family resemblance between the two women was suddenly intensified. Mavis was darker and more angular, but she had the same round blue eyes and well defined cheekbones. She was a couple of years older than Mrs Askew. There was a strong bond of friendship between the two women, although as they lived in different cities and Mavis worked, they saw less of each other than they would have liked.

Eventually Christmas Day drew to a close, and a few days after the bells had rung the new year in, Louis saw his first snow. He was amazed at the immaculate whiteness covering the streets, the roofs of houses, and the backyard of the Askews' house. On waking that morning he had noticed the light seemed strange, as if reflecting upwards through the curtains. When he drew them he realised that during the hours of darkness a covering of snow had silently descended and transformed the view from his window.

'Snowball fights!' shouted Bob, when his friend, Alan, called for him. 'Come on, Louis, you've never seen snow before, let's have a game!' The touch of snow was so strange, the cold hardness moulded into a rough ball in his hand, the curious elation he felt, dodging the missiles from the two boys, and managing to hit them both with an accurate aim.

'Never mind larking about with snowballs,' called Mrs Askew from the back door. 'Mek a pathway to the gate. Tinker doesn't like the snow, but he'll go into the yard if there's somewhere for him to do his business. I don't want to bother with his litter tray if I can help it. And don't you throw a snowball at him, Bob.'

The dazzling whiteness of the first snowfall only lasted a short time, to be replaced by grey slush. People tramped around in wellington boots, beneath sunless skies. The winter wore on, with snow alternating with wind and rain, and sometimes freezing fog. The worst was when it froze over the half melted snow and hard, slippy ridges made it treacherous underfoot. Through it all, the buses kept running, with Jim stoically driving on, sometimes through lashing rain, sometimes on sanded roads with half melted snow piled in the gutter, and, most worrying to Louis, occasionally through a fog. When that happened the traffic went more slowly, the city sounds were muted, and car headlights were on all day. It was like a hideous grey-yellow cloak enveloping everything, so bad sometimes that passengers had to ask Louis if they were at the stop they wanted. The drabness of everything, even the smell of cold, wet clothes as people got on and off the bus, depressed him beyond measure.

'Cheer up, lad, the fogs are nowt as bad as they used to be,' said Jim kindly. 'We'll get over it, you see.'

Then 'flu began to rage through the city. 'People are dropping like flies,' said Mrs Askew. 'Half Bob's school are away, kids and teachers. I hope nobody in this house gets it, although Mrs Hawkins reckons people like you from hot countries go down like ninepins with it. No resistance.' Mrs Hawkins was a next door neighbour, a cheerful, friendly woman, always pleasant to Louis when she saw him.

A few days later Bob became a victim and was confined to his bedroom for a week. Fortunately his mother escaped it, and so did Louis, despite Mrs Hawkins' rather pessimistic comments. There was 'flu at Jim's house, too, but like Louis, he kept well, unlike many of the transport workers. It meant there was plenty of overtime on offer at the bus depot.

Mrs Askew had a wheeled shopping basket in which she put the week's washing to take to the newly opened launderette a short walk away.

'It's a godsend,' she remarked to Louis. 'I can get everything washed and dried there. I can dry them in the yard in summer, but we don't want wet washing draped around the place in winter. It's miserable enough.' Hard though that winter was, Louis was growing more accustomed to life in England, and to working on the buses. The streets he walked along to the depot were familiar now. The grimy brick houses no longer appeared strange, with their tall chimneys which seemed to be topped by jagged crowns. The empty cigarette packets in the gutter, the wind blown dirt, and the occasional dog mess to avoid became everyday objects on his daily journey. He knew the house with the torn lace curtains at the window, and the house where a woman was constantly shaking mats outside. There was a tiny corner shop where he sometimes bought cigarettes, to be greeted always by a tail wagging black mongrel dog. In his working hours, Jim was always ready to give him advice, particularly on how to deal with drunken passengers. They often got on the late buses, and sometimes they were noisy and insulting.

'Ignore 'em as much as possible,' said Jim. 'If they get really tough, stop the bus and let me know. We'll pull up at Bridge Street Police Station, and have the buggers run in.'

On one occasion when the bus was full, three drunken men got on and rang the bell before Louis could get to the platform.

'You all have to get off at the next stop,' he told them. One of them was sitting on the stairs singing. He made them get off, but once clear of the bus they stood shouting curses at him.

'Roast in hell!'

'Wall-eyed get!'

'You black bastard!'

'Haul you tails away!' yelled Louis, ringing the bus on. He stood on the platform, muttering curses in Hindi. Afterwards he told Jim about it.

'They call me a black bastard!'

Jim laughed. 'It would be them bloody Irishers from Bright Street flats—never worry about them, they call everybody names, and a right set of bastards they are anyway. The Micks are streaming into Ruddersleigh now, with all the building going on. They've been clearing the slums since the Thirties, but half the houses they are knocking down now are better than the ones they put up, as for them high rise flats...' He shook his head in disgust. 'We've always had the Irish and the Jews in Ruddersleigh, then we got showered with Poles and Czechs and God knows what after the war. Then the Pakistanis, and you lot from the West Indies, and the Chinks opening restaurants! Talk about there'll always be an England—have you changed the indicator yet, lad? Come on, let's get back to the depot.'

Life had a lighter side, though, even as a transport worker. In the mornings Louis often had sweets and fruit offered him by women shoppers, and cigarettes by men, usually at night. As the weeks passed, he felt less of a stranger in Ruddersleigh. He had good lodgings and a steady job, and he and Jim got on well together. He had not planned for the future, he felt that to have achieved what he had in a foreign country was enough for the time being.

But now another face had turned in the crowd. A lovely fair face, framed in softly waving auburn hair. It was this face which kept Louis awake, and filled him with restless longings and desires. This face, with vivid blue eyes, and dimples that came and went in the rounded cheeks, as the tender mouth curved in a smile. He turned over in bed, savouring the sweetness of her presence even though she was not there, and hearing again the sound of her girlish laughter.

Chapter 5

Helen had help with the housework every Friday morning. A Mrs Garside had been coming once a week for several years now. She lived on the big council estate in Fordham where she had been re-housed in the Fifties. At first Helen wasn't sure that she was going to get on with her, she was so uncompromisingly Yorkshire. Outspoken and blunt, she said what she thought, and sometimes Helen found this disconcerting. She had a kind heart, though, despite her caustic tongue, and she was totally trustworthy. Helen grew to like her. She always made a cup of coffee for both of them as soon as Mrs Garside arrived, and they sat at the kitchen table to drink it. This was an opportunity for some conversation, a rather one-sided one, as a rule, as Mrs Garside would either talk about her family, or regale Helen with some piece of gossip from the estate. Helen was always careful to be very non-commital about anything Mrs Garside told her. She was often reluctant to hear unpleasant details about certain matters, but Mrs Garside was very uninhibit-ed in that respect. She was a strong, middle-aged, heavily built woman, with short grey hair and a prominent nose and chin. She had big red hands, with her wedding ring half buried in the flesh, behind swollen knuckles. Her topic this morning concerned a neighbour of hers who had miscarried on her fifth child.

'Well, she swore she wouldn't have it—she swore she wouldn't. She was in agony... collapsed in a pool of blood... the ambulance rushed her off to hospital. Of course, she did all sorts to herself... it takes more than hot baths and a drink of gin to shift 'em—don't I know it? Anyway, she's got shut of it now. *He's* no use, of course, drinks like a fish.' Husbands were always referred to as "he" by Mrs Garside.

'Poor woman. It's time abortion was legalised,' said Helen hastily, putting down her cup. She knew all about the eternal female battle against pregnancy, but she didn't want to hear a blow by blow account of a sordid, self-induced abortion.

'They shoulda legalised it long ago. I wouldn't have had five lads, I can tell you. Still, they're all married now except our Tom, I expect he'll be off in a few years, he's been out with enough lasses already.' She stood up, buttoning her flowered print overall.

'You can start upstairs as usual,' said Helen. 'I expect Eddie's room is in a bit of a mess.'

'Aye, it is that.' Mrs Garside stood with the vacuum cleaner ready, surveying Eddie's room. Then she went and looked in Barbara's. 'His sister's room is a bit of a tip too,' she called downstairs. 'Lasses these days don't seem to frame up to being tidy, do they?'

Helen thought that it was easy for Mrs Garside to talk like that, having only sons herself she had no daughters with whom to draw comparisons. Still, sons brought their problems. Standing at the sink washing up the breakfast dishes, Helen wished for the hundredth time that Eddie had been a bit brighter, and passed the eleven-plus, so that they wouldn't have to pay fees at a private school. She didn't begrudge the money, of course, but the fees had gone up again, and Barbara seemed to need so many clothes these days, and they had to keep increasing her pocket money. It seemed a bit ironic that the girl should win a free place at Ruddersleigh's most expensive girls' day school, while the boy couldn't even scrape through to the local state grammar school. George had sold the car at the beginning of the year, they seemed to need so much money for other things. Being without a car was inconvenient, though. They always had to make arrangements for Barbara to be brought home from late dances and parties. It was all right if she went anywhere with Shirley Beck, because Shirley's father would pick them up. It was no problem if Barbara's boyfriend, Roger Leffey, took her anywhere, of course. He usually had the use of the family car.

Occasionally, if there was some unmissable late night function on in Ruddersleigh during the week, Barbara had stayed overnight with her aunt and grandad in Parkleigh. They made a great fuss of her, which she enjoyed, and it was handy for school the following day. Sometimes Helen thought now the children were older, she should manage the housework without Mrs Garside. Perhaps she ought not to go to the hairdresser every week either. On the other hand, why should she give up her two modest luxuries? Unlike most of her friends, she didn't smoke, although smokers didn't seem to consider that habit a luxury. Catch George giving up his pipe, or his golf...

If he managed to get promoted at the next Board, things would be better. He'd failed other promotion Boards, though, but that was the Civil Service. You could be stuck in the same grade for years, until you retired, in fact. She swished the water out of the washing up bowl, and stood looking through the kitchen window. The back garden was sodden, after a night of heavy rain. There were two mature trees down at the bottom, a sycamore and a beech just inside the boundary fence, which separated their garden from the one at the back. When the woods had been cleared to make way for house building, some of the trees had been spared. Occasionally, a tiny copse would be left standing between a group of houses, and quite a number of gardens had trees in them. Flowering trees had been planted on the wide grass verges bordering the pavements, which gave the place a very pleasant appearance. It also ensured that any mention of Fordham in the *Ruddersleigh Evening Chronicle* began with: "In the leafy suburb of Fordham—"

The garden shed stood down by the sycamore tree, and outside the kitchen door was the rabbit hutch containing Ezra, the grey Netherlands dwarf rabbit, now in his fifteenth year. The back lawn was bordered by perennials, the bedding plants had not yet been put in. There was a small plot set aside for herbs which Helen used for culinary purposes. George had no need to have a greenhouse, or grow vegetables, as his father was a dedicated gardener, and supplied them with tomatoes, strawberries, and a variety of fresh vegetables in season. There was always more than he and Violet required. This generosity was much appreciated by Helen and George, they liked fresh vegetables, but preferred flower-bordered lawns back and front in their own garden.

'You'll settle,' George had said when he had been posted to the local office of the Ministry of Pensions and National Insurance in Ruddersleigh, after he had been demobilised from the army. He had been delighted, having applied for that posting. After all, Ruddersleigh was his home town, his father and sister lived there, so did a couple of aunts, and sundry cousins. There were also friends he had known since boyhood.

'What?' Helen had cried scornfully. 'Settle in this place after growing up in Eastbourne?' How she had hated it, the cold, the dirt, the bluntness of the people, the glottal Ruddersleigh twang. When they had first moved there the fogs had been appalling. They still had fogs, but nothing like they used to be, and the city had been cleaned up considerably since then.

'You wouldn't think now that it had been one of the most atmospherically polluted cities in England,' George remarked. He thought the council had done a great job cleaning up Ruddersleigh. 'Every building was black when I was a child. I didn't know it was dirt, just plain dirt. The Town Hall, the parish church, the market buildings, everywhere, jet black. They look grand now. Of course, the dirt in the city never bothered us, we could get out into the country so easily. We had the Dales and the moors practically on the doorstep, and places nearer than that, we cycled everywhere when we were kids. I can remember Fordham when it had a village green, so did Dudley. The one at Dudley was big, they used to have cricket matches on it. I used to go blackberrying there, it was just a nice four mile cycle ride from the city. There's nothing wrong with Ruddersleigh now, it's a splendid shopping centre, four big department stores, three theatres, plenty of cinemas, a famous market.'

'I know what it's like. I'm living here. It doesn't help to tell me how much worse it used to be.'

'You can't expect a big industrial city to be like a seaside town on the south coast. You never complained about it before you came to live here. You used to like coming here before we were married, and after we were married for that matter. After Babsy was born you and your mother came here to show her off to Vi and my father. You loved a couple of weeks here.'

'Yes, I know. That was different, though. Spending holidays here was all right. Living here permanently is a different thing altogether.'

'You haven't given it much of a chance. There might be a bit of promotion before long, and I don't know where I might get posted to then, it could be anywhere. We may not be living here permanently at all. I think you should try to make the best of things, anyway. I'm just thankful I came home in one piece, which is more than a lot of others did.'

Conversations like this went on continually when they first moved to Ruddersleigh. Helen's brother, Tony, had been killed in the war, then her father had died. These deaths had placed an enormous emotional burden on her. Her own happiness when she and George had got married seemed out of place in that house full of memories and photographs.

George had been brought up in Parkleigh, where Barbara now went to school. It was a long established residential neighbourhood, set on a hill, above the city's smoke and grime. The houses were solidly Victorian, many of them stone built, roomy family houses with attics and cellars. As well as busy roads there were plenty of trees, quiet little lanes, and a lingering air of gentility behind the walled gardens. When they had first moved to Ruddersleigh after the war, Barbara had been a toddler, and they had stayed at the family home, the same house that George and his sister Violet had been born in. George's mother had died during the war, and Violet's young husband, an RAF pilot, had been shot down and killed. Drawn close by shared grief, father and daughter had continued to live together.

There had been suggestions that George and Helen and their lively infant might care to live there, too.

'Plenty of room here, George. House prices will come down I expect. If you don't want to buy, though, you and Helen and little Babsy are welcome to live here. I know Vi likes having you here, and it's company for Helen. It's handy for you to get to the office from here, too. If you and Helen want to go anywhere together, you can always leave Babsy with us.'

George was tempted. If his wife had been agreeable to the idea, he would have been inclined to take up his father's offer. However, Helen made it very plain that she wanted her own house, and she didn't want to live in the Parkleigh neighbourhood, either. She had nothing against George's family, she liked his father and his sister, who both adored Barbara, and were always ready to look after her. Much as she appreciated her kindly in-laws, she didn't want to share a house with them. Nor did she want to live as close to the city as Parkleigh was, although it was convenient in many ways, as his father had pointed out.

She and George looked round all the suburbs, balancing what they would like against what they could afford, and finally settled on Fordham. It still had a countrified appearance in those days, and after living at Parkieigh for six months, Helen and George moved to Fordham. George knew that his wife had not been happy up to then, but he thought that she would settle down once she had her own house.

He had no idea of the desolate homesickness she was enduring, something which she had been quite unprepared for. She had fits of weeping sadness which irritated George, although he tried to understand.

'It's not as if we're in a different country. You can always go back for a few days with Babsy, see your mother, and everyone there.'

Eddie had not yet been born. 'I thought you would have settled down now we're in our own house. What is so awful here? You have me.'

'I miss my mother. She's alone there now.'

'She's not totally alone. Your Aunt Hilda only lives five minutes walk away, and she has friends and neighbours she's known for years.'

'It's not the same as having her own family. You don't understand. I don't feel as if I belong here... I miss the sea,' she would murmur forlornly, but that was only part of it. George would put his arms around her.

'You can't be very far from the sea anywhere in England,' he would say lightly, or he might suggest a couple of days in Whitby. Then he would point out that he'd had to go abroad during the war, and how being homesick had been the least of his worries. Helen knew all that, but it didn't alter the way she felt. She could not explain to her husband the terrible yearning which seemed to come from the bottom of her being. She longed for her mother, she longed for familiar surroundings, for her girlhood home, and the friends she'd had since schooldays. What people called homesickness was a sense of place, a feeling of being torn out by the roots, and thrown down on alien soil. She had looked forward happily to George's demobilisation and return to Civvy Street. She wanted a proper family life instead of just having him for brief army leaves, and waving goodbye again. Of course, it had all been exciting at first, having George home for good, but living in Ruddersleigh was the price she was having to pay. Until she moved north she had not realised how strong was the tie which bound her to her mother and to Eastbourne. At the same time, she felt guilty for being homesick, as well as feeling guilty about leaving her mother alone in Eastbourne. Her mother's brave smile when she had kissed her before she left to live in Ruddersleigh had wrung her heart. Unshed tears were very hard to bear.

George's father had helped them financially, lending them the deposit for the house in Fordham. Young couples who had married in war time or just after were all desperate for somewhere to live. Most of them were crammed in with relatives, and council housing lists grew ever longer. It was the post-war period of austerity, people were still rationed, bedding and utility furniture were on dockets, only allowed to recently married couples. Violet gave Helen a beautifully embroidered tablecloth, which she had intended to be part of her bottom drawer, for when the war ended, and she and her husband had their own home.

'You might as well have it, Helen. I shan't ever use it,' she had said with a sad little smile.

'But Vi, you'll meet someone else, you'll marry again—'

'No, I shan't. We were both war brides, but I drew the short straw. You're lucky, you have everything, a nice home, and George and Babsy. As for me, well, I have a decent job with the building society, and I quite like being an indulgent aunt. It's probably my natural destiny.'

Behind the brave words, Helen glimpsed the hidden grief, the lost dreams, the concealed emotions of her sister-in-law. Compared with the pain of bereavement, her own homesickness scarcely merited a mention. She gave Violet a quick hug, and afterwards to all outward appearances, she settled down in Ruddersleigh. She was soon caught up in the domestic trivia of everyday life, coping with post-war rationing, to which there appeared to be no end in sight. Barbara was a lively little girl, very hard work, demanding attention all the time. Helen had never imagined that running a home with a husband and toddler to look after could be so exhausting, nor how lonely the days could be. Sometimes Violet came to babysit for them, and she and George managed an evening out together. Gradually she made a few friends, and then Eddie was born. Her mother came and stayed for a month, to help out. Barbara was extremely jealous of the new baby, who seemed to scream incessantly, and took so much of her mother's attention away from her. Magazines and books offered plenty of advice on how a young mother should cope. "Give extra love to the first-born child, and don't let your husband feel neglected, etc". Not a word about the shattered wreck you might feel after a night when the baby had woken up screaming every couple of hours. No mention of an overflowing nappy bucket, or when the older child gave the baby whooping cough or something. Still, that phase didn't last for ever. The children grew older, and then you were faced with a fresh set of problems.

Helen turned away from the window, depressed by the drab, wintry outlook. Spring cleaning, that would be the next thing. The kitchen badly needed painting, and she didn't want it painted cream again. A cheerful, sunshiny yellow shade would be better. She went upstairs. 'I'm going to the hairdresser now. I've locked the back door and left your money on the kitchen table,' she told Mrs Garside, who was busy in Eddie's bedroom. Helen stood in front of the dressing-table in the room she and George shared, and ran a comb through her hair. Once it had been the same colour as Barbara's, but it had darkened slightly. No grey hairs yet, she thought, with a certain satisfaction, and she still had a trim figure. She wasn't tall, though; five foot two, eyes of blue, and Barbara was the same. The Grangers were all tall, and Eddie was growing rapidly, he seemed all arms and legs. In a fawn poplin raincoat, with the rain beginning to patter on her umbrella, she walked quickly along Sycamore Avenue towards the parade of shops. She knew that Mrs Garside would carry on doing the housework without any supervision, and she would make sure she closed the front door firmly before leaving.

Flowering plum trees were planted at intervals along the grass verge that bordered the pavement, their tiny new leaves just thrusting through to give a promise of spring. Mrs Bell from the end house was braving the unsettled weather, too. She was a plump, lynx-eyed woman in her forties, with a gushing manner, and a loud, tinny laugh. She was one of the biggest gossips in the neighbourhood, sifting every scrap of news like a prospector panning for gold. Helen didn't mind hearing the odd bit of gossip, but she made a point of choking Joyce Bell off. She considered the Bells' common, but weighed against this lack of refinement was the galling fact that they seemed to get on very well in the world. Still, there was some consolation in the fact that their son was no brighter than Eddie, like Eddie he had failed his eleven-plus, and attended Westcliffe Grammar School.

'Good morning. Awful, isn't it?' called Mrs Bell, when Helen drew level with her. 'Was your Eddie home late from school last Friday night?' She gave a knowing little smile.

'Last Friday?' said Helen. 'I can't remember as far back as that.'

'Our Ian said he got into trouble with one of the prefects, and had to stay behind in detention for ages.'

'Really?' Helen's voice was icy. 'It must have been a change for Ian to come home at the proper time.'

'Oh, well, I suppose boys will be boys.' Joyce Bell gave her ear-grating laugh. 'Your Barbara won't be able to play tennis so much with her friends if this weather continues.'

'No, it's not very good for outdoor games, is it? It doesn't stop the youngsters, though, quite a few are already playing regularly on the court at Fordham park. Barbara says if it rains they all just pile into the park shelter. The bowling green there must be absolutely soaked, anyway it's not likely to be needed for a while yet.'

'Well, of course some people take their pleasures inside. If you go playing bingo every afternoon it doesn't much matter if it's raining or what it's doing.'

'It's certainly a very popular pastime—perhaps that's why.'

'You'd be surprised at the people who do go playing bingo. I know I got a shock one afternoon when I was walking past the Palais in Ruddersleigh. They were all coming out after a session, and who should I see tripping out but Mrs Eggleston, who lives at the back of me. You know who I mean—'

'Excuse me, I must dash, I have an appointment at the hair-dressers. 'bye,' said Helen, mustering a smile. Detestable woman, she thought, and her sneaking, sly-faced son. No wonder Eddie hated him. They were the only two boys in Sycamore Avenue who attended Westcliffe Grammar School, but they were none the fonder on that account. In fact Eddie and his friend "Mousy" Marfitt waged ceaseless war on Ian Bell.

Helen quickened her pace towards the parade of shops where the hairdresser had her salon. Most of the front gardens that she passed displayed rain soaked, wind flattened daffodils, with a few battered tulips making a contrasting splash of red beside the yellow. Here and there a forsythia bush made a brave show, but the general effect was very much an end of winter look for the gardens, with the promise of a cold, wet spring.

Before she reached the hairdresser, Helen met Mrs Rodley, another acquaintance. She was just leaving her house to take the Labrador for a walk. She had a daughter, Karen, who was the same age as Barbara. The two girls had been friends at Fordham Junior School, and they had both sat for the eleven-plus, and for the Parkleigh High School Scholarship. Barbara had passed for both, but although Karen had passed the eleven-plus for the newly built Fordham Grammar School, she had not won a place at Parkleigh High School. Once they were at different schools, the friendship foundered. Helen knew that Karen's mother had never quite forgiven Barbara for succeeding where her own daughter had failed. However, Karen had a younger brother, Jeremy, who had passed the eleven-plus, and was now at Fordham Grammar School, like his sister. Mrs Rodley knew that Eddie had failed to get a place there, and was at a fee paying school. She would somehow manage to bring the subject of education into the conversation if she and Helen happened to meet.

She would say how well both her children were doing at Fordham Grammar School, how Karen was going to take A levels, how expensive everything was, and thank goodness they weren't having to pay school fees for either of them.

'Good morning, can't stop, hair appointment. Awful weather, isn't it?' Helen called cheerfully, hurrying along. Mrs Rodley looked slightly taken aback, but a hair appointment was a legitimate excuse not to stop and talk, so she returned the greeting, hushing the dog, who had given a couple of barks.

Helen decided to have a look round the shops that afternoon, so she took the bus into Ruddersleigh. She did quite a lot of home dressmaking, and she was very good at it, having attended classes at night school. Barbara had asked her to have a look at some material which she had seen in Gibsons, a large department store. Helen also tried out some new perfume that was being sold there that week. It was called Olive Adair Sweet Pea, and the delightful fragrance enchanted her as the salesgirl sprayed it on her wrist.

'I shall be selling it in another town next week, madam. You can't buy it in any shop, only from this counter while I'm here...'

Helen bought two bottles, one for herself and one for Barbara. It would be a nice surprise for her when she came home from school. She also had a look at the new season dresses in the shops. There was a whole rack of crimplene frocks in one of the big department stores, all in bright jewel colours.

'Easy care, drip dry, madam,' said the smiling assistant, but Helen was not to be tempted. She was not too sure about all these easy care man-made materials appearing in the shops, although Eddie was wearing terylene trousers. They were certainly hard wearing, and looked smart, but as Eddie was growing so fast she was doubtful if they were such a good buy.

"Outgrown before outworn" was the proud slogan in one of the department stores, but it meant that a perfectly wearable but too short pair of trousers would end up at a local jumble sale. On the other hand, boys were rough and careless with their clothes, and cheaper trousers soon looked shabby. As for drip dry, with the present weather there was plenty of drip everywhere, but not much chance to dry. Anyway, it was less trouble to take something to be dry cleaned than dripping it dry, and then finding that you had to iron it after all. Helen purchased some knitting wool, and two pairs of nylon stockings. The busy, well lit department stores were a pleasant contrast to the wet cheerlessness of the city streets.

Shortly before four o'clock she stood in the bus queue for Fordham, along with several other people. They were mostly women shoppers, umbrellas held aloft, with a few under school age children. The queue lengthened, and there was a general feeling of relief when the familiar yellow bus came into view. Wet umbrellas were shaken and furled, oozing dampness, as the bus filled up and started on its journey. There were frequent stops on the way to Fordham, with the standing passengers lurching and swaying alarmingly every time the vehicle pulled up.

'Fares please.' The conductor asked people to move further along when it was quite obvious that nobody could move any further along. Children were hauled up onto people's knees, and peevish mackintoshed toddlers wailed intermittently. Helen glimpsed a couple of familiar faces bound for the terminus at Fordham, and smiled accordingly. She knew when they stepped off the bus they would all grumble about the weather as they dodged the puddles on the way to their respective homes.

When Barbara arrived home from school she was delighted with the unexpected present of scent.

'Oh, it's gorgeous! I've just about finished all the scent I got at Christmas... Shirley will be green with envy.'

'Well, they might still be selling it tomorrow at Gibsons, but not next week. Are you going into Ruddersleigh with Shirley tomorrow?'

'I'm going into Ruddersleigh, but not with Shirley. I'm going to the Reference Library to see what there is about Trinidad. I want to get that essay done that I told you about.'

Barbara seemed to have forgotten about the dress material, and Helen decided not to remind her. Either she was busy thinking about that essay, or she was thinking about Roger Leffey. Not that Helen disliked Roger, as a boyfriend for her daughter she distinctly approved of him. He was an engineering student at Ruddersleigh University. With light brown hair, an athletic build, and clean cut good looks, he made a handsome escort for Barbara. He was a pleasant, steady young man, well mannered and always well dressed in a discreetly up to date way. Although his hair was somewhat longer than that of his father's generation, it was never allowed to get too long, and was kept carefully trimmed. He was ambitious, an only child who lived at home in the sprawling, ever growing suburb of Dudley. His father was a pharmacist with a thriving shop there, but he had put no pressure on his son to follow in his footsteps. The fact that Roger knew what he wanted to do, and had obtained a place at Ruddersleigh University delighted both his parents. It meant they would have him at home for a few more years, unlike most of his contemporaries from Ruddersleigh Royal Grammar School. They had been dispersed to various universities throughout the country. Roger found Barbara rather abstracted that evening. When he kissed her goodnight, and asked what she was doing at the weekend, she said she was going to be busy writing her essay.

'You have several weeks to write it in, though,' he objected, his grey eyes slightly puzzled.

'I know, but I want to write a lot while it's fresh in my mind— she broke off. 'I mean I'm going to the Reference Library tomorrow. I don't want it hanging on for weeks. I'd rather write it and get it over with.'

'Next week, then, darling?'

'I'll see you Monday, and we'll go and see "The Sundowners" at the Odeon in Ruddersleigh. It's supposed to be very good, and there's nothing worth seeing at the Orion in Fordham. We don't get much homework on Mondays.'

So he had to be content with that. But she squeezed his hand and dimpled at him so disarmingly that he didn't mind. And on Saturday Barbara spent a considerable time in the Reference Library, adding to her knowledge of Trinidad. That evening she surprised the rest of the family by neither watching television nor going out. Instead, she sat in her bedroom and made a rough draft of the essay. And as she wrote, the things Louis Ramdeen had told her mingled with the more prosaic notes which she had taken at the library. The vividness of his spoken words gave her writing a power and vitality she knew could never have been possible just from cold facts taken out of books. A sense of elation filled Barbara. She would give Pringle a run for her money, and all the other Sixth Form Pringles in Ruddersleigh, male or female. So she wrote on, checking and altering, considering what to put in and what to leave out, until Eddie thumped on her bedroom door.

'Well, what is it?' she asked, frowning.

'Mum's making coffee, and she says if you want a drink and biscuits or a sandwich, you'd better come downstairs now,' announced her brother. She was still occupied with the essay for a good part of Sunday, in fact, by the time she had done her homework as well, she felt very tired. It was with a good deal of pleasure that she looked forward to Roger's company on Monday evening. When he enquired about the essay, she told him that she was getting along fine with it. In fact, she was so pleased with herself that she was particularly agreeable towards him, and they had a very pleasant evening. Sitting in a double seat on the back row of the balcony at the Odeon cinema in Ruddersleigh, they indulged in a good deal of surreptitious kissing and petting. They were both in a very happy mood when later they stood talking and laughing, waiting at Marsh Street bus stop for the number sixteen to Fordham.

They were at the front of the queue, and while they stood, Roger talked about the university dance to be held in May. Barbara was so interested in this when they boarded the bus and went upstairs that she didn't notice the conductor on the platform. When he came to collect the fares she saw that it was the young man from Trinidad, and felt oddly embarrassed. She wondered whether he would smile, or make any sign of recognition, and if he did, what would Roger think? Louis made his way along the upper deck, trim in his navy blue uniform. There was a greeting in his eyes for Barbara when he took the fares, even though he didn't smile. But from that look she knew that he would be waiting for her the following Monday. She watched him covertly while Roger talked, noticing how quickly the impassive expression returned to his features. At the terminus he was on the platform, seeing the passengers get off. Barbara knew that he was watching her, but she kept her eyes fixed straight ahead. The hazy sodium lighting at the terminus turned everyone an unbecoming shade of yellow-green. She shivered slightly in the chill spring evening, and Roger put his arm round her.

'Are you cold?'

'No, not really. I'm awfully tired, though.'

'It's all the work you've been doing on that essay. You know you're not used to work.'

'Cheek! I work harder than some people I could mention.'

He laughed, and squeezed her waist. They walked past the familiar shops, and the semi-detached houses with their hedged gardens. A dog barked somewhere in the neighbourhood.

'Look, I won't come into the house with you, if you are really tired,' said Roger, who usually took the short cut back to Dudley on foot, when he came without the car. 'But what about tennis this week, Babsy?'

'Thursday—if the rain keeps off, of course. I shan't have time any other night.' He took her to the gate, and they parted with a good night kiss.

After a prolonged session in the bathroom, Barbara tumbled into bed. The enjoyable film she had seen, Roger Leffey's company, the look in the eyes of the strange young man from Trinidad, all these things kept her awake even though she was tired. So did the restlessness which came upon her at intervals, particularly when she considered her future. Not the immediate future, because that pattern was fairly regular at the moment. Coffee in

Ruddersleigh on a Saturday morning with Shirley, a good look round the shops, perhaps to buy a new record, or see some article of clothing to pester her mother for. Rambling with the East Ruddersleigh Rambling Club, going to school, doing homework, watching television. Smiling when the black-blazered Sixth Formers from Ruddersleigh Royal Grammar School wolf-whistled her. Sharing confidences with Shirley, bickering with Eddie, going out with the adoring Roger. Spending hours in front of the mirror, trying out all the beauty hints in the women's magazine her mother took. That was the sum total of her immediate future. But what was beyond that, enchanting, mysterious, exciting, this was the future which Barbara's romantic imagination etched with glory. She was absolutely certain that her life was going to be quite out of the ordinary. She hoped to go to university of course, but not Ruddersleigh University. It was different for Roger, doing engineering. There were always plenty of would-be engineering students applying for Ruddersleigh, Roger was lucky to be living on the doorstep, so to speak. Barbara fancied doing Psychology, she hoped after graduating to enter the teaching profession. She dreamed of emigrating to Canada or America, or perhaps Australia; she wanted to go somewhere where teachers were highly paid, and life was glamorous. Of course, there would be romances along the way, and eventually marriage...

She had not mentioned these ideas about teaching abroad to her mother, she had a number of other ideas which she kept to herself, too. At no time did she even remotely imagine leading the same kind of life that Helen led. She supposed that it was all right for her mother, but most decidedly not for her. It was a mystery to her what her mother did all day, anyway. It was certainly not what you could call work, and yet she got so irritated during the school holidays if Barbara objected to washing up, or otherwise helping her.

Of course, Barbara was willing to admit it must be a bit dreary stuck around the house most of the time, a kind of existence, in fact. But millions of women led that kind of life, she thought contemptuously. Her mother's friends were all the same, the same jokes, the same sort of conversation, dry-rot and school fees, and all about their families. Her mother attended a Keep Fit class, and she was in something called the Cabbage Club, where women discussed various subjects, but nothing domestic. Then they had those silly little Tupperware parties at each other's houses, buying kitchen gadgets and containers. It was all very boring, but that was certainly not going to be her life, just sort of living, never doing anything. However, until this glittering and enviable future opened out for her she would have to make the most of the present. She finally turned over and slept.

Chapter 6

It rained heavily on and off for the rest of the week. It was dry at the weekend, and then heavy storm clouds brought the rain back on Monday.

'Are you going out?' enquired Helen, putting her head round the door of Barbara's bedroom that evening.

'Yes, I'm going to Shirley's, she's had some records lent her,' lied Barbara.

'You're going to get awfully wet, then.'

'Oh, don't fuss, Mummy. I'll take the short cut to Dudley, I'll dodge between the drops.' Somehow she felt obliged to go and meet this young man, having made use of him. After tonight she wouldn't be seeing him again. There were still things which he could tell her, though, and this was what spurred Barbara on to face the cold and wet of the evening. It was windy, too, so it was no use taking an umbrella. She squelched along to the bus terminus in her sensible school shoes. Stiletto heels were forbidden within the confines of Parkhurst High School. Miss Pickersgill was not going to have her parquet floors ruined by any passing fashion, and the ban included her staff, as well as the Sixth Form pupils.

By the time she got to Ruddersleigh, Barbara was wondering if he would turn up at all on such an evening. But he was already there, in the tiny park shelter, his black hair clinging damply to his forehead. He hurried forward to meet her.

'Hello—you did get wet!' he laughed, and they went back into the shelter together. Barbara took out her handkerchief and rubbed the wet tendrils of her hair which had escaped from under the hood of her grey school gaberdine.

'Isn't it awful?' she exclaimed.

'It terrible. *Oui*.' He paused, his dark eyes watching her. She felt sure the rain had washed away every scrap of make-up from her face. She opened her handbag and had a sly peep in her powder compact mirror.

'You looking okay,' he told her, and she had to laugh. She felt none of the nervousness which she had experienced at their first meeting.

'The essay—it finished?'

'Well, I've written it out roughly, but there may be a few more things I ought to put in it.'

'But we ain't stay here in this. We go somewhere,' said Louis. He pulled a very damp *Ruddersleigh Evening Chronicle* out of his raincoat pocket. 'If you like, we go see a film.' He turned to the entertainments page. Barbara was at a loss for a moment. Of course, they couldn't stay here in the driving rain, that was obvious. But if they went to the cinema together, that would leave no time for any further information regarding Trinidad.

Apart from that... going to the cinema with him! She felt she must draw the line at that. 'It's a three hour show at all of them,' she objected. 'It would leave no time to talk about Trinidad.'

'Is the rest of the week,' said Louis. 'Look, it have a good film at the Plaza—"Guns of Navarone".'

Suddenly she couldn't resist his boyish eagerness. 'Well, as it's such an awful night I suppose it's the only thing to do.'

'You can go straight home after the film,' said Louis, as they walked round the corner to the Plaza. He hesitated. 'It too late?' he enquired.

Barbara could see that there were things which he wanted to know, and she had a good idea what they were. He knew that she was still a schoolgirl, and he was obviously being a bit cautious. He probably thought she was younger than she was.

'Of course it's not too late,' she answered, a little impatiently.

'No later than you went home last week,' said Louis.

She felt a twinge of annoyance at that remark, but they were in the Plaza now, with the usherette determinedly flashing her torch towards the double seats on the back row of the balcony. The place was practically deserted; apart from one other couple they had the entire back row to themselves. The usherette went away.

'We can put we wet coats on the seat beside me,' said Louis, taking off his raincoat. Barbara was somewhat reluctant to do this. She didn't want to sit in a wet gaberdine for three hours, but she was rather apprehensive about sharing a double seat with him, wearing a skirt and jumper. But she took her coat off, as he was waiting to put it beside his. At least, in the darkness of the cinema she didn't have to worry about anyone seeing them.

Before long he lit a cigarette. He had bought some in the foyer of the cinema, while Barbara had been glancing round nervously. He must have bought chocolates as well, because he handed her a small box.

Why, he's sweet, really, she thought, and it was true. He had a funny, endearing charm all his own. He had more than that, though. Sitting beside him, Barbara found herself becoming intensely aware both of his masculinity and his undeniable good looks. Excitement stirred in her, in spite of the fear that he might start getting familiar. She didn't want that to happen, of course. She glanced sideways, and caught him looking at her. She kept her eyes on the screen after that.

When the main picture was half way through, she felt his arm going round her waist, very cautiously. She would have to tell him that he needn't think he could start anything like that, just because she had agreed to go to a film show with him. But more disconcerting than his behaviour were her own reactions. She didn't find his arm around her in the least objectionable, anything but, in fact. He must have eased himself closer to her by a fraction of an inch at a time. Certainly they were very close now, and highly disturbing Barbara found it.

The novelty of the situation intrigued her. Because of that essay on Trinidad she was sitting in the Plaza Cinema with an Indian bus conductor, and in a double seat, too. She tried to imagine what Roger Leffey would think, or Shirley. Or her mother... but she knew well enough what her mother's reaction would be.

And as she sat there with Louis, another feeling came over her. Why shouldn't she please herself what company she kept? Her mother was always so keen to know where she was, and with whom. Well, tonight she was with someone her mother didn't know about, and wouldn't approve of if she did. Barbara's ideas were no more and no less conventional than those of Shirley or any of her friends. Yet something in her reached out to protect this boy from what other people might think or say.

A few minutes before the end of the programme he withdrew his arm. Surprisingly it had stopped raining when they got outside.

Barbara had enjoyed the film, indeed, she had enjoyed the whole evening, guilty though she felt about deceiving her mother.

Beside her walked the strange young man, handsome in the street lighting. 'You go out much at night?' he asked.

'Not really. I'd go out a lot more if I didn't have so much homework to do.'

For a while they walked along the wet pavements in silence. Then he asked if she had heard all she wanted to about Trinidad. Evidently he hoped to see her again. Barbara considered whether to meet him once more, or thank him and say she had enough information about Trinidad.

'Well... perhaps I should put in something about elections.'

'Is okay. When we go meet again?'

She considered. 'Friday evening?'

'Is at seven, *oui*?'

She laughed. 'All right. I hope it doesn't rain.'

'It was one good picture, though.' Evidently Louis had no regrets about the inclement weather.

'Any evening you want, you can go out?' he asked suddenly.

'Why do you keep asking questions like that?' She spoke a bit irritably.

'You still at school,' he reminded her.

'I happen to be nearly eighteen,' said Barbara somewhat haughtily, not being quite truthful about her age. 'I'm old enough to go out every night in the week if I want to. I please myself what I do.' She looked at him and burst out laughing. 'Go on, tell me nice girls don't go out much where you come from.'

Louis laughed too. 'It true,' he admitted. 'They ain't have too many dates—not with a lot of different fellows, anyway.' He looked very hard at Barbara when he said this.

'Nice girls where you come from seem to have rather a miserable time of it,' she observed. 'I wonder they put up with it. Tell me what else they don't do.'

'They ain't go smoke, smoke, smoke, like I see some girls here,' said Louis, with unconcealed disgust.

Barbara began to understand why he never offered her a cigarette. 'Go on. What else don't they do?' she enquired with amused contempt.

'I see women going into bars, drinking, in Ruddersleigh. It

have nothing like that where I come from. No nice girl do that.'

When Roger had the use of his father's car he frequently took Barbara for a drink in The Barley Mow, a pleasant country inn well away from Ruddersleigh. She had never had more than a gin and lime there, or perhaps just a soft drink. Certainly she could see no harm in it. At the same time, as she was not yet eighteen, she didn't mention these little jaunts at home.

'I'd hate to be a girl where you come from,' she told Louis crushingly. 'I've never heard such peculiar, narrow-minded ideas in all my life. Living in a place like Ruddersleigh you should be able to see for yourself how out of date things are in Banana Grove, or whatever it's called.'

'You think everything is good idea in England?'

'I think it's a good idea for girls to enjoy themselves,' she said with spirit. 'Have lots and lots of dates, go out dancing – and smoke and drink if they want to, exactly the same as men.'

'But they ain't men,' said Louis, with devastating simplicity.

Barbara realised with growing irritation that he disagreed entirely with her last remark. 'It's convenient that things are different here, anyway,' she snapped. 'I've met you twice, and you want to meet me again, don't you? Well, I might as well tell you that nobody else knows anything about our meetings.'

'M-mm, you think best hads keep it quiet, even though you go please yourself about everything. *Oui*,' agreed Louis.

Barbara was utterly at a loss how to reply.

'What do you mean?' she asked him, after a pause.

'If they know at home you meeting me, it have one big row. Not so?'

'They wouldn't like it. It's true,' she admitted. Her irritation with him vanished as if it had never been. The strange mixture of compassion and tenderness rose in her again, drawing her towards him. She didn't care how odd his ideas were, nor how old-fashioned his views.

'I thought it better not to mention our meeting. I knew they wouldn't understand,' she explained. 'They know who I'm with usually when I go out. And I never talk to strange men like I did to you. I just thought that you could help me with the essay, if you didn't mind doing it. And you didn't.'

She smiled at him, and he smiled back. She could tell that he was pleased by part of what she had told him, anyway. They were getting near the bus stop now.

'You want to know so much,' she said, a little teasingly. 'I'll start asking you a few questions next time.'

'It have nothing else but questions when we first meet.'

'Yes, questions about Trinidad, not about you.'

'Let we stand in this doorway five minute,' said Louis, consulting his watch. 'Then you go catch bus, smartever, Barbara.'

She laughed, and stood in an unlighted shop doorway beside him. A curious, half-shy happiness enfolded them. Passers-by splashed along the wet, dreary pavement without seeing them. Barbara slipped her hand into his, again he clasped it, again she felt excitement at the contact.

'You best hads go now, Barbara,' he said. 'Or you miss bus. I see you Friday. Good night.'

'All right, Friday. Good night.' She was gone, into the drenching darkness of the night.

Sitting in the bus to Fordham, she reviewed the week ahead. Stay in tomorrow night, a date with Roger on Wednesday and tennis on Thursday, weather permitting. If the present wet spell continued, it didn't look as if the weather would permit. Barbara's mother had pointed out that it was really too early in the season for tennis, and Shirley's mother had said the same. Although the girls agreed privately with the parental judgement, they continued to risk the elements to play with Roger and Steven. There was always the park pavilion to huddle in when it rained. She would see Louis again on Friday, and she was expected for tea at Roger's on Sunday. On Saturday she would shelve everything and try to get the essay finished. Thinking about the essay, she was soon thinking about the young Indian again, and of the evening they had spent together. He's a nice boy, she thought. As nice as plenty of English boys, a lot nicer than some, if it came to that.

Two days later she got on his bus at home time. This time he smiled at her openly and she smiled back, feeling slightly embarrassed. She knew how young and school-girlish she looked in her grey and maroon uniform.

'Is better weather,' said Louis softly, as she held out her school bus pass. At the terminus a glance passed between them, which caused her to be rather preoccupied that evening.

The weather had improved; the rain had stopped and had been replaced by a chilly wind. Roger had the use of the family car, and they went for an evening drive into the Dales, stopping in the little village of Thorpe.

Roger parked the car at the back of The Barley Mow, the local public house. For the most part Thorpe was a huddle of cottages, with some newer houses built since the war. There was a village school and a few shops, including one which was a general store and post office. There was also a beautiful ancient church, St. Botolph's, surrounded by a somewhat untended churchyard, with listing headstones set higgledy-piggledy in the rough grass. The Barley Mow was old, too; solidly stone built, and seemed so much a part of the surrounding countryside that it was hard to imagine that there must have been a time before it existed. Roger knew that it was not a smart place to take a girl, but it was cosy, it had character, and Barbara liked it. Apart from that, he knew that while her parents weren't really strict, they would not be very pleased at the idea of their seventeen-year-old daughter drinking in pubs. Out in the Dales mid-week at this time of the year it would be highly unlikely that anyone who knew Barbara's family would be in The Barley Mow. Roger knew only too well the gossiping that went on in Fordham and Dudley. Young girls in particular were watched by older people, usually women. They were talked about, their clothes criticised, their boyfriends discussed, and very often their whole way of life condemned. He always felt this was grossly unfair, certainly the girls he knew were simply normal modern girls wanting dancing partners and boyfriends, and to enjoy themselves, to have fun, in fact.

Barbara was like that, but she was not quite like that, she was someone very special, and Roger wanted to keep on the right side of her parents. He knew when they went to The Barley Mow she always had a packet of some tiny sweets which took away any hint of alcohol on her breath. For a young man to be steady, reliable and trustworthy were not very exciting attributes, but it was a good image to project as far as parents were concerned. In any case, he did want to take care of Barbara, although he was careful not to get too possessive as she had a very independent streak.

There were not many people in The Barley Mow, just a few locals exchanging gossip and banter with each other in the smoky, tobacco laden atmosphere of the bar room. The landlord, a stout middle-aged man in a bright red pullover greeted them cheerfully, and every male eye was upon Barbara. She was well used to admiring glances from men, and her calm acceptance of this silent homage made Roger both proud and slightly irritated. They went into the room leading off from the bar, known rather quaintly as The Best Room. Like the bar-room it had a low-beamed ceiling, but there was a welcoming log fire in there, permeating the atmosphere with the faint smell of wood smoke. A harness and a few horse brasses were hung up around the place, and a shelf displaying pewter tankards and old plates and jugs ran along the wall over the fireplace. There was an unmatched, motley assortment of chairs and tables, and on a sort of trestle in a corner of the room was a stuffed fox in a glass case. The carpet must have been new at some time, but the pattern of roses on a green background had faded to a soft dullness.

There was only one other couple in there, a middle-aged, long-married looking pair. The husband's eyes sparked with sudden interest when Barbara walked in. There was a high-backed oak settle upholstered in worn tapestry near the fire, and Barbara sat down on it. Roger went to the bar, returning a few minutes later with a gin and lime and a pint of best bitter beer for himself.

While he was being served Barbara looked more closely at the framed sepia photograph on the wall by the fireplace. It was of a group of men in white flannels, and underneath was written, "Thorpe Cricket Team, 1910". The men's faces were young and eager, curiously innocent looking, even those who were sporting moustaches. She knew that the First World War had broken out in nineteen fourteen and for a brief moment she wondered what had happened to those men. Her grandfather had been in that war, she had seen a photograph of him wearing khaki in an album that her Aunt Violet had shown her one day.

Roger sat down beside her, putting their drinks on the much-scratched oak table. He gave her hand a little squeeze before he picked up his beer. It promised to be an enjoyable evening with Barbara all to himself. They discussed the changeable weather, and the possibility of it being too wet to play tennis that week.

'If it really pours like it has been doing, I suppose it will look a bit silly setting off to play tennis. If it's all right when we go to the

93

park it doesn't matter so much if it rains while we're there,' said Barbara.

'I don't mind a bit if it rains while we're there. We can cuddle together in the park shelter.'

Barbara laughed. 'And I thought you were only interested in improving your game.'

As usual when they were together the time passed pleasantly enough until Roger asked if Barbara could attend a party with him on Friday evening.

'Two students who share a flat in Ruddersleigh are having some sort of celebration and I've been invited, with a friend, if I have anyone special I would like to take along.'

'Friday evening? No, I'm sorry, I won't be able to. I've been out quite a lot this week.'

'Have you?'

Barbara began to feel that matters were getting rather complicated.

'Yes. I was at Shirley's on Monday; I'm out with you tonight and tennis tomorrow... I've homework and all sorts to catch up with.'

'I was particularly asked to go to this party and take a friend.'

'A girl friend?'

'Not necessarily. Just bring someone else along.'

'You have other friends.'

'I know that.' Roger spoke moodily. 'I don't want to go without you, Babsy.' He sat silent for a while, looking at her. 'Make an effort and come.'

'I'm sorry, Roger, but the answer is no,' she told him firmly.

He didn't pursue the subject any further. He began to talk about his course work and which firms he would be applying to for a job after he graduated.

'Assuming you do graduate.'

A remark like that from Barbara was usually part of the rather teasing attitude they took towards each other's studies and ambitions. Normally there would be an equally facetious reply from Roger, but Barbara's refusal to attend the Friday party with him had taken much of the pleasure from the evening.

'I'm not anticipating failing,' he said stiffly.

'In that case you'd better cut down on your social life a bit.'

Barbara spoke quite tartly, but she knew that was an unfair remark, and that Roger was a keen student. Unlike some of them living on the university campus, he led a comparatively quiet life. It was true that he made time to see Barbara, but that did not necessitate skipping any lectures. His parents had turned one of the bedrooms into a study for him at home. He was never disturbed when he went in and closed the door behind him, and he could get through a lot of work.

'Actually, getting a place at university is quite a thing,' he said thoughtfully. 'Some people can do quite well with their O levels, but don't manage to scrape through at all with their A levels. Or if they do, it's with very low grades. No decent university would want them.'

'An indecent university might want them, though. Personally, I wouldn't mind going to an indecent university. I shall look around for one of those next year.'

Nonsensical though that remark was, Barbara knew that it would annoy Roger. If he thought he could get digs in at her about A levels, she knew exactly what line to take with him. Roger finished his beer, and glanced at his watch.

'Yes, we'd better not be late home. You'll probably want to be in your study, burning the midnight oil.' Barbara picked up her handbag.

'Are you sure you don't want anything else, Babsy? I mean a soft drink, juice of some sort?' Roger was always very careful about Barbara's drinking.

'No, thank you. There's something I want to watch on television, anyway.'

'You've never mentioned it before. We don't have to go yet,' Roger protested.

'Yes, we do. I saw you looking at your watch. I don't wish to take up too much of your valuable time.'

Exasperated, but trying not to show it, Roger followed her out of The Barley Mow into the blue-grey dusk of the evening. All around them stretched the wild, rugged beauty of the Yorkshire countryside, yet in less than half an hour they would be back in Fordham. The wind had dropped, but they were high up here and it was bitingly cold. Barbara looked down across the valley of Scardale and saw the yellow lights of the town below winking in the vaporous twilight. She shivered suddenly in the raw moorland air, buttoning up her camel coat. Without speaking, Roger opened the door of the green Morris Oxford, and held it open until Barbara was comfortably ensconced in the passenger seat.

'I shan't have to borrow this for an evening out after this year. I've been promised an MG sports car for Christmas. A sort of combined Christmas and birthday present, really.'

'Well, lucky old you.'

He started up the car, and began the long descent from Thorpe, during which they met one solitary car driving up towards the village. A fox sped across the road in front of them, causing Roger to brake sharply. Barbara gave a little cry as she was jerked forward.

'Gosh, that was close thing,' she said. There was just a grunt from Roger. He was subdued and distant beside her, concentrating on the road ahead, white between the darkening countryside. Barbara knew that it would be easy to bring a smile back to his face. She had only to break her date with Louis, and go with him to that party on Friday. She turned this over in her mind. Not to be there on Friday evening, to leave him waiting for her in that dreary little park. As she pictured this, she knew that she could never do it, not for Roger, not for anyone. But why couldn't she do it? She became aware that Roger was sulking. She disliked such treatment from her admirers. She sat without speaking either, until they were back in Fordham. As soon as the car pulled up out-side number twelve Sycamore Avenue, Barbara opened the door and scrambled out before Roger could make a move.

'I see you're in a hurry tonight, so don't let me detain you for a moment,' she said cuttingly. 'And thank you for the pleasure of your charming company. Good night.' She banged the car door behind her. Roger heard the gate click, and the next moment she had closed the front door a good deal more forcefully than was necessary.

Little madam, thought Roger. He wouldn't put up with such treatment from any other girl, but then, she wasn't any other girl. She was Barbara, and she was so lovely... she knew it, too. If he stopped taking Barbara out, he knew she wouldn't be without a male escort for long. It was exasperating. Roger sighed, and start-ed the car. If she didn't appear at the tennis court tomorrow, he would be round to see why.

Barbara stood smiling behind the front door that she had just closed so vigorously. That would teach him. Helen and George didn't find it so amusing, though.

'Do you have to bang the door like that?' enquired her father testily. Her mother frowned and compressed her lips when her daughter appeared. She didn't say anything, but Barbara knew from the expression on her face that slamming the door had not been a good idea as far as her parents were concerned. Freckle-faced, sandy-haired Eddie was in his bedroom and from the vantage point of his window he had witnessed the farewell his sister had bestowed on Roger. Then he heard the door bang. He had mixed feelings about it. Although he and Barbara sometimes argued, he would always take her part against anyone else. At the same time he liked Roger Leffey, who had given him a good stamp album, and a few other items which he no longer required. He had also slipped him the odd five shillings from time to time. Of course, Barbara was no angel, she had quite a temper, Eddie reflected. She used to be a right scratcher in her younger days, too. Leffey didn't know the half.

* * *

The following evening Barbara and Shirley were both in Barbara's bedroom, prior to their game of tennis with Roger and Steven. When Helen's mother came to visit from Eastbourne she shared Barbara's room, which overlooked the back garden. The twin beds made it a bit cramped for space, but most of the time Barbara used the unoccupied bed as a useful place to put things on. Shirley was sitting on it, having pushed aside an assortment of magazines, records, schoolbooks, stockings and sundry articles of clothing. Barbara sat at the dressing table, brushing her hair with a tortoise-shell-backed hairbrush, part of a set, which had been a Christmas gift from her grandmother. Both the girls were wearing pleated grey flannel skirts and Arran cardigans. There was a spill of face powder across the dressing table, amid the clutter of jars and bottles. The whole room reeked of Olive Adair scent. If Helen ever complained that it was untidy, Barbara merely said that it had a lived-in look, and that her mother should see the state of Shirley's room.

97

'Remember I was at your house on Monday evening if Roger or Mummy happen to mention it,' said Barbara. 'You'd better say your father was out, too, because that's what I told my mother when I got home. She thought your father would have given me a lift home in all that rain.'

'Well, he would have if you'd been at our house.' Shirley lolled on the bed, idly poking the cream coloured tufts of the candlewick bedspread. 'Instead of two-timing Roger.'

Barbara had told her a tale about accidentally meeting a boy she used to know, and having a date with him.

'Funny, you've never mentioned this boy before.'

'Because we were just kids when I knew him. He lived in Fordham a long time ago. In fact, I didn't recognise him at first.' Barbara was a bit surprised at the ease with which she was lying to Shirley. Fortunately she was still brushing her hair, so she was not obliged to face her.

'Where did you go, anyway?'

'Oh, just the Plaza.' That at least was true.

'But why all the secrecy? Come on, give. What's he like? Roger would go hairless if he knew.' She rolled on the bed, laughing, and Barbara joined in. 'Now my bra strap's broken,' said Shirley, still giggling. She sat up and pushed her dark hair out of her eyes. 'I don't know how you can two-time that poor lad. Have you got a safety pin handy?'

From Eddie's bedroom came the loud twang of a guitar. It had been a birthday present from his parents, a much-wanted gift for which they were now suffering.

'And what's the name of this dreamboat?' Shirley raised her voice slightly above the din. She fiddled with the safety pin that Barbara handed her.

Something held Barbara back from even divulging Louis' Christian name.

'Very ordinary, John,' she said. 'John Hall.'

'And what is he like? Tall, dark and handsome?'

Barbara laughed, 'That would describe him very well.'

'Still, there's nothing wrong with Roger,' mused Shirley. 'You're not thinking of ditching him, are you?'

Living in the ever-growing suburb of Dudley, Shirley had known Roger by sight for a long time, and she liked what she saw.

At Christmas he had been helping his father in the shop as he sometimes did at holiday times, and Shirley boldly asked him to her birthday party in January. He accepted her invitation with some surprise, but obvious pleasure.

'And bring a friend if possible, and I don't mean a girl,' said Shirley, smiling. 'I can supply those.'

'Yes, I can manage a friend, and thank you very much for the invitation,' Roger replied.

The friend turned out to be Steven Crowther, another Ruddersleigh student, but not a local one. Steven was in a flat in the city, and Shirley thought he would do very nicely for Barbara, but things did not work out as she had planned. As soon as Roger met Barbara, he had eyes for nobody else. A double date was speedily arranged, and the four of them went to the theatre, Roger with Barbara, and Steven with Shirley. Steven was a pleasant, easy-going sort of young man, but Shirley would have exchanged him any time for Roger. Later in the year they all played tennis when the weather allowed, but they were not always in a foursome. It was quite obvious to Shirley that Roger was besotted with Barbara, and dating her at every opportunity. It was a galling situation to be in, but she had enough pride to keep her feelings to herself. Apart from that, Barbara was her friend, and Shirley knew her to be quite flirtatious in her dealings with the opposite sex. It was possible that she might leave Roger for somebody else before too long. There might be a bit of hope for Shirley then, but the worst part was that it was usually Barbara who attracted new males. On this occasion when Shirley had managed to do it, it was still Barbara who walked off with the prize.

The doorbell rang. 'Heavens, Babsy! That'll be Steven and Roger calling for us. They must think we're not turning up, even though it isn't raining. We're coming, boys! Babsy's coming, Roger, she's two-timing you like mad, you poor misguided nit!'

'Sh-sh!' hissed Barbara, flushed with laughter. 'See who's at the door, Eddie,' she called.

'You know who's at the door,' shouted Eddie, strumming away.

'Little beast,' muttered his sister, hurrying downstairs to greet Steven effusively, and Roger with cool politeness. But before long he was restored to favour, and nothing more was said by him concerning the forthcoming party.

The following evening Barbara went out to keep her third appointment with the young man from Trinidad. She told her mother she was going to the Reference Library again. It was a dry, windy day. She put on a blue tweed coat, which intensified the colour of her eyes. Again Louis was waiting in the shelter. He came eagerly towards her as she walked along, smiling.

'Hello, is better weather tonight,' he said, his dark eyes looking her over admiringly. Barbara noticed that he had a *Ruddersleigh Evening Chronicle* in his hand.

'If we go to the News Theatre, Barbara, it have a short film show. We can get a drink of coffee afterwards where we went before. I can tell you about Trinidad there, it quiet, and nobody trouble we.'

She thought he was going to suggest something like this. She stood hesitating. The News Theatre was not very far away, but it was broad daylight, and they could be seen by anyone. At the same time, it was a pleasanter way of spending the evening than huddling in a park shelter.

'All right, then,' she said, and they walked along together. Louis shortened his stride to accommodate Barbara, tip-tapping along in court shoes. She was no longer nervous of him, nor was she afraid of going into that little café. It was merely that she felt conscious of what other people might think should she happen to meet anyone who knew her.

However, nothing of that nature occurred, and they were soon installed in a double seat on the back row of the News Theatre. She sat smiling to herself in the gloom, as once more he lit a cigarette, and handed her a box of chocolates. He was the strangest boy she had ever met, she was thinking. Then she felt his hand close over hers, and the physical contact set her pulses racing. Excitement quickened in her, and she could feel her heart beating so loudly that she was half afraid he might hear it too. By the time they came out of the cinema a new intimacy had sprung up between them. They walked along, smiling and talking about films and film stars, and how nice it was in the News Theatre, and other unimportant matters as they made their way through the dingy streets where Barbara had been so afraid to go only a fortnight before. Suddenly Louis linked his arm in hers, and absurdly happy, they walked the last few yards to the café in that manner.

There was someone else at one of the tables tonight, a dark-skinned man. Barbara didn't like this at all. She had no wish to be surrounded by coloured men. Louis noticed her apprehensive glances.

'It okay,' he told her. 'Nobody speak to you but me, Barbara. Just ignore.'

'It's not that,' she began. 'It's...'

'You mean you not accustomed to place like this, with coloured people? It funny little joint, I know, but where else do we go? You not so keen to go in white people café with me, and the coffee-bars are full of limers.'

She felt a bit ashamed. 'What is this place called?' she asked.

'You not see the name outside? It call the Taj Mahal Restaurant,' said Louis with a smile. Barbara smiled too. 'It serve good food. Is what matters.'

'Where's the little boy tonight?'

'Ganesh? It like he's in bed early, or he come running out to see me, sure thing.'

While they sat drinking their coffee the door opened again, and two Indian women in saris came in, accompanied by two men. They sat down at the next table, the women chattering excitedly. Barbara had always known there was quite a large coloured element in Ruddersleigh, but she had never before given it a passing thought. The women wore coats over their saris, and she thought how incongruous they looked.

'Why do the women trail around in those things, while the men wear European clothes?' she asked in a low voice.

'Men couldn't wear *dhoti* in England—the cold would kill them,' said Louis, laughing. 'Too, besides, they looking funny.'

'You found it cold here?'

'It powerful weather. I never saw snow before. At first it looking pretty, then it all turn to mud. Then it freeze on top, bus skidding, then sand on the road, dark come about three o'clock! I wished I was back in Trinidad.'

Barbara smiled sympathetically at his remembered misery.

'Now the days grow longer,' he said thoughtfully.

She felt his wonder at the lengthening days, and the coming of the chill northern spring, after the long, bitter winter. There was a burst of laughter from the next table; one of the Indian men appeared to be recounting something very funny. The other man joined in, while the women listened with much amusement. It was an incomprehensible jabber to Barbara.

'Goodness, what on earth are they saying?' she asked unthinkingly.

'I don't listen to other people's conversation.'

'Neither do I.' Barbara coloured up. 'How am I to know you understand their language?'

Louis realised he would have to be diplomatic. 'Of course you're not to know,' he said gently. 'They Hindu people, Barbara, and they speaking Hindi. Was my mistake, don't vex with me.'

She was quiet, and he sat looking at her anxiously. 'You wanting to know more about Trinidad?'

'It doesn't matter.' She suddenly stood up, hurried to the door, and was gone.

Louis jumped up too, and rushed after her, leaving his coffee half finished. In the dusk he saw her running along the deserted street as fast as she could go in her rather unsuitable footwear. He dashed after her and caught her quickly, just as she was about to turn off into the wrong road. She gave a little cry of terror when she felt his hand on her arm.

'What you think you're doing?' he demanded angrily. 'You think it smart go run away alone down these streets?'

Barbara stood panting, petrified in his grasp. While they stood there a coloured man emerged from the dark, narrow lane running parallel with the road. He walked silently past them. Barbara began to cry. Louis put his arm round her and drew her into the doorway of a dilapidated corner shop.

'Now you hush,' he said. 'You go bring this on yourself. It have nothing smart to run away like that, but you okay now. You with me.'

'You shouldn't have brought me to this place,' she sobbed. 'It's full of coloured people.'

'I ain't bring you here to run off like one silly girl,' he said sternly. 'No reason at all for you to go leave me like that. You making one big fuss over nothing, and cause me a heap of worry, too.'

'You won't have to worry about me after tonight.' Barbara dabbed her eyes.

'I say you behave like one silly girl, and it true. You vex with me over nothing, and not care how much it scare when you run off like that.'

She knew then how much her behaviour had worried him. 'I'm sorry, Louis,' she whispered.

He tightened his arm around her. 'How come you like this?' he asked softly. 'What you so 'fraid of? We were happy together, then you start making misery.' He stroked her hair. 'You're all upset... what you upset about, Barbara?'

'You lied to me when we first met!' she said accusingly. 'You told me you only spoke English, and that French *patois*—but you understood what those people were saying! You speak Hindi as well.'

Louis was quite taken aback. 'It important? You not think it my private business, anyway? How come you think you can ask me questions like that? You a policeman?'

'What about you?' countered Barbara. 'All those questions and hints about whether I go out at night, and have dates—you think I don't know what you're trying to find out?'

'I think we both like to know things... I speak a little Hindi, *oui*. It matter? It make me different? I know what wrong with you, Barbara. You think I'm too Indian, and it suddenly scare. Not so?'

She admitted that he was right. He understood her panic stricken exit from the Taj Mahal. He laughed. 'You one silly girl. They were Hindus, real Indian people. It have no comparison. You know I'm Christian, Barbara. What difference it make if I speak a little Hindi?'

'I was afraid other things you told me might not be true.'

'Well, they are true. My tanty speak Hindi in the house sometimes, so I answer her in it.'

'Your tanty?' exclaimed Barbara. 'Why, that's neither proper French nor proper English. You mean auntie, or *tante*.'

'I'm always in trouble with you over speaking. I best hads keep quiet,' said Louis, with resignation.

'You best hads,' she agreed, but she was smiling. He could see that all was well again. He was holding her very close. The excitement of having a white girl in his arms for the first time made him tremble uncontrollably. The temptation to kiss her was overwhelming. He suddenly pressed his lips to hers, and felt his kiss returned with such warmth that passionate delight stirred his senses.

'You like me a bit?' he whispered.

'Of course I do. Would I have met you again, otherwise?' She was nestling up against him as though it was the most natural thing in the world. 'You like me too?'

'You know I like you, Barbara—' he broke off, and kissed her again. They clung together, kissing and whispering in that deserted shop doorway. Again, a wonderful shared happiness enfolded them as they stood there. Barbara's resolve not to meet him any more faded into the background. Already he was talking about their next meeting, kissing her gently, and holding her close. All her confidence was restored now; the revulsion that she had experienced in the Taj Mahal had vanished completely.

'Come on, *ma petite*, we get back,' he said softly. 'It getting late.'

With his arm around her waist they walked through the mean streets and back into the city centre.

Chapter 7

As they walked along Barbara chattered away, secure and happy with Louis' arm around her. 'I'm definitely going to finish that essay tomorrow,' she said, after asking him several more things about Trinidad.

She was quiet for a moment, while a rather unpleasant thought occurred to her. 'Louis, do you realise I don't even know where you live? You don't live anywhere around here, do you?' She indicated the unsavoury neighbourhood they were passing through.

'No. Now don't go making misery again. I live with a white family in Dinningley. Is just Mrs. Askew, and her boy, and me.'

Barbara had passed through Dinningley occasionally in the car or on a bus, always on the way to somewhere else. She knew that it was a big, working class district, starting in Ruddersleigh with back-to-back houses, and stretching beyond the city. She knew that it was a built-up area, but it was considerably better than the district round the Taj Mahal café. In fact it was a relief to know that he was the only lodger in a respectable English home. She had entertained a vague fear that he might be living in some ramshackle house with about twenty other Indians. She had read about such things in the newspaper, immigrants sleeping about a dozen in a bedroom, and other unpleasant details.

They were getting back into the city now. 'We have one goodnight kiss before it too public,' said Louis. They stopped beside a high wall, and embraced again. In spite of his happiness, something appeared to be worrying him.

'I'm working every night next week,' he said, frowning slightly. 'So we go meet a week on Monday.'

'Yes.'

'What you do every night next week, then?'

Barbara had a feeling he was very concerned about this. 'Play tennis with a girl friend, and so on. Do homework, watch television, nothing much,' she said, thinking of Roger Leffey.

Louis walked along without speaking.

'Why do you want to know?' she asked.

'You like to know things about me,' he said, smiling. Tenderness welled up in Barbara, an indescribable tenderness towards him, and with it the knowledge that Roger Leffey was not going to last much longer. Looking ahead she felt both confused and worried, in spite of the wonderful emotions she had experienced during their first, sweet exchange of kisses. If they were going to continue meeting each other, numerous difficulties and complications lay ahead. Engrossed in these thoughts she was not even aware that they were standing at a busy crossing, waiting for the lights to change. She began to walk off the pavement, and Louis caught her arm.

'Is not time to cross yet,' he said anxiously. 'Do you always do that? You wanting to get run over, or something?'

She looked at him blankly for a moment.

'I think you often in one big dream, Barbara. You go leave books on buses, and begin to cross roads, don't mind the lights are all wrong! You make a heap of worry for people.'

'I shouldn't be allowed out,' she said, smiling.

'You okay with me. I'm ready for anything now, running down streets after you, pulling you away from car-wheels, you hard work. *Oui*.'

She had to laugh at his comical English, but he had conveyed his meaning quite plainly. They parted with a last handclasp, and a warning to Barbara from Louis to be careful and look where she was going. He, too, was engrossed in his own thoughts, going back to Dinningley. He found himself having some difficulty in concentrating on Mrs. Askew's conversation after he got in that night.

'Are you tired, love?' she asked, after a pause during which he had answered no, when he should have answered yes to something she was saying.

'Yes. I think I best hads go to bed. Do you want me to get Tinker in?' Tinker still had the fancy to prowl at night, particularly now there were signs of spring, but he was always brought in without fail before the family retired. Sometimes he had to be tempted in by the sound of a spoon being rattled on a saucer outside the back door, accompanied by much calling of his name. Louis often performed this task, just to oblige Mrs. Askew. He thought they made a ridiculous fuss of the animal, yet he knew that in the Askews' house the whole family revolved round a fox terrier. This aspect of English domestic life baffled him, but he was too tactful to comment on it. He went into the kitchen, picked up a spoon and saucer, and opened the back door.

'Tinker! Tinker!' he called. There was no sign of the cat, and he shivered in the cold night air. 'Where are you, you old fool?' He banged the spoon on the saucer, and walked out into the yard, muttering curses under his breath. After a while there was a hoarse mewing sound, and Tinker jumped over the wall.

'Get inside, you worthless cat,' said Louis in disgust, while the ageing Romeo rubbed up against him, purring wheezily. He liked Louis to speak to him in a soft voice when he brought him in at night. So did Mrs. Askew, she thought it had a comforting sound. Louis was glad she couldn't hear what he was saying sometimes, particularly on cold nights when Tinker was a long time putting in an appearance.

After locking the back door, Louis went into the tiny bathroom, which had been built onto the kitchen. Then he said goodnight to Mrs. Askew, and went upstairs to his room. But once in bed he lay awake, as he had done so often lately, thinking ceaselessly of Barbara. He thought of the warmth with which she had returned his kisses, and the passion he had felt when she had been in his arms.

As he lay awake, thinking about her, Barbara, several miles away, lay thinking about him. She turned restlessly in bed until her blue baby-doll pyjamas were nearly round her neck. Why did this strange young man exert such a fascination for her? This fierce, undeniable attraction! Yet it had turned to repugnance in the Taj Mahal. Surrounded by other Indians her flesh had crawled, there was no other word for it. Yet that wonderful happiness when she had been in his arms was something she had never experienced in her life before. She knew that he had felt it too, a deep, instinctive closeness. One thing was certain, she no longer wanted Roger Leffey's kisses, but how was she going to work everything out for her own convenience? Take Shirley into her confidence? No... She wondered what Shirley's reactions would be, anyway. She might be incredulous, shocked, amused or disgusted, or perhaps all those things. Before she finally went to sleep she resolved to get the essay finished at the weekend whatever happened, and despite the complications besetting her life, Barbara kept to this resolve.

The following week she handed it in, completed, to a gratified Miss Pickersgill. Having done that, she lay on her bed that evening playing her most recently purchased record: "Don't treat me like a child" over and over again, until her mother was nearly distraught.

'If she plays that once more I'll scream,' said Helen putting down the pullover she was knitting for Eddie.

'It's certainly getting a whacking tonight,' agreed George. 'It's a change from Elvis Presley, anyway.' He shook his head with a resigned air and lit his pipe. He had been telling Helen that Chorley, the office manager, had applied for early retirement on the grounds of ill health. He had been off sick for several weeks following a heart attack. George had taken charge in his place and Helen had remarked that George should get through his Promotions Board this time, as he was actually doing a higher-grade job.

'It won't make a ha'porth of difference,' he assured her, puffing away. 'That's the idiotic thing about the Boards, you can be doing the job...' He broke off and shrugged. He was a tall, slim man with a humorous mouth and keen hazel eyes. From Barbara's bedroom the sound of Helen Shapiro belting out the latest hit started all over again.

'Every time I walk into the sitting room I seem to trip over young Leffey's legs,' went on George.

'Well, it's been Roger for several months now. He seems to be lasting. I suppose one of them could have a change of heart any time—in which case you might be tripping over someone else's legs before long.'

'Some girls are never satisfied,' said George. 'She's got that boy drooling at the mouth, and the use of his father's Morris Oxford. I hope she does stick to him; he's as nice a lad as she's likely to met anywhere. He's pretty keen on her—if they do split up I bet it won't be his doing.'

'She's very young to get serious with anyone.' Helen picked up the pullover again.

'Yes, but I've an idea he's pretty serious about her. Still, women don't know how to enjoy what they've got.'

'Are you sure enjoy is the right word? You could substitute "endure" with quite a number of women.'

George had just thought up a very good reply to this when the doorbell rang. He went to answer it and came back into the room with Roger, who explained that Barbara wasn't really expecting him but as nobody was using the car he thought she might like a run out.

Helen cast a vaguely benevolent smile in his direction. 'She probably would, Roger. She just seems to be playing records. Sit down a minute.'

George began to talk to Roger, and Helen went to the foot of the stairs.

'Barbara!' she called. 'Here's Roger for you.'

There was no reply, only the sound of singing and music. She ascended the stairs and opened the door of her daughter's bedroom.

'Roger's here,' she announced. 'He's got the car and he thought you might like a run out somewhere. It's not a bad evening.'

'Oh.' Barbara looked quite startled. She was lying on the bed in her school skirt and blouse. 'Yes... tell him I'll be down in a few minutes.'

Helen lingered in the doorway. 'Are you going to wear your new suit? You might as well, I don't think Roger's seen it yet.'

'He hasn't. Nobody has. I didn't expect to be buying clothes at that new shop in Fordham.' She put the record player off.

Barbara had seen the suit in the new dress shop that had just opened on the parade. It was of fine green tweed, beautifully made, and she had noticed it in the window on her way home from school.

'Mummy, it's a special opening offer—it's gorgeous, it's a bargain, it's my size, and if I don't snap it up someone else will. Anyway, I need something new for spring.'

'If it's a case of needing, you don't really need anything—' began Helen, who was preparing the dinner.

'Oh, Mummy! I'll put my pocket money towards it; I can go and get it now—' George had looked up from the local evening paper. 'For the sake of peace, let her buy it. How much is it? Here,' he handed Barbara some notes.

'Thanks, Daddy.' Barbara dashed out, to return in triumph with her purchase. Her mother admitted that it was a good buy, it fitted perfectly, and the delicate shade of green suited Barbara's colouring.

This would be her first date since she had bought it, so it was a chance to show it off to Roger. As she was getting changed into it, a feeling of guilt and unease spread through her. There was no doubt that Roger was becoming more and more one of the family, and his parents were very nice to her. Everyone approved of the friendship in fact, but as she got ready to go out with Roger, it was of another man she was thinking. A foreign man, one who spoke strange English in a lilting voice, who had dark, long-lashed eyes, and the power to make her heart thud with excitement. A handsome man, a man who walked and ran with the lithe, effortless grace of an animal. But a man who was not white, a man of whom nobody sitting in that room downstairs would approve.

About fifteen minutes later, Barbara went downstairs to join them. She knew that she looked lovely in the new suit even before Roger's eyes told her so.

'I'll give you a penny for luck,' he said, as following the local custom, he slipped a coin into her pocket.

'Well, if we're lucky it won't rain,' said Barbara, laughing.

'No more Helen Shapiro tonight, anyway,' remarked George, as the car drove off. 'No guitar either. Eddie's gone to the pictures with Mousy. I think there's a decent play on television tonight.'

'People are a bit fed up with some of these BBC plays. So many of them don't have a proper ending.'

'Well, we can have a look at it I suppose. I know it's supposed to be spring now, but the ground is so waterlogged I'll have to wait for it to dry out before I dig around the borders. The house needs painting, too—'

'For goodness sake don't start listing all the things that need doing when the weather improves, I could add to the list indefinitely. Let's look at that play you mentioned.'

George switched on the television. 'Where will those two be going for a run out, anyway?' he asked.

'I don't know, and I don't think we should expect Babsy to tell us everything now. She's growing up, and Roger always brings her home at a decent hour.'

'Well, wherever they go, they'll need to stay in the car. We're well into April, and we're not really having a spring at all.'

'It's the same as most springs here,' was Helen's comment. 'Cold and wet, only if anything it's been a bit colder and wetter than usual.' She settled down to watch television with her husband.

As soon as he started the car, Roger asked Barbara if she fancied a drive out to The Barley Mow. She laughed. 'Just the place to christen my new suit in.'

'You know you look gorgeous enough to be taken anywhere, but I don't want to be seen taking you into pubs. We might as well take advantage of having the car for the evening.'

'I'm all for it. The Barley Mow it is.'

'Yes, give the locals a treat. Before long they'll be treating us as regulars.'

Although Barbara enjoyed the evening, and kisses were exchanged in the car, a part of her was not really happy about the situation.

'Penny for your thoughts,' Roger had said on the way home.

'They're worth more than a penny.' Barbara smiled as she spoke, but she would certainly not have shared her thoughts with anyone, least of all Roger. She was thinking about Louis, and their next meeting.

A few days later she again went to keep a secret rendezvous with him. She wore the new suit, which had drawn admiring comments from Roger, and on her mother's insistence she carried an umbrella. Before going out she had sprayed a few drops of the sweet pea scent on her wrists and throat. As soon as she alighted from the bus in Ruddersleigh, she walked briskly along to the park. Some children were playing there, they looked poor and dirty, neglected looking, like the scruffy little park itself.

Feeling considerable distaste for such surroundings, she paced up and down, glancing at her wristwatch from time to time. She waited ten minutes, fifteen minutes... if he should not come! She was trying to face up to this awful possibility when he came hurrying along, the lock of hair falling over his forehead, his expression anxious.

'I'm so sorry! There was accident on the road; the bus from Dinningley was delayed. You think I ain't coming?'

To Barbara's consternation she found that she was unable to speak for a moment, but he seemed to understand. He looked round quickly, and gave her hand a reassuring little squeeze.

'I'm here, Barbara. Where shall we go?'

For a few moments the ragged children stopped shouting and running around, gathering to stand silently and stare at the couple.

'I don't mind where we go. Anywhere... let's get out of the park, anyway.'

'It okay at The Plaza, then? "Greengage Summer"?' enquired Louis as they walked along.

Barbara was a member of the school film society, and from time to time she went into Ruddersleigh to see a particular film, usually accompanied by Shirley. She had led her mother to understand it was a film society evening, and that she might be a bit late home.

'I know it's late to go now, but it okay if we see the main film. *Oui?*'

'Yes, I've heard it's very good.'

Louis was unable to take his eyes off her; she was so lovely. Other men must look at her too, white men. Thinking of this his smile faded.

'You did play tennis last week?' he asked.

Barbara smiled. 'You arrive late, and start asking questions straightaway. Some people have a cheek.'

'I've got one terrible cheek. I want to know what you were doing last week.'

They walked along to the Plaza, Barbara looking around as usual. She told Louis some of her activities since she had last seen him, omitting any mention of Roger. The usherette flashed her torch towards the double seats, and, as always, Barbara felt relieved in the darkness of the cinema. When Louis lit a cigarette she held out her hand, smiling at him.

He laughed. 'I know you're making joke about the chocolates. You go be surprised if I didn't buy them.' He handed her the usual box.

Before long, Barbara felt his arm around her, and she leaned back, the physical contact making her pulses race. The sweet, haunting fragrance of the Olive Adair scent emanated from the warmth of her body. His arm tightened, and their lips met in a long kiss, a lingering, intimate exploration, not like those first gentle kisses in the doorway. She had unfastened her jacket, and he suddenly slipped his hand under, and put it lightly on her breast.

112

Barbara caught her breath; she knew that she would have to put a stop to this. She turned and looked at him in the dim light. These emotions, these frightening emotions sweeping through her, threatening to swamp common sense! She would have to scold him, push his hand away, do something, if only for the sake of appearances. The next moment their lips met again, and the thrill that tingled through her senses was like nothing she had ever thought possible. Nevertheless she whispered that he would have to behave himself, and he did, for the space of about ten minutes. Then the kissing started all over again, and Barbara was obliged to remonstrate with him once more. In this manner they spent the next couple of hours.

Out in the foyer they were both shining-eyed, and Barbara's face was burning. Louis asked her if she had enjoyed the film, and she said she had. The fact was that she had missed quite a lot of it, so occupied had she been fending off Louis' advances, and not really wanting to. He had smoked one cigarette, and between them they had eaten three chocolates. The time had gone very quickly; in fact everything seemed to be moving so swiftly for Barbara that she felt a bit dazed.

He seemed to realise this, and kept a watchful eye on her while they waited to cross a busy road outside the Plaza.

'There's been one terrible accident in Ruddersleigh tonight,' he reminded her. 'I wish you would be more careful, Barbara. You're one dreamy girl.'

'Not when I'm alone.'

'I go make you dreamy, then?'

'Now you're trying to find out things.'

'Let we find a quiet place for five minutes. Five minutes, Barbara, so we can talk.'

They stood in a doorway down a dimly lit street near Ruddersleigh market, and exchanged passionate kisses. He asked her how she had managed to get out and meet him again, and if there had been many questions.

'Goodness, it's not so hard,' she said. He wondered about this, but he knew she got annoyed if he pressed her for more details on the subject. So he asked if she would be able to see him again that week.

'I think so,' she said, her face close to his. 'Friday?'

'Why Friday? You going out all the other nights?'

'No. I just don't have to do homework on a Friday.'

Louis was quiet for a moment; he seemed unconvinced about the no homework reason to see him on Friday.

'You having other dates?' he asked. 'That fellow you were on the bus with—you seeing him?'

Barbara stood hesitating, looking down, unsure what to say.

'I don't want any other fellows liming around,' he said suddenly. 'If you seeing anyone else, it have no use meeting me. I want you to be my girl, Barbara. If you are not wanting that, we best hads not meet again. Anyway, I'm coloured, you wanting white men, not me. So maybe we best hads not meet again in any case.'

'If I like you, Louis, that's all that matters —'

He gave a bitter laugh. 'You ain't kidding me, Barbara, and it have no use kidding yourself. I'm just a coloured immigrant; you're a white girl from a good home. You say if you like me it all that matters—you think your parents say that too? I know well enough what they say. You know too.' She was silent, faced with the truth.

'They think I'm 'bout good enough to punch you a bus ticket, and mind I don't touch your hand when I go giving change.'

'Louis!' she cried. 'It's not as bad as all that.'

He made no reply.

'Very well, if you don't wish to see me again...'

'You know I do! But this thing making misery between us.'

'I thought you were happy when we were together,' said Barbara, trying to keep her emotions under control. 'You weren't nasty to me like this when we were in the Plaza, I know that. I'm going now.'

She couldn't trust herself to speak any more, and if the tears were going to come she didn't want Louis to see them. He was in an emotional state too. For a moment neither of them spoke, then they were in each other's arms, clinging together as though nothing could part them.

'We'll try and work everything out, darling,' she whispered. 'We'll have to talk things over the next time we meet.'

'We do that, *ma petite*,' he said tenderly. 'You not seeing other fellows?'

'Of course not,' she answered. 'I'll see you any evening. Wednesday?'

'Okay. Wednesday.' Moving out of the doorway they walked along, his arm round her waist. 'Now I have to watch you,' said Louis with resignation. 'You go walk along in the middle of the road.'

Barbara laughed. They were happy again, and that was all that mattered. She was thinking they would work things out between them, because she wasn't going to stop seeing him for anyone. She would have to shake Roger off somehow, gently but firmly, and yet not let her mother know. In order to go on meeting Louis she would have to pretend she was still seeing Roger, and she would have to use Shirley, too. That wouldn't be easy, in fact Shirley might be a bit of a problem. Her mother would wonder why Roger no longer came to the house. Pondering on all this, she had no idea where she was going. She walked unseeingly along beside Louis, relying with childlike faith on the touch of his arm. He knew this, but it didn't matter as long as his arm was there, his arm, and nobody else's. As he walked along thinking this, she asked where they would go on Wednesday.

'I've never been to the cinema so much for ages,' she added.

'You don't have to look. I don't mind if you go to sleep.' He laughed as he said this, and so did she. 'I like to go to the pictures with you, Barbara.'

'I think you like the double seats.'

'It have nothing like them,' agreed Louis. They stopped walking, having reached the place where they usually parted. 'You best hads go straight away for your bus, *ma petite*. It getting late.'

They managed a swift, sly kiss before she went to join the bus queue. On the way home she decided that if Roger rang up to make a date for Wednesday, she would put him off. If he stopped calling at the house or ringing up, her mother would probably guess that someone else had taken his place. That would be all right for a time, then she would think if there was someone new, why did he never come to the house? Barbara tried to imagine Louis calling for her. Her mother would probably mistake him for a man selling something. They had quite a number of Indian peddlers in Ruddersleigh. Mummy would pass out, she thought. As for her father... better not to think about it.

Louis' unpalatable words in that doorway had been no more than the truth, but overriding these facts had been her feelings towards him.

'I want you to be my girl,' he had said, and it was as though he had put fetters on her. She had seen him less than half a dozen times, and she knew scarcely anything about him, except that he was an immigrant from Trinidad. She both feared and wanted a closer relationship with him. And for him she was going to turn her back on Roger Leffey, in spite of knowing how deeply he cared for her. His affection, his good allowance and bright prospects and the use of his father's Morris Oxford seemed unimportant now. It had all happened so suddenly, Barbara tried to make sense of it. A short while ago she had been unaware of Louis' existence, and now thoughts of him dominated her mind.

The following day, Roger rang her up. Barbara said that she had promised to give a friend a home-perm on Wednesday. She didn't want to play tennis that week, either, she told him, because she had strained her wrist, although she couldn't remember how it had happened. She had to wash her hair on Friday, and she would be helping her mother with the spring-cleaning on Saturday, her wrist being all right by then. They had better leave things for the time being.

She sensed Roger's disappointment at the other end of the phone, along with her own sense of guilt about telling such lies. She had told Shirley the same lie about a strained wrist, adding that she was getting a bit fed up with the tennis playing, anyway.

'Fed up with the tennis, or fed up with Roger?' asked Shirley, rather taking Barbara by surprise.

'Well, just a bit fed up with everything,' said Barbara lightly.

'Do you want to have a look round the shops on Saturday?'

'Yes, why not?' Barbara didn't want to disrupt her usual routine too much, or Shirley might sense things had changed. After Roger's phone call she went upstairs, and threw herself onto her bed. She jerked up her school satchel beside her, and without enthusiasm began to do some homework.

The following evening she walked along Sycamore Avenue, and noticed the fresh greenness everywhere, and saw the tender young leaves tossed in the wind. The days were lengthening rapidly now, children were out playing, and people were busy in their gardens. The smell of privet hedges and freshly mown grass seemed to fill the air in Fordham.

She had told her mother that one of the girls was having a

record playing evening, and several of her form mates were going. She added that it was at Moorleigh, another suburb of the city.

'Well, don't be back too late,' said Helen, who was feeling rather exhausted after a day spring-cleaning with Mrs. Garside. The kitchen had been really bad after the long, dirty winter, but at least it was ready for painting now, and a change of colour scheme. George said he would paint it in the evenings, but they would have to get a decorator in to paper the hall and sitting room.

Louis was waiting for Barbara in the park, hurrying forward to meet her, seeing the colour rush to her face as soon as she saw him.

'Hello, how you keeping? I'm early tonight.'

An old man sitting in the shelter watched them curiously.

'Hello,' said Barbara. 'It looks as though the shelter is getting a bit more popular lately.'

She knew that Louis was eager to hold her hand, put his arm round her, have some sort of physical contact. But it was a light, bright spring evening, and there were people about. In the end it was Barbara who couldn't hold out. She reached up, and with a swift movement pushed the little lock of hair away from his forehead. They decided to go to the News Theatre and talk things over in the Taj Mahal afterwards.

'But I don't want another bacchanal like last time,' said Louis. 'You ain't go run away like last time, will you?'

'Of course not,' she smiled, as they walked along in the direction of the News Theatre. Once inside, comfortably seated on the red-plush double seat, it was a repetition of their last visit to the cinema, with Barbara emerging in a very flushed and flustered state, but extremely happy, too. In between their passionate kisses Louis had told her how much he cared for her. She had whispered back her feelings towards him; it had the effect of making him more ardent than ever. They were both excited when they left the News Theatre, and had Louis been as dreamy as Barbara they would have been in dire danger at the first busy crossing.

This time she scarcely noticed the dreary streets they were passing through on the way to the Taj Mahal. He told her it wouldn't be so busy on a Wednesday evening, and to his relief as well as hers, it was empty when they arrived.

Ganesh came and sat on Louis' knee, chattering to him in singsong Hindi. 'We have to speak English, Ganesh,' said Louis

117

severely. 'You go get me into one big row, you worthless boy.'

Barbara smiled. 'I don't mind with Ganesh,' she said. He was an engaging little boy, very attractive with his great dark eyes and wavy black hair. 'He's bonny, but very thin,' she added.

'Not for an Indian boy. You okay, Ganesh-Baba.'

A young woman in a pink sari appeared from behind the curtain. 'Ganesh!' she called.

'There, your *mai* wanting you,' said Louis, putting him down.

Barbara thought how pretty she was. She wondered if Louis thought so too, as she sat drinking her coffee. Every minute they spent together was precious, yet neither of them was saying much. It was not necessary, the love and happiness was flowing between them, filling even that dingy little place with radiance. Because she was there with Louis, Barbara was oblivious to the garish ugliness of the yellow painted chairs and tables, the hideous red flock wallpaper, and the lingering smell of curry. After a while, she spoke.

'I don't really know anything about you, darling.' She pressed her foot against his. She felt that it was only right for her to know more about him, now that the emotions between them had ripened so swiftly.

Louis realised this. She knew that he had been brought up in his uncle's home, but little else. He gave her a bare outline of his life in Bamboo Grove, and his decision to come to England. But as in everything he told her about Trinidad, he carefully sieved the facts, omitting a good deal, and dwelling on the pleasanter side of things. There was so much that would have shocked her, so much that she would not have understood. He knew that whatever he told her she could never grasp a way of life so different from the one she was accustomed to. Backwardness, ignorance and superstition, poverty, drunkenness, endless petty thieving, threats, racial insults, violent quarrels and fights. And yet, in spite of that, a robust, high spirited way of life, a gaiety, an easy-going uncaringness, but how horrified she would be at the idea of his uncle stealing from him!

'So you wanted the adventure of coming to England,' she said, finishing her coffee.

'You not sorry?'

'Of course I'm not sorry. How else would I have written my essay?'

'Is that all you think about me?'

She laughed at him, teasing with her eyes. 'Yes, that's all I think, darling. That's why I tell all sorts of stories at home, so that I can get out and be with you.'

'You like to have jokes. We go to the park and sit in the shelter two-three minutes, *ma petite*.' They walked back to the park, and found it quite deserted. In the darkness of the shelter they embraced without speaking.

'We haven't talked much about what we're going to do, darling,' said Barbara, nestling up against him.

'We go have to think carefully about things. You know I want you to be my girl, Barbara, but it's not going to be easy for we. You know why.'

They sat and considered the situation in their separate ways. Barbara was fully cognizant of the social and racial gulf that lay between them. Never for a moment did she delude herself that her parents would approve of this attachment. They would be appalled at the idea. So Louis would have to be kept very much out of the way. She would have to meet him in secret, and practice endless deceptions in order to do so. That in itself was going to be a complicated enough task. And where was it going to lead them in the end? In the dim light she looked at Louis, and felt to the full this strange, overwhelming desire to be with him. To be with him... to be with him. She couldn't understand why, his spoken English was dreadful, his ideas quite different from hers; sometimes his foreign ways repelled her. And yet, how could she expect anything else from an Indian who had spent all his life in some outlandish Trinidad village? Because of this she could make allowances for his quaint English, with its curious sprinkling of *patois* and American slang. She could not eradicate that strong foreign accent of course, but she could certainly help him to improve his hopeless grammar. She could not have endured such grammar from an Englishman, but again, she realised it was different in his case.

Hindi—that was another thing altogether. She didn't really like to think that he spoke it at all; it seemed to cut him off from the West completely. He denied having much knowledge of it, but she suspected that he was not being quite truthful about this. However, that was just a minor detail. She was intrigued at the idea of helping him; in a way it was a challenge. He had plenty of intelligence, she could not have tolerated him otherwise, and it was not his fault that he had had so little opportunity for self-improvement. Well, he could join the library for a start. As for his old-fashioned ideas, she would soon bring him up-to-date.

Yes, she loved him, and she would change these odd ways, very tactfully, of course, but she would change them. In a few months he would be moulded a great deal nearer to her heart's desire. She was quite confident about this. She would make his whole outlook more sophisticated, for after all, she had grown up in a great city, and she knew more about the world than he did...

Strangely endearing, disturbingly exciting, he sat beside her. He had only to come close to her, take her hand in his, for her heart to start hammering. When his lips met hers, thrills of delight went through her; one look from his dark, long-lashed eyes was worth a dozen from Roger Leffey. She knew all this, although she didn't know why, but she felt the compelling vitality that streamed from him. It was as if he was life itself. Life vigorous, elemental, uncompromising, and it was to this that her senses quickened. She didn't know where these intense feelings were leading her, and somehow she didn't care. She only knew that she must be with him at all costs, however much she had to plot and plan and deceive.

Things would work out for her somehow, anyway, in a few years time she would be able to do as she liked, be friendly with whom she pleased. In the meantime she was still going to be friendly with whom she liked, only she would have to be discreet about it. She and Louis would get out of the city, into the countryside between Ruddersleigh and the mill town of Netherby. She would walk with him in the valley of Ruddborough, where the river flowed sweetly, with grey mills clinging to its banks, and long farmhouses dotted here and there. She would take him to where the dry-stone walls stretched for miles, where the glories of scenic Yorkshire began. She would take him up on the moors, which rolled away, billow upon billow, where the wind did your breathing for you, where the enormous sky met the earth in a sweep of infinite grandeur.

There they would find privacy, there would be no prying eyes, only the eyes of the moor sheep, the curlews, and the other wildlife. For always on the moors there was solitude if you wanted it, space, endless undulating remoteness, with the bare, basic rocks jutting out, and the passing clouds making great shadows on the earth. She knew that this was Louis' first spring in England, and that he had as yet scarcely stirred beyond the boundaries of Ruddersleigh. Together, then, they would hear the lark and the curlew; together they would walk through meadows thick with wild flowers; together they would see the beauty of the Yorkshire countryside in spring. So Barbara made her plans and dreamed her dreams, as she sat hand in hand with Louis.

He, too, was thinking about their future. He was wondering how she was going to continue meeting him, and still keep it a secret from her parents. She appeared to have a great deal of freedom, but he was unable to fathom out how much. He had a strong feeling that she resented any parental control at all. Then he considered the financial side of things. The wise words of Teacher Ramlogan came back to him: "As soon as a man starts to prosper and catch himself a bit in the world, along comes woman, bringing misery". Well, here was woman all right, woman incarnate, in the form of Barbara. With the inherent thriftiness of his race, he wondered how much he could afford to spend on her. He worked this out mentally, automatically changing English money into "Beewee" dollars, and then changing it back again. But in either currency it didn't amount to much, nor did it matter, clearly this was of no interest to Barbara, all she cared about was that they should be together. Where were they going to go, though? They couldn't keep sneaking into the back row of the cinema all the time, but they would have to be very careful where they went for Barbara's sake.

Another thing worried Louis. If they were going to continue meeting each other, did she think he was going to be content with hugs and kisses for an indefinite period? If things could have been different... but he was too much of a realist to pursue that line of thought. Her parents would never approve of her being friendly with him. He sat struggling miserably with his feelings, wanting Barbara, loving her, and yet hesitating.

'We'll meet each other and get right out of Ruddersleigh,' she said. 'I know the countryside round about, darling. There are plenty of places where we can be alone.'

'But what you go tell your parents?'

121

She shrugged. 'I'll tell them I'm out with Shirley or Rog—I've plenty of friends. Anyway, there are always school clubs and activities going on in the evenings. As long as Shirley still comes to our house sometimes they won't worry.'

'You sure?' He was not happy about all this deception, but she began to pout, and said if he didn't want to meet her again he jolly well needn't. Even as she spoke the tears were gathering in her eyes. He couldn't bear to see her like this, and yet he was torn two ways.

'I thought you wanted us to meet again,' she said reproachfully. 'Didn't you mean what you said in the News Theatre? I try to plan things so we can meet—' her voice began to tremble. 'Now you don't seem bothered. Well, I've plenty of other boy friends—'

'Barbara!' he cried. 'You tell me I'm the only one—you not letting other fellows lime around you?' This appalling thought drove all others out of his head for the time being.

'No, I'm not,' she said sulkily. 'But don't imagine you're the only one interested in me.'

He didn't imagine that, far from it. Moreover, the other men were white, and had every advantage over him. The next moment they were in each other's arms again. It was inconceivable, impossible, that he could let her go. And when he felt her soft, pliant body against his, her kisses on his lips, pride as well as desire rose in Louis. He was just a coloured immigrant, one of hundreds in Ruddersleigh, but this beautiful white girl cared for him, and that gave him every advantage over her countrymen. Here in the grey and grime of this busy Yorkshire city, an English rose was blooming for him.

'If you can manage it, of course we go meet,' he said tenderly. 'It just because I was thinking it going to be hard for you, *ma petite*, getting to see me. And I ain't want one big row at your house, or anyone vex with you.'

Barbara wanted something wonderful to happen, which would make everything all right for her and Louis. He had no such flights of fancy. He accepted the situation as it was, and told her they must see each other when they could, and make the best of things.

'And we see you not out late at night,' he added. 'If you're in early, nobody vex with you and ask questions.'

Barbara realised the wisdom of these words, albeit reluctantly.

'By the time we've got out of Ruddersleigh and away from every-one, it'll be time to get back. We won't have much time together, will we?'

'It better to have little time together than long time and one big row waiting,' said Louis. 'Too, besides, I ain't bear you home, so I want you in early, anyway.'

'Bear me home?' Barbara giggled at the word, it sounded so quaint.

'You know what I mean. I want you in early, but don't be down couraged, *ma petite*. Sometimes we go meet in the afternoon, as well, and when I'm on late turn I see you one night, instead of working banger.'

They made arrangements to meet again on Friday, and parted after many whispered endearments.

For the next two days Barbara found it increasingly difficult to concentrate on her schoolwork. The image of a swarthy young man floated before her, and blotted out reality. A line of half for-gotten poetry kept running through her head, to the exclusion of all else.

"A stranger loved the lady of the land—" Byron had written that, she was sure. He had gone to Italy, and fallen in love with an Italian girl...

'You don't seem to be paying much attention, or taking any notes, Barbara,' said the history mistress. 'None of you girls hop-ing for good A level results can afford to waste time. Because your O levels were good, it doesn't mean you can rest on your laurels. A levels demand a much higher standard.'

Thus reproved, Barbara made a determined effort to concen-trate, but she felt miles away, utterly removed from the classroom. She knew that Miss Brent was speaking, but it was just like watch-ing television with the sound turned off. It seemed to her that everyday living was a dream, and only her feelings for Louis were real.

Chapter 8

It was the last Saturday in May, warm and sunny, but breezy as well. Wearing a white nylon petticoat, Barbara was standing in front of her open wardrobe, deciding which summer dress to wear. She did this to the accompaniment of a calypso record, one of several she had bought lately.

There had been other changes in her life besides her changed taste in music during the past few weeks. She no longer saw Roger Leffey, or brought Shirley home with her to play tennis. She and Roger had one last date at The Barley Mow, where she told him she thought they were seeing too much of each other. She had added that she intended to work very hard throughout the summer term. Rather flushed, with a glass of gin and lime in her hand, she had talked about the importance of her schoolwork. Roger had listened to her somewhat rambling excuses, noticing her heightened colour and evasive manner.

'Babsy, if you've met someone else you might as well say so, instead of trotting out all this stuff. I thought you liked going around with me, and you know I like it. If you're really keen to tackle more work, we'll cut down on our dates for the time being. I'm pretty busy myself, with exams coming up. But if it's someone else, why don't you say so?'

'You men always think of that.' Barbara was the more annoyed because it was absolutely true.

'Well, tell me who it is, anyway. Is it that idiot in the Ramblers' Club who got stuck in a pothole at Craw Fell last summer? Perhaps he thinks he's going to get you on that pot-holing lark—'

'What? Stan Ward? Don't be ridiculous,' Barbara interrupted crossly. 'I had supper with him once at Harry Ramsden's, and he got ideas.'

'Oh, I know he fancies his chance, like a lot more—and you think you only have to crook your little finger—'

'So I have, and don't you forget it! I've told you I want to catch up on some work this term, but if you don't believe me, you can believe what you like.'

Roger sat looking at her. He desperately wanted to believe her. He asked her if it was really true about the swotting, and she assured him that it was.

'Well, perhaps we can start seeing each other after the exams are over,' he suggested. He was very upset, much more so than he intended Barbara to see. He knew that for a few weeks things had not been satisfactory between them. Barbara had made many excuses not to see him when he had rung up to make a date. Sometimes when he had the car he had called at the house without telephoning first. Occasionally it was to find her out; if she was in the house she would come out with him, but she seemed reluctant, somehow. It was as if she had put up a barrier between them, where before they had talked freely about so many things. As for kissing, 'I'm not in the mood,' was her response to that. He had pretended not to notice anything was wrong, hoping that it was just a passing phase. Roger finished his beer, and they walked outside to the car park in silence.

The tennis playing stopped, too. When Shirley suggested that her wrist must be better now, Barbara told her that she was bored with tennis, anyway. She added that she and Roger weren't seeing so much of each other these days. Shirley looked at her quizzically.

'Come on, give. It's that other dreamboat, isn't it? Roger's been on his way out for a few weeks now, hasn't he? Ever since that mysterious date of yours, John what's-his-name.'

'That?' Barbara tried to sound casual. 'No, I'm not bothering with anyone in particular at the moment.'

'You'll be going to the university dance though, the big one, won't you? Steven was talking about it.'

'No, I won't be there. You can count me out of that, too.' Barbara was filing her nails, but although she was looking down, she could sense Shirley's curious gaze.

'Turning into quite a little stay-at-home, aren't you?'

'Could be.' She went on filing her nails. She had no intention of taking Shirley into her confidence. At the same time, she didn't want Shirley to stop coming to the house altogether, as she was a useful alibi to have. They were in Barbara's bedroom, and she put the nail file down on the dressing table.

'I'm not such a stay-at-home,' she said briskly. 'We'll go into Ruddersleigh on Saturday, and have a look round the shops. Where did Laura Haxby get that super nail varnish?'

'She wouldn't tell anyone, but she told me in confidence. She got it from a stall in the market, dirt cheap, and it lasts for ages. They have a huge range of colours.'

'We'll make the market a priority then.' To keep up some appearance of normality when nothing in her life was normal called for some ingenuity on Barbara's part.

'You never know who we might bump into,' went on Shirley. 'Everyone makes for Ruddersleigh on a Saturday.'

Barbara knew one person they wouldn't bump into, and that was Roger's mother. Mrs. Leffey thought it was common to be in Ruddersleigh on a Saturday, although she knew it was different for Roger and his young friends. Two of the better-class department stores in the city closed on a Saturday, because they knew their customers wouldn't shop on that day. The girls continued to talk until Helen called upstairs to say she had made coffee and some sandwiches.

By dint of much deception, and using Shirley's name a good deal, Barbara had managed to continue meeting Louis, and not just in the evenings, either. On several occasions they had met on a Saturday afternoon, when Louis had been on early turn. She had made some excuse not to see Shirley, and they had taken a bus out of the city and strolled happily in the rural district of Ruddborough. They had also met each other frequently during Barbara's Whitsun Holidays; she had delighted in showing Louis the attractive scenery only a few miles beyond the fringes of the city. Smiling at her enthusiasm, he had admired the wooded slopes, the winding roads with their characteristic dry-stone walls, and the grey cottages. Sometimes they had gone further afield to where the houses crept up to the very edge of the moors, and hand in hand they had walked along. Louis looked at her as they climbed the steep slope of Blacktarn Gill, and saw her pride and pleasure in showing him these local beauty spots.

'You like these old moors, Barbara,' he said teasingly.

'You've nothing like this in Trinidad.' She was a little out of breath.

'It have nothing like these winds, either.'

126

'You get your Trade Winds.'

'You think Trade Winds is like this? Let we sit down a minute.' He spread his raincoat on the sheep-cropped grass. They sat down together, and looked beyond at the impressive moorland. Below them lay the panorama of Rudderdale, with the river winding along. The wind made the telegraph wires on the moorland road hum with a strange high-pitched sound, which intrigued Louis. It blew his unruly forelock about, and made Barbara tie a silk head-scarf over her hair. At the foot of a bracken-covered hill they were quite secluded. Barbara put her face beside his, and looked at the grandeur of the scenery, but Louis was more interested in looking at her. Nor was he content merely to look, before long, as usual, she was admonishing him for his too ardent caresses.

'Okay, I go behave,' he said sullenly, lighting a cigarette. He smoked in silence for a few minutes.

'I think we'd better start getting back, darling,' said Barbara, hating to see him look like that. He never sulked for long, though.

'Come on, then, *ma petite*. It have a little café at the bottom of the road—you wanting some tea?' They had never been in a café together except the Taj Mahal, but away from the city Barbara felt less apprehensive. It was still possible to meet people she knew, but not quite as probable.

They went into the pretty, low-beamed room and sat by the window. Several of the tables were occupied, and Barbara knew that she and Louis were getting plenty of glances. She was about to pour him a cup of tea, when to her utter amazement he told her that he didn't drink it. Instead, he had a cup of milk, and sweetened it. As they had previously only had coffee together, she had not known this.

'What do you drink, then?' she had enquired, wide-eyed. 'I mean apart from coffee.'

'Cocoa mostly. And milk.'

'Cocoa!' she repeated. She hid her astonishment as best she could, regretting nevertheless that she was unable to pour his tea out for him. Gradually they were getting to know one another better. Barbara had broached the subject of his spoken English, very tactfully.

'It so bad?' Louis had asked.

'It terrible, darling,' she said smiling. 'It very funny English.'

She kissed him, drawing him close, with all her love showing in her eyes. 'We'll have to do something about it. If you joined the library and read some really good books it would help. It's no use coming to England and just getting stuck in a rut.'

She knew that he had taken the first job available in Ruddersleigh, but she wanted much better things for him. The wonderful future she had dreamed about for herself now included Louis. She imagined him working hard to improve and educate himself, so that somehow, some day, he would be acceptable to her parents. She suggested that she should correct his grammar when they were talking together.

'It okay if you don't do it too much.'

'I shan't do it too much, darling. Anyway, I don't want you talking like a BBC announcer. It wouldn't sound like my Louis.'

'Ah, now you is sweet-talk me.' He laughed.

He called her *ma petite* and by the little Creole pet name "*doux-doux*". On this sunny Saturday she was meeting him so that they could spend the afternoon and evening together at Burnham Bridge. She finally decided to wear a blue and white polka-dot cotton dress. Her mother thought she was meeting a girl from the Rambling Club, going to a film show in Ruddersleigh, and having tea at the girl's house. There were times when Barbara almost forgot which story she had told her mother, she seemed to tell her so many these days. She picked up her off-white duster coat, and smart white, summer handbag, and went downstairs. Standing in front of the hall mirror, she put on her coat.

'I'm going now. 'Bye, Mummy,' she said, pulling on her gloves.

'Have a nice time. 'Bye darling,' said Helen absently. She was in the kitchen baking. George was busy in the front garden. He looked up as Barbara went out. She smiled at him, and his eyes followed her with fond pride as she walked down Sycamore Avenue.

Waiting for her in Gower Street bus station was Louis, pride in his eyes, too. It was the big bus station in Ruddersleigh, always very busy, with long distance buses travelling all over the country. There was a Netherby bus waiting to go out, and they boarded it and went upstairs. Sitting on the back seat together they clasped hands, and laughed with sheer high spirits. What if Barbara did have to scheme and deceive in order to meet him? They were together and that was all that mattered.

Burnham Bridge was a pretty little village halfway between Ruddersleigh and Netherby. It was in the valley and the gentle slopes on either side had not yet given way to hills and moorland. The country here was wooded, secluded, with trodden paths, devious lanes, and streams gushing along in the most unexpected places. Louis and Barbara had their favourite walk here, up a steep lane that gradually narrowed until it became just a path, with the trees growing more and more thickly on either side. Finally it merged into a wood, with long grass underfoot and a beck tumbling along between the trees. Bluebells were in luxuriant bloom everywhere, filling the air with their delicate fragrance. Barbara stooped and picked a few, holding them up to her face, revelling in the heady scent of the blue loveliness.

'I won't pick any more,' she said. 'I shall have to leave them here; I can't take them home and put them in water. I'm supposed to be in Ruddersleigh with a girlfriend this afternoon.'

She and Louis had looked around here and found a place with a little patch of short grass, yet completely surrounded by bracken and bushes. It was at the foot of a birch tree, and Barbara had declared it was specially made for them. They sat down in this secluded spot. The dappled sunlight slanting through the trees turned Barbara's hair to burnished copper in parts. Somewhere in the woods a cuckoo cried, ceaselessly, plaintively. The wild, sweet smell of grass mingled with the scent of bluebells, and the faint fragrance of Barbara's Olive Adair perfume.

Louis took her in his arms, but before long his passion reached such a pitch of urgency that as usual, she told him to behave.

'I'm fed up,' he said. 'It's behave, behave. Yet you come out with me, and bring we to lonely place together. You want me to kiss, and then you start all cagey-cagey. Is not reasonable.' He pronounced it reasonable.

'What do you mean?' asked Barbara, although she knew perfectly well what he meant.

'It going to stop.'

She sat without speaking. He didn't know how afraid of her own feelings she was, how hard it was for her to tell him to behave. Yet she was fearful of taking the final step which would make them lovers.

She was afraid of so many things. Her mother had talked to

her about the dangers that could lie ahead for a girl. No... she simply daren't, and yet, she wanted him. Desire was strong.

'I go love you properly today, self, or we don't meet again,' said Louis.

'Darling!' she cried, the tears starting. 'It's not fair to make conditions like that. You don't understand—I've never thought of doing anything like that until—' she broke off.

He kissed her passionately. 'It not fair to me,' he said softly. 'I do love you *ma petite*. It have nothing to wait for, no marriage, nothing like that. You tell me you love me.'

'You know I do! But I'm afraid...'

'What you so 'fraid of?' he asked gently. He could see that she was shy, as well as afraid. 'Tell me what you 'fraid of,' he coaxed. 'It your Louis who love you, remember.'

'I'm afraid of... of doing that. Girls have babies...'

'It all right. Nothing like that will happen to you, *doux-doux*. I will take great care'

He began to kiss and caress her, his soft, lilting voice murmuring persuasively. Barbara was torn by her emotions, fear and desire fought each other, but Louis sensed that she was weakening. Exultant joy rushed through him, he was doing things she had never allowed him to do before. He was kissing her fiercely, his hands roving without restraint, pulling at her clothes, touching the secret places of her body. He was determined to possess her, and against the ardour of this sudden, breathless onslaught, her last defences were undermined. Fear was still strong, but desire was stronger, at last she was compliant in his arms. She heard him whisper that he would be gentle, she scarcely understood what he meant before moans were forced from her lips, and tears rolled down her cheeks. It was cruel, agonising, she was being wounded, butchered, torn asunder... it was nothing at all like it was supposed to be in the books she and Shirley had read. When it was all over she lay, shaken with sobs, shocked and bewildered by the reality of sex. She turned away from her lover and covered her face with her hands. Deeply concerned, Louis knelt beside her, wiping away the perspiration that was streaming down his face. He stroked her hair and tried to comfort her, saying he had never meant to hurt her, and he was sure things would be better next time. A querulous voice, muffled by a handkerchief said there wasn't going to be any next time.

So Louis let the future take care of itself, and concentrated on the present.

'I'm in a mess,' gasped Barbara, between sobs. 'I didn't know—'

For the next twenty minutes or so Louis was kept busy, kissing and fussing over her, lending handkerchiefs, and generally rendering first aid. He did this with such untiring patience and tenderness that at last he was rewarded by a faint smile.

'Darling, my head aches dreadfully,' she murmured, 'and we must get down to the village, to the shops—'

'We go buy Aspros, and you can have tea in the little café there, you'll feel better after a cup of tea.' Louis knew that Mrs. Askew always had an Aspro and a cup of tea if she had a headache, and he simply felt he could not do enough for Barbara. She suddenly caught the expression in his eyes.

'Why,' she exclaimed shyly, 'you're as pleased as anything with yourself.'

'Sure thing,' he agreed, smiling happily. He covered her face with kisses.

'You still love me a bit?' he whispered.

For answer she clasped her hands tightly round his neck. She had been through a shattering emotional and physical experience, and yet, painful and frightening though it had been at the time, it had drawn her so close to him that the very intensity of her feelings bewildered her. Everything else faded into nothingness beside her love for Louis. She was overwhelmed with the events of the afternoon, the physical shock, the violent weeping, the new relationship between them.

'When you're ready, *ma petite*, we go down into the village. We go to that chemist shop for you.'

He waited until she had put on some make-up, and combed her hair. When she put her powder compact away he helped her to her feet and held her close for a moment without speaking. On the recently vacated patch of grass lay a handful of crushed bluebells and a couple of cigarette butts. They walked slowly down the hill to where the dry-stone walls began again, and the lane led back into the village. A couple with two little girls carrying bluebells were walking in front of them. Barbara, white faced and subdued, clung tightly to Louis' arm. Very solicitous he walked beside her, aware that her emotions were in a vulnerable state. Because of this he thought it wiser not to look too pleased with himself, although pleased was not the word for what he was feeling, he could scarcely contain his pride and excitement. This beautiful white girl... she was his, his! It was the most wonderful thing that had ever happened to him. He could have sung a calypso about it; he could have done handsprings all the way to the village.

Chapter 9

'You're a bit early this month, aren't you?' Helen was sorting through the linen basket, getting the clothes ready for washing the next morning.

'Yes, it was a bit of a surprise.' Barbara spoke casually, being careful not to meet her mother's eyes.

'I hope you're not going to start being irregular again.' With that, the matter was dismissed, much to Barbara's relief. A couple of weeks later she took to wearing a very pretty and unusual bangle.

'I saw it in the little antique shop near the market,' she told her mother, who had been admiring it. 'It was only ten shillings, so I decided to have a splash.'

'It's very unusual for that price,' said Helen. 'What's it made of?'

'Oh, some sort of metal, I don't know, really.' Barbara spoke hurriedly. 'Anyway, I thought it was a bargain, so I couldn't resist it.'

'I don't know, Babsy,' said her mother, laughing. 'The things you can't resist. Wait till you're earning your own money, we'll see how you budget then. Spending your pocket money on bangles.'

'What's this all about?' enquired George, coming into the living room. 'What's she squandering her pocket money on now?'

Barbara was growing rather flushed. She knew that they were only teasing her, and that neither of them minded in the least how she spent her money. Only it was rather embarrassing, as she hadn't bought the bangle at all. It had been a gift from Louis. A few days after they had become lovers he had taken a small, flat parcel out of his pocket, and handed it to her.

'What's this, darling?' she asked, opening it and taking out a bangle with a delicate pattern of flowers traced on it.

'Is a present for you. An Indian gold bangle. It was my mother's, a gift from my father when they did marry. It was handed down to him. I kept it after they both dead.'

'All those years?' asked Barbara in amazement. 'But you were only a little boy.'

'I know. But I kept it. I did take great care of it.'

She was deeply touched at so young a child keeping his mother's bangle with such care. Her sense of surprise communicated itself to Louis, and looking back on the household he had grown up in, he himself felt a little surprised that the bangle had survived the ups and downs of the Chittaranjan family.

'You must treasure it very much.'

'Most precious possession,' he said simply. 'I want you to have it, *ma petite*.'

'No, I can't take it, darling. If you've kept it all these years, no, I just can't.'

For answer he took her hand and slipped the bangle on. Barbara was nearly in tears. 'But your most precious possession...' she murmured.

'Is why I want you to have it.'

Barbara looked at the bangle on her arm, and wondered how many slim brown wrists it had encircled. She knew that it was more than just a present. There was something deeply symbolic in the giving and receiving of this bangle. 'I'll always treasure it,' she said. 'Always.'

'It look pretty on your arm, *doux-doux*.'

'I suppose I'm the first white girl to wear it.' She laughed, but her laugh was a bit shaky. Louis was in an emotional state, too. He put his head on her shoulder, and they sat in silence for a few minutes. The wonder and the tenderness of being lovers overwhelmed them both. Barbara looked from the bangle on her arm to the dark head resting on her shoulder, and the emotions that rose in her at that moment transcended anything she had ever known. She felt that as long as life was for both of them, the place for his head was on her shoulder. As long as life was, home for her was in the encirclement of his arms. She didn't attempt to reason all this out, she had stopped trying to reason things out for some time now. She simply felt, with a deep, sad, instinctive feeling that he was the other emotional half of herself. It was as though he had journeyed many miles across the ocean to find her waiting for him. He was not of her race, but that didn't matter. Her parents would never approve of him, but that didn't matter either. None of these things mattered. All that mattered was the enthralling beauty of their love for one another; all that mattered was that her fair face could be where it belonged, beside his dark one, for as long as life was.

To continue meeting him, Barbara was kept busy thinking up plausible stories to tell her mother. When Helen noticed that Roger no longer came to the house, she was told that it was because he was too busy.

'He had important exams this term, so he's really having to work. I still see him though, mostly at his house. He's no time for tennis at the moment, so we listen to a few records, or go to Shirley's.'

Helen accepted this although she thought it odd that Roger no longer brought Barbara home in the car in the evenings.

'His parents are out in it now the weather's fine, and I tell him not to bother coming back with me. I'm not in late.'

That was true. She was always home in good time now, reflected Helen. So she said no more, and Barbara congratulated herself on the way she was managing things.

One June evening she and Louis were walking up the lane to the woods at Burnham Bridge.

'What you go do these nights when you're not with me?' Louis asked.

'Nothing very special. I do my homework, play a few records, watch TV. Sometimes Shirley cycles round from Dudley to see me.'

'This Shirley, what is she like?'

Barbara rummaged in her handbag. 'I've got a snapshot of her somewhere... I stopped playing tennis because we always played in a foursome. Someone took this photograph of us. That's Shirley.' She handed him the snap, with Steven and Shirley standing together, and herself with Roger smiling proudly beside her. Louis took it from her and scrutinised it, his face growing angrier and angrier. He was not looking at Shirley, but at Barbara and her partner.

'That fellow—you did have dates with him. I saw you once on the bus together.'

'Yes, that's right. Roger Leffey,' admitted Barbara.

Louis suddenly tore the snap to fragments in front of her, and threw the pieces on the path. 'You keep away from that son-of-a-bitch!' he snarled, his face a mask of jealous rage.

Barbara was too shocked to speak for a moment, and then she

was filled with indignation. 'I told you I didn't play tennis any more—and that wasn't your snap to destroy, you had no right to touch it. And don't bully me like that, and use awful expressions, either, I'm not accustomed to it, and I'm not going to have it!'

She was completely taken aback, both at his high-handed action in tearing up the snap, and the way he had spoken to her. After all the recent tenderness between them it seemed unbelievable. And calling Roger that! It sounded so low and horrible, and uneasy fear stirred inside her as she glimpsed another side to her lover's nature.

Louis put his arms around her, and tried to control the violent jealousy that had shot through him like a flame at the sight of that snapshot.

'That fellow,' he said. 'He went to your home? Your parents did like you to be with him?'

Barbara admitted this. She tried to understand the bitterness and jealousy that Louis must feel at seeing this snap of another man who was accepted so unquestioningly into her family circle. He himself was compelled to skulk in the back streets of her life. Seeing the baffled misery on his face she forgave him, and their lips met in a long kiss.

'I was vex, *doux-doux*. I'm sorry.'

'Louis, sweetheart,' she murmured, 'I can't always say I'm with Shirley. Sometimes I say I'm with him now, when I'm with you. But what else can I do?'

Much as he hated the idea, he was obliged to accept it. 'As long as you are not,' he said. 'Let's don't talk about it any more.'

They began to walk through the woods together, with their arms entwined. Barbara realised that she would have to be more careful in future. If jealousy made Louis like that, then she would avoid giving him the least cause for being jealous. He never bewailed the situation they were placed in, as she often did, and Barbara had thought that he was reconciled to it. Now she began to suspect that he felt certain matters very much, although outwardly he accepted things as they were. Certainly he never entered into any racial discussions with Barbara.

'It have no use go talk about all that again,' he would say with a touch of impatience.

'Darling, if only you were white,' she whispered once. Her lover saw little use in these flights of fancy.

'If I was white, how could I be the same fellow? Have you heard me go wish you were Indian girl?'

'But that would be different.'

'How come it different? England full of white fellows—if they so wonderful why go pick on me? I ain't wanting to be white, I've got my Barbara. It more than any white man done, anyway,' he added with a grin.

'All right, you needn't sit crowing about it like that,' she said, giving him a little push. Louis laughed. He was filled with pride every time he looked at her. However cut off he was from her everyday life, he was her lover, nevertheless, even if he was just an immigrant from the West Indies. In his arms she had realised herself as a woman, in his arms she had known the horizon of pleasure, the anguish and ecstasy of physical love. He knew now that there were dimples on her shoulders, he had traced with his fingers the tiny blue veins just visible on the white skin of her neck and breasts. He had kissed the funny, surprising black mole on her stomach, and the small brown birthmark on her right hip. Every secret of her body had been revealed to him, but never all at once, and never for longer than a few minutes at a time. For although they were secluded enough under the birch tree, Louis was not the only one who found Barbara's flesh sweet. Burnham Bridge was full of midges, and she was continually having to take precautions against these small pests. Before she went out she would rub her legs with lotion to keep them away. Louis would sit blowing cigarette smoke at them, once he lit a tiny fire to get rid of them.

'They ain't bother me,' he said in perplexity. 'If mosquitoes get you they finish you off altogether. It lucky you in England.'

On the evening when he tore up the snapshot Louis had brought a sharp penknife out with him, because Barbara wanted their initials carving on a birch tree. She sat on the grass, while he cut deeply into the bark, making the traditional heart shape.

'Is that okay, *ma petite?*' Every few minutes he asked for her approval, and stood back to appraise his handiwork.

'Yes, keep going. That's lovely, darling.' Barbara was only too pleased to see him happy again. She wanted to forget that unpleasant incident concerning the snapshot. She was listening to the cuckoo, noticing how its cry had changed. 'It's doing the double cuck,' she said.

'What you say?'

'Just the cuckoo changing its cry, sweetheart.'

'Changing its cry? How come it do that?'

'In June, change my tune; in July prepare to fly, in August, away I must; cuckoo goodbye to you. It flies to a warmer country in August.'

'Is sensible bird,' was Louis' comment. 'Look, *doux-doux*, it finish now.' He stood back to admire his carving. 'It deeper carve than any of the other trees.'

The wood was by no means exclusive to Barbara and Louis, and other couples had the same idea about carving their initials.

'You've done it beautifully,' said Barbara. 'Your carving will be on that tree long after we're gone and forgotten.'

'Unless that old bomb come, then the tree and all go. It ain't matter what colour we are then.' He seized her and swung her round and round, laughing, until she squealed and told him to put her down.

'There, you've made me all dizzy now.'

They walked down the hill hand in hand as usual. When they came to the place where Louis had torn up the snapshot, they both averted their eyes from the pieces still lying on the path. He gave Barbara's hand a little squeeze, which she knew meant she had to think no more about it. But Barbara did a good deal of thinking these days about various aspects of their love affair.

Nothing could have happened any differently was the conclusion she reached. She didn't regret it, either, she told herself. It wasn't as if your eyes changed colour, or anything like that. Nobody was any the wiser. She felt infinitely experienced now. Sometimes when Shirley was talking she could scarcely hide an impatient smile. Shirley... why, she didn't know what day it was! And to think that she had been like that herself not so long ago. Her attitude towards her mother changed, too. She felt a certain amused tolerance towards her when she thought of the things Helen had told her, and warned her against. It seemed such a fuss, now she knew about such matters. For the most part, though, she spent her time thinking of Louis. Even when they were not together, the magic of his caresses lingered with her. In bed at night she lay thinking about him; when she slept she dreamed about him, and he was her first waking thought in the morning.

The joy that she now experienced in his embraces seemed to flow out from her, filling even the prosaic world of school with a curious glow. It was also a secret, wonderful flame within her. Louis commanded her physically, and physically she gave with delight. Beside this fact nothing else seemed of much importance. Only sometimes in the mornings when her mother opened the bedroom door and asked if she was getting up, a guilty sadness would settle over Barbara.

The faint odour of frying bacon would waft up the stairs, and the milkman would be coming along Sycamore Avenue, jingling bottles. She would lie looking at the wallpaper that she had chosen, with the pattern of tiny pink roses, and the matching curtains that her mother had made. There were six Peter Scott prints hanging up, and a framed sampler that her great-grandmother had worked as a child. On top of her wardrobe was her rather battered teddy bear, presiding over the scene as he had done since her childhood. There were mornings when she would feel like a stranger there, an impostor, not the girl who used to lie there between the candy-striped sheets. Immersed in her thoughts she would sometimes stay in bed so long that Helen would stand at the foot of the stairs and call her again, not without irritation. By that time Eddie would probably be in the bathroom, and Barbara would bang on the door, telling him to hurry up because she wanted to go in.

For whatever strange and wonderful things were happening to Barbara, life was going on as usual for the rest of the family. Helped by Mrs. Garside, Helen had finished the spring-cleaning, much to her relief. The paintwork on the outside of the house had been looking shabby for some time, and George had decided to save money by repainting it himself. It was now blue and cream, a colour scheme which Helen had chosen, although she was not sure now whether green might have been better... still it did look quite smart. Anyway, George had finally finished, and he was tired of the sight and smell of paint, and of brushes soaking in turpentine. It took him the best part of one evening to return the ladders that he had borrowed from a neighbour, and to clear up the mess of brushes and paint tins in the garden shed. He came into the dining room and flopped into a chair.

'Where's Eddie?' he enquired.

'Lying on his bed, reading, not doing homework. And

Barbara's in her room too. It doesn't sound as if she's busy, either.'

From above came the beautiful sound of Edith Piaf singing "No Regrets".

'Barbara's in as big a dream as Eddie these days. She looks quite startled sometimes when she meets me around the house.' George lit his pipe. 'I didn't tell you about Norman Smith at the office, did I?' He knew Helen would be interested in this bit of gossip.

'Why, what's happened to him?'

'It's not him, it's his daughter. He's had to take leave to go chasing up to Gretna Green after her—she's run off with some boy. She's only eighteen, and she wants them to consent to her getting married, and they won't. I should think not either. Norman doesn't know how on earth she picked up with a type like him in the first place, a real layabout by all accounts. He hasn't even got a job—and she wants to marry him! I hope Norman finds her and brings her back.'

'There'll be a bit in the *Evening Chronicle* I suppose,' said Helen. 'Runaway lovers, and so on.'

'She's drawn out her Post Office savings, I believe,' went on George. 'So that's a good start. She won't be able to keep both of them on that for long, though, not if she's anything like Babsy.'

Helen laughed, and George smiled, too. 'Still, it's tough on her parents,' he said. He sat thinking about it. Poor old Smithy. You spent years of your life bringing up a golden girl, and then she ran off with some long-haired lout. If it had been Barbara! But then, of course, Barbara was different.

'Two girls at the secondary modern school down on the estate are expecting babies,' said Helen. 'Mrs. Garside told me. The boys responsible are still at school, too. None of them even fifteen yet.'

George shook his head at the ways of modern youth.

'Our two could be doing a lot worse than lying on their beds, not doing their homework,' she added, and her husband was bound to agree with her.

So the long June days slipped by. George played golf most weekends, and he and Helen both went to the bowling green adjoining the tennis court on fine evenings. Eddie went his happy, harmless way, lolling around, playing his guitar, and visiting Mousy Marfitt. With the rest of the family thus occupied in the evenings, Barbara continued to meet her lover, lying glibly if Helen ever asked her where she was going.

Chapter 10

Barbara had been buying a new dress in Ruddersleigh. It was a soft shade of green, with a delicate tracery of white flowers.

'It is pretty, darling,' said Helen when she saw Barbara trying it on. 'I like the sheath style.'

'I'll have to shorten it.'

'Not very much. Just turn it back the width of the hem.'

'No, that's still too long.'

'Well, do what you think, then.'

Barbara turned it up, but as soon as she saw it in the mirror she knew that it was a bit too short, although when her mother said so, she insisted that it was the right length. The following evening she wore it when she went to meet Louis. At Gower Street bus station in Ruddersleigh a bus for Netherby was about to pull out, and they had to hurry for it. Instead of going upstairs as usual, her lover bundled her inside, and sat frowning all the way to Burnham Bridge.

'What's wrong with you?' enquired Barbara, when they alighted from the bus. 'You've never smiled once since we've been together. And why did you push me inside like that?'

'Because your dress is far too short. Is disgusting. Girls don't know what they show when they go up bus stairs in skirts as short as that.'

'But you seem to know what they show!' cried Barbara indignantly. 'You must be standing looking.'

Louis made no reply to this accusation. The hemlines of Barbara's summer frocks had been a source of concern to him for some time. He decided to speak his mind about this matter. There was a wooden seat near the bus stop at Burnham Bridge, and Barbara crossed the road and sat on it.

'All right,' she said. 'You don't have to walk two yards with me. We'll sit here until the next bus comes, and I'll go back home.'

Louis sat down beside her. 'It wasn't as short as that when you bought it,' he said, actually turning back the hem for a second, to her intense annoyance. 'It could go down another two inches, and Barbara, it damn well need to.'

'Does it?' She gazed straight ahead. 'You seem to know a lot about home dressmaking. I suppose nice girls where you come from don't wear dresses as short as this. Go on, why don't you say it?'

'It true, they don't. I ain't liking you in these short dresses. It have all the fellows staring at your legs.'

'I'll wear a sari then. You'd like that, wouldn't you?'

'Is no need to say things like that. I'm telling you that dress is too short. All your frocks is too short, but that one is worse than any.'

'Don't you think it's nice?' she asked appealingly. She liked Louis to admire her clothes.

'"Course I do.' His attitude softened considerably. 'You know you looking lovely in it, *ma petite*. But you go please me very much if you make it longer. All the other frocks could go longer, too. I been looking at the hems, *oui*.'

'Well, of all the nerve!' She laughed in spite of her annoyance, and Louis joined in. He still wanted to get the matter of her hemlines settled though.

'Don't let this thing go making misery between us. It please me very much if you make your skirts longer.'

'But Louis, they're no shorter than other girls wear theirs.'

'I know that. I ain't caring what other girls wear, though.'

She sat thinking for a moment. 'All right, then, darling, if it means so much to you.'

He slipped his hand in hers, and he was obviously pleased and relieved. She had to smile. They walked along to the woods, with Louis making a great fuss of her.

Helen, too, was gratified when she saw Barbara letting down the hem of her new dress. It showed she took some notice of what her mother said after all. Then she saw that Barbara was busy every day after school, letting down all her dresses. Even George remarked on her industry. 'Babsy seems to be doing a lot of sewing lately,' he said one evening.

'She's letting down all her clothes,' explained Helen.

'Letting them down!' George was astonished. 'I've never seen her do anything but take them up. Have they been saying something about it in Paris?'

'Not to my knowledge. I don't know what's got into her. Still, they could do with letting down, most of them.'

George was going to do a few jobs in the front garden, but as he walked into the hall, the telephone rang. It was Roger Leffey for Barbara. A little flustered, she took the receiver from her father, who went into the kitchen. He told Helen it was Roger on the 'phone, and she remarked that he had been working very hard, and that was why he hadn't been round so much for Barbara lately.

Meanwhile, Barbara was dealing with Roger. He had rung up several times like this to try to make a date, and unknowingly he had benefited her by so doing. Because he rang up occasionally Helen took it for granted that her daughter was with him when she said she was. Sometimes she wondered why Shirley didn't come to the house so often these days, but then teenage girls frequently changed their friends she thought.

One Saturday when Barbara met Louis they went right into Netherby, instead of getting off at Burnham Bridge. They sometimes did this because in Netherby they could wander round freely and look at the shops without worrying whether they were being seen. They could also go to the cinema there, and visit Burnham Bridge on the way home.

Conveniently close to Netherby bus station was a Chinese restaurant called The Golden Palace. They were afraid to patronise a Ruddersleigh café, but they always went there for a meal when they visited Netherby, because East and West were served equally well. Barbara, who disliked Chinese food, usually had an omelette, while Louis ate Chow Mein. She was beginning to realise certain things about her lover, by now. He had his own ideas, and they didn't include eating English food if he could possibly avoid it.

It was a warm day, and Barbara was not feeling very well, so they went to see a film, and decided not to visit Burnham Bridge at all. There was a large, pleasant park just off the bus route outside Netherby, and Louis suggested that she might like to sit there for a couple of hours.

'I must get some cigarettes, *doux-doux*,' he said, as they went through the gates. 'Just sit on this seat and wait for me.'

Barbara sat down on an empty seat, and looked at the neatly laid out flowerbeds. It had not rained for several days, and the air was sultry. Before long a man approached from the opposite direction, a florid-faced, shifty-eyed man in his thirties. There was no one else about in that part of the park, and to Barbara's surprise he sat down beside her.

'Lovely evening, isn't it?' he enquired, his unpleasant eyes running over her offensively.

'Yes,' she answered coldly and without interest, looking away from him.

'I wonder what a nice girl like you is doing, sitting in the park on your own,' he continued. Barbara didn't reply. She thought if he spoke again she would get up and walk out of the park. He did speak again, making an objectionable suggestion. She stood up and began to walk towards the park gates, but not before he had called out an offensive remark about her figure.

She flushed with disgust, and quickened her pace, reaching the park entrance just before Louis did.

'What you doing here?' he asked in surprise. 'You think I get lost, or something?'

She slipped her arm through his. He glanced into the park, then, and noticed the man on the seat. 'That fellow,' he exclaimed. 'He been trying a fast one? He say something to you?'

'Let's go and sit by the boating lake,' said Barbara hastily. She pulled at his arm, but he wouldn't move.

'He did say something to you,' he protested. 'It make you get up and walk away. What he say, *ma petite?*'

But she was not going to tell him that. 'I didn't like sitting there, so I came to meet you,' she explained. By now the man evidently realised that there was some discussion going on about him, and he rose and hurried off in the opposite direction. Barbara clung to Louis' arm as he stood, half ready to dash after him, but unable to get any information out of her. His face was murderous.

'Louis, darling, let's sit down,' she said. 'Why should we upset ourselves over things like that?'

She was holding onto his arm so tightly, and her eyes were so beseeching that he was finally persuaded to sit down on a seat in front of the boating lake. He lit a cigarette, but she knew that he was still thinking about that other man.

'What did he say to you?' he asked again.

'If I told you, you would be angry. Can't you see I just want to sit here and be happy with you?'

'But I want to know what he said. He's gone now, anyway, *doux-doux*. I go sit here whatever he said. I promise.'

On that understanding he finally got it out of her. 'You should have told me!' he exclaimed angrily. 'He say that to you and get away with it!' He was enraged, as she had known he would be.

'Darling, do you think I care about him getting away with it? Don't fuss so.'

Louis sat without speaking for a few minutes. Barbara knew that he was doing fearful things to that man in his imagination.

'When I'm not with you,' he began. 'These fellows liming around—'

'Oh, stop it,' she said fretfully. 'If a man makes a pass at me I ignore it. It happens to all girls. You take too much notice of things like that.'

'You think I'm going to stand scratching while other fellows say what they like to you?' he demanded.

Barbara decided to keep quiet and let him simmer down. She knew by now that there was a hot-headed streak in her lover if he was roused. Sometimes when she attracted admiring glances from other men she would catch the expression on his face as he glared back. It was no wonder they soon stopped looking. Louis' intense jealousy had caused more than one argument between them. He had objected to some lipstick she was wearing one day, and told her to wipe it off because it was too bright. For a few seconds Barbara had stared at him in astonishment, and then indignation had taken its place.

'I'll do no such thing,' she said. 'You're not going to tell me what shade of lipstick to wear. Whatever next?'

'It too bright,' repeated Louis, doggedly. 'It have you looking like a—like a—'

'Like a what?' cried Barbara, her face flaming.

'Never mind. I don't like it.'

'You don't like it,' she mocked him. 'Well I do, and that's all that matters.'

They sat in dignified silence for a few minutes, and then Louis spoke again. 'I ain't having you go walking round painted up like that.'

'It's nothing to do with you,' she said coldly.

Louis was justifiably indignant about this remark, and she followed it up with racial insults, which she was inclined to do when they disagreed. 'I thought Indians liked bright colours.'

'Not on your face.'

'The trouble with you is that we've only partly Westernised you. You still have the Eastern attitude towards women.'

She hoped this would cut him cruelly, but he merely remarked that it was a sensible attitude, and very necessary with some women. She sat hesitating between a choice of outrageous replies.

Louis thought it was time to change tactics. '*Ma petite*,' he said, laughing. 'I'm only making a joke. I go buy you some lipstick that suit your skin. Who say that colour suit my Barbara?'

'Well, Shirley said—'

'Maybe it suit her,' said Louis cunningly. 'It ain't suit a girl with hair and skin like yours.' He put his arms round her. 'You care about pleasing your Louis?' Clasped in his arms, with his soft voice murmuring, his urgent kisses on her lips, Barbara's annoyance melted into a different emotion. Before the week was out she was wearing a very quiet shade of lipstick, to the satisfaction of Louis, and the perplexity of Shirley.

'You're wearing very pale lipstick these days, aren't you?' she remarked, on one of her increasingly rare visits to Sycamore Avenue.

'Because it's the most up-to-date look. Most people haven't caught on yet. Pale lipstick, and emphasis on eye make-up. Just you look around.'

'Yes, I have seen a few like that. But they're wearing masses of eye shadow, and false eyelashes too, most of them. I mean you're not emphasising your eyes, are you?'

'Possibly not,' said Barbara, leaving Shirley totally puzzled. She knew that there was a big change in her friend, but she was unable to understand how or why it had come about. Shirley was well aware that she was a pleasantly ordinary looking girl beside Barbara, but one of the advantages of being Barbara's friend had been the number of attractive young men available. These days there was no talk of boyfriends, in fact Barbara seemed to have lost all interest in the opposite sex. She was getting quite dowdy lately, too. She'll be like Pringle before she's finished, thought Shirley, except that Pringle's schoolwork was going up and up, while Barbara's was going down and down.

146

* * *

Louis slipped his arm round her as they sat on the park seat. 'You feeling better, *ma petite?*' he asked, remembering why they were there.

She shook her head.

'Lean on me then, if your back ache. He stroked her arm. 'I eat you up one day. You're as nice as Curry Cascadoo.'

'What's that?'

'Is cascadura fish. When it's cooked we call it Curry Cascadoo.'

'I remember something about it when I wrote that essay. Isn't there a little rhyme about it?'

"Those who eat the cascadura, will, the native legend says, wheresoever they may wander, end in Trinidad their days," he quoted softly.

'I expect you've eaten plenty, darling.'

'Plenty. I did use to fish for it with a bucket and basket.'

She put her face against his, and she was quiet for a long time. It was over three months now since they had first met. Louis' spoken English had improved slightly, but his ideas had not changed at all. Barbara's social life away from him was practically non-existent now. Her hemlines had crept down to a more modest length, and her make-up was very discreet. Yet whatever had happened to Barbara, whatever changes other people might notice in her, she was living every second of every minute with an intensity that she had never dreamed possible before she met Louis. She had stopped even thinking and planning for the future; she was far too busy living for the present. By now she knew that there were things about Louis that she could not alter, or at least it would take longer than she had thought at first. So although she would worry about the situation sometimes, in the main she shelved everything, and gave herself up to the joy of having her lover. To meet him and go to Burnham Bridge where they could be alone together, that was the important thing for Barbara. All that mattered was that he should tell her of his love, hold her in his lover's arms, and kiss her with his lover's lips.

And this he never failed to do, caressing her passionately, straining her to him, bruising her with his hard young body.

147

Chapter 11

It was July now, and the gardens in Sycamore Avenue were a blaze of colour, scenting the air with fragrance. George's roses were exceptionally good this year. Many hued butterflies and moths fluttered around the flowerbeds, and the bees went swiftly and efficiently from blossom to blossom. Fledgling birds were everywhere, feeding themselves now, and practising flying. Birdsong started at dawn and went on intermittently all day. People were out in the evenings mowing their lawns and talking over the clipped privet hedges to their neighbours. After spending the afternoon in deck chairs in the back garden, Joyce Bell and her sister were sitting in the front room, while Ian sprawled on the red and purple patterned carpet reading comics. The room contained a wine-coloured, crushed-velvet three-piece suite, and a brown leather "recliner" chair. There were a couple of occasional tables, and a big mahogany display cabinet crammed with china and glass. The wallpaper was blue with a diamond shaped raised design on it in crimson, with several popular prints from Boots hanging on the walls.

They had just finished watching an episode of Coronation Street on the big television set. Mrs. Bell pulled back the heavy gold-coloured curtains, which she had drawn across the window so that they could view the screen more easily. It had been a fine, warm day, and the evening sun blazed into the room. Joyce Bell sat bulging out of a green crimplene dress, her face, neck and arms burnt a bright pink. She switched off the television and remarked that she hadn't missed an episode of Coronation Street since it started.

'Well, hardly one,' she added. 'Ken doesn't watch it, though.'

'Bill watches it if he's around when it's on. He likes that Elsie Tanner.' Mrs. Bell's sister was a younger, slimmer, more attractive looking woman than her sibling. She was a hairdresser in a Ruddersleigh salon. She lived in Frinton, a village on the way to

Netherby, where her husband worked, but she often took the bus from Ruddersleigh to Fordham to visit her sister when she had a free afternoon from work.

'Ken will run you home when you are ready to go—I'll come along too, just for the drive out,' Mrs. Bell was saying. 'Watch Ken stop trimming the hedge to look at Barbara Granger when she goes past.' She nodded towards the window.

'Who's Barbara Granger?' asked her sister.

'A young girl who lives further down the avenue, her brother goes to the same school as our Ian. There, I told you! Look at Ken gawping after her.'

'What, *that* girl? I know her by sight. I work late at least once a week, and I've seen her time and again getting the Netherby bus from Gower Street bus station. She meets a young coloured chap, and they go upstairs and get off at Burnham Bridge, the stop before Frinton.'

'A coloured chap? Are you sure it's the same girl?' Joyce Bell's eyes were bulging with excitement.

'Positive. I've stood near her in the queue sometimes. Everyone looks at her, I mean, that lovely auburn hair! She's a real head turner; Ken's not the only man who gawps at her. She wears a lot of blues and greens, doesn't she?'

'Yes, that's right.'

'Hasn't she a dark brown suede jacket? And a green suit, and an off-white coat?'

Her sister recognised all these as being Barbara's clothes. 'What's the man like?' she asked, avid for every detail.

'Very young. Not bad looking, I suppose. Indian, I should think, probably from Pakistan. Quite smart, neat looking. He usually wears a rust coloured sports jacket.'

'She keeps him well hidden, then. He's never been seen round here. Earlier this year she was going out with a university student, he was always at the house. I think his father has a chemist's shop in Dudley.'

'I suppose this one might be a student, too.'

'I doubt it, Rita. I've seen Barbara Granger and her friend with a few university boys, but none of them coloured. There's something funny going on there... you say they get off the bus at Burnham Bridge?'

149

'Yes, and they're pretty keen on each other, I can tell you. He comes rushing along as if he's won the pools when he sees her, and he can hardly keep his hands off her even before they get on the bus—' She broke off, catching a warning look from her sister. Ian was listening open-mouthed on the carpet.

'Ian,' said his mother, 'I can hear the ice cream man somewhere. Go and get one each for us, here's the money. Ask your dad if he wants one.'

When the two women were left together they resumed their conversation.

'What are the girl's parents like?'

'Toffee-nosed, particularly the wife. She's from the south, you know. The girl goes to Parkleigh High School; she won a scholarship there. They don't pay school fees.'

'She must be clever, then.'

'Well, the boy isn't. Our Ian gets better marks at school than him. Of course, they hoped he would pass the eleven-plus, but he didn't. I know they had him privately coached.'

'What does the husband do, then?'

'He's in the Civil Service. Just because Ken's a rep they think they can look down on us; the wife does, anyway. She thinks herself far above me.'

'I know the sort. We have one like that at Frinton. Her husband's firm supply him with a car, and they've just bought a bubble car for the wife. Her "little runabout" she calls it. Talk about showing off. Tuppence ha'penny looking down at tuppence.'

'The Grangers can't even afford to run a car now; they have to cadge lifts. Granger gets a lift into Ruddersleigh and back every day, and he had to paint the outside of the house himself this year. When they go on holiday it's always to Eastbourne, where the grandmother lives; they can't afford anything else. Granger still plays golf, though, and madam has someone to help her clean the house every week. That's the scene there, Rita.'

'All top show. You know the old saying, fur coat and no knickers,' Mrs. Bell's sister laughed as she spoke. Mrs. Bell joined in with her own raucous laugh. 'That's something I've got and she hasn't, a fur coat.'

'And knickers too—there's Ian coming back with the ice cream, Joyce.'

'Better talk about other things then, seeing Grangers' kid's at school with Ian. It's certainly given me something to think about. Keep your eyes open at the bus station, then, Rita, and let me know any further developments. Now I come to think of it, Barbara Granger's girlfriend from Dudley doesn't seem to be round these parts much now. I'd like to bet that little minx has got something going with that coloured lad on the quiet. She's keeping him well away from Sycamore Avenue—hello, love, your dad didn't want an ice, then? I bet he'll have a beer instead.'

Later in the week Barbara was seen at Gower Street bus station by her aunt. Violet's Morris 1100 had recently developed clutch trouble, and as a result was having attention in the garage. Violet was with an office friend, and they were both going to visit a colleague who had fallen down some steps and broken her ankle. She had been discharged from hospital, but she lived some way out of Ruddersleigh, and the only way to get to her was from Gower Street. As the two of them were waiting in the queue for Brampton, Violet caught sight of Barbara. She was just about to board a Netherby bus, but she was not alone. Violet was amazed to see a young coloured man obviously with her, they were talking together, and Violet saw the look of tenderness and possessive pride on his face. The next moment the Netherby bus pulled out, and Violet and her friend got on theirs. The two women had known each other for a long time; sometimes Edna's chatter got on Violet's nerves, but on that particular journey she was glad that she was only required to nod, and appear to listen. In actual fact she was thunderstruck by what she had seen. The expression in that young man's eyes when he looked at Barbara... poignant memories came back to Violet. Someone had looked at her like that a long time ago, but he had been killed... she knew that look though; it was the look of love. Did George and Helen know anything about this?

The following Sunday she and her father went to Fordham in the afternoon, Violet's car was fully serviceable again now. They took tomatoes and some strawberries with them, much appreciated by Helen.

'You've had the sitting room decorated, it looks lovely—have you been buying a new suite, too?' Violet looked round the room admiringly.

'No, Helen re-covered it herself,' said George proudly.

'I thought it was a new suite! I know you went to upholstery classes in the winter. It looks lovely, beige, with that pale gold thread in it.'

'We chose the wallpaper to tone with it,' said Helen. 'We bought new curtains, too. Mrs. Garside cleaned the carpet, so we are quite pleased with the room now.'

'I should think so.' Violet followed her sister-in-law into the kitchen. 'I would like to make some changes at home, but Father just seems to want to keep everything the same as when Mummy was alive. When we have any painting done, it's still brown paint. God, I hate brown paint, but it's not worth arguing about.'

'I suppose our parents were the brown paint generation, certainly I can understand it in Ruddersleigh, with all the dirt,' was Helen's comment.

'No brown paint here, anyway,' said Violet, looking round the kitchen. 'It looks super. Buttercup yellow and white. We haven't managed a trip out here for ages, Father not being well, and one thing and another. George has popped in to see us now and again in his lunch hour.'

'We miss having the car; we can't get about the same. We'll have these strawberries at tea time, Vi.'

'Where are the children, anyway?'

'Eddie went out with Mousy this morning. They both had sandwiches with them, and went off somewhere on their bikes.'

'And Babsy?'

'She went out about an hour ago, to Shirley's, she said. I expect she'll stay there until tonight.'

'I saw Babsy one evening last week. She was in Gower Street bus station with a young man. I was with my friend, Edna; we had to get the bus to see someone because the car was in the garage. She caught a Netherby bus. She didn't see me.'

'She would be with Roger, I expect. I don't know why they would be going to Netherby, though.'

'No, it wasn't Roger. I've met him here, remember? This young man wasn't English, definitely not. Very dark—' Violet hesitated.

'Not English?' Helen raised her eyebrows. 'It would be one of Roger's friends from the university, then. Roger would be with them, I expect, but you must have missed seeing him. They have a good few foreign students there, they all congregate in that coffee bar near the college. I'll mention it to Babsy, though.'

'No, don't. She'll only think we've been discussing her, you know what these youngsters are, and I don't want her to think I've turned into a prying old aunt. When she was little we used to be such good friends, but now she's very reserved about her affairs as far as I'm concerned. I don't want her to push me out into the cold altogether.'

Helen heard a wistful note in her voice, a sadness that her young niece no longer rushed into her arms crying: 'Auntie Vi, guess what's happened since I last saw you!'

'Well, she doesn't exactly confide in George and me. I get the bare outline of what goes on, and that's all. I won't say anything then, Vi. There goes George, showing your father round the garden. I expect he'll be telling him the latest scene in the office.'

'Why, what's that?'

'Well, they all detested the manager, Mr. Chorley. Then he had a heart attack a couple of months ago, and George had been acting up in his place ever since. Now it seems he's taking early retirement on health grounds. Nobody is sorry, least of all George.'

'Will it make any difference to George's chances of promotion?'

'It should do, but knowing the Civil Service...' Helen shrugged.

'I think I'll have a look in the garden, too,' said Violet. She stepped out of the kitchen door and joined the two men on the back lawn. Helen thought how alike Violet and her brother were. Both tall and slim, both with good features and hazel eyes, and both keen golf players...

Anyway, she was pleased with the strawberries and tomatoes, very handy for Sunday high tea. They would have salad, strawberries and cream, and the Victoria sponge cake that she had made that morning. She busied herself in the kitchen, while George and his father and sister talked together in the garden. After a few minutes Violet came back into the house, pausing at the back door to peer into the rabbit hutch. A small grey lump of fur looked back, nose twitching.

'Ezra still going strong, I see.'

'George says he'll see us all out. His fur's going a bit brown in places, well, it can't go grey as it's grey to start with.'

'Now what can I do to help? Have you been buying a new tea service, Helen?'

'No, a friend bought me that as a thank you present for helping her cover a sofa. I know she got it from Gibson's, I've seen them there. It's very modern, the way the cups are shaped, very streamlined. Do you like it?'

'Yes, very much. It's such a lovely shade of blue, too... I'll butter the bread rolls, shall I?'

When Violet visited she didn't expect to be waited on. Capable and efficient in a smartly checked shirt-waister dress, she bustled around in the kitchen, shelling hard-boiled eggs, washing lettuce, slicing tomatoes and generally making herself useful.

Meanwhile, unaware that anyone who mattered had seen her with Louis, Barbara continued to meet him. She was busy just now thinking about his twenty-second birthday, and the gift she had bought him. It was a very handsome cigarette case, with his initials engraved on it; she had also bought a pretty, sentimental card, with a loving message written in it.

His birthday fell conveniently on a Saturday when he was on early turn, and she went off to meet him in the afternoon. Louis always dressed conventionally, and usually wore a tie, but as soon as she saw him, Barbara took a violent dislike to the one he was wearing. She thought it was loud and vulgar, with hideous bright colours, and that she would tell him so when the opportunity presented itself. There were more important things to think about, first, though. On the bus going out of Ruddersleigh, she handed Louis his present. He was delighted with it, and the birthday card. They sat smiling at each other, with their hands tightly clasped all the way to Netherby.

They were celebrating Louis' birthday by going to the cinema, and then to The Golden Palace for a meal. Afterwards they were catching the bus to Burnham Bridge. Louis particularly wanted to see a John Wayne western film that was showing at the Odeon in Netherby. Barbara was not so enthusiastic, but it was his birthday, so she said she would like it too. With her lover's arm round her she sat through the endless shoot-ups, the whooping redskins, and the thundering hooves of the sheriff's posse. Then they went to The Golden Palace, and she was struck afresh with the vulgarity of his tie. She asked him if it was a new one.

'M-mm, I got it this morning, a present from Mrs. Askew. Why?'

'I don't like it very much,' she said candidly.

'It all right,' said Louis, with a note of obstinacy in his voice.

They finished their meal at The Golden Palace and caught the bus to Burnham Bridge. Haymaking was in progress in the surrounding meadows, and scarlet poppies made a bright splash of colour in the cornfields. The hedges were a tangle of wild flowers, white roses and masses of white elder blossom mingled with the pale pink of blackberry blossom. Purple foxgloves reached up from the verges, along with nettles and grasses, clover, buttercups and daisies. It had been a fine, dry day, although with a breeze, the scents and sounds of the country filled the air, the hard cry of the starling was heard, mixed with the chirping of tree sparrows, and the flute-like notes of the blackbird. Burnham Bridge, basking in the glow of high summer had never looked lovelier, and never, to Barbara, had any tie looked as unsightly as the one her lover was wearing. Hand in hand they began the ascent to the woods.

'Don't wear that tie again,' she said suddenly. 'It's horrible. I hate it. It shows what taste that Mrs. Askew has, buying you a thing like that.'

'It all right,' repeated Louis calmly. 'She was pleased when I put it on.'

Annoyance rushed through Barbara. *She* was pleased, indeed! 'Well, I'm not pleased. You look awful in it.'

'Okay, I look awful.'

She became so angry with him then that she withdrew her hand and stopped walking. She demanded that Louis should take off his tie, and wear his shirt open at the neck. He flatly refused to do this. Barbara became so incensed that she made a snatch for the offending tie, but he jerked away, laughing. She hated him then, as she had not thought it possible to hate anyone. She was angry as she had never been angry before, hurling insults at him, every cruel and hurtful thing she could think of. Finally she called him a dirty Indian, fairly spitting the words out in her rage. Louis retorted with a remark which made her hysterical.

In a frenzy she tried to claw his face with her nails, unable to do that she struck wildly out at him, raining blows on him with all her strength. For a few seconds he warded them off with his arm, then, his eyes glinting angrily, he seized her wrists and loosed on her a stream of oaths in Hindi. She didn't understand a word, but she knew that he was calling her worse than dirt. It was too much for Barbara. To be glared at with such venom, to have Louis swearing at her in some unknown language, and holding her helpless like that, she crumpled up, sobbing, terrified. The next moment his arms were around her. A young couple were approaching them from the direction of the woods. They had obviously witnessed the unpleasant scene that had just taken place. Louis led Barbara away from the path, holding her close. As the other two came nearer, the man looked askance at Louis, almost as if he was inclined to interfere, but his companion said something to him, and they walked past in silence.

Barbara's legs were trembling so much that she could hardly stand, and in contrast to all the abuse she had been heaping on her lover, she was absolutely speechless for several minutes. Louis held her in his arms and waited for her to recover. How two people so much in love could quarrel like that was a mystery to Barbara. True, they had different opinions on various things. There had been little sulks and arguments before, but never anything like this. How she could descend to that level, feel such hatred for Louis, and utter such deadly insults was beyond her understanding. Why, she had even struck out at him in her rage, and screamed like a fishwife! But how could he have looked at her like that, and abused her so vilely, even though it wasn't in English? It must be all his fault, so she would make him apologise for everything.

What Louis wanted after such a frenzied scene was peace and quiet again, and to make love to Barbara under the birch tree. But first he had to say he was sorry for looking at her like that, even though he protested that he didn't know he was looking at her like that. Anyway, he was sorry, and of course he had to apologise for swearing at her. He didn't deny that he had been swearing, although after all, it wasn't in English. Then he even had to be sorry because Barbara's hands were red and stinging from contact with his arm. It was Louis' private opinion that this served her right, after assailing him so vigorously, but to Barbara he was duly regretful. And he had to be sorry for holding her wrists so tightly; he had to kiss the red marks. It seemed he had committed endless crimes for which he had to be sorry, and Barbara was not going to let him get away with anything. Pale-faced, with traces of fear still lingering in her eyes, she extorted the last apology out of him. Louis had been too angry at the time to realise how much his behaviour had frightened her, but it had certainly been effective. There was no further mention of the tie.

When they had made it up, and Barbara had forgiven him, very sweetly he put his arm round her, and led her to their secret place. And there, crushing the dark fern fronds beneath them, he made love to her, passionately, ecstatically, straining her to him, a panting, trembling thing in his arms. Afterwards they lay quietly for a long time, locked together. But Barbara still felt uneasy about the angry scene between them. She had never behaved like that since she had been a child, fighting with Eddie. She had made Louis take the blame for everything, but in her heart she knew that she had provoked him.

'Darling,' she whispered, 'I'm sorry I said those awful things, and hit you like that. I've spoilt your birthday.'

'Oh, *that* bacchanal?' Louis laughed. 'You were sure vex with me, *doux-doux*. You were hell self.'

'And has it... do you love me any less because of it?'

'Woman, haven't I show you enough I don't love you any less? Or maybe you still not satisfied—you wanting more?'

'Louis!' she spoke reprovingly. In spite of her passionate responses to his lovemaking, she could still feel shy if he teased her with a saucy remark. Knowing this, he was unable to resist teasing her sometimes. 'I mean were you shocked by my behaviour?'

'Shocked? Just because we had one big row?' Louis fondled her breasts gently. 'Nothing to shock,' he said softly. 'All women are hell self sometimes. You okay when I sweet-talk you a bit.'

Evidently to Louis violent quarrelling was a normal pattern of human behaviour. He had seen her at her worst, but his feelings towards her had remained unchanged. He just accepted her as she was, even when she was "hell self". She found herself wondering what Roger Leffey would have thought, had he witnessed her in that rage...

In a vague sort of way she felt that Louis should be shocked, and yet there was something tremendously comforting in knowing that he was not. One thing was certain, after that exhibition she would no longer be able to get digs in at him about not being properly civilised. She had an uneasy feeling that as the white member of the partnership she had somehow let the side down.

'You still worrying, *ma petite?*'

'I was terrible, darling!'

'You were terrible, *oui*. I never had such licks in my life—I thought you were going to leave me for dead! Praise the Lord I found the strength to defend myself —'

'Oh, stop it! You're laughing at me,' she said, hiding her face in his shoulder.

'Why don't you laugh as well?' he asked. 'Is the only sensible thing to do.'

He stroked her hair, and kissed it, but she still kept her face hidden, for the most galling part about the whole business had been the futility of her behaviour. Although certain garments had been removed for the purpose of lovemaking, afterwards Louis had put the hated tie back in place. It lay across his chest, the colours glowing as gaily as a Caribbean sunset.

Chapter 12

Westcliffe Grammar School was an ugly, Victorian building situated a couple of miles from Fordham, where the main road to Ruddersleigh forked off into a less desirable district. The original building had been a Board school, but over the years it had undergone various problems. It had been considered structurally unsafe at one time, then having been repaired, was to have been demolished to make way for a road-widening scheme, which was abandoned as being too expensive. The council had sold it off eventually, and it had become a fee-paying boys' school. They had also sold off the dreary piece of wasteland beside it, which had been turned into a playing field. Parts of the school had been built out and modernised, but most of the high-ceilinged, sash-windowed classrooms were still reminiscent of an earlier period. Even when they were redecorated, which happened about every five years, it was always the same pale yellow walls and dark brown paintwork. All the desks and chairs were old and scratched and carved on, there were radiators in the rooms and assembly hall, but it was still cold and draughty in winter. George called it Dotheboys Hall when he and Helen had occasion to go there for a parents' evening.

'It always makes me think of an old workhouse,' he would say. 'It's positively Dickensian. I don't know how they have the cheek to charge the fees they do for this place.'

'Still if the boys get the individual attention they're supposed to, I don't suppose the surroundings matter all that much.'

'Individual attention doesn't seem to do Eddie much good.'

'It's either Westcliffe or the secondary modern down on the estate. You know the score.'

This sort of conversation went on constantly between Helen and George. It never resolved anything; Eddie was not academic. Facing up to the fact that they had a bright daughter and a not-so-bright son was much harder than if things had been the other way

159

round. If Barbara had been the non-academic one, she could have gone to a commercial college and learnt shorthand and typewriting. She would have been sure of a nice little job in one of the many pleasant offices in Ruddersleigh.

'He doesn't seem to have any aptitude for any subject at all,' George would say gloomily. In many ways he was a tolerant father, but now that Eddie was growing up it concerned him greatly that his son was not clever.

'Well, we can't just write him off at his age. He might be a late developer.' Helen was ever hopeful, and Mr. Stokes, the headmaster at Westcliffe, talked a great deal about late developers. It encouraged the parents of eleven-plus failures to enrol their sons at his school. For the sake of appearances they had to pass an entrance exam before they were accepted for tuition. However, if they did not pass, Mr. Stokes would say, 'Well, I think he should be given a chance, just the same. He's probably a late developer.'

Mr. Stokes was a big, middle-aged, balding man with a genial manner and an air of confidence. He was justified to some extent about his talk of late developers, because not all the boys at Westcliffe remained academic failures. Some of the boys were in fact late developers, and managed to do quite well when they took O levels, and even A levels. The school uniform was dark green, with the initials WGS in bright yellow on the badge. Long hair was not encouraged, although it was allowed up to a certain length with the older boys. As long as they were in school uniform Mr. Stokes expected a decent standard of behaviour from them. Of course there was a certain amount of drinking and smoking among under-age pupils, and occasionally an irate parent would see him about it, as if the school was responsible for their son's misdemeanours. On these occasions Mr. Stokes' attitude never varied.

'If you can tell me how to stop boys from drinking and smoking, I would be very pleased to hear it,' he would say, his genial manner never flagging. Behind his smile lay many years of experience in such matters. Nobody had ever yet come up with an answer to that, and he knew that nobody ever would. If a boy was caught smoking on school premises he was threatened with expulsion. Westcliffe School did not take boarders, so after school hours they were their parents' responsibility. Occasionally at assembly Mr. Stokes would lecture the boys briefly about any alleged   misbehaviour that had come to his attention, emphasising that he didn't want the school to get a bad name. This was the important thing to him. The fact that a few of the kids did a bit of drinking and smoking on the quiet didn't trouble him unduly. What he cared about was getting a new influx of pupils every autumn, and he certainly wanted the school to have a reputation for being a good establishment.

Corporal punishment was not used at Westcliffe, detention and writing lines were deemed more appropriate for failure to do homework, carelessness, forgetfulness and the usual myriad offences normal in a boys' school. Mr. Dodds, the maths master, had been teaching boys for nearly thirty years now, and he had no time for these modern ideas, appealing to their better natures, or anything like that. Early in his teaching career he had concluded that they simply didn't have any better natures. To him they were all liars, idlers, wasters, dodgers and potential criminals. He believed in corporal punishment. Although he did not possess a cane he had a long, folding ruler, which when folded could be brought down smartly on someone's hand. He had wielded his ruler on countless miscreants in an attempt to eradicate what he considered to be the natural viciousness of boyhood. Whether he had succeeded or not was another matter, but he had the satisfaction of knowing that he had never spared the rod. He was not popular with the boys, but he did not court popularity. His role was simply to force knowledge into their heads, if at all possible. Not surprisingly he was known as "Flogger Dodds".

'Well, tell me boy, where is your logbook? Where is it then?' He stood frowning over Eddie, who had been frantically rummaging through his books.

'I don't know, sir,' he faltered, and in fact he was completely bewildered. He knew that he had put his logbook in his locker two days ago, and yet it was nowhere to be found now. But he *knew* that he had put it in...

Mr. Dodds stood over him, his eyes gleaming ferociously behind his horn-rimmed spectacles. He was not in the best of moods to begin with. He was trying to get used to a new set of teeth, but there seemed to be something radically wrong with them. He would have to go back to the dentist at the earliest possible moment. And now, this wretched boy, this uneducable youth, couldn't produce his logbook, didn't have the faintest idea where it was.

'I thought as much. You're a waster, a complete waster. You can take two hundred lines, and see me at the end of the period.'

Edie sat gloomily, knowing what to expect. That beastly ruler, and two hundred lines, all because his logbook was missing. And yet he knew that he had put it in his locker. The maths period ended, and Mr. Dodds beckoned Eddie forward.

'Come here, boy, I want to see you,' whistled the new dentures.

As Eddie stood up, he happened to catch Ian Bell's eye. A suspicion formed in his mind, but for the next few minutes Mr. Dodds claimed his full attention. At break he sought out his friend and ally, Mousy Marfitt. Eddie was stinging from Mr. Dodd's ruler. He stood drinking his milk through a straw, his thoughts centred on the missing logbook.

'I put my logbook in my locker, I know I did. I knew I wouldn't need it till today. I wasn't going to leave it in my desk, and there was no point in toting it home in my satchel,' he told Mousy. 'Somebody's taken it out, I'm sure of that. I bet Ding-Dong's had summat to do with it.'

At home Eddie spoke reasonably good English, but to Mousy and his other friends he lapsed into the local twang. It was a recognised thing, down in the locker room the broad Yorkshire and hard swearing could not have been bettered on the shop floor of any Ruddersleigh engineering works.

'Is your locker door bust?' asked Mousy, draining the last of his milk from the bottle, and making a hideous gurgling noise with his straw in the process.

'Course it's bloody bust. Do you know any locker down in that place that isn't kicked in, within a fortnight?'

That was true enough. Locker doors were kicked in, locks were picked and hinges unscrewed every day of the week.

'Let's have a look down there at lunchtime,' suggested Mousy, putting down his milk bottle. Some time later, after a meal of cottage pie followed by apple crumble and custard, the two boys went to inspect the locker room.

'Eh—look at Ding-Dong's new lock!' exclaimed Eddie.

'I suppose he thinks he's safe,' sneered Mousy.

'I'm flipping sure my logbook's in there. You should have seen

162

the look on his face when old Flogger called me out. If it's in there I'll clobber him till he can't stand up. He won't be looking so chuffed when I've finished with him.'

'We'll soon find out,' said the resourceful Mousy, who always kept a screwdriver handy. 'I'll tek the door off its hinges. Keep a look out, Ed.' Mousy began to unscrew the hinges rapidly. The door hung on its lock, and Eddie pocketed the screws. He began to rake through Ian Bell's books, throwing them on the stone floor in all directions. Suddenly his hand closed round his own logbook.

'It's here, Mousy! I was right... the swivel-eyed get! I'll belt him for this! Of all the stinking, lousy tricks, getting me into a row with Flogger!' Eddie's eyes were blazing. 'That's because I punctured one of his tyres a couple of weeks ago!' His language became obscene.

'I'll get him before he goes home,' he said, throwing Ian Bell's books back in his locker. They left the door with its hinges unscrewed, and at four o'clock there was a fight in the locker room between Eddie and Ian Bell. Such things were quite commonplace, in fact rarely a day went by without a skirmish. The Second, Third and Remove forms shared this locker room; it was usually in an uproar when it was time to go home.

Ian Bell was heavily built, although shorter than Eddie, and it took a good deal of preliminary scuffling and some assistance from Mousy before he was down on the floor. On these occasions nobody worried about good sportsmanship, or any of the lofty ideals that the games' master tried to instil in them. Ian Bell was not a very popular boy, anyway. He had certainly had some rough handling, during which a button had been ripped off his blazer and his recently bought terylene trousers were clicked and snagged.

Eddie thudded on top of him, digging his bony knees into Ding-Dong's chest. 'Let the rat get up now, Ed,' advised Mousy. 'We want him to live a bit longer, because we haven't finished with him yet. Gerrup,' he added, prodding Ian Bell with his foot.

Eddie rose and dusted himself down with his hands. Helen often wondered how his clothes got so dirty and smelled so dusty from time to time. This usually depended on what scores there were to be settled in the locker room at home time. Ian Bell, very red in the face, also got up. He slung his school satchel over his shoulder, and shouted a last remark to Eddie as he went out of the locker room.

'You want to tell that sister of yours to keep Britain white! She's knocking around with wogs—you'll be having wogs in the family before long!' He disappeared from sight while Eddie and Mousy picked up their satchels and went along to the cycle shed. They could see Ian Bell already cycling down the road.

'What did he mean about that last crack about your sister?' asked Mousy, looking puzzled.

'I don't know. Summat to say, I suppose.'

'But she doesn't, does she?'

'What?'

'Knock around with wogs?'

'She's going out with Roger Leffey as far as I know. Wogs—pooh, could you see it? Babsy! It just shows you how daft Ding-Dong is.'

Eddie tossed Ian Bell's words to one side, but after he had cycled home and put his bike away in the garden shed he began to wonder what had made Ding-Dong say that. Now he thought about it, he hadn't seen Roger Leffey around for quite a long time. It was a ridiculous thing to say, but in spite of this, somehow Eddie couldn't get the words out of his mind. Helen noticed him hanging around the kitchen when she was washing up that evening. She thought he must be wanting a sub from his pocket money.

'Is Babsy still going around with Roger Leffey?' he asked casually.

His mother looked blank. 'Yes, as far as I know,' she said slowly. 'Why?'

'Nothing. Only he used to come here a lot, that's all.'

'He's been very busy this term. If you want to get anywhere in this world you have to work hard.'

'But...' began Eddie. He had been going to say that the exams were all over now, and the students were on vacation, but Roger still didn't come to the house. Then he realised the folly of bringing up the subject of work at all; his mother had already held Roger up as an example. Whistling loudly he went outside to see if Ezra needed any carrots, or fresh water, or anything else to add to his comfort. Helen stood frowning. A few minutes later she went upstairs and confronted Barbara in her room.

'Are you going out this evening, Babsy?'

'Yes... why?'

'Are you seeing Roger?' Barbara was thankful that she was bending down putting on a clean pair of stockings. She had an excuse for growing flushed.

'Not tonight. I'm going to a special film show in Ruddersleigh. You know some of the girls in my form are in the Film Society, and I've been invited to go tonight.'

'What film are they showing?'

'Some French film. I can't remember the title.'

'Do you still see Roger?'

'Of course! Why all the questions? What is this, the Spanish Inquisition? Anything else you want to know?'

'There's no need to use that tone of voice... yes, there is something else I want to know. Are you going to Edinburgh for your holiday with Shirley, or coming to Grandma's with the rest of us next month? If you're going to be too bored with us, go to Edinburgh by all means. I know Grandma would love to see you, but don't let that influence your choice. Just please yourself.'

'Don't worry, I will,' said Barbara, fastening her suspenders, her eyes carefully averted from her mother's. Helen went out of the room without another word, leaving Barbara guiltily remorseful. She knew well enough that she was irritable and impatient with the rest of the family, sulking around the place, and spending hours in her room. One evening a couple of weeks before, her father had told her not to be so uncivil. It was very rarely he said anything like that to Barbara, and she had flounced upstairs and banged the door of her room behind her.

There were times when she was snappy and moody with Louis, but if he told her about it she would burst into tears. He would hold her close, then.

'What all the bacchanal about?' And in these sad moments, when the hopelessness of things overwhelmed Barbara, when Louis gave her the silent, animal comfort that she sought, they were closer perhaps than in their most intimate embraces.

She finished her toilet, spraying on a mist of the sweet pea scent. She was reminded that her mother had bought it for her, and on her way out she apologised to Helen for her rudeness. On the bus to Ruddersleigh she considered the question of holidays again. Every year they went to Eastbourne to stay with her grandmother.

Her father only stayed a fortnight because they were unable to spare him for longer than that from the office during the holiday season.

Last year she had gone to Norway with the school, so she hadn't minded three weeks in Eastbourne. But Shirley had asked her if she would like to go to Edinburgh with her, the first two weeks in August. She had an aunt there who would be pleased to have both of them to stay. Barbara considered this as she went to meet her lover. The truth of the matter was that she had no desire to leave Louis for a fortnight to go anywhere. It was bad enough when he was on late turn, and they could only manage one evening together.

Louis had a few days holiday due, she remembered. If he took them during the third week in August she could travel back to Ruddersleigh after a fortnight, and there would just be her father and herself in the house that week. He would be at the office, which meant she would be able to meet Louis every day. But should she go to Edinburgh with Shirley, or travel south with the rest of the family? She decidedly favoured the idea of Edinburgh.

She broached the subject of holidays to her lover.

'What you wanting to go to Edinburgh with Shirley for?' he asked straight away, drawing his black brows together. She had half expected this.

'Well... it would be a change from Eastbourne,' she suggested, a little hesitantly.

'But Shirley will be wanting to meet fellows—have dates on her holiday—not so?'

'Of course she won't—' Barbara broke off. She didn't sound very convincing, even to her own ears.

'Of course she will! You not going with her—she single girl!' he said hotly.

'Well, so am I...' her voice faltered.

'What you mean by that?' he demanded.

Barbara really didn't know what she meant. He seemed to have tied her in a knot. 'It was just a suggestion Shirley made,' she said hurriedly. 'I don't mind either way. But I won't go to Edinburgh, I'll go to Eastbourne with the rest of the family.' She smiled at him coaxingly. She had left home feeling guilty towards her mother; it would be the last straw if Louis became difficult.

However, he seemed mollified at the speedy way she had given in over the question of holidays. They were sitting under the birch tree at Burnham Bridge. He lifted her onto his knee, and they were quiet for a few minutes. She put her face beside his.

'I'll come back after a fortnight, darling. There'll only be my father and myself in the house. If you have a few days off then, it will be wonderful. I'll write to you from Eastbourne, and we'll soon be together.'

They discussed this, both looking forward to it. Barbara ruffled his hair.

'Yes, I soon get into trouble with you,' she said teasingly. 'I shan't know what you're up to while I'm away, though.'

'Oo la la! I won't be up to anything,' grinned Louis. 'You think I'll be chasing after some other slick chick? I ain't wanting any more cuties—I got enough with you.'

'That's what you tell me. I shan't know, though.'

'You find out soon enough. I'll have it all saved up... he give you licks when you get back to Ruddersleigh. *Oui.*'

'You awful thing, Louis Ramdeem. I believe you're looking forward to it already.'

'Is the thought that keep me going while you're away.' They sat, kissing and talking. Then suddenly Louis put Barbara off his knee and jumped up, complaining of cramp.

'That's nursing you, you fat girl!'

'Who's fat? Cheek, calling me fat!'

'You got one fat bottom, anyway,' he said hopping about, trying to get rid of his cramp.

'And glad you are!'

'Have you heard me complain? Give my leg a rub, it hell self.'

Barbara rubbed vigorously for a couple of minutes. She began to get quite breathless. 'Hasn't the cramp gone yet?'

'Yes, it gone. I just like to keep you working hard with massage.'

He hugged her to him, laughing. 'Come on, we better go now, *doux-doux.*'

They walked back to the village. The corn was ripe now in the fields at Burnham Bridge.

'Days changing again,' said Louis. 'Growing shorter. Is a funny thing.'

'Don't talk like that. It's still summer, darling.'

'Is not much of a summer, is it?'

'We've had *some* fine days,' she reminded him. He smiled, without answering. Barbara fell silent, too, and sitting alone some time later in the bus on the way back to Fordham, she wondered uneasily why her mother had asked her about Roger like that. She decided she had better make an effort to be pleasanter in the home. She knew it would please her mother if she went to Eastbourne instead of Edinburgh, it would please her grandmother too, and there was no doubt at all that it pleased Louis.

The following day she told Shirley that she was going on holiday with the family. 'Mummy seems to think Grandma would be very disappointed if she didn't see me. Thank you all the same, Shirley, and thank your aunt for inviting me.'

'All right,' said Shirley, and turned away without expressing any regret. Barbara knew that this had widened the growing gulf between them.

Soon she noticed that Shirley was forming a friendship with another girl, Vida Shippen, growing daily on more intimate terms. Sometimes she would go into the cloakroom and see them exchanging confidences. When they saw her they would cough pointedly, and change the subject. On one occasion she saw them whispering together when they were getting ready to go home. Barbara knew instinctively that they were discussing her. She put on her blazer, and walked straight past them, her head held high. She told herself that she didn't care who Shirley was friendly with, anyway. She was just a silly, scatterbrained girl.

Barbara did care, though. She remembered the many times that she and Shirley had slept in the same bedroom, either at her house or at the Becks'. She thought of the whispered confidences between them, the giggling that had gone on until far into the night. They had shared the same lipstick on occasions, discussed other girls with unashamed cattiness, and tried each other's clothes on. They had sent away for samples of perfume and cosmetics, read unabridged paperbacks in secret, and wondered together what it was really like. Well, she could never get back to being like that.

A new maturity was born in Barbara. She kept herself aloof at school. She had no intimate friends now, and she was quieter at home, too. There had always been a bit of sibling bickering between Eddie and Barbara, but she had withdrawn from that, and as a consequence some of the zest went out of Eddie's life. Helen, too, noticed a change in her daughter. She was certainly less irritable, and she had agreed to go to Eastbourne with them, in spite of the tempting alternative offered by Shirley. Yet there were times when she caught a look on Barbara's face that was old, far older than her seventeen years warranted. Even George noticed that Barbara seemed quiet.

'We grumble about her whatever she's like,' said Helen. 'I know she's difficult at times, but after all, growing up isn't easy.'

'I suppose you're right. And even if she's moody, she's never given us any real worry.' George picked up a book that had slipped down the side of the cushion on his chair. 'Who's reading this?'

'I've seen Barbara with it. I think it's required reading for English literature.'

'What? "The Catcher In The Rye"? Have you read it?'

'No, but the title's familiar. I don't know what it's about, though.'

'I read it not long after it was published,' said George. 'It's about a feckless, lazy, useless lad, and we've got enough of those around. If I remember rightly the only thing he thought he would like to do is catch kids in his arms when they ran through a field of rye. If that's what they call literature today...'

'If that's what it's about I hope Eddie doesn't read it. It might put ideas into his head.'

'Judging by his last school report, "The Catcher In The Rye" couldn't put any ideas into his head that aren't there already.'

'He's no worse than Mousy.'

'Probably not. They should never have stopped National Service. It did give these youngsters a taste of discipline. They'll regret having stopped it in years to come. There won't be enough fields of rye for all the useless, idle catchers we're breeding.' George lit his pipe, and turned his attention to the *Ruddersleigh Evening Chronicle*.

'Where's Roger going for his holidays?' asked Helen one evening when there was just herself and Barbara in the house.

'He and Steven Crowther are going to Spain together—in fact, they'll be there now,' said Barbara promptly. She knew this because she had met Steven Crowther in Ruddersleigh one Saturday morning, and he had told her about their proposed holiday in Spain.

'He doesn't seem to come here these days. He was never off the doorstep at one time.'

'It was mostly the tennis playing that brought that little crowd round here, and I went off tennis after I strained my wrist that time. Roger and I are still friends, but I don't want anything serious, and neither does he.'

'Of course not,' agreed Helen. It was rarely they talked together like this these days. 'I think a holiday will do you good,' she continued. 'I think you've looked a bit tired this term.'

'I feel all right.'

Lately Barbara's dependence on her parents had irked her dreadfully. She had ample pocket money for the girlish things that took her fancy, and plenty of clothes. She had always taken this for granted before, but she was beginning to think of things in a different way now. To be independent, earning her own money instead of still being a schoolgirl, that was the thought very frequently in her mind. To leave school and start work instead of taking her A levels and applying for university... to live her own life...

Helen glanced up from her knitting, and saw the sad, thoughtful look on her daughter's face again. 'Is anything wrong, Babsy?' She asked.

Barbara suddenly felt a great desire to tell her mother, to unburden her soul, and put her heavy load on those maternal shoulders. There were times when she felt crushed beneath it. To tell her, oh, to tell her! To tell her that she was in love with an immigrant from Trinidad, and that she was deceiving them all the time. To tell her that she was meeting him secretly, and that she was crazy about him, and hadn't been able to help herself. If she could only make her mother understand—but how could her mother possibly understand? The impulse passed.

'Of course there's nothing wrong, Mummy.'

'Do you want some new trews for your holiday, darling? Or one of those denim skirts?'

The conversation turned to the forthcoming holiday, and Barbara put on a show of being interested. Her parents' loving concern for her welfare pricked her conscience, so that she often lay wakeful and restless in bed. It was an effort to get up sometimes, and Helen grew annoyed when she came downstairs too late for a proper breakfast. The schools would soon be breaking up though, so there would be no need for rushing round in the mornings. Eddie had always been a bit of a sluggard, but recently Barbara had been nearly as bad. With Eddie, missing books and gym shoes, homework not done, lost pens and pencils, a suddenly remembered essay; Helen knew and hated the morning ritual. George silent and abstracted, detaching himself as much as possible from the rest of the family, and now Barbara tumbling out of bed at the last minute. The sheer relief when Helen was finally alone in the house was indescribable.

Now that the children were older, they didn't need their mother to organise various treats and amusements during the summer vacation. Eddie would spend most of his time with Mousy, and Barbara had her friends, although Helen hadn't seen Shirley around the place recently.

When the schools finally broke up, Judith Pringle had a very good report, Barbara's was not bad, but it was not good, either. Eddie had a poor report, but Helen and George had ceased to hope for anything better.

Chapter 13

During the third week in August the temperature soared and the sun blazed down on surprised holidaymakers. Back in the stuffiness of the office, George smiled wryly. Whoever was on holiday this week had picked a winner.

The extra few days in Eastbourne would do Helen and Eddie good. Eddie always enjoyed Eastbourne because a boy the same age as himself lived next door to his grandmother. Each year they picked up the threads of friendship from the previous year and found much to do together. George wondered why Barbara had been so insistent on coming back with him. It was not that he saw much of her. He saw her in the mornings before he went to the office, and again at night before he went to bed. She seemed to have somewhere to go every day. Certainly she appeared to be enjoying herself and George didn't begrudge her that. Only he was getting a bit tired of coming home to an empty house every evening.

In the mornings Barbara would hurry out to the new serve-yourself shop in Fordham. Clutching a wire basket she would dart from shelf to shelf, buying with more speed than care. Back in the house she would make a salad for her father's evening meal and go off to meet her lover. For this was their wonderful week together, with Louis on holiday as well as herself.

'It's too good to be true, darling,' she told him. 'It's absolutely perfect.' They were spending the day at Ryewater, a pretty and secluded village in Rudderdale. Barbara had been there before with the Rambling Club, and she liked pointing out places of interest to Louis. She became quite serious and instructive about this, as they stood hand in hand, looking at the beauty and the indefinable sadness of the Dales scenery.

'I'm telling you about the course of the Rudd. It's very changeable. The becks and rills drain into it, so that it's a growing river by the time it reaches Ryewater.'

It was walkers' country here, with rich grass growing on the pastures. But further along the valley were jutting crags, and caves with their gaping mouths showing the exposed limestone.

'Over there they've found remains of Bronze Age man.' Barbara pointed across the valley.

'It bronze man you wanting?' asked Louis, kissing her ear. 'Matter soon fix for you. Bronze man going to settle in lonely place any time now. Afterwards people come and find remains, cigarette ends, empty bottle of lotion to keep the flies away from his woman—'

'Louis Ramdeem, you don't deserve to be educated. I'm telling you things of local interest, and you're not at all grateful.'

He laughed and held her close. It was so wonderful to have her to himself again, after their separation. They walked along, looking for somewhere to sit.

'It's lovely to feel complete again,' she said, after a few minutes silence.

'Ah, you felt like you were only half of something, *ma petite*,' observed Louis, surveying a likely piece of grass. 'Come on, let we sit here. Everything mash up without each other, it was hell by the second week. But I got letters okay, two of them, and it done you good—you looking lovely. *Oui*.' He gazed at her with loving pride, and as soon as they sat down he began to tremble, his physical need for her swamping everything else.

'All right, bronzed man,' said Barbara with a smile. 'I suppose you'll listen to things of local historical interest afterwards.'

She was wearing a denim skirt, with a very attractive crisp, white broderie anglaise top. Louis put his arms round her and kissed her. They were well concealed by the tall grass and the wild tangle of shrubs and bushes. They stayed there for a long time; it was evening before they began to walk back to the village.

* * *

The next day was hot and cloudless too, and Barbara put on a sleeveless blue cotton dress with a full skirt. She had bought a pair of white sandals in Eastbourne, late summer bargains, and she was pleased to be able to get a few days' wear out of them before autumn. Louis was casually dressed for the weather, too, in an

173

open-necked, cream-coloured shirt and fawn trousers. They went to Millborough, a riverside beauty spot about fifteen miles from Ruddersleigh. Louis had never been there before, but Barbara had always loved it. She had brought a picnic lunch for them, having bought a barbecued chicken in Fordham. She knew Louis would eat it, and she left some for her father, to have with his usual salad when he came home from the office. Holding hands they walked down the tree-lined slope to the river. Rowing boats and punts were out, and music from transistor radio sets was coming from all directions.

'Shall we get a boat out, darling?' asked Barbara.

'It making very hot on the river.'

'Are you scared of a bit of sunshine?'

'I don't want you getting burnt, *ma petite* or getting a headache, that's all. You know you can't stand the sun for long—you tell me so yourself. It better sitting under the trees.' They sat and watched the boats going past and under the wide bridge. It was intensely hot, and the sunshine glaring on the water was so bright that Barbara put on her sunglasses.

'So we've come all the way here to sit and watch,' she said after some time, sighing gustily.

'Okay,' Louis spoke with resignation. 'We take a boat out. But we finding shady place under the trees along the bank.' They went for a boat, and Louis took the oars and began to row. Barbara sat back dreamily, and watched him. After a while he removed his shirt, and rowed stripped to the waist. She closed her eyes for a few minutes, listening to the rhythm of his rowing, but when she opened them again, she was highly displeased at what she saw. A rowing boat with four girls in it had moved quite close to them. There was much splashing of oars, and Barbara realised indignantly that the girls were whispering and giggling together, all eyes on her lover. She had a good idea of the kind of idiotic remarks they would be making, too. In bright cotton sundresses they looked very attractive, which added to her displeasure. She cast a look in their direction, baleful enough to sink the boat.

'All right, we've seen enough beefcake,' she snapped at Louis. 'You can stop playing at being Tarzan now, and put your shirt on again.'

He looked at her in amazement, wondering what was wrong.

Then, hearing giggles across the water, he turned his head and saw the all-female rowing boat. He smiled at them, realising that he was being watched with some interest.

'They admiring my suntan, *doux-doux*,' he laughed, but his face soon changed when he saw the expression on Barbara's. He pulled on his shirt hastily, and rowed up the river as fast as he could, putting as much water as possible between them and the other boat.

It was quite tiring, rowing so quickly in all that heat. He felt in need of a rest. He was not out of disgrace yet though, by the look of Barbara's pouting underlip. He steered the boat towards the bank, where the trees hung over and shaded the water. Then he sat back and wiped his face and hands with his handkerchief. The silence between them became oppressive, and then at last Barbara spoke.

'How would you feel if I just had a bikini on, and a lot of men were staring at me—and I sat smiling at them?'

Louis looked at her imploringly. He would feel like murder, pure and simple, and well she knew it. 'You know that would be different,' he protested.

'Oh yes, of course it would be different! You always twist things round for your own convenience. Look what you can be like, but if I say anything, I'm making a fuss over nothing.'

Louis felt beyond arguing after rowing so hard in that heat. 'Don't spoil our day, *doux-doux*,' he said coaxingly. 'You know I'm only intristed in one girl, the one that wearing my bangle.'

He hoped that would do the trick, and much to his relief, it did. She gradually came round, and they sat under the trees, watching the other boats go by.

'It have any lonely places in this lime?' he enquired, when he felt sufficiently restored in her favour.

'I thought you would be wanting to know that before long,' said Barbara, who knew her ardent lover. 'We'll go back and buy some lemonade at that shop, and then we'll find a nice place. I'll row now, darling.'

'M-mm, it making very hot,' ventured Louis. 'Is a long way back.' He was afraid her hands would get blistered, and he was quite sure it would be too much for her, but he still had to be tactful about things. Reluctantly he relinquished the oars, but halfway back to the boathouse he could tell she was tiring.

'It too much for you in this heat. Let we change over.'

'Don't be silly. I'm not tired at all.'

When she was like this, Louis prayed for patience. After a few more minutes he could see the strain showing on her face.

'*Oui papi*, you damn silly girl, give me the oars,' he exploded. 'You going funny in the head or something because it making a bit of sunshine here? I see now it ain't good for English people, it sending them crazy. It have nothing like wind and rain to keep them normal. Now give me the oars.'

She changed places without another word, and Louis rowed the rest of the way back.

On the bank of the river there was a shop with a café upstairs. It was very old, with paintings of Millborough Bridge hung on the walls. Louis bought some lemonade and coca-cola, and he and Barbara walked around looking for a place where they could be unseen and undisturbed. By the time they had found somewhere, Barbara was so tired and hot that she just sank down exhausted, and complained of a headache.

'Try and go to sleep when you've had something to eat,' said Louis. 'It nice and shady here.' He looked at her anxiously, and thought that she had better keep out of the sun for the rest of the day. He wished that he had been more insistent about them staying under the trees on the bank, instead of taking a boat out. Barbara said very little while they were eating their lunch, and she lay down afterwards.

Louis smoked a cigarette. There was not a breath of wind. He had never known a day so hot since he had left Trinidad. After a while he saw that Barbara had fallen asleep and was breathing gently and evenly. From somewhere he heard voices and laughter, and then it was quiet again. He lay down beside her, and before long he fell asleep too.

Later in the afternoon a breeze sprang up and cooled the air slightly. Barbara was the first to wake; her headache had gone, and she felt refreshed. She drank some lemonade, and sat combing her hair. Before long Louis stirred, and opened his eyes.

'You feeling okay, now, *ma petite*?'

'I'm fine, darling.'

She smiled at him and he held out his arms invitingly. 'Nobody can see we here. It safe.'

A high, time-mellowed, sun-warmed brick wall concealed them on one side, and grass and trees on the other. Young passion swept through them, while the breeze trembled the leaves overhead, so that one or two of them broke away and fell, showing that it was late August in spite of the heat.

'You finished all the lemonade, *doux-doux*?' asked Louis, after they had been quiet for a long time, lying in each other's arms.

Barbara laughed. 'I thought you were going to say something romantic.'

'It have enough romantic for a while.' He reached for the lemonade bottle. 'Is this for me?'

She nodded, still smiling. He drank what was left, and then eyed the bottle thoughtfully. Barbara had brought a tea-knife out with her, and he struck the blade on the bottle, making a pinging sound.

'I saw a tin on the ground over there,' he said. 'I'm going to get it.'

Propped up on her elbow, Barbara watched him lazily. He went off, looking in the long grass, and returned presently with an empty tin.

'What on earth do you want with that, darling?'

'We can have a band with these.' He shook the tin, and Barbara heard it rattle.

'I been putting pebbles in. This is the *shak-shak*. Here, you go shake it like this—it clean tin, so don't make hubbub about it. We make calypso now.'

'What, with these? We can't possibly.'

'You'll see,' said Louis. 'Now I'll bang the bottle, and you shake the *shak-shak*.' He began to beat out a rhythm on the bottle. He was quite serious about it, but Barbara giggled as she shook the tin.

'You're not much good with the *shak-shak*,' he told her. 'Try again.'

This time he began to sing, and Barbara recognised the genuine beat of the calypso, caught in spite of the improvised musical instruments. She was quite enchanted—how did he do it? He began to sing about her:

'Barbara has a lovely face, and I know she is just as lovely down below—'

The words grew saucier and saucier, and she pretended to be very indignant. When he got to the last few words she threatened to hit him with the *shak-shak*. 'So that's what goes on in your mind, is it?'

He leaned forward and kissed her. 'Only singing how nice you are. It the best way of telling things.'

She didn't really mind these tender carnalities from her lover. She realised that he was singing her a love song, in the strange music of his own country.

'Well, just be careful,' she cautioned him. 'Or I'll sing one about you.'

'Try then, with the bottle,' he offered. She had a try, although she didn't seem to be able to get the beat, or make the words fit in. But she enjoyed doing it.

'Louis Ramdeem had a mind so bad, they were very pleased to see him leave Trinidad—' she paused, having run out of inspiration.

'It takes a lot of practise,' he said. 'Don't be down couraged.' He added that some people had been very sorry to see him leave Trinidad.

'I wonder which people,' said Barbara thoughtfully. 'Those nice girls who are only allowed to go dancing about once a month, I suppose.'

There were no limits to her curiosity regarding these "nice" Indian girls who led such sheltered lives, but she could never extract more than the barest information out of Louis. She thought of another line for her calypso.

'Indian girls are very prim, Louis couldn't get one to go out with him - '

She hoped this would rouse him to some comment, but he just sat with the impassive look on his face that she knew so well. Suddenly the thought that he had ever had dates with other girls was unbearably painful to her. She sang a bit more. 'So he came to England, to Ruddersleigh, and he doesn't ever want any girl but me.'

She put down the lemonade bottle, wound her arms tightly round his neck, and pressed her face close to his. 'Tell me it's true, darling,' she whispered.

'You're one silly girl,' said Louis. 'I sing calypso about how much I love you, and then you sing calypso and get all upset. It the sunshine affecting you, woman.' He held her close, his soft voice murmuring reassuringly. Before long she was smiling again, listening to his account of a Hindu wedding.

'Were you invited even though you're not a Hindu?' she asked wonderingly.

'Sure. I been to plenty. Everybody goes to Hindu weddings—don't mind if you're not invited, you can still go if you want to.'

'But how do they cope with all the washing up?'

'They use sahari leaves instead of plates.' He anticipated her next question. 'No knives and forks either. It all food you can eat with fingers.'

'Oh... what is it then?'

'All sorts, *ma petite*. Curried green mangoes, dahl, boiled hearts of palm and rice, of course. And sweet things as well—not food that you would like though. The pundit is there to perform the ceremony, and the bridegroom has to eat kedgeree while he gets the dowry. The girl wears a yellow sari, and the man wears a pink robe, with a sort of crown of gold beads. They have to have baths and do all sorts beforehand.'

Barbara was always fascinated by these glimpses into such a different way of life. Her essay had been concerned with more general matters.

'Then they both get covered over by a blanket thing, and the bridegroom unveils the bride while they're underneath.'

'Do they know each other?' she asked, wide-eyed.

'Nowadays, yes. But at one time it was quite usual for them not to. He would see her face for the first time when he lifted the veil.'

'How ghastly! But suppose she didn't want to marry him?'

'It all arranged. The girl had no say at all, the boy only a little—'

'How perfectly disgusting! And he wouldn't know what was under that veil.'

'He would know it wasn't a fellow, anyway.'

But that remark didn't please Barbara. She wanted him to be as horrified at the idea of an arranged marriage as she was.

'She might be ugly.'

'She might bring nice big dowry, though.' Louis laughed. 'It no use looking on the black side. It have a story about one fellow lifting up the veil and finding the wrong girl under it, not the one he thought. I don't know if it true, though.'

The idea evidently amused him, but Barbara didn't find it funny. Sometimes when he told her things about Trinidad she stumbled upon ways and customs that seemed nothing short of repugnant to her. It was not only the customs themselves that troubled her; it was her lover's casual acceptance of them.

'I'm only telling you intristing things,' said Louis. 'If Hindu parents have a daughter they love very much, they wanting to get good husband for her—don't you see, *ma petite*?'

'No, I don't,' said Barbara. 'I think it's a revolting idea. I know I would just die if I were a Hindu girl, newly married, and a husband I didn't love lifted up my veil.'

'These arranged marriages... they not all bad.'

'But you're glad you're a Christian, aren't you, darling? It must be pretty horrible to be a Hindu in any case.'

He agreed fervently that it must be absolutely dreadful to be a Hindu.

'I ain't notice it making them very unhappy, though,' he added.

Barbara however, was not going to admit to the possibility of a happy Hindu. Louis possessed a racial and religious tolerance that was difficult for her to understand. She loved him, but she thought that love set him apart. She didn't really like to think of him as mixing freely with other immigrants or identifying himself with them. She wanted him to consider himself different from them, and superior to them, because he was her lover. Louis, although he was intensely proud of her, had no such ideas, but he was careful not to upset Barbara. He had become friendly and had an occasional night out with two of the young West Indian transport workers, but Barbara, for her peace of mind, knew nothing of this.

* * *

George arrived home in the blistering heat that evening to find a salad and some cold chicken waiting for him. Barbara was out as usual, and he sat down rather gloomily to his solitary meal. It had been stifling at the office, and he faced an evening of swotting up for his Board, which was the following week. For some time now he had been reading The Observer in preparation for it, although it was not a newspaper he took as a rule. But a Board was a signal to take The Observer, and to study carefully the trend of world affairs. It was a signal to swot up on insurance too, because you never knew what questions you were going to be asked. It might be something about Africa, or else some fiddling question purely about work. George sat down with a cup of coffee and began to trawl through some of the notes he had made about current affairs. Well, they wouldn't waste time asking him who was President of the US now, or the name of the first man in space. That still left an awful lot of other things they could ask him, though. There was the Queen's tour of India and Pakistan earlier in the year, the failed "Bay of Pigs" invasion of Cuba, Sierra Leone became a member of the Commonwealth, South Africa became a republic... what else? George Blake, spy, sentenced to forty-two years, but the most topical was Britain applying to join the European Economic Community. That and East Germany closing the frontier between East and West Berlin, and the very latest, this wall they were erecting...

The telephone rang, breaking in on his train of thought. He knew that it would be Helen, as they were taking it in turns to ring up, and it was her turn. After the usual greetings, Helen asked if everything was all right at home and if Barbara was around.

'Everything normal here, another sweltering day in the office of course. No, Babsy isn't around, she seems to be making the most of the nice weather. She's fine, though. I see her in the morning and at night; she leaves a salad in the fridge for me every day. Yes, I'm getting a proper meal at lunchtime in Ruddersleigh... yes, I gave Celia some money for looking after Ezra; she is a good kid. Of course, her mother said there was no need to give her anything, but she knew we would, anyway. I'm just studying some notes for this wretched Board next week. Tom said he would pick me up tonight if I wanted a drink at the golf club with him. I don't know whether to go or not.'

'You might as well go. Relaxing a bit might do more good than staying in reading The Observer.'

'Yes, I think I'll give Tom a ring after I've watered. Everything is really dry now. Have you been anywhere today?'

'No, we've just sat in the garden with Aunt Hilda. We don't see much of Eddie; he's busy with Alan next door. If you go out with Tom, Babsy always has a key with her, so if she's home before you she'll let herself in. Oh, here's Eddie, he wants a word with you...'

'Hello, Dad, did you remember to get a new inner tube for my bike? Is Ezra all right?'

'Hello, I expect you're having a good time with Alan. Ezra's very well. Mrs. Collins and Celia have both been looking after him. I'll get the inner tube before you come home.'

He had a brief conversation with Eddie, and then Helen came on again. After the usual chatty interchange, mainly about domestic affairs, George put down the receiver and proceeded to dial Tom Bingley's number. He was an office colleague who lived in Dudley, and he had been giving George a lift to and from the office every day since he had been without a car. Having arranged to be picked up a bit later in the evening, he went into the garden and began to do some watering. He had a few words with Mrs. Collins next door, who was also watering. George knew that she was the keen gardener at that house. She remarked that she had seen Barbara going off somewhere every day.

'Can't blame her for that,' said George. 'She leaves a salad in the fridge for me every day.' He smiled ruefully.

'Well, that's something.' Mrs. Collins laughed. She was a big, cheerful sort of woman, the type men feel comfortable with, and George was no exception. She finished her watering and went back into the house, smiling at him. Although he returned her smile, the melancholy of the summer evening seemed to press down on him. The play cries of children, tennis, cricket, dogs being walked in the park, birdsong, and brightly coloured butterflies in the garden, watering cans, and earwigs in the dahlias... summer. Over it all was the sombre, all pervading sense of his own depression. The sweet perfume of night-scented stock filled his nostrils, but even that did not lift his spirits. He went into the house and upstairs to the bedroom, to select a clean shirt for the evening. He pushed the one he had worn to the office into the laundry basket. It was getting quite full, with his washing and Barbara's. He knew that everything would just pile up for when Helen came back, and he knew that Helen knew, too.

'Yes, the spoon in your hand the minute you set foot in the

house,' she had remarked to a friend of hers who was complaining that after being away on a three-day painting course her husband and children hadn't lifted a finger to do anything. They had been discussing it in the kitchen, and George happened to go in to get a knife for some purpose. Having caught the gist of the conversation he had departed swiftly, with a sheepish grin on his face. What they were saying was the truth, but he didn't wish to hear it. He was certainly missing Helen's presence in the house, and he would have appreciated it if Barbara had been at home just once when he came back from the office, but she never was. This Board hanging over him... you could swot up until you were black in the face, and get asked the very things you hadn't swotted up. You could be asked all the right questions, though, and answer them capably, yet you still wouldn't get through the Board. You never knew why. On the other hand some people were convinced they had made a mess of the interview, and found to their astonishment (and delight) that they had been promoted. The only thing to do was to prepare yourself to the best of your ability, and to keep calm when the time came.

George had been pursuing this policy for years without a grain of success, but he was still unable to think of any better plan. Helen was probably right that relaxing would do him more good than being alone in the house, stuffing his head with knowledge that probably wouldn't be any use to him at the time. It was with some relief that he heard Tom Bingley ring the doorbell.

Chapter 14

In a rather abstracted frame of mind, Roger Leffey was driving the family car through Dudley. Fit and tanned after his holiday in Spain, life back at home seemed particularly dull and flat. When the new term began it would be better, but just now a number of his friends were still holidaying. Steven Crowther had gone back home to the North Riding for the rest of the summer, and Roger had been considering what to do with himself that evening. He had been offered the use of the car, so he intended to drive somewhere, although he wasn't sure where. Somewhere out in the Dales, perhaps. He was just passing Dudley library when a familiar figure emerged, casually dressed in a denim skirt and white T-shirt. It was Shirley Beck. He stopped the car and hailed her.

'Hello, Shirley! What are you doing with yourself these days?'

She came down the library steps, smiling. 'Hi! Nothing much at the moment. My parents are away this week and I have an aunt staying with me. I'm at an awkward age you see.'

'How do you mean, awkward?'

'I'm too old to trek around with the parents and too young to be left alone in the house. They're in France, and my aunt is teenage-sitting. I wanted to have a look round the shops in Ruddersleigh this morning and she came with me. We had lunch there, but the heat was too much. We've been sitting in the garden this afternoon. I've just been returning an overdue book to the library, but I couldn't be bothered looking for another. I left Auntie Jean lying on the sofa.'

Roger got out of the car and for a moment he didn't speak. Shirley stood looking at him, with one thought in her mind. The same thought was in Roger's, but for different reasons.

'Your aunt will be expecting you back fairly soon then,' he said finally. 'I was wondering...'

'Auntie is very easygoing.' Shirley's big brown eyes gazed into his.

'If I ran you back home, and you told her you were going out with a friend for the evening, would that be all right?'

'It would be fine with Auntie. Who is this friend?' Shirley burst out laughing, and Roger joined in.

'Get in the car,' he said, opening the passenger door. Shirley needed no urging.

The Becks lived in the newer part of Dudley, in a cul-de-sac of detached houses, part of the ever-growing sprawl of the suburb. It was nowhere near Roger's home, a stone-built house in what was left of the old village.

'Well, you'd better come in and meet Auntie, so that she can see that you're respectable,' said Shirley, when Roger drew up outside the house. 'I'd better go in first and break the news.'

She disappeared into the porch-way and Roger stood for a couple of minutes, remembering that it was in this house that he had first met Barbara. He could scarcely take his eyes off her during the whole evening, although he had to give some attention to Shirley, as it was her birthday party and she was the hostess. He and Steven Crowther had expected to have an enjoyable time there, but nothing had prepared Roger for the powerful feelings that Barbara had roused in him right from that first meeting. While he was thinking this, Shirley appeared at the door, and beckoned him in.

He was introduced to her aunt, a pleasant woman in her fifties.

'Sit down a minute,' said Shirley. 'I'm just nipping upstairs to get changed.'

Roger sat down, prepared to make polite conversation with the aunt until Shirley was ready. However, he soon realised that he was required to say little; he was a captive audience.

'I've come down from Edinburgh for a couple of weeks— Shirley was up staying with me not so long ago—with a friend. I'm not a Scot, of course, but I married a Scotsman for my sins! Have you been to Edinburgh at all? You have?' She paused for breath.

'I toured Scotland with my parents a couple of times when I was younger—'

'You'll have been in the Highlands then. We like to go right up north—we've been to Orkney of course, the islands are beautiful. I like to come back to Yorkshire, of course. Have you been on holiday yet?'

'Yes, I've not been back in England long. I went to Spain with a friend.'

'I've been to Spain twice, and both times I've had tummy trouble. I said never again after the last time. It gets very hot, too, a bit too hot for my liking, mind you, it's been hot enough for Spain here lately. Shirley wanted to go to Ruddersleigh this morning, and we had to get the bus—I came here by train, I've never learnt to drive, never wanted to. It was so hot on the bus, and after we'd had some lunch I told Shirley I wanted to rest in the garden this afternoon. I sat in the shade, but Shirley sunned herself, she has that sort of skin, you know, she goes brown. Of course, if you have a fair skin you freckle, I always freckled when I was young—'

Roger sat and listened, nodding his head when appropriate. He knew that she was Mrs. Beck's sister, round-faced and brown-eyed like Shirley and her mother. He didn't mind the fact that she was a chatterbox; she was bright and jolly, and quite charming in her own way.

In her room upstairs, Shirley was deciding what to wear. She hadn't got round to making her bed yet, but that wasn't high on her list of priorities. Getting ready to go out with Roger was. On the way to her house he had suggested a drive out to The Barley Mow. She rummaged frantically through her wardrobe, throwing dresses on the unmade bed, finally selecting a pink two-piece in a fine, silky material. It was short sleeved, with a heart shaped neckline, plunging quite low. She decided a gold locket and chain would look right with it. Should she wear stockings? She picked up a pair of nylons. She had been barelegged all the afternoon, and her legs were nicely brown. Stockings would mean a suspender belt... no, she would stay barelegged. She didn't need a petticoat either; the two-piece was lined with a very thin material. She would only need panties and bra. She put on her outfit for the evening, adding a pair of very dressy sandals, then combed her hair, and put fresh make-up on. She didn't need much, she was quite tanned, pale lips and heavy eye make-up was the trendy look. False eyelashes were essential for the best effect, but one of hers had gone missing. It had fallen on the carpet from her dressing table, and disappeared up the vacuum cleaner when her mother's cleaning help had been busy in the house. After a desperate search the mystery was solved.

'Sorry, love, I thought it was a dead spider...' Her parents had thought it was funny, but Shirley saw nothing humorous about it. She finished off her toilet with a squirt of the treasured Olive Adair. With a last glance in the dressing-table mirror, she picked up her handbag and went downstairs.

'Well, you do look nice. Doesn't she?' The aunt appealed to Roger, who smilingly agreed. 'Where are you planning to go, then?'

'We're just having a run out into the Dales,' said Roger, who had stood up, ready to go when Shirley appeared.

'Just the evening for it. I'm going to have a nice long soak in the bath, Shirley, then I'm coming down in my dressing gown and I shall watch television. You won't be too late home, will you?'

'No, of course not, Auntie.'

'If you are a bit late, you'd better take a key, anyway. I'm a bit tired; it's been so warm today. I might be in bed when you come home.'

Roger thought Shirley was right about her aunt being easy-going. They finally waved goodbye and got into the car. Shirley's eyes were shining. She was determined to make the most of the evening, which had promised to be a very dull one. Instead, she would be spending it with Roger Leffey, someone she had long fancied. Steven Crowther had faded out of the picture after the tennis playing stopped. There had been a couple of dates with him afterwards, but she had an unpleasant feeling that he was just being polite. However, since she had become friendly with Vida Shippen she had made the acquaintance of a few other likely young men. It didn't alter the fact that Barbara's behaviour had left her feeling both baffled and hurt.

Roger headed in the direction of Scardale, leaving the boundaries of Ruddersleigh behind, taking the winding country roads at a speed that would have horrified Mr. Leffey senior.

Roger had sent Barbara a postcard from Spain. She had found it on the doormat with the rest of the mail that had accumulated while the family had been in Eastbourne. He had made several attempts to get in touch with her, but without receiving any encouragement at all. He felt sure that he would be able to get some information about her from Shirley, without it seeming too obvious, of course. Before long they were ensconced in The Best Room at The Barley Mow. After such a hot day the place was crowded, but there were a few wooden benches and chairs at the side of the pub to take the overflow, most of whom consisted of young people. Roger had never been there since his last date with Barbara, but it was obvious that the landlord recognised him from the way he greeted him, in spite of being busy. His glance took in Shirley, and he seemed to Roger to have a knowing look in his eye as he smiled at them. A couple were just on the point of leaving and indicated their seats to Roger and Shirley.

'What do you want to drink, then?' asked Roger, when they were settled in the recently vacated seats. When he and Barbara had gone there, he always knew what she would be drinking, and he took care that it was never very much. He was careful about his own drinking too, as he was driving.

'Do you fancy a gin and lime? Or perhaps a soft drink, seeing it's such a hot evening?'

'I'll have a gin and lime, please.' The room was crowded, smoke filled and noisy, but Shirley didn't mind that, she had Roger's exclusive company, something she had long wanted. With Barbara now out of the way, she might get him for herself; an unexpected date could be the start of something bigger. Roger had to wait quite a time to get served at the bar, although there were two people helping there, as well as the landlord.

Finally Shirley was sitting with a gin and lime, and Roger with a modest half pint of beer. They began to talk about holidays.

'You haven't told me all the details of your Spanish holiday. What did you and Steve get up to? I've been to Torremolinos twice, and to Majorca three times, but when I was a kid, with my parents, of course. I went on holiday to France with them last year, and I decided never again. That's why Auntie is staying with me now.' Shirley laughed.

'We went sightseeing mostly. We were staying in L'Estartit on the Costa Brava, and we had trips out to different places. We went to Barcelona—a great place—and we went to Girona, a fascinating old town. I like the Costa Brava. That part of Spain is really Catalonia. They have their own language. We did a bit of sunbathing, and took a boat out a few times. Anyway, what about your holiday? You stayed with your aunt in Edinburgh, so what happened there?'

'I took a friend with me, and we had a good time. I asked Babsy to come first, but she didn't, so I took another girl.'

'Why didn't Babsy go to Edinburgh with you?' enquired Roger, trying to sound casual.

'She made some excuse and went to Eastbourne with the family. I wasn't surprised, though. I'm not surprised at anything she does these days.' Shirley gave a dismissive shake of her head and asked Roger when the autumn term at university started.

'In about a month... I shall probably go in to see what's what in a couple of weeks. This is my final year, and then it's finding the right job. I've been testing the water with a few firms, and I don't think I'll have any difficulty getting fixed up.'

'This is going to be my final year at school,' said Shirley, sipping her drink. 'I might manage a couple more O levels before I leave. I won't get any A levels, and I couldn't care less. I'm not a career girl, and I won't be testing the water with any firms, looking for a job. There's a job waiting for me in my father's office if I want it.' Her father was a partner with a firm of solicitors in Ruddersleigh. 'I've taken up horse-riding,' she added. 'I could always be a stable maid, or whatever they call them. On the other hand, it can be rather a smelly occupation. Riding is fun though, even if it makes you use muscles you never knew you had. I think I'm getting fitter, though.'

'You look fit enough to me.' Roger felt honour-bound to give Shirley some sort of compliment, and to look at her admiringly. At the same time he was afraid of overdoing things. They were sitting quite close, and the faint fragrance of her scent rose up from the warmth of her body. He could tell that she was wearing very little under her silky two-piece, and just for a moment her bare leg touched against his. He very discreetly moved his legs slightly. He quite liked Shirley, and he had always felt a bit guilty that he had gone to her party at her invitation, and then gone off with her friend. He was uncomfortably reminded that even when she was with Steven her eyes had signalled certain feelings towards him. They were doing that now in an unmistakable way. She was looking thoughtfully at her empty glass, too.

'Perhaps you would like a soft drink now, orange juice or something?' Roger suggested.

'I'd rather have another gin and lime. I'm a big girl now.' He

189

went up to the bar again. The crowd there had thinned out a bit by now. He was thinking that Shirley had better sip this one slowly, and he was wondering if taking her out for the evening had been a good idea after all. What he had really wanted was to try to find out things about Barbara, but Shirley had dismissed any details about her with a shake of her head. He also had a curious feeling of loss and nostalgia; this was where he and Barbara used to come sometimes, and he regretted the impulse that had made him think of The Barley Mow. He ran a finger round the inside of the collar of his open-necked summer shirt; he was stickily hot. Earlier in the day he had been wearing shorts around the house and garden. He was glad that he had changed into trousers for the evening, thinking of Shirley's nudging leg. When he left the bar with the drinks, he had made up his mind to find out more about Barbara. He gave Shirley her gin and lime, and sat down.

'I gather you went to Edinburgh with another friend, instead of Babsy,' he said. 'I'm a bit surprised; you always seemed to get on so well together.'

Shirley hadn't intended to mention Barbara, but suddenly her feelings of resentment against her rose to the fore. She considered that she had been very shabbily treated by her former friend. If Roger still thought Barbara was Little Miss Wonderful, it was time he was disillusioned. Without any explanation or reason she had turned against Shirley, and thrown her friendship in her face. Shirley took quite a gulp of her drink, and released some pent-up feelings about Barbara to Roger.

'I suppose you never see her now?'

'No, she more or less told me to sling my hook ages ago.' Roger tried to speak lightly.

'Well, you're not the only one. She's told us all to sling our hooks. She stopped playing tennis—just when the weather was getting decent, too. She dropped out of the Rambling Club, and that was after getting me to join!' Shirley took another gulp of her drink, and continued her diatribe.

'And she wouldn't give any reasons. Babsy, who was so mad-keen on the Rambling Club! She never wants to go anywhere these days—and she doesn't look half as smart as she used to—'

'She told me she was going to do a lot of swotting,' put in Roger. He wanted information about Barbara, but he didn't intend listening to a lot of catty remarks. There was no stopping Shirley now though.

'Swotting! Babsy! Her work's gone down and down. I imagine she had a poor report at the end of last term. She's been told off again and again for daydreaming in the classroom and not paying attention. She's just not switched on these days. I can't understand what's happened to her. She always seems to be on the defensive somehow, as though she's hiding something—'

'Don't you go to her house now?' asked Roger, who felt deeply concerned at this report.

'I don't. Not any more. I've made friends with someone a bit livelier. If Barbara wants to lead a life without any kicks, I don't. She's really square these days.'

'Does she seem miserable... unhappy?' He was unable to keep the anxious note out of his voice, and Shirley heard it.

'I wouldn't know. We just don't bother with each other now. She stopped confiding in me ages ago. She suddenly shut up like a clam. She doesn't bother with anyone else at school either.'

'It doesn't sound like Babsy.'

'It's what she's like now. I don't think she has any friends at all now. Stan Ward, the secretary of the Rambling Club, wrote asking her why she had dropped out. He told me she never even answered his letter. He was always keen on her, you know. At one time she used to lead him on no end.'

'Did she?' Roger's voice was cold.

'Well, you know how Babsy is—how she was anyway. Everything in trousers was a challenge to her, she thought she was quite irresistible.'

Shirley's tongue was well loosened by now. 'She did have a date with somebody else when she was going around with you in the spring.'

'Well, that's not exactly a crime.' Roger had a feeling that sitting listening to gossip about Barbara was anything but creditable on his part.

'She told me in confidence about it, but I don't suppose it matters now, anyway. You don't see her these days.'

What Shirley had just said had given Roger an uneasy jolt. Barbara had persistently denied that there was anyone else when they had stopped dating earlier in the year. Either she had been lying, or Shirley was making it up.

'It's funny though; it was round about that time that she began to change. I particularly noticed. And there's been no swimming in the Lido at Prodmore Park for Babsy this summer. She's never been once with me, and you know how she fancies her figure! Last summer she used to parade up and down in a green bikini, fairly lapping up the wolf whistles. It wasn't the swimming she was there for of course, it was the men.'

Roger felt that he had heard enough. He knew that Barbara liked admiration from the opposite sex, and she had the looks that drew it. He also knew that she was a strictly moral girl, and he didn't care for the way Shirley was talking.

'You know what I think—' she continued.

'You know what I think, Shirley?' he interposed, 'I think you've had quite enough to drink. I think we should be getting back to Dudley.'

'All right,' said Shirley, draining her glass. She was certainly very flushed and bright-eyed by now. She picked up her handbag; then put it down.

'What I was going to say is I can't imagine Babsy changing overnight into a man-hater. All this dropping out of social life... and even when we were still friendly she never mentioned men at all. In fact, the last mention I ever heard was that date she had with some dreamboat in Ruddersleigh. And then she seemed secretive about it, somehow. I wonder if she's up to something?'

'I think you're letting your imagination run away with you,' said Roger. 'Steven bumped into her in Ruddersleigh before we went to Spain, and they had a few minutes talk. He didn't appear to notice the deterioration you mention, anything but, in fact. As for Barbara being dowdy, I think you must be exaggerating a bit.'

'Well, not dowdy, exactly. But you know how with-it she used to be; she wasn't just with-it she thought she *was* it. She hardly uses any make-up at all these days, and you know how she used to lay it on with a trowel.'

'I don't seem to remember her using as much as all that,' said Roger dryly. 'I've often seen her without a scrap of make-up on when I've called at the house. I should say she's not the type to need much, in any case.'

He changed the subject quite pointedly, and they went out

into the slightly cooler air of the evening. The car park was emptying rapidly now.

'It's a green car, isn't it?' asked Shirley, who was feeling just a bit muzzy-headed now that they were outside. The car park had been gravelled since the winter, and she was having to walk carefully in her high-heeled sandals. Just before they reached the car she nearly lost her balance. Roger felt obliged to put a steadying hand under her elbow, and she immediately drew it in, and trapped his hand against her warm body. He was not sure if that stumble had been accidental. He pulled away from her and unlocked the car, opening the passenger door. The stifling heat from the interior enveloped them, and Roger wound down the windows. He had no intention of getting involved with Shirley, but at the same time he didn't want her to feel snubbed. It was a difficult situation to be in. He had made use of her to find out things about Barbara, but taking her to The Barley Mow for the evening hadn't been exactly a penance, it had been quite enjoyable, in fact. On the drive back to Dudley he tried to keep the conversation as impersonal as possible, deftly fending off any hints at future dates. Shirley was pushy, that was the trouble. Even if he had fancied her, that pushiness would have put him off, but the fact was he didn't fancy her, although he quite liked her. At the same time he was guiltily aware that it was through her pushiness that he had first met Barbara.

Back in the winter he had been both intrigued and amused that a customer at his father's shop had invited him to a party, now he half wished that he had never gone. He had no doubt that Shirley would have liked him to stop the car in some isolated spot, for them to indulge in a bit of snogging. Even if he didn't fancy her, it was somewhat disturbing sitting so close to her. The scent she had on was the same that Barbara had used; only it was the wrong girl wearing it.

It was with considerable relief that he finally drew up outside Shirley's home. The porch light was on, but the rest of the house was in darkness. He got out of the car, and opened the door for her.

'It looks as if Auntie has gone to bed,' she remarked, standing on the pavement.

'Very sensible. I'm a bit tired myself.' Roger spoke rather hurriedly, fearful that Shirley would ask him in for the dreaded cup of coffee. There were plenty of offers of coffee among the students in Ruddersleigh. If a girl had a pad of her own in the city, and she invited you in for coffee late at night, she fancied you, and if you accepted, you had better fancy her.

'It's been a lovely evening, Roger.' She was holding up her face in some anticipation.

'Yes, it's been great. We were lucky to meet up like we did.'

'Weren't we? We must do it again some time.' They exchanged mutual thanks, and Roger gave Shirley the kiss she was clearly expecting.

'Good night, take care, Shirley. See you around.' She waved to him just before she entered the house, and he waved back. On the way home he thought continually about her remarks concerning Barbara. He wondered if he had adopted the wrong tactics towards her in the past, just ringing up and trying to make a date. Suppose he booked a couple of seats in the dress circle at the Theatre Royal in Ruddersleigh for tomorrow evening, and called at her house in the morning? It was supposed to be a good play "Heaven's Heights". He wouldn't say the seats were already booked of course. There should be a few vacant seats left; anyway, with the present heat wave, some people would want to spend their evenings out in the fresh air. Even if Barbara turned him down, he felt he had nothing to lose... well, two theatre seats... in that event, he could always go alone. If he offered them to his parents they would think it rather strange, his mother would guess that he had planned to take a girl. Take Shirley? Definitely not, that would be tempting fate. He wanted to think positively about the visit to Barbara, though. She was probably at a loose end just now, like most of his friends and acquaintances. She might be only too pleased to see him. He thought of every possible eventuality concerning his idea, even that Barbara could be out when he called. It was worth a try, anyway. He put the car in the garage, having made up his mind to try bold tactics with Barbara.

Chapter 15

The following morning Roger booked the theatre seats, and walked briskly into Fordham, taking the short cut. For the first time in nearly four months he rang the doorbell of number twelve Sycamore Avenue. Barbara's mother opened the door, and her face expressed both surprise and pleasure at seeing him.

'Why, hello Roger, you're quite a stranger! Come in. Babsy won't be more than a few minutes, she's just gone to the shops for me.'

He stepped inside, smiling. Certainly Mrs. Granger seemed pleased to see him.

'You do look well,' she went on. 'Babsy said you were holidaying in Spain. She told me you were very busy last term; too busy swotting to come to the house. I hope you did well in your exams.'

'Better than I expected,' said Roger modestly. 'I'm in my final year now.' He was wondering why Barbara had made up a story like that, about him being too busy to come to the house. 'I don't know if Babsy has any plans for tonight. I thought she might like to see that play at the Theatre Royal, Heaven's Heights.'

'She's not going out as far as I know. She's coming into Ruddersleigh with me this afternoon, and she mentioned washing her hair later on. I'm sure she'll be delighted to go to the theatre with you... isn't it hot today? We're having an Indian summer. I'll make some coffee as soon as Babsy gets back. Oh, she's here now. Babsy, there's a visitor to see you,' she called.

Helen was in the sitting room with Roger. Barbara walked into the room, and he stood up, smiling, hoping to hide his nervousness. She went white with shock, seeing him there, and then she tried to regain her composure.

'Hello, Roger,' she said, managing to force a smile.

'I was just saying, he's quite a stranger here. I expect we'll be seeing a bit more of him now that the exams are all over, and he's back from his holidays. I don't suppose you'll be washing your hair tonight after all, Babsy. Roger wants to take you to that play at the Theatre Royal, Heaven's something. I know it had a good write up in the Chronicle.'

Helen sat smiling at them both, while Barbara wondered how on earth she could get out of it. Her mother had obviously as good as made the date for her, taking it for granted that she would want to go. She couldn't turn it down very well, either, or her mother would wonder why, knowing that she was doing nothing else that evening. And she daren't appear on anything but friendly terms with Roger, after all the times she had pretended to be with him—and would have to go on pretending. She was hoist with her own petard...

Both Roger and her mother were waiting for her to speak. There was only one course open to her under the circumstances. 'What a nice surprise,' she said. 'I'd love to go.' She would have to go out with him this once, and put him off very firmly regarding future dates. 'Thanks for the card from Spain,' she added.

Roger could scarcely believe it had all been so easy. The seats were booked, and she was quite agreeable. His eyes ran over her admiringly. She was looking very well, and absolutely adorable in a pair of dark green trews and a sleeveless white blouse. The sun had caught her slightly, and there was a delicious dusting of freckles across her nose. What nonsense Shirley had been talking! She was prettier than ever.

Helen went into the kitchen, saying that she would make some coffee. If it had just been for herself and Barbara, she would have used the instant, but as Roger was with them as well, she reached for the percolator. She hoped there were a few decent biscuits left; she knew Eddie pillaged the biscuit tin constantly.

Alone with Barbara in the sitting room, Roger was quite unable to take his eyes off her, and yet he could think of nothing to say for a moment. He could see that she was nervous as well; his sudden appearance had taken her completely by surprise. He controlled a strong impulse to kiss her. Shock tactics had been successful up to now, but he didn't want to rush things too much. Barbara spoke first, asking him about his holiday in L'Estartit. Helen came in with the coffee, and found them talking together, quite happily, she thought. And yet, Barbara had seemed so taken aback when she first saw him. Her mother wondered if there had been a tiff, or some sort of altercation between them. All seemed well now, anyway.

'I must wash my hair this morning, then,' said Barbara, as soon as they had finished the coffee. Roger stood up to go, it was obviously a hint.

'I'll see you later then, Babsy. I'll have the car.'

After he had gone she stood for a minute staring blankly in front of her. She would have to go to the theatre with him, under the circumstances. But should she tell Louis, and risk his frenzied resentment? He would be very angry, she knew. He was on late turn this week, but she would be seeing him on Thursday, his day off. She would think about whether or not to tell him after tonight, and she would be very cool towards Roger, discouraging the least familiarity. Reluctant though she was to have this date with him, Barbara spent quite a long time getting ready that evening. In this she was abetted by Helen.

'You'll be wearing that lovely new dress that Grandma bought you in Eastbourne, won't you? You might as well; it will probably be the last chance this summer. The warm weather can't go on forever, and you'll want to look nice for a trip to the theatre.'

'Yes, of course I'm wearing it,' said Barbara. She put it on. It was of duck-egg blue, figure skimming, with a scooped neckline, and the slight drape from the hips was caught by two bows near the hemline. She slipped her feet into white court shoes, and picked up a small, matching handbag.

Her mother was still in the bedroom. 'Are you putting some of your sweet pea scent on?'

'It's just about finished, Mummy.' It wasn't really, but she had promised Louis not to use it unless she was with him. Her mother left the room, and before Barbara realised what she was doing, she had returned with her own supply of Olive Adair, and sprayed a fine mist over the girl.

'There... you won't need a coat if Roger has the car.'

When Roger called at the house, though, he was very apologetic. 'I'm sorry, Babsy, but I couldn't get the car for the evening. My parents had already made arrangements to go out. I've had it such a lot that I took it for granted I would have it for tonight. We'll just have to get the bus into Ruddersleigh.'

'You'd better take your white, lacy jacket, then,' said Helen. 'I know it's very warm now, but when you come out of the theatre it'll be cooler.'

Roger looked the epitome of casual elegance. He was wearing grey whipcord trousers, and a Ruddersleigh University blazer. The dark green and grey stripes looked very smart, with the city coat of arms on the pocket.

'I know it's very warm, too hot for a suit or sports jacket, but I felt I couldn't take you to the theatre in shirt sleeves,' he explained. 'I don't wear my blazer much, really.'

'Well, as I said, it will be a bit cooler later on. I'm sure you'll enjoy the play.' Helen smiled brightly at them both.

Barbara picked up her lacy jacket and matching gloves, slipping the gloves on as they stepped outside.

''Bye, Mummy.'

'Goodbye, Mrs. Granger.' Helen watched them walk along Sycamore Avenue together.

It was very reassuring to see Roger around again, as devoted as ever. She had been worried about Barbara for several weeks. This was mainly because her friendship with Shirley appeared to have fizzled out, and nobody seemed to come to the house for her now. She still went out, she always seemed to have somewhere to go, very often it seemed to be the film club in Ruddersleigh, yet pressed for any details about it, she became irritable with her mother. Helen had felt uneasy without being able to say exactly why, but when she tried to share her feelings with George, he merely said she worried unnecessarily about the children. Perhaps he was right. Teenagers, they went through all sorts of phases and outgrew them. Men, though, they were an even bigger nuisance. George had come home far from happy after his Board. It had been hopeless, the worst ever, he told her. Helen had tried to cheer him up, but he had made it quite plain that he didn't want to be cheered up. She watched Barbara and Roger until they turned the corner of Sycamore Avenue.

Barbara was quiet, thinking uneasily that they would have to go into Ruddersleigh by bus. There *was* a chance that Louis would be the conductor. The thought kept her rather apprehensive. Meanwhile, Roger was talking about the Theatre Royal, and how splendid it looked now, after a recent redecorating. He intended to get onto more personal subjects later in the evening. He would take her to Ferraris for supper after the theatre. It stayed open until very late. To Barbara's great relief the conductor was not Louis, and she began to take a good deal more interest in what Roger was saying.

She smiled, showing her dimples in the old, enchanting way, and he had a sudden rush of confidence that he was going to get her back. That was what he had wanted ever since their last date. As they sat on the bus, Barbara thought how fair he looked after growing accustomed to her lover's darkness. It was Roger who seemed unfamiliar now, but he was as charming and attentive as ever. The conversation between them was light chit-chat, the holidays, the surprisingly hot weather, and the autumn term looming ahead for both of them.

Yet somehow it seemed to Roger that Barbara managed to carry on a conversation which was curiously impersonal. She never mentioned anybody apart from her family. Once inside the theatre, there was the usual air of excited anticipation from the audience, although the place was half-empty. The exotic décor, all crimson and gold, the magnificent ceiling with its enormous chandelier, the opulence of the whole interior seemed to transport people temporarily into another world. Roger had obtained excellent seats in the dress circle, and Barbara experienced a sense of relief that it didn't matter who saw them. In spite of her reluctance to spend the evening with him, she was enjoying the play, although the atmosphere in the theatre was rather too close for comfort. She had a drink of orangeade during the interval, and Roger suggested that they should go to Ferraris for supper afterwards. She had been there before with him; soft lights, tables in little alcoves; Roger was evidently hoping to do some high-powered talking. As she sat considering the idea, he was wondering why she had invented stories about him being too busy to come to the house for her. He wanted to get to the bottom of all this mystery. Why had she become such a recluse, dropping all her friends, leaving the Rambling Club, and other things? He glanced at her covertly. There was a change in Barbara. Shirley had been right in a way, and yet he couldn't really place what and why the change was. There was a reserve, but that was understandable, they had not been out together for a long time. There was something else, though, something indefinable. He looked at the sweet, well-remembered curve of her cheekbone, and the wide, blue eyes. He was baffled.

'I don't know about going to Ferraris,' she said dubiously.

'But why on earth not, Babsy?' A lot of questions were trembling on the tip of his tongue, and he was determined to get the answers before the night ended.

Barbara sat hesitating. She had a feeling that Roger was hoping for a heart-to-heart talk with her, and she wanted to avoid that. At the same time, if they went to Ferraris she would be able to make it plain that there was to be no more of this surprise dating. She finally agreed to go with him. They walked out of the theatre into the darkening blue of the August night. It was cooler; Roger helped her into her lacy jacket, as worn by top models, and faithfully copied by her mother from a knitting pattern in "Woman".

The soft lighting in Ferraris shone on her newly shampooed hair. There were very few people in the restaurant, and she and Roger sat in a secluded alcove.

'I'm not very hungry, Roger.'

'Well, you don't need to have much. Have something cold. I'm going to. Here's the menu... have smoked salmon salad, or whatever you fancy, and we'll have a bottle of wine.'

'I shall only have one glass.'

'A half bottle, then,' said Roger, with resignation. The waiter hovered, and took their order. Barbara glanced round, thinking that it was some time since she had been in Ferraris, not since the winter, in fact, when Roger had first started dating her. He was remembering that occasion, too, the light-hearted laughter between them, and his delight at being in her company.

He waited until their order had arrived before he got onto more personal topics. 'What do you do with yourself, these day, then, Babsy?' He tried to sound casual.

She shrugged. 'Just get around, I suppose.'

'You don't get around to any of your old haunts. You're never seen in Mumbles, or anywhere else for that matter. You must have a new set of friends.'

Barbara said nothing, and Roger began to realise that Shirley had given him a very good assessment of the truth, after all. Barbara *was* on the defensive. But why? 'I understand you told your mother I was too busy to come to the house for you last term.

Why did you say that, Babsy? You know I'd never be too busy for that.' He spoke gently, but he saw her colour up.

'Mummy's always asking me questions, Roger, that's why. I may have told her a little white lie—but don't say you've never done it with your mother.'

He could hardly say that, so he let it pass. 'Don't you see Shirley these days?'

'Have you brought me here to ask me a lot of questions about my private affairs?'

He hated the way she said that. At one time he had been very much a part of her private affairs himself.

'Of course not,' he said quickly. 'Only it's such a long time since we've been anywhere together. I'm just interested in how you're getting on.'

'I'm getting on very well, thank you.'

Very well without me, thought Roger. She still pouted, he noticed. *That* certainly hadn't changed. For a few minutes they sat eating in silence. Roger had a sip of wine, and then cleared his throat nervously.

'Babsy, I thought perhaps we might see a bit more of each other now.'

'Well, I'm sorry, Roger, but the answer is no. Quite definitely.'

'But won't you tell me why? I haven't changed towards you— I'll never change. You liked me well enough at one time. What's wrong? Is there something the matter, darling?' The old, tender endearment had crept back while he was speaking. She saw the love in Roger's candid grey eyes, and she felt unable to meet his gaze. She had used his name, and involved him in the web of deceit she had been obliged to spin so that she could keep seeing her lover. She sat battling with an overwhelming sense of shame and guilt, knowing the sincerity of Roger's feelings towards her.

'Haven't you enjoyed yourself tonight?' he asked.

'Very much. But don't ask me for any more dates, please.'

'But, Babsy, if you would only tell me why—' The atmosphere between them was beginning to get emotional, which was precisely what Barbara had wanted to avoid.

'I just don't want to go out with you any more,' she said, hating having to speak to him like that, but unable to see any other way.

Roger was silent for a moment. If she adopted that attitude there was nothing he could do about it. 'Is there someone else?' he blurted out miserably.

'I don't have to tell you about my private affairs,' she answered, her eyes evasive.

Roger had a strong feeling that there was someone else, and that there was something wrong, too. Had Barbara got herself into some sort of emotional tangle? These things could and did happen to the best of girls. She was headstrong, yes, but there was also a kind of trusting innocence about her. Suppose some unprincipled type was attempting to ensnare her? A married man, even. Looking at the sweet loveliness of her face, he felt an overwhelming desire to protect her. She needed looking after, he was sure of that, and he was the one to do it, if she would only give him the chance. He could see all too plainly though that he was not going to get the chance.

She began to discuss the play they had seen, expressing her regret that another theatre in Ruddersleigh was going to close down.

'It sounds as though you haven't been to the theatre for some time,' observed Roger. 'You used to be very keen on it. Will you be coming to the students' Rag Show in October?'

'You're looking a long way ahead,' she said smiling.

'It'll soon come. And the Rag Ball at the Scala Ballroom—can't we make that a date, Babsy?'

But when he began pressing her to see him again, she withdrew in that strange, evasive manner which so baffled him.

'If you feel like that, why did you come to the theatre with me tonight?' he asked. He hadn't intended to be as blunt as that, but he had reached the point where he felt that he had nothing to lose.

'Well, my mother practically took the decision out of my hands, didn't she? She hadn't seen you for months, and then suddenly, there you were. She took it for granted that I would be agreeable to go out with you tonight. You had already told her your plans for the evening.'

'You sounded quite keen this morning...' Roger broke off, catching the eye of the head waiter.

It was late; they had sat in Ferraris a long time. They would have to go, to catch the last bus to Fordham. There was a fare stage quite close to the restaurant. The main stop where Barbara usually caught the bus was further into the city centre. There was nobody else at the bus stop, and Barbara stood, feeling uneasy again, wondering if the conductor would possibly be Louis. It was just a chance, and yet it could as well be her lover as anyone else.

'It might get full at Marsh Street,' said Roger. 'Perhaps we should have come out of Ferraris sooner, and walked back to the main stop. Anyway, it doesn't matter. If we can't get on, we'll get a taxi home.'

Two men came and stood behind them, and the next minute the familiar yellow double-decker came round the corner.

'It looks pretty full, darling,' said Roger, the endearment slipping out automatically. 'Most of them will get off long before we reach the terminus, though.'

The bus pulled up, and Barbara caught one agonising, disbelieving glimpse of the conductor pushing his way forward to the platform. It was Louis! Petrified, she half turned away, but at the same time Roger steered her onto the bus in front of him. Distraught, panic-stricken, she rushed upstairs, not knowing what to do. My God! My God! she thought, looking wildly round. She saw an empty seat halfway along, and sat down, her heart thumping painfully.

A minute later, Roger and the other two men came upstairs, having given Louis their fares on the platform. Roger sat down beside Barbara and began to talk, but she was so agitated that she could scarcely follow a word of what he was saying. She was trapped now, sitting on the bus with the very man Louis had told her to keep away from. She remembered his anger that evening at Burnham Bridge, when he had torn the snapshot to pieces.

Oh, God, why do things like this happen to me? she thought. She had never been anywhere except with her lover for months, and yet, on this one occasion they had to get on his bus. She should have insisted on a taxi when they came out of Ferraris... she should never have taken the risk... Roger was only too eager to please. She looked desperately out of the window, into the darkness of the night. If there was only some way of getting off that bus unnoticed by Louis... but it was no use. She would have to go down those stairs.

Clammy perspiration broke out all over her; she could feel it trickling down her back. What would Louis think when he saw them together? Would he think she had been seeing Roger regularly? Surely not! More harrowing still, what would he do? She thought of the look on his face if another man so much as glanced in her direction. Barbara began to pray. Up to the age of sixteen she had prayed every night, but Shirley had laughed at her once when she had slept overnight at the Becks', and she had not prayed since. She prayed now, though. She prayed for Louis not to come upstairs for any fares. She prayed to be able to slip off the bus unnoticed at the terminus. Even if she didn't deserve it, she hoped God would help her, because she had a feeling she was going to need His help before the night was over.

She cowered in her seat, staring through the window, but it seemed as if her luck was holding. A few passengers went downstairs to get off at various stops, but evidently everyone upstairs had a ticket.

'Are you all right, Babsy?' asked Roger, ever solicitous.

'Oh... yes...' she scarcely knew what he was saying throughout the long torture of that journey. Never would she risk anything like this again. She dreaded reaching the terminus.

Oh, God, she prayed, make Louis not see us. She wondered frantically what he would do if he did see them. Suppose he was too angry to be discreet? Suppose he started a row with Roger, and let the whole cat out of the bag? But she was seeing him on Thursday; surely he would wait and let her explain? Surely he would... under the circumstances, what else could he do? What else? Oh God, don't let Louis see me with Roger. I'll pray again every night if you don't let him see me with Roger this once...

But Louis did see her. At the terminus he stood on the platform, watching the passengers get off. Barbara came down the stairs after Roger, and her lover looked at her in amazement. He had never taken her fare, and what was she doing out late at night like this? She gave him a quick, nervous glance, and then Roger turned to help her off the platform.

Realisation came to Louis then. His ticket machine was lying on the long seat nearest the platform, and with one quick movement he slipped off his money bag and put it there too. He sprang off the bus and raced after Barbara. She felt his hand on her arm, gripping it cruelly, jerking her away from Roger's side. She gave a gasp of fear, the next moment she received a slap on the face so hard that a cry of shock and terror rose in her throat.

Roger turned round in astonishment, and Louis, muttering words almost unintelligible with rage, smashed at him with his fist. It all happened with such speed that Roger was completely taken by surprise. He took the full impact of that first, vicious blow, which sent him staggering to the ground. But there was only one thing to do—get up and fight back, and the next moment a group of amazed passengers witnessed the two of them in combat under the eerie yellow glow of the sodium lighting.

Louis was wearing the thin, fawn jacket of his summer uniform. Roger was hampered by his university blazer. Barbara stood, stunned, trembling, crying helplessly, not believing this could happen to her, not knowing what to do. She had never seen violence like this at close quarters; it was terrifying, it was like a nightmare. And she was responsible for it—and yet how could things have been any different? What had she done that this horror should break over her head?

They were mostly men standing watching, but nobody seemed inclined to interfere up to now. And there was no doubt Roger was taking some punishment from his incensed opponent, even Barbara's inexperienced eyes could see that.

Jim Askew sat, still at the wheel, oblivious of all this, smoking a cigarette before turning round for the depot. He decided not to bother getting out, as they wanted to be back as soon as possible. He wondered why Louis didn't come round to see him, and to change the indicator. He had the window open as it was a warm night, and a man appeared suddenly beside it.

'There's a fight going on at the back between the conductor and another chap,' he said. Jim was out of the bus immediately, and hurrying to the scene of the struggle, with the man beside him.

'It'll be them bloody drunken Rockers, or whatever they call themselves,' Jim told him. He hated the louts and yobs on these late buses, not that Fordham had many, but there were a few on the council estate. Doubtless they had provoked the boy beyond endurance. Jim pushed through the straggling little crowd of onlookers, and assessed the situation. Louis and another lad knocking hell out of each other, and a young girl crying hysterically. But it wasn't Mods or Rockers trouble. It was a university student judging by his blazer. What was left of it, anyway, for it looked as if the old Trinidad blood was up tonight with a vengeance. Louis was lashing into Roger with unspeakable ferocity—this couldn't be allowed to go on, Jim could see that.

'What happened? Who started it?' he asked another man who was watching.

'The conductor started it. The other chap never did anything that I saw—he was with that girl.' He nodded towards the distraught Barbara.

'Get the police!' shouted someone.

Jim went into action then. Assaulting a passenger—instant dismissal if you were reported. He rushed at the assailants. When Jim took the plunge, two other men came to his assistance, and hauled Louis away from Roger, not without some difficulty.

'Louis!' sobbed Barbara, pushing forward, oblivious of the onlookers, and standing beside her panting, dishevelled lover. She wondered how much longer her legs would be able to hold her. Roger stood, swaying slightly, the blood on his face ghastly in the ugly lighting. He looked straight at Barbara, ignoring Louis completely.

'Are you coming with me?' he asked, speaking between gasps. There were two men holding her lover, and she could have walked away with Roger then, and out of Louis' life, but he held her, as he had held her right from the start. She just shook her head, and without another word, Roger turned and walked away.

Jim Askew took charge of the situation. 'The show's over for tonight. We're off for a sit-down,' he announced to the goggle-eyed onlookers, who dispersed rapidly. He propelled Louis towards the bus, with Barbara beside him. 'You can have a couple of minutes together,' he told them, hustling them both inside. He went round and changed the indicator, then he lit a cigarette again, and walked up and down...

He knew that an intensely emotional conversation was taking place inside the bus. He could hear their voices murmuring as he passed. Accusations, recriminations, explanations, faintly borne onto the air of a summer night. It was deserted now at the terminus, not a soul got on the bus to go back to Ruddersleigh. And on the long seat nearest the platform, Barbara sat, shocked and bemused to learn the full extent of Louis' frenzied jealousy and suspicions. She could scarcely follow the dark workings of her lover's mind. He had thought of things that would never have occurred to her. She had known that he would be angry, but she had not imagined that such suspicions about her would have entered his head.

'Louis,' she said brokenly. 'How could you think such things about me? How could you...' but she was unable to go on.

And looking at her pale, tear-stained face, with the red mark flaming down one side, he didn't know how he could. This girl, who had come to him as pure as a blossom drifting down from an immortelle tree... he was filled with shame. But he couldn't explain to her that he hadn't thought, or reasoned, or done anything logical at the time. He had seen her with that other fellow, and he had just gone mad.

It was like some hideous nightmare, and now she was beside him again, and the other fellow had gone. He wanted her to let him know that everything was all right between them, because he felt so sore and weary. He loved her so much, his need for her was overpowering. She must surely understand that the sight of her with another man had driven him crazy—she *must* understand.

He was quite beyond speech. He put his head on her shoulder and wept. He wanted Barbara to comfort him, even after he had wronged her, even after he had struck her. She held him close, without speaking, her tears mingling with his. She was stunned by the reality of what had just taken place, the suspicion, the violence, and after all that display of savage aggressiveness, Louis was like a little boy, needing her tenderness now.

She thought of Roger Leffey, the innocent victim of that assault, and there were feelings of guilt that she was ultimately responsible for the whole wretched business. She couldn't believe that she was involved in anything as distasteful as a public brawl; it was unthinkable.

She wanted to think that it hadn't really happened, that she would wake up in her bed at home, relieved that it was just a bad dream.

The driver stood on the platform and coughed. They were locked in each other's arms. 'Come on, love, we've got to get back to the depot,' he said to Barbara. A few whispered words, a last kiss, and she stepped down from the bus. She looked so pitifully young, and so overwhelmed with everything that Jim was strangely moved.

'What have you been up to, love? Running two chaps at once?' he asked in a low voice. He had a feeling that he wouldn't get any information out of the boy, and he thought he was entitled to know a few details after being so accommodating.

Barbara thought so too. There was something very comforting about this bluff, down-to-earth man. She shook her head. 'No, just Louis. I went to the theatre with a friend because it was arranged, and I couldn't get out of it. And—' her voice faltered— 'he should have had a car, and didn't, at the last minute. He lives in Dudley.'

'Ah,' said Jim sympathetically. 'And you just happened to be unlucky, getting on this bus.'

She nodded. 'Thank you for being so kind, anyway.'

Jim Askew looked at her curiously. Such a nice girl, with her ladylike air and refined voice... what was she doing running around with Louis?

Jim knew that his Ruddersleigh was the Ruddersleigh of a working man. There was another Ruddersleigh, though, and the men who belonged to it went to Ruddersleigh Royal Grammar School, or somewhere similar. Then they went to university, and they didn't have jobs, they had careers, and they usually didn't earn a penny piece until they were in their twenties. The young ones affected an informal style of dress; duffle coats in winter, sweaters and corduroys, or jeans. In summer they wore blazers and well-cut whipcord trousers with a casual elegance. They strutted around the city as if they owned the West Riding, patronising certain coffee bars and public houses. They never used bad language in front of women, and if they were walking with one they pranced round like horses every time they crossed a road so that she would be on the inside of the pavement.

Jim didn't belong to that world, and he didn't want to, but neither did he resent its existence. He knew that no less than it needed its bus drivers Ruddersleigh needed its professional men. He also knew that in spite of their pansified manners, and the posh noises their mouths made when they spoke, they were Yorkshiremen, just the same. And you couldn't push them around.

Much as he liked Louis, he was glad that the Ruddersleigh boy had stood his ground and belted him back. But suppose he reported the incident?

He asked the girl about this, but she assured him that there was no fear of that happening. She evidently knew the other boy pretty well. She knew that he wouldn't tell tales—involve her—or anything like that. Too much of a gentleman, thought Jim, and that was his trouble. Fancy giving the girl a choice like that, after the fight had been stopped! He should have grabbed hold of her and marched her off, back where she belonged. Because *she* belonged to that other Ruddersleigh, too. He couldn't see her knocking about with any transport workers, white or coloured... how had Louis got hold of such a classy little piece in the first place? He would like to bet her parents knew nothing of this attachment. She was a peach of a girl too; any man would fancy her. So where did that leave Louis? In a state of insane jealousy, by the look of things.

Jim stood for a moment, hesitating. He was greatly inclined to tell her to keep away from the Indian boy, and stick to her own sort. He had a daughter just about her age. But he finally decided not to give her any good advice; it was never taken, anyway.

'Your cardigan's in a right mess,' he told her gently. Barbara looked down. Louis' blood, tears, sweat, yes, the lot, all down the front of that beautiful lacy white jacket. It was the last straw in a catastrophic evening.

'There's a cut on his face. It won't stop bleeding,' she said tremulously.

'I've got a bit of plaster with me. I'll put some on it. Don't you worry.'

'And his hands—'

'Well, he'll have to see how they are tomorrow. Can't expect owt else—what about that poor devil on the receiving end? Now you hurry along home, love. It's late.'

He stood for a moment, watching her retreating figure. They would have to make up some yarn about drunks, to explain Louis' appearance to Annie. It would never do for her to know the truth, because there was something distinctly unsavoury about the whole business. It didn't show the young Indian in too good a light. Jim knew that his sister-in-law and nephew were very fond of their lodger, and after all, he, Jim, had persuaded Annie to take him in the first place. He remembered uneasily her remark about not knowing what to expect with coloured men. Still, it wasn't fair to judge the boy's behaviour when he was half crazed with jealousy like that. What a night, though! Scrapping and kissing—better than the telly any day.

Chapter 16

Roger felt a disgust for Barbara so intense that he could not have put it into words. He felt contaminated by the events of that evening. He walked along, taking the short cut from Fordham to Dudley. His head ached violently, one eye was rapidly closing, and his knuckles were throbbing with a raw pain. But even worse than his physical distress was the shattering blow to his self-esteem. Barbara had actually preferred that man to him, and had stayed with him.

That Barbara could form an attachment with a man of that type, an immigrant worker, good God, it was unthinkable! What had happened to her pride?

Barbara: so haughty, so independent, and with a bevy of eager males to choose from. And yet, she was completely under the influence of this man! Now he knew why she no longer had any friends, why her manner was so evasive.

How had she met that Indian in the first place? He must have made a pass at her on the bus. He would never have made her acquaintance any other way. Plenty of men made passes at her though, that meant nothing. She could freeze a man at twenty paces with one look, if she chose. The more he thought about it, the more ugly and sinister it seemed. He had no doubts at all as to the relationship between them. It was clear that this man considered Barbara his property. Yet Barbara was no pushover. Sweet though her kisses were, they were not silent promises. She made that very plain. So how had that man gained such power over her?

Roger didn't pursue his thoughts in that direction, they were too unpleasant. But bewilderment mingled with his other emotions; he ached for the girl he had known only a few short months before. If she had only come with him, and broken away from that other influence, he would still have cared for her, he would have helped her. If she had only come with him instead of choosing that man! But her sole thought had been to soothe him—to explain to

211

him. Explain—ugh! Roger's head swam dizzily; he was compelled to lean against a wall for a few moments. She wasn't worth tuppence after all, this girl whose lovely face and vivacious charm had captivated him ever since he had first met her. And yet, he knew that wasn't strictly true.

He could see how she had changed from the carefree girl who had been so happy in his company before this other man had come into her life. He had been right when he had suspected that Barbara was involved with someone else, and that there was something wrong. He could never have envisaged anything quite as wrong as this, though. It was positively bizarre.

It would have been different if it had been anyone on the same footing as himself—if it had been any of the university crowd who ogled her so avidly in Mumbles. But the ignominy of being ousted by a man like that was well nigh unendurable. Why, the fellow had even slapped her in the face, and still she had chosen to stay with him!

The memory of that degrading incident brought on a fresh wave of nausea. And how she had lied... Roger could see it all now. She had lied to him about being busy swotting, and she must have lied endlessly at home. He understood Mrs. Granger's attitude towards him now. It was obvious that Barbara had used his name and pretended she was with him, making excuses as to why he no longer came to the house. She had only gone with him to the theatre because she couldn't get out of it. To think she had it in her to be so deceitful! Her parents would go mad if they knew the truth, but he was certainly not going to tell them. Let Barbara paddle her own canoe. That was what she had always wanted to do, anyway. Occasionally in the past she had complained to him that there was a fuss sometimes if she arrived home late at night, as if she jolly well couldn't take care of herself.

Well, it was a sad comedown for a girl who could take care of herself, that was all he could say. He wished with all his heart that he had never had this idea about taking her to the theatre. If he had only known how the night was going to end... a couple passed him under a street lamp, and glanced curiously at his dishevelled appearance. But Roger didn't notice anyone. His only desire was to get home, to shut himself away, and blot out the night's painful memories.

He had no idea how he was going to explain his appearance to his parents. He would have to think up some cock-and-bull story. They would be in bed by now, anyway. He could clean himself up, and face his mother's anxious gaze in the morning. Things could have been worse. He had always kept himself fit, and he was glad of that, and he was glad that boxing had been compulsory at Ruddersleigh Royal Grammar School.

So that was what a girl wanted. Physical violence, brutality, a slap in the face! Primitive, yes, the man was primitive, an ignorant savage. He saw again that swarthy face filled with jealous rage—and Barbara—an intelligent, well brought up girl like Barbara cringing in fear of him, clinging to him submissively. Disgusting, disgusting, disgusting! The word went through Roger's mind again and again.

Barbara had gone native. He knew that he had got it the wrong way round, but however mixed up it appeared she had somehow managed to go native in Ruddersleigh. Civilisation? Women hadn't any use for it beneath the surface. Violence, bestiality, elemental emotions—they were food and drink to them. Look at the way they screamed: 'Flog them! Hang them! Bring back the cat o' nine tails!'

Those sort of women showed their feelings in a refined way, for the sake of law and order. And if it didn't take them one way, it took them another. Young girls stood up in court and proudly declared their love for some thug about to do a life sentence. However brutal the crime, however far removed from all decent standards of behaviour, it never put a woman off. It was all bunkum and rubbish about them having finer feelings than men. Finer feelings! Stick any one of them in a grass skirt, and put her on a desert island with some Tarzan type male, complete with club, and she would be in her element. Then if another male came along, she would reach the pinnacle of feminine glory watching them fight for possession of her, just for the use of her body, nothing else. And girls like Barbara were no different from the rest.

The grass-verged streets of Dudley were quiet, almost deserted. Here and there a car revved up, or a couple walked along, closely entwined. He was approaching home now. The detached, stone-built house standing well back from the road was in darkness. With a curious pang he remembered that Sunday in winter when he had first taken Barbara there to meet his parents. He had been so pleased at their obvious approval, their delight in having what they clearly considered "the right type of girl" around the house. When she stopped coming they had asked after her at first, until they realised there had been a rift.

Roger let himself into the silent house. If there was one thing he needed it was a drink of whisky. He poured himself out a good stiff one, added a squirt of soda and crept upstairs with it to the bathroom. The last thing he wanted was to disturb his sleeping parents. He closed the bathroom door quietly behind him, and stood leaning against it, sipping his tot of Bell's. His right cheekbone felt numb. He wondered if it was broken. He would have to assess the damage—see the doctor if necessary.

He wanted to forget the events of that night altogether, but he felt that he could never forget as long as he lived. Never. He told himself that he hated Barbara, despised her, was disgusted with her. And yet... if she had only stayed with him...

Chapter 17

Barbara scarcely slept all night. Towards morning she fell into a doze from which she awoke pale and heavy-eyed. Fortunately, only her father had been downstairs when she arrived home after her disastrous evening with Roger. She had put the stained part of her jacket in a bowl of cold water in the kitchen. She would have to tell her mother she had spilt something down it in Ferraris. Looking in the dressing-table mirror she was horrified and ashamed to see the slap from Louis had bruised her face. She would have to try to hide it under make-up, and say someone had opened the door unexpectedly in the Ladies room at the restaurant. Her arm, too, was darkly discoloured and sore where he had gripped her so roughly.

She wondered how Roger had fared. She knew that he would never gossip about her, neither would he tell tales to her parents, but didn't know who else had witnessed the events of the previous night. She might have been known to one or more of the onlookers, she had been too distraught to care at the time. She was glad that Louis' muttered words to Roger had been almost incoherent with rage. The memory sent waves of shame through her; she had never felt so mortified in her life. Nor would she ever be able to look Roger Leffey in the face again.

Oh, Louis, she thought, how could you? He had slapped her, shamed her before other people, and involved her in a disgraceful scene. He hadn't cared in the least about making such a scene, either. Yet, in spite of all this, she still loved him. She loved him, but she was quite unable to understand such violent, hotheaded behaviour, such uncontrolled jealousy. She didn't care to think what might have happened if the fight hadn't been stopped. And if he had only waited until they next saw each other, she could have explained everything. So Barbara weighed her lover in the balance, and deeply as she cared for him, she found him sadly wanting in some respects.

Louis saw the matter rather differently. He had simply behaved in Ruddersleigh as he would have behaved in the same circumstances in Bamboo Grove. He had caught his girl with another man, and he had given his rival "licks". He was deeply sorry afterwards for the distress he had caused Barbara; he was miserably ashamed when he saw her bruised face, and filled with remorse for having struck her. But never at any time did he express the slightest regret for what he had done to Roger Leffey.

Barbara was, however, quite justified in feeling uneasy as to who else had witnessed that scene at Fordham bus terminus. One spectator had been extremely interested, only he had been unable to tell his mother about it that night, as she had gone to bed. There was no time the next morning, either, but on Wednesday evening he was able to give her a detailed account.

Mrs. Garside was busy in the kitchen when her youngest son, Tom, came home from work.

'You're a bit early, aren't you?'

'Got a lift 'ome,' said Tom briefly.

'Well, did you have a good time last night?'

'Aye, but the best part came at the bus terminus, Mam.'

'What do you mean?'

'There was a scrap between the Pakistani bus conductor and one of the passengers.'

'What were it all about?'

'You'll never guess! Wait till I tell you,' said Tom, who was enjoying recounting this to his mother. 'It were over Grangers' lass—you know, you go to help her mam in the house.'

'Never! You've made a mistake, Tom. It would be another lass, not her. What happened?'

'It were her all right. You pointed her out to me a few years ago. I've seen her many a time since, she goes to Parkhurst Girls' School. She used to be a tubby little kid, auburn sort of hair. She's slim enough now, though, although she's got plenty where she should have it.'

'Tom!' said his mother, pursing her mouth primly.

He grinned, and went on talking. 'I came downstairs after her on the bus, and the chap she were with was standing waiting for her to get off. They walked away together, but the conductor suddenly jumped off the bus and hared after them. He pulled her away

216

from the other bloke and clouted her one in the face. Then he started on the chap and nearly knocked him into next week. It was grand while it lasted.'

'I don't believe it was Barbara Granger. She wouldn't have anything to do with Pakistani bus conductors—why, it's a guinea to look at her!'

'It were worth more than a guinea to look at her last night, getting a slap in the face. She didn't half squeal.'

'And what happened to stop the fighting?' enquired his mother.

'The driver and a couple of other chaps stopped it. Not me, I was enjoying it too much. But the Paki got her, Mam! She went off with him—the driver took 'em both to sit in the bus. He didn't want the police there, he said. I came home then. There's one thing certain, she won't go out with the other bloke again. I know who he is, too.'

'Go on, you don't,' said his mother disbelievingly.

'I do that! When we first moved into this house I used to go to Dudley church, and I were in the choir, weren't I!'

'Aye, that's right. You and Arnold Gee, you joined the Scouts and the choir.'

'He sang in it. They have a chemists' shop in Dudley, and he's a bit older than me. He used to go to Ruddersleigh Royal Grammar School—and a right set of pansies that place turns out, too! He's called Something Leffey, and he had to leave the choir when his voice broke. Though how it broke I'll never know. He was that pampered if it spit of rain they'd bring the car to take him home! He's at the university now.'

'And what happened to him after the fight?'

'He went 'ome—to tell his mam, I should think. He was in a right mess, too, and he hadn't even got the lass to show for it. I think the Paki put the fear of God into the pair of them last night.' Tom paused ruminatively. 'His mam 'ud pass out when she saw him.'

'If it had been you, you'd have happen come home a sight faster than he did,' said his mother caustically.

'Me? If I'd had that bugger after me I'd never have stopped running. I'd have set up a new world record.' He burst out laughing. 'Anyone who fancies taking Grangers' lass out is welcome.

She's a tempting bit of stuff and all the rest of it—but the thought of that bloke hanging around! Not for me, Mam. I'd want a bloody good pair of spiked running shoes, for a start.'

'She wouldn't go out with you, lad.'

'Oh, I know that. She's too toffee-nosed for the likes of me, but not for the likes of that Paki bus conductor, evidently. As for Leffey, I bet he thought Judgement Day had come. I'll say this for him, though, he's not yellow, for all he's such a mother's darling. If they hadn't stopped the fight, though, the Paki would have put him in hospital.'

'Why, was he a lot bigger, or summat?'

'No, it wasn't that... he's a scrapper, you could tell. I bet he's been in more fights than Leffey's ever seen. Mind you, Leffey didn't put up such a bad show, either. I think that first thump from the Paki set him back; he wasn't expecting it. But the Paki was raging mad. They say them chaps carry knives, well, he must have forgotten his last night, or he would have knifed Leffey, if he'd had his handy.'

'Well, he hadn't and he didn't. Don't make things out to be worse than they are, Tom. Fancy, though. Grangers' girl.'

'She's a stuck up little bitch, and never was owt else. And Leffey's the same, just about her mark. I wasn't sorry to see either of 'em getting a belt in the chops.'

'You shouldn't say that. The Grangers are a right nice family, Tom, and if their girl has got herself mixed up with one of them fellows, I'm sorry for her mam and dad because they won't know owt about it, you can depend on that. Her dad would go barmy if he knew! He thinks the sun shines out of her bottom.'

'From what I've seen she wants her bottom tanning,' said Tom. 'She nearly got it tanned, too, with the Paki. From what I could mek out, Leffey and the lass had got on the very bus that they shouldn't—but that's life, isn't it?'

Mrs. Garside was so interested in Tom's account of the previous night's happenings that she didn't notice that the chips were beginning to burn. 'Well, I don't know what to think—'

'Don't say owt over at Grangers',' warned Tom. 'It's nowt to do with us.'

'I'll not say owt; don't fret yourself. But when I think of that lass, and all the fuss they mek of her, the posh school she goes to, and the clothes she gets—and *that's* how she frames herself! Running around with coloured riff-raff. I can't understand it.'

'If she were my daughter, I'd tek a strap to her,' said Tom.

His mother suddenly remembered the chips. 'Oh, would you?' she said scornfully. 'Well, wait till you're bringing up your own family, and see what kind of a mess you mek on it. I don't wish you owt worse than five lads, like me and your poor old dad's had to put up with.'

'You could have had worse than us, Mam,' said Tom, laughing. 'None of us could ever bring any little white bundles home to you—like Grangers' lass will be doing if she's not careful. Only hers might be a bit off-white.'

'You think you know all the answers, don't you?' retorted his mother. 'Well, happen you do now, but I can tell you this, you won't when you're my age. Here's your tea, gerrit down you.'

For the rest of the evening Mrs. Garside sat watching television, outwardly having dismissed the matter from her thoughts. But this was far from being so. She was turning the whole thing over in her mind. While she didn't relish the idea of telling Helen about Barbara, at the same time she thought it was wrong to keep quiet. She had been going to the house for several years now, and she liked Helen, or she would have given up the job long ago. It was true that Helen didn't talk about her own family as freely as Mrs. Garside did about hers, but the other woman had a good idea of what was going on, most of the time. And she was quite certain that neither of Barbara's parents knew anything about this business with a coloured bus conductor. She thought of Barbara's father, and how pleasant he was, always pulling her leg if he was ever at home when she was there.

As for Barbara... Mrs. Garside remembered the chubby little girl who had always bought her a Christmas present. True, she could be a "madam" these days, but then so could most teenage girls. Besides, it was impossible to know all the circumstances leading up to the incident that Tom had described. Barbara might be trying to break away from this man; she may be afraid to tell anyone about the affair; she may have gone with him to avoid further trouble.

Her mother should be told, but not in an obvious way. Mrs. Garside sat wondering how she could tell Helen, and yet spare her feelings as much as possible. She decided to repeat the whole story as a piece of gossip, leaving the girl and the university student unnamed. She would soon know from Helen's face if it had struck home.

And so, with a good display of casualness, she regaled her with a detailed account, the following Friday morning. 'Anyway, our Tom said she went off with the Pakistani,' she wound up. 'And the other lad, the university one, went home by himself. As for the lass—doesn't it make you wonder what the young girls are coming to, these days?'

Once, as a child, Helen had fallen from an apple tree, and been winded. She remembered the torturing sensation of being unable to move, and waiting for her breath to return in agonising gasps. That was how she felt now. A whole jigsaw of bits and pieces suddenly danced in front of her eyes, and fitted together. Mrs. Garside saw her change colour, and knew that she had said enough. She turned away hastily, saying that she must get on with Eddie's room.

Helen stood, quite unable to move, while the full shock spread in ever widening circles through her, like a pebble thrown into water. She sank down onto a kitchen stool. *This* then was what Barbara had been up to all summer! She sat, thinking feverishly. Barbara had been on the last bus from Ruddersleigh to Fordham that night. George had stayed up, and he had told her that Barbara came in very late, and that she had told him that she and Roger had been to Ferraris for supper after the theatre. Helen had assumed that Roger had seen her to the gate, and taken the short cut home to Dudley. That bruise on Barbara's face, the way she had picked at her food all the week; no further sign of Roger Leffey...

God, how blind I've been! thought Helen. Blind and trusting in the face of everything. How many other people knew about this, and were gossiping with malicious interest? Roger Leffey... but whatever had occurred that night he would discuss it with no one. She knew this as surely as Barbara had known it. But did Mrs. Garside know the girl was Barbara? Did she? Why, even Vi had seen them together—a foreign young man she had said—and Helen had dismissed the matter casually. She knew now that Barbara had merely been using Roger's name. No wonder she had looked staggered on Tuesday morning to see him at the house.

Lies, lies, lies, she thought bitterly. That's what she's been telling me for months. But a Pakistani bus conductor! It couldn't be true—it couldn't. Their adored and only daughter, their lovely Barbara, what in the world had happened to her? Their child, hers and George's—it *couldn't* be true. Barbara could pick and choose her boyfriends, and if they didn't come up to scratch, they didn't last long. She simply wouldn't look at a man of that type. It was ridiculous. And she wouldn't, she *couldn't* let her parents down like that, after all they had done for her. Helen thought of the ample pocket money and the attractive clothes which Barbara had always had, and more than that, the love which had been lavished on her since babyhood.

She and George had made sacrifices to give Barbara and Eddie as much as possible, and they had counted such sacrifices well made. It was not that they wanted repayment, or anything of that nature. They just wanted to see their children getting a good start in life, and not becoming juvenile delinquents. Where have we gone wrong? thought Helen. Her mind was going round in circles. She had always put the family first, she had never gone out to work; she had always been ready to listen to the children's troubles. She and George had made allowances for their daughter's moods and sulks because she was an adolescent.

Why, then, had Barbara struck up a friendship as unsuitable as this? But no, it wasn't a friendship. Obviously it was considerably more than that. Oh God, how far had it gone? She was trembling and shivering, although the day was close. Mechanically she began to make some coffee. If she took an Aspro the trembling might stop. She told herself that perhaps it had been a mistake after all. Perhaps the girl wasn't Barbara... perhaps it wasn't true. It couldn't be true—of course it couldn't. But what was the use of trying to fool herself? It was true, all right.

By the time Mrs. Garside had gone, Helen's mind had moved on to another stage. This affair must be stopped, and stopped as soon as possible, but how? What about George? She ought to tell him of course, he was Barbara's father, and it was just as much his business to know about it. And yet, if it could be managed, if she could possibly handle the situation without telling him, she would.

She considered it from all angles. It was strange that she could think so clearly. George was irritable and preoccupied these days, the aftermath of his unsatisfactory Board. If she told him about

Barbara he would be as shattered as she was, but there would be another reaction. He would think she was somehow to blame. There was no logical or sensible reason why Helen should be one whit to blame for Barbara's behaviour, but she knew that her husband would hold her responsible. She was Barbara's mother, he would reason, a member of the same troublesome, unpredictable, irrational sex, and therefore it was up to her to look after her daughter's welfare.

Suppose she had a confrontation with Barbara before she considered telling George? The thought of this also filled Helen with alarm. Girls nowadays had a way of defying their parents, and running away with the object of their affections. She thought of poor old Smithy at the office, and his erring daughter. If Barbara suddenly vanished with this young coloured man—the publicity—the gossip! The mere thought horrified her. She envisaged them having to make Barbara a ward of court. Good Heavens, what would her own mother think? Or George's father, and Vi, and all his other relations? Everyone in Sycamore Avenue and half of Fordham pointing and gossiping; Joyce Bell, George's colleagues at the office—Barbara's name dragged through the mud. But what to do? What to do?

The trembling seemed to have moved inside her now. She went upstairs and sat down in front of the dressing-table. There was a silver-framed photograph of Barbara on it, taken when she had been elected Rose Queen at her Sunday School anniversary celebrations. She had been eight years old then, and Helen remembered how she had stayed up half the night to finish making that white, frilly dress. She and George and little Eddie had been at the chapel to see her crowned. How proud they had felt that day, especially when Barbara had sung a solo in her sweet, childish treble:

"God make my life a little light,
Within the world to glow,
A little flame that burneth bright,
Wherever I may go."

Up to now Helen hadn't wept, but suddenly she was engulfed in grief. An agony of weeping swept over her. Their adored, darling daughter, hers and George's! She felt that she couldn't possibly cope with this situation; that she couldn't possibly be expected to. But what to do? What to do? Tell George, and have him blame her, on top of everything else? For blame her he would. Have it out with Barbara, and risk her doing something really crazy? Thinking about this, Helen was filled with fear. For if Barbara was capable of carrying on a clandestine affair, she was capable of anything. But what other action was there to take? She lay on the bed, with the sunlight falling in slanting beams across her, and the sobs choking in her throat.

After a while, a third possibility presented itself, and she decided not to take any drastic action yet, but to make absolutely certain of the facts. The more she thought about this, the more sensible it appeared to be. Having faced the worst, she would now take steps towards breaking off the affair, but she would keep up an appearance of normality in the home.

It was a long time before she rose from the bed, and attempted to hide the ravages of her weeping. She must keep a firm grip on herself. Barbara was shopping for some new school blouses in Ruddersleigh and Helen had told her to lunch there as well. Eddie was spending the day at his grandfather's, so that meant it would be several hours before anyone came home. Some time later she went downstairs and picked up the classified telephone directory. The trembling inside her began again, but she flicked the pages over until she found what she wanted. She would have to engage the services of a private detective agency, distasteful though the idea was. But this was the only way she would find out who the man was, where he lived, and if Barbara was still seeing him. That was all she wanted to know. For the other possibility, which Helen had considered, was to see the man himself, before she did anything else.

If he lived in some terrible house in Gantridge, though, she would have to abandon the idea and tell George. The thought of meeting this man filled her with angry bewilderment. How could Barbara...? She must have picked up with him on the bus. Helen realised that as he was on the Fordham run he had probably punched a ticket for her on the odd occasion. She thought about the bus conductors on the Fordham route. There was quite a good sprinkling of immigrants among them. They seemed to be a quiet, self-effacing set of young men, and she had simply never taken any notice of them. Well, it looked as if she was going to have to take notice of one of them, whether she liked it or not. On Monday she would go into Ruddersleigh and see what could be done about tracking down this particular man. They would probably have to follow Barbara to start with. The whole business was highly unpleasant, yet Helen meant to stick to her plan.

Meanwhile she would keep up an appearance of normality. She made a cake for the weekend, although it was an effort. She could see the strain on her face when she looked in the mirror; she would have to use heavier make-up than usual before the family arrived home.

She suddenly found it rather ludicrous. Barbara had been trying to hide her bruised face under make-up ever since Wednesday morning. What a godsend cosmetics are to women, she thought. Make-up could help to conceal worry, age, grief and bruises. She laughed aloud; she walked into the dining room laughing. It was all too ridiculous for words, but when finally she stopped laughing the tears welled up again. She bathed her eyes, rouged her cheeks and went into the front garden. She took deep breaths, and forced herself to think about inconsequential matters.

George would have to do a bit of dead-heading and weeding at the weekend. The lawn needed cutting, too. It was almost September, but how warm and sunny it was. Mrs. Stone, a cheerful, chatty neighbour passed by, and remarked on the Indian summer they were having, little knowing how ironic her choice of words sounded to Helen. Barbara had certainly been having an Indian summer, she thought.

That evening the whole family sat and watched a play on television. Helen behaved as if nothing untoward had happened that day. But when she got into bed that night, the trembling began again, and she felt the full reaction to the shock she had received. It was all so unbelievable, so unthinkable when she saw her daughter innocently watching television. Yet when Barbara turned her head, the bruise was plain on her face, and her mother knew it had not been caused accidentally. Improbable though the situation seemed, it was true.

Chapter 18

Helen had never been in Dinningley in her life before. She had to go into Ruddersleigh first, and then catch another bus. There seemed to be endless rows of terraced streets, but from the bus she could see great empty spaces where houses had once been. Tower blocks stood there instead, with the occasional public house still standing. It was like looking at a wasteland.

After having to ask the way to Rothwell Road, she finally stood in front of number seven, her heart thumping with nervousness. It was halfway through September now, but the fine warm weather continued, and the mellowing sun glinted on the well-polished doorknocker. She had to knock twice before she heard movements from within. Mrs. Askew opened the door and looked enquiringly at her.

'Good morning. Does a—have you a Mr. Ramdeem living here?'

'Yes, that's right.' Mrs. Askew smiled, and Helen thought what a pleasant faced woman she was. 'Do you want to see him? Come in, I'll tell him. Were you knocking for long? I've been in the back.'

Helen stepped over the cream, donkey-stoned doorstep and into the little hall. It was rather dark, but with a brightly patterned paper on the wall. There was a small table with a vase of white chrysanthemums on it, and their sad, funereal odour mingled with the smell of polish.

'Er... is he expecting you? He hasn't said anything—' Mrs. Askew paused. She was agog with curiosity. Who was this elegant looking woman, and what did she want with Louis?

'No, he's not expecting me. Just tell him it's Mrs. Granger.'

'He's shaving at the moment, I think.' Mrs. Askew walked into the kitchen, and tapped on the bathroom door. 'Louis, there's a lady to see you, love.'

Helen heard the faint sound of a man's voice, and recognised the distracted cry of the male, disturbed at his toilet. Then a door

225

opened, and there was a hurried, murmured conversation. Mrs. Askew reappeared, and asked her to come into the front room. 'He won't be many minutes if you'd like to wait here.'

Helen followed her into the rather crowded sitting room. It was full of odds and ends, and contained at least three chairs too many for its size. 'Lovely day, isn't it? I'm off to the shops now. If you'd like to sit here—'

'Thank you,' said Helen, sitting down and forcing a smile. Mrs. Askew retreated. Helen sat, her mouth dry, her hands cold and clammy. She had removed her gloves, but she put them on again. She looked round at the ornaments and the family photographs, clogging up every available corner. She felt thankful that she didn't have to dust them. But she could see that it was a very respectable little house, respectable, and scoured and polished with vigilant care. She heard Mrs. Askew go out, and then the sound of footsteps going upstairs. For a frightening moment the room seemed to spin round; she knew she must be strong though, however stressed. She removed her gloves again, and took a deep breath of the polish-laden air. There were footsteps on the stairs again, and a minute later Louis entered the room.

'Good morning,' he said politely, and for a moment Helen was quite unable to reply. All the sleepless nights she had endured on this man's account, all the hours of heart searching and wondering...

'Good morning,' she said at last. 'I'm Mrs. Granger, Barbara's mother. You're Mr. Ramdeem, aren't you?' For a moment Louis seemed to grow blurred in front of her. This was the man, all right. He was neatly dressed in a green casual shirt and fawn trousers. She looked at the regular features, the black wavy hair, the dark, lustrous eyes, nor did she miss the appeal of his well-proportioned figure. In fact, she stared at him as if she had never seen a man in her life before. No need to ask what Babsy saw in him, not in *that* sense, anyway. But with all this blinding handsomeness, one salient, significant fact remained. He was coloured.

Louis was gazing at her, too. Somehow he had never imagined Barbara's mother looking as young as this. She didn't look old enough to have a daughter Barbara's age. And Barbara was so unbelievably like her mother that he suffered a double shock. The same blue eyes, the same face, mature, but still lovely. She was a bit

226

plumper than her daughter, but very shapely in a well-cut grey suit.

'You wanted to speak to me?' he asked. His eyes were watchful.

He knows what's coming, thought Helen. When I can get it out. 'You're friendly with my daughter, I believe?' she began, speaking with an effort.

Louis sat down opposite her, clasping his hands over his loosely crossed legs. 'It true I'm friendly with Barbara,' he said.

She noticed the soft, foreign lilt of his voice. There was nothing hostile about his manner, it was boyish, almost placating. He was very young, not more than twenty-two at the most. Helen began to get a grip on herself. She took the plunge.

'Well, I don't think it's a very suitable friendship,' she said briskly. The young man made no reply, so she continued. 'Not at all suitable. Barbara has her own circle of friends, young people we know and approve of. She knows perfectly well we would never approve of this—she's been behaving in a thoroughly deceitful way for a long time now. She's been sneaking off to meet you, and telling me a lot of lies. She never did things like that before she met you—' She broke off, her feelings getting the better of her, and Louis spoke.

'Does Barbara know you find out about we?' he enquired anxiously. 'Mrs. Granger, have you say things to Barbara?' Under the calm exterior that he was trying to maintain, he felt mounting agitation. His English slipped right back into the island Creolese, causing Helen's lip to curl.

'As a matter of fact, I haven't spoken to Barbara yet,' she said. 'Her father doesn't know anything about it, either. I want as little fuss as possible... I decided to see you first. She only started back at school this week—' she paused, not sure how to go on.

'You come to see me in the morning—' Louis looked mystified. 'You knew you would find me in?'

'I expected to find you here in the mornings this week. I've gone to some trouble to find these things out. I wanted to be sure it was true about you and Barbara. It must stop as soon as possible, this *friendship*.' She didn't care to give it any other name.

'You object because I'm coloured?'

'That's one of the main objections—yes. You're Indian or something, aren't you?'

227

Helen's emotions began to turn to anger. She wanted to insult him for daring to look at her daughter, for having the sheer nerve to exert such an influence over Barbara, and for putting her, Helen, in this odious position.

'I'm Indian,' said Louis, with just a hint of sharpness in his voice.

'Then you know perfectly well you've no right to be seeing Barbara at all. All this deceit—'

'You think Barbara should have told you about we?'

'I don't think she should have struck up this friendship at all. You must have known it was wrong. You must have known we would disapprove if we found out. I'm not saying that it's all your fault,' added Helen, a little more kindly. 'Barbara knows as well as you do; only she happens to be our daughter, and not even eighteen yet. She's only a child.'

'She not a child—' began Louis, but Helen pounced on him.

'Not according to your ideas, perhaps, but according to ours she is, and we're responsible for her.' She spoke scornfully, but the next moment the question, the awful, tormenting question, the truth about Barbara's behaviour blotted out all other thoughts. How far had things gone between these two? Had Barbara...? No, she couldn't, she wouldn't—not after the way Helen had brought her up, and talked to her about such matters. But had she? These things went on all the time, always had done... but surely Barbara wouldn't... of course not. It was unthinkable. But had she? She stared at the young man, trying to read the answer in his impassive face. And now that calamity had actually overtaken Barbara and himself, Louis made a desperate bid to win her mother's approval.

'Mrs. Granger, we been meeting each other and keeping it secret. It was wrong. We talk about it for a long time when we first know we love each other. It ain't been easy for we—it making *doux-doux* unhappy many a time. You go say it bad and wrong, you vex with we—you don't know how much we love each other. But she say you wouldn't understand, she frighten to tell you—we go on meeting. *Oui.*'

'And where did you think it would get you—going on meeting like this?' Helen was trembling uncontrollably again. The emotion in his voice had revealed the passion between them even more than the rapid singsong words he had spoken.

'We had to be together!' he cried. 'Barbara loves me—don't mind I'm coloured—and I love she. Won't you give me a chance? It all we wanting, to be together. Don't vex with Barbara, she cry many a time about it all. I know it shock you to find out now, but don't vex with she.'

His deep concern for Barbara, and his wish to protect her was not lost upon Helen, but she was not in the least deflected from her purpose.

'Listen to me for a moment,' she said. 'You know perfectly well your background is entirely different from Barbara's. You're coloured, you have nothing in common with her. Your ways are not our ways, and where do you think it can lead to, this friendship? Only to unhappiness for Barbara, for both of you, if it comes to that.'

'But if you would only let we see each other,' said Louis distractedly. 'It mean everything to we. I know some things is different in England, but *doux-doux* is happy with me—'

'Is she?' Helen spoke coldly. 'I know you've exerted an influence over Barbara these past few months—and it hasn't been a good one. She was a happy girl with a happy life until she met you. She had the sort of boyfriend that we approve of, and the house was always full of young people. I'll tell you what's happened to Barbara—she has no friends now, and no social life. If she isn't sneaking off to meet you, she's mooning around the house, lying on her bed, or doing something equally aimless. Because she doesn't care about anything these days. Her last school report was poor—her work went steadily down right through the summer term. She was keen enough to stay at school and try for a university place at one time, but lately she's dropped one or two hints about leaving school. And apart from that she's been moody and weepy all summer—and you say she's happy.'

'It the circumstances making she unhappy,' protested Louis. 'Mrs. Granger, if you say okay, we can go about together, she'll be the happiest girl in Ruddersleigh. It make all the difference to Barbara, *oui*.'

'If we say you can go about together,' repeated Helen. 'With what end in view? Marriage?' She could scarcely get the word out; it was so distasteful.

'You think it cheek of me. I know I ain't got much for Barbara now, but I'm not afraid of work. Look, I've not been in this country for long—if you just give me a chance, I'll have something to offer she later on. Don't mind I'm coloured, Barbara don't mind—I know she'll wait for me if you give me a chance. I work hard and save—I get business later on—'

'What, one of those grocery shops in some slum?' Helen pictured herself telling her friends that Barbara was getting married, and that she and her husband had a corner shop in Gantridge. 'We want something better than that for our daughter...' she broke off hastily, before she could add 'and better than you'.

'So do I! You'll see! Barbara has given me a list of books to get from library. She say I can go to night school and study—Barbara promise to help me.'

Helen was filled with dismay. She looked at his pleading eyes, his eager, boyish face. She saw the shining aspiration on it; she saw that he meant every word that he said. It was clear that he was prepared to go to any lengths, scale any heights to get Barbara.

'Even if you say wait till she older, it all right,' he went on. 'Whatever you say—if you just let we write to each other—and let Barbara decide when she older—'

'You think we want Barbara walking around with a name like Ramdeem?' asked Helen crushingly.

For a moment Louis was taken aback. He didn't think it was a bad name as Indian names went. Still, he wasn't going to let that stand between himself and Barbara. 'I soon get that changed if you're wanting she to have an English name.'

'That couldn't change other things.' Helen spoke contemptuously. 'You're an Indian—an Asiatic. You've got an Asiatic mind, nothing can alter that.'

'It so different?' enquired Louis bitterly. 'I don't know what you mean, but I know if I got the chance to marry Barbara I'd do everything to make she happy. I'd take great care of her, as much as any white man.'

'I'm afraid I'm not impressed. I know what went on at the bus terminus one night last month. You say you'll take as much care of Barbara as any white man, but if she married you I'd never sleep at night. You put that bruise on her face, something she's never had from any of her English boyfriends—and don't deny it. You were seen.'

230

Louis was silent for a moment. He didn't need anyone to remind him that actions speak louder than words. All the talking in the world couldn't alter that bruise on Barbara's face. He thought of saying that it was only a slap, and that she bruised very easily, anyway. Then he realised that that remark, although true, would in no way advance his cause.

'I know it looking very bad,' he said at last. 'But you don't understand the circumstances—'

'Oh, yes I do.' Helen could feel her anger and resentment against him rising to boiling point. 'Barbara had been spending the evening with the boyfriend she had before she met you. He is the sort of young man we like her to be with. And you made a horrible, jealous scene, slapping her and attacking that young man. What kind of life would she have married to a man like you—a man with cruelty in him?'

Louis didn't know how to reply to this. He couldn't explain to anyone how he had felt that night; Barbara herself had scarcely understood. Useless to tell her mother that cruelty like that was completely alien to his nature; he certainly didn't consider giving Roger Leffey licks as being cruel. He felt the monstrous injustice of her accusation, and yet there seemed to be no way of defending himself.

'Your background,' said Helen. 'I know nothing about it, but one thing I do know, it's very different from Barbara's. Are you from Pakistan?'

'No. I belong to the West Indies. I'm from Trinidad.' Louis spoke dispiritedly. It was true that his background was very different from Barbara's but he was not to blame for that. When he said Trinidad, it struck a faint chord in Helen's memory, but she couldn't quite place it.

'Then my advice to you is to marry a girl of your own race... anyway, I thought you Indians had arranged marriages.'

'Not when we change religion to Christian. My family all converted to Christianity long ago. Missionaries very active in Trinidad.'

Helen inwardly cursed the zeal of those dedicated missionaries. 'What kind of social life would Barbara have, married to you? What kind of friends?'

'The friends she likes,' said Louis indignantly.

'Think again. Do you imagine her circle of friends would accept you? How could they? Barbara would be a laughing stock. If she had young married friends, she would expect them to come to the house with their husbands—she would expect to do some entertaining. You wouldn't allow a young white man over the doorstep! I know what Barbara would get out of marriage to you— black eyes and a string of coffee-coloured babies!'

She knew it sounded crude and beastly, but she was past caring. She saw sudden anger blaze in the young man's eyes, but she went on recklessly.

'You should get back to Trinidad. You should never have left your island—they should never have allowed you people to come here in the first place. You should keep your eyes off white girls, that's what causes all the trouble. I know what's behind the colour-bar in these other countries—we don't want England full of half-castes and Anglo-Indians.'

'They got plenty of those in other countries,' said Louis. 'Only it different, they having white fathers. It making a change, having white mothers. I could tell you plenty things about how white men behave in countries with coloured people. You think they don't look at coloured girls? I could tell you bad things they done—' He paused. He had heard the older people talking; he had heard stories about the white men in Trinidad, about the overseers pushing the young Indian girls down in the cane fields. And worse than that.

He looked into Helen's icy blue eyes, and a burning resentment rose in him. A handful of her countrymen had ruled over millions of his for years; they had ruled over the coloured races in the farthest corners of the earth. They had forced their language onto people of all shades and all tongues.

'The British should have stayed on their island in the first place,' he said. 'It saving a lot of trouble. They go into other people's countries, and think they behave how they like with coloured girls, but it different when the coloured fellows come here and start looking at white girls—'

'Stop it! I won't listen to this disgusting talk! You're to stop seeing Barbara, or we'll take drastic steps to have it stopped.'

'Well, tell Barbara that,' Louis flung at her. 'Forbid she to meet me again—see what she does!'

Helen was extremely frightened. It was plain that he was confident of his power over her daughter. But she was not going to let him see that she was afraid. 'She'll do as we say,' she said angrily.

'You'll find out!' Louis, too, was past caring what he said now; he was so stung by her insults. 'She'll do as I say—remember that—don't mind I'm coloured! She'll do as I say, and nobody else... anything I tell she,' he added.

For a moment Helen was speechless with fury. Now she knew the answer to the question that had tormented her. She drew in her breath sharply. Barbara, their adored, darling daughter had been seduced by this man.

'Oh, God...' she suddenly broke down completely. 'I wish she'd never been born...'

Louis stood up and walked over to the window, while Helen sobbed into her handkerchief. He wished he hadn't spoken like that, but she had goaded him cruelly. The sound of her weeping was all too much like Barbara's though.

'Don't cry so,' he said, although he could scarcely speak himself, for emotion.

'You don't know how much we love her,' sobbed Helen. 'And she was a good girl until she met you—you must have persuaded her—'

He was silent. He couldn't deny that he had done some persuading, but he was sure that he was not the only man who had attempted to seduce Barbara. The others had tried and failed; he had succeeded. But it merely showed him in a more villainous light, while Barbara's white boyfriends appeared in the roles of angelic, pure-minded males. Louis knew that was ridiculous. Men of whatever race were much the same in some respects, but telling Barbara's mother that simple fact wouldn't help matters.

'Mrs. Granger, don't cry so,' he implored again, overwhelmingly aware that she was Barbara's mother. '*Doux-doux* safe and sound, doing she lessons, while you're making misery like this. I never knew she talk about leaving school, or anything like that.'

Something in his softly coaxing voice calmed Helen, as it had calmed her daughter on occasions. Her sobs subsided.

'Don't think too bad of me,' went on Louis. 'I know you're thinking I'm a worthless fellow, but I do love Barbara. I only ask you to give me a chance. Remember she loves me very much, too, although maybe you don't think it.'

'I realise she must be very fond of you,' said Helen wearily.

The conversation continued, with Louis entreating to be given a chance. He pointed out that he was a Christian, that there would be no religious differences. He asked to be allowed to see Barbara's father, but Helen wouldn't hear of it. He tried to make her understand how impossible it was for him to walk out of Barbara's life; that it was utterly cruel, utterly unfair to Barbara. In spite of herself Helen was moved by his impassioned pleading, his fear of hurting her daughter.

'You should have thought of all that before,' she told him. 'I know she's going to be upset, but it's better than her whole life being ruined. I don't doubt you want Barbara, but you don't care about her welfare. Marriage is hard enough for a woman with a man of her own race—I don't want it to be any harder for Barbara than it would be normally. And if she decided to marry you later on, she would start with a big social handicap. I can see you care for her, but it's not difficult for a girl like Barbara to inspire affection in a young man. And when men are in love, they all sing the same song—what counts in marriage is how they behave when they're no longer madly in love. If I saw Barbara married to a man like Roger Leffey I should know he might neglect her a bit after the first few years, but that would be all. I've never heard Indians make very good husbands.'

Again, Louis could think of no reply. She was prejudiced, he could see that, but what did she know of the closeness of a happy Indian home? He thought of Teacher Ramlogan's house, where he had never seen anything but love and thoughtfulness. The thought of a home with Barbara as his wife, and their own children filled him with despairing longing.

'You're thinking of the old days,' he said at last. 'These are modern times, everything changing.'

'People are gossiping about Barbara,' went on Helen. 'I don't know how many people know about this, but don't you care about her reputation at all?'

'Of course I care,' protested Louis. 'I don't want people saying things about Barbara, but if they gossiping it's because I'm Indian. Don't mind if she going out with a bad white fellow, they won't talk. But if she seen with a coloured fellow—everything wrong!'

'Yes,' said Helen dryly. 'And not without cause. However much you say you love Barbara, certain facts remain. It's you who've influenced her away from her friends, and made her lose interest in the career she was so keen on. You've persuaded her to do wrong, and Barbara was brought up to lead a decent life, not to cheapen herself with men. And it's you who've put bruises on her face—is it any wonder I want you to keep away from my daughter? If you love her as you say you do, break off the association without driving us to take further steps. Because I warn you, Barbara will suffer more in the long run. We'll send her away from Ruddersleigh.'

She was determined to let him see that even now she knew they were lovers her attitude towards him remained unchanged. If he were naïve enough to imagine they would want him to marry Barbara because of that, he was mistaken. It was obvious that he would be only too eager to make an honest woman of her, if he got the chance. But he was not going to get the chance. Because of his constant pleas for her not to be angry with Barbara, Helen saw the way to defeat him. She began to bluff, making threats as to how they would keep Barbara away from him, how they would punish her. Mercilessly she played on his love for the girl.

And although Louis had said that she would defy her parents, he was very unsure of his ground. He didn't know how much pressure they would put on her, and he was not sure how he would stand in the matter. He had no knowledge of how white people handled these domestic affairs; he was, in fact, quite out of his depth. And conflicting with his love for Barbara were his old, deeply rooted ideas, those unshakeable ideas from a foreign culture. Much as he cared for her, a part of him felt that it was right for a daughter to do what her parents wanted.

Even though he had tried so hard to win her mother's approval, he had known from the start that it would be hopeless. The man that Barbara married must have certain qualities, and he knew well enough that he didn't possess any of them, least of all, the first and most obvious.

'No, don't vex with *doux-doux*!' he cried suddenly, his eyes filled with pain. Helen could scarcely bear to look at him, but she knew the battle was over. With a woman's instinct, she knew it.

'I do what you want,' he said, speaking with difficulty. 'I do it if you promise not to vex with she, not to blame she. If you say you'll be kind, help her to get over it. It going to be terrible for Barbara, promise you won't vex with she.'

'I promise that,' said Helen, and she meant it. Relief flooded through her. She was prepared to be more charitable towards him now.

'She'll be terrible to live with—you'll have to have a lot of patience. She'll be hell self to live with—don't vex with she, though! She'll be missing me—' He broke off for a moment. He knew how much of Barbara's nature leaned on his, and yet in other ways he was just as dependent on her. He wanted to explain to Helen that Barbara wouldn't feel complete without him, but he could see no way of putting it.

During this pause in the conversation, Mrs. Askew returned from her shopping, and tapped on the door to enquire whether Louis and his visitor would like a cup of coffee. She added that she was making coffee for herself anyway. The stressed, unhappy atmosphere in the room communicated itself to her. It was plain that whatever business the unexpected caller had with Louis, it was not anything good. They both seemed distraught, but when she took the coffee in, Helen forced a smile, and thanked her. She felt calmer after drinking it, during which time they discussed Barbara.

'Couldn't you break it off without saying I've had anything to do with it?' she suggested. But Louis was not having that.

'Tell Barbara I'm tired of she? You got no heart? No, I'm not telling lies.'

'It's only that I don't want her to turn against me,' explained Helen. 'I know she's going to need me. I don't want her to feel I'm not sympathetic or anything.'

'She won't turn against you,' he assured her. 'She's always known you wouldn't want us to see each other. She's always known there would be one big row if you found out. No, I tell Barbara in my own way, when I see she next week.'

'Well then, use your influence to make her understand I've acted in her interests,' urged Helen. She hesitated. 'If she makes other suggestions—not wanting to break it off, don't be talked round by her. If she has any wild ideas about leaving school, or leaving home, make her see it's not the sensible thing to do.'

'I promised, didn't I? She won't do anything silly, I'll see to that. I'll say she best hads do what you want.'

A silence fell in the room, while Helen finished her coffee. There seemed to be nothing left to say. Now that Louis was going to stop seeing Barbara, some of her hatred and resentment melted away. She had said some vile things to him in her fear and anger, now she saw only the unhappiness in his dark eyes. She wondered what strange affinity had drawn her daughter so close to this man, when she had plenty of young Englishmen to choose from.

His personable face and form, his soft, lilting voice, his strange accent, barely understandable at times... was it just the attraction of something different? But no, there was more to it than that. Yet Barbara was so much better educated... still, he was no fool. Helen could see that. Unsophisticated he may be, unintelligent he certainly was not. What was the strange little name he had called Barbara, Doodoo, or something? How long had they been lovers, and had they considered the possibility of Barbara becoming pregnant? The thought made Helen shudder. More important, had they done something about preventing such a calamity?

What had they talked about together? What could Barbara possibly have in common with this Indian boy? These questions and many more passed through her mind, but she knew they would remain forever unanswered. She rose to go.

'I'm sorry things have had to be like this,' she said, hesitantly. 'I'll do everything I can to help Barbara, though. Goodbye.'

She was out in the street again, where Tinker sat washing himself in the warm September sunshine. She knew now that she had taken the right course of action in saying nothing to Barbara, and in seeing her lover first. There was a chance, of course, that he would not keep his word, but she had a feeling that he would. Helen walked along the unfamiliar street, thinking about it. Her head ached, and she was distressed beyond measure by the whole wretched business. She had prepared herself for the worst, yet it in no way minimised the shock she felt at knowing how far things had gone between those two. Barbara... at seventeen! Still a schoolgirl, and with a man so unsuitable that Helen couldn't believe that she had actually found herself discussing marriage with him.

The trembling inside her began again, she was becoming used to it now. But at least, if things went the way she hoped they would, George need never know.

Chapter 19

The following Monday something completely unexpected happened in George's life. The results of the Boards came out, and his name was included on the list of promotees. In a daze he rang up Helen, and told her about it.

It seemed incredible after all these years, and after such an unsatisfactory interview, too. He was filled with a sense of anticlimax; that he should get through when he least expected it. That evening he and Helen would have a drink to celebrate, later on they could organise a proper party. He was still acting up in Chorley's place; the vacancy had not been filled as yet. George decided to put in for it without delay. After all, he knew the job; he was doing it. It was just a matter of consolidating his position.

That evening Barbara congratulated her father, and then went out to meet Louis. George had imagined Helen would be absolutely thrilled at the news of his promotion, but she seemed quiet and preoccupied. She knew well enough who Barbara had gone to meet, and she could think of nothing else but what was going on between them, and whether the Indian boy would keep his promise.

As soon as Barbara met Louis she knew there was something wrong. She could detect the strain on his face.

'What's the matter, darling?' she enquired, before they had been together five minutes. For his worries were her worries, and the deeply emotional scene between them after the fight with Roger Leffey had drawn them even closer together. Whatever Barbara thought of her lover's behaviour on that occasion, she accepted it, as she now knew she would accept everything about him, whether for good or otherwise.

'Come on, *doux-doux*, we go to Burnham Bridge,' he said.

Upstairs in the bus, he scarcely spoke. They sat pressed close together, and a cold uneasiness stirred in Barbara. The sense of foreboding that had lingered ever since that disastrous evening in August began to grow. Nervously she removed her gloves, and thrust one hand into the pocket of her suit. It closed over a coin; she drew it out in surprise, and looked at it. Then she remembered how it had got there. Roger Leffey had slipped it in for luck, on a blustery spring day when she had worn it for the first time.

Louis sat beside her, silent and unsmiling. It was growing dusk when they alighted from the bus at Burnham Bridge. There was an autumnal look about the place now; the leaves were falling. He slipped his arm round Barbara's waist as they walked up the path.

'What's the matter, darling?' she repeated. 'I thought you wanted to see that film at the Plaza tonight.'

'I want to talk to you, *ma petite*,' said Louis. His voice sounded strange; suddenly all Barbara's senses alerted to danger.

'There's something wrong!' she cried. 'It's about us, isn't it? Tell me, Louis!'

He saw the apprehension in her eyes, and thought of what lay ahead, and how he had gone over it in his mind until he was nearly crazy.

'Wait until we get into the wood,' he told her. She didn't reply, but he saw her eyes widening, as they always did when she was afraid.

'Aren't you going to kiss me?' she asked a few minutes later, as the leaves rustled under their feet. He put his arms round her, and held her for a long time without speaking. She clung to him with all her strength.

'I got something to tell you,' he said at last, forcing the words out.

'Go on then.' Her voice was very small and choked.

'There's been one big row about we seeing each other, *ma petite*.'

She knew it. She knew that something awful had happened. The blow had descended, as she had always known it must.

'Someone's said things to you?' she cried in bewilderment. Why not to her? Barbara began to tremble, as Helen had been doing on and off for the past three weeks.

'Your mother knows about we. She came to see me one morning last week—'

'She came to see you?' Barbara was incredulous. 'She came to see you—and never said a word to me! Mummy's never said a thing about it to me, and she's seen you!' For a moment she was too astounded at her mother's duplicity to think of anything else.

'Well, you been seeing me for a long time—you ain't tell your mother about it,' Louis reminded her. Under happier circumstances he would have smiled at her indignant astonishment. Instead, it only served to show him how extremely young and defenceless she was.

'But how did she find out where you live?' she asked.

'It have ways. You know that as well as I do.'

'You mean that Mummy's deliberately found things out about you? That she's had us watched?'

'It looks like it, *doux-doux*.'

'Oh!' Barbara stood, trying to assimilate the full significance of her mother's visit. 'Does Daddy know?' she asked, between chattering teeth.

'No. She don't want him to, either. Pull yourself together,' he urged, with growing alarm. 'I think we best hads sit down.'

'Does she say we must stop seeing each other? Answer me, Louis,' she cried, her voice rising on a shrill note.

In the dusk she could see the answer on his face, and the trees began to grow misty around her. She knew what was happening, but she was unable to speak, and warn him. It had happened before on odd occasions, once in assembly at school, once when her mother had taken Eddie's part in an argument, once during a game of hockey. The blackness rolled over her in waves, she shivered, and icy perspiration broke out all over her. Louis felt her go limp in his arms, something he had not been prepared for. He had steeled himself for every reaction he could think of from Barbara. Tears, hysterics, pleading, but he had never imagined she would just faint silently away.

Terribly agitated, he lowered her gently onto the leaf-strewn grass, and looked around, wishing with all his heart for someone to look after Barbara. If only they were not so alone, if only there was a woman available who would know what to do for her. She was cold, like stone, and the sweat of fear began to run off Louis. How long would she be like this? Was it just a faint, or something worse? Kneeling beside her, he put his arm under her shoulders and called her name again and again.

Anything would have been better than this, even abuse, even her clawing finger nails. He felt utterly helpless, alone in the woods

240

with an unconscious girl. He ascertained that her heart was still beating, and wondered whether to carry her back to the nearest cottage and ask for help. He was beyond caring what people might think. Then she came round, making moaning noises that frightened him dreadfully. He wondered if there was anything wrong with her that he didn't know about; had she had a heart attack or something?

Her eyelids fluttered, finally her eyes opened, tears streaming from them. She was shivering violently. He had brought his raincoat for them to sit on, and he wrapped it round her.

'You warmer now, *ma petite*?' he asked anxiously. She had not spoken yet, only sobbed and moaned. He wanted so much to say: 'Don't mind, *doux-doux*, we'll find a way. Don't cry, let we talk it over together.'

But he knew that he must not say it. Instead, he asked if they should go back to the village as soon as she could walk, so that she could have some brandy at the inn there. Struggling back to consciousness, Barbara realised what a fright he must have had to suggest taking her into a public house.

'No,' she whispered. 'I'll be all right in a minute. It's just a faint, darling. It was the shock... don't take me where there are other people.'

He held her silently, while she recovered.

'Louis,' she said, after a while, 'what did Mummy say? Was she very angry?'

He repeated part of the conversation between himself and her mother.

'But didn't you tell her how we feel about each other?'

'I tell her that. *Oui*,' said Louis, his voice husky with emotion. 'I tell she if she give me a chance I work and study and do everything so I can take care of you properly. I ask if I can see you father—she say no. I promise to keep away from you till you're older if she just let you write to me—she say no. I offer to have my name changed to an English one, she say it making no difference, I got an Asiatic mind.'

'What does she mean by that?' asked Barbara tearfully.

'I don't know, perhaps it the wrong colour. It making no difference what I say. She think I got no business to look at you in the first place. Your mother think you much too good for me—she

241

think it damn big cheek for a common coolie boy from Trinidad to love you and want to marry you. It right, too, *ma petite*.' His voice broke on a sob.

Barbara knew then how hard he must have tried to win her mother over. The strange protectiveness that she had always felt towards him came to the surface. She drew his head onto her shoulder.

'Does Mummy know about us? I mean about us... making love together?'

'She guessed that. She ain't think we been picking daisies all the summer.'

'Does she think I'm very bad?' she asked querulously.

'She think I'm very bad, *ma petite*. She don't mind I love you— she ain't caring I want to marry you. She say however hard I work it making no difference. She think I'd be a worthless husband any-way—' Louis's bitterness against Helen got the better of him. That icy stare, those cruel insults that he could never forget...

'What does she mean by that?' Barbara was mystified. How could Louis be anything but the dearest husband in the world?

'She think I would ill-treat you—I don't want to talk about it,' he said. He couldn't bring himself to mention the black eyes and coffee-coloured babies.

'Louis! It was that night! Someone saw everything, and told her.'

He nodded wretchedly. 'It have no use saying again I should have behaved different. Don't go blame me now, *doux-doux*, it mak-ing enough misery. You know I was all mash up—'

'I'm not blaming you, sweetheart,' she said sadly. They clung together silently, and Louis tried to control his emotions.

After a while Barbara spoke. 'I don't care what Mummy thinks,' she said, and there was a note in her voice as determined as the one which had been in Helen's when she had gone to see Louis. He recognised it straight away. He thought of her mother, still slim and attractive, and of how closely Barbara resembled her. And not just in looks, either. He realised that now. From the wil-ful, pouting girl would develop the woman of determination and character. He remembered the cold fire in Helen's eyes, the tongue that could cut like a whiplash; the tenacity of will which would not be deflected from its purpose. From such stock was Barbara bred,

242

and he knew now the tremendous inner strength, untried as yet, which lay behind the dimples and the soft, full mouth.

Had she not plotted and planned right from the start, defying conventions and everything else, so that she could be with him? Had she not suggested their first meeting because of her determination to find out about Trinidad, even though she later admitted to him that she had been frightened to death? When he had held back and hesitated in the early days, she had pushed forward. When his desire had become so over-powering that he had told her they must part or become lovers, she had yielded rather than lose him. And now, already she was seeing ways and means of defeating her mother.

'We'll stop seeing each other for a while, darling, but I'll write to you, and I'll make arrangements with the post office so that you can write to me there. I'll leave school and start work—'

'No,' said Louis, raising his head. 'Don't go doing anything like that.'

'Very well. I'll stay at school and do what they want me to, then.'

However stubborn she was, she was seldom so with him. Goaded by Helen, he had boasted of his influence over her daughter, but he had not exaggerated in the least.

'I'll stay at school, but we'll write to each other, and start meeting again when things blow over a bit. We'll have to be even more careful, and not meet very often, I know. But when I'm twenty-one I can please myself, and we'll get married. If you'll wait for me,' she added.

If he would wait for her!

'I know I'm not much good at cooking, or anything like that. But I'll get one of those cookery books with how to make curries and things in it—'

'Oh, God, don't. I can't bear it,' said Louis, and it was true. Her pathetic plans to wait for him, and prepare herself to be his wife moved him unendurably. She was ready to fight with everything in her in order not to lose him. He knew that he had only to say the word and she would wait for him, and defying everyone, she would marry him at twenty-one. He saw the loyal, valiant heart of her, ready to wait, to suffer, to endure, for him. He had only to say the word.

243

'*Doux-doux*,' he said. 'Your mother talked to me—she loves you very much. It true what she says, that we best hads stop meeting. It been selfish of me to want to keep you away from your friends— it would be more selfish to expect you to wait for me—'

'Don't talk nonsense,' she said sharply. 'Do you think I would-n't rather be with you a thousand times than with any of those friends Mummy talks about?'

The scene that Louis had dreaded now took place. Just as he had pleaded and fought with Helen to keep Barbara on any terms, so now Barbara pleaded and fought with him. Faced with the pos-sibility of losing her lover, she argued and coaxed and implored, but he remained obdurate until she worked herself into a frenzy.

'You've listened to Mummy, you've agreed with her—it was all planned before you met me tonight! And she knew I was coming out to meet you—she knew what was going to happen! I hate you both!'

She burst into tears again, and Louis was distraught; the situa-tion was too unbearable. He had promised Helen, but he was riven at the sight of Barbara's suffering. He wished that her mother could be here now, to witness the anguish of her daughter. And this, this, was for Barbara's ultimate happiness! He was tremen-dously tempted to break his promise to Helen. Let them say what they liked, but he and Barbara belonged together. He wished that he had never agreed to her mother's conditions, and then he thought of how she had said they would send Barbara away if he didn't. He thought of all the other threats. He held her close, but she struggled in his arms.

'Go on, go then! Get another girl!' she sobbed. 'I bet it won't be long before you do! You wouldn't leave me like this if you real-ly loved me!'

He tried to calm her, but he was in such a state himself that he scarcely knew what he was doing. To keep his word to Helen, and to have to witness Barbara's agony of grief—he felt it was more than could be asked of any man.

'I don't care what happens to me now!' she cried hysterically. 'You don't care, so I don't care! I'll sleep with every man I meet! Go on, leave me—'

Louis felt as if his insides were turning to water, but he knew from experience that it was best to be firm with her when she got like this.

'You worthless girl,' he said angrily. 'You got no shame at all, talking like that. I'm disgusted with you, Barbara. You think I'm leaving you to lead a life like that? You don't know what you're saying. You go lead the same sort of life you did before you met me—or give me back my bangle. I didn't give it to a bad girl to wear—is not going to stay on your arm. Give it back!'

He had no idea what he would have done if she had given it back, but instead she was suddenly quiet in his arms. Seeing his opportunity, Louis held her close and began to talk, using all his influence towards directing her future life. She was not to imagine he wouldn't be thinking about her, he would be thinking about her all the time, he told her. He cared very, very much what happened to her. And she mustn't be angry with her mother, because her mother loved her, and she wasn't angry with Barbara about it all. Louis impressed this point upon her, because he knew she was going to need her mother in the future. She was to work hard at school, and be a credit to them all, not sit around moping. She must go out and enjoy herself, too.

'But behave yourself,' he added at this point. 'It going to be hard without each other, I know. It going to be hell. Promise you wear the bangle all the time. It making me feel happier if I know that.'

She promised, in a subdued voice. For now she knew that she was not going to keep her lover, no matter how much she argued and pleaded. The cold future lay ahead of her, bringing with it the responsibility for her own life, her own happiness, without Louis. She was dazed, acquiescent, agreeable to anything he suggested. And Louis racked his brains, trying to keep the bond between them still powerful without his physical presence.

She was to be very careful crossing roads, and not to start day-dreaming unless she was in some safe place. She must kiss the bangle every night before she went to sleep, because he would be thinking of her, too. She must take great care of her skin when the cold winter winds blew through Ruddersleigh. He extracted end-less promises from her; he hedged her daily life around with do's and don'ts. He knew that it was important for Barbara to have all these charges laid on her, particularly during the first few terrible months without him. For Louis had no illusions about that. He knew that she would weep; she would ache for his arms, as he

245

would for hers. And because of the tremendous love and responsibility he felt towards her, he was fearful for her future.

He realised that it must be getting late. He glanced anxiously at his watch. 'Come on, *doux-doux*, we best hads go now, and I'm taking you right home tonight. Don't mind who sees we, you're not going home alone.' He helped her onto her feet. 'Don't go to school tomorrow if you don't feel well. Your mother will understand.'

She still seemed dazed, in a kind of dumb bewilderment over everything. They walked back to the village. The air was still; the moon was enormous, brilliant. The leaves rustled faintly underfoot. An owl hooted somewhere in the woods.

'Louis,' she said, suddenly breaking her silence. 'What will you do without me?'

He wanted to tell her that he had no idea, that the very thought of being without her was agonising. He wanted to lay his head on her shoulder, so that she could give him the sweetness of her feminine comfort, as she had always given him it in the past. He wanted to say that he would be as lost and hopeless without her as she would be without him. But he knew that he must put on a more cheerful front than that. For the time being at least she was dry-eyed, and he had to get her home.

'Well, I'll be thinking of you all the time. You must remember that. And I'll work a lot of bangers, so I won't have much time to go feeling sorry for myself.'

'But suppose I get on your bus?'

'I've thought of that. I know it would upset you, *ma petite*. I'll put in for a transfer to another run. *Oui*.'

She was silent, apathetic once more. But Louis talked incessantly, impressing on her again and again all the things she must do, and must not do. He kept saying: 'You listening, *doux-doux*?' and she would rouse then, and answer mechanically.

They were on the bus going to Ruddersleigh now. Still Louis talked to her in a low voice, still frantically issuing instructions as to how she was to conduct her life without him.

He scarcely knew what he was saying; he suddenly realised that he was speaking in Hindi. Even more disconcerting was the fact that she showed no signs of noticing which language he was using. By the time they were on the bus from Ruddersleigh to

Fordham he was beyond speech at all. He sat as silently as Barbara right up to the terminus.

'I'll walk to the end of your road,' he said, but when they got to the parade of shops, Barbara stopped suddenly. Panic filled her.

'I can't give you up, Louis,' she said. 'I *can't* live without you. I'm not strong enough.'

'Don't be down couraged, of course you can. You never find out how strong you are yet. I know life is giving you licks, but are you telling me you can't fight back? They say you the breed that fight them on the beaches—you making poor show. Well, shame on you for your blue eyes and white skin, then.'

'What difference does my skin make?' she asked despairingly. 'It makes no difference to my feelings.'

'Mine making no difference to my feelings, either. Only I got to put up with some things because of mine—you got to live up to some things because of yours. You supposed to be brave in danger, see fair play, help underdog, set example—keep stiff upper lip— you know all that stuff.'

'It's a lot of rubbish,' she said bitterly.

'It have something, though, *ma petite*. You never lived in a colony. They kicking the British out everywhere, then when things mash up they bawling the British should have seen to it. Why did- n't the British do this, that, the other? Worthless British, they say. Then hurricane, famine or flood comes along and they bawling where the British? They coming to help we? Course they com- ing—it making a funny world if they ever don't come.'

'I don't care about all that. I don't care about behaviour or fighting back, or being brave—or anything else. I don't care about anything except us. And I haven't got a stiff upper lip, and I'm not going to pretend.'

'I know this; you got one damn stiff bottom lip. I've had to stand up to it many a time. I never noticed you being so weak, *doux-doux*.'

'Don't give me any more pep-talk,' she said, with a kind of sad dignity. 'You only asked for a chance. I know it's all over, and I know how you've been treated. I shan't forget—ever.'

They stood for a few moments without speaking.

'Well, remember all the things I've told you then,' he said finally. 'Don't go let me down, *doux-doux*.'

They walked along to the end of Sycamore Avenue. There was nobody about, and they embraced for the last time. He watched her walk away in the moonlight, a small, dejected figure, taking his love with her. She opened the gate of number twelve, and a moment later he heard the door close behind her. He had given her back to her people.

For a minute he stood looking down the deserted street, then he turned and walked back to the terminus, where the bus to Ruddersleigh was waiting. Less than a month ago he and Roger Leffey had exchanged vicious blows there. Tonight the great full harvest moon irradiated the place brilliantly, making mock of the sodium lights.

Back in Dinningley he was glad that Mrs. Askew was watching television. He wished her goodnight, and said that he was going straight to bed, as he was tired. That was true enough. He felt drained after the battle with his own feelings, the anguish of Barbara; the finality of their parting. He went to bed, but was unable to sleep. He heard Mrs. Askew come upstairs later, and the house was silent. A beam of moonlight streamed into his bedroom though a gap in the curtains where he had not drawn them properly. Lying there, he felt the utter nothingness of his existence.

A coolie boy from Trinidad, an East Indian from the West Indies, a faceless immigrant tramping the bleak pavements of a foreign city. But a beautiful and educated white girl had loved him; loved him still. She would be lying in bed now, weeping for his arms to hold her, and for his lips to kiss her. His thoughts went back over those wonderful unreal months he had spent with Barbara. He remembered their first meeting, and how they had sat in that windswept little park together, while she had asked him questions about Trinidad. He heard again her sweet, serious voice:

'First there were the Arawaks, then the Caribs. It was discovered by Columbus... conquered by the Spanish... colonised by the French... ceded to the English...'

Ceded to the English. He turned on his side and covered his face with his hands. And Louis saw an island in his mind's eye, an island with Moslem mosques and Hindu temples. An island where many races work and play, laugh and weep, quarrel and love, beneath the hot, Caribbean skies. The Land of the Humming Bird, the home of the calypso; an island where the sun shines fiercely, where the rain falls in torrents, and the earth steams. A place where the orchids grow wild in the forests, where the oysters cling to the mangrove roots in the swamps, and where the scarlet ibis roosts. Where the perfume of frangipani fills the air with its penetrating sweetness; where a Hindu father hangs out a red flag to indicate that he is the possessor of marriageable daughters.

Louis saw all this, and more. He saw the burnt trash blowing in the wind at crop season; he saw the men working in the cane fields, cutlasses glittering in the sunlight as they swung their arms and with one blow felled a cane. He saw his uncle, Roopchand Chittaranjan, staggering home, drunk on rum. He saw foolish, shiftless Zilla, and his swarthy, thin-legged cousins, running after him, pulling at him with their sticky fingers.

'Louis! Louis! Make we *shak-shak*! Sing to we—play with we! Lou-is! Lou-is! Lou-is!

And, finally, he saw the banana boat.

Chapter 20

When Barbara arrived home that night her father had gone to bed, but Helen was waiting up for her. For the past half hour she had been very worried; Barbara was home earlier than this as a rule.

When she heard the door close, Helen went into the hall, but the girl walked straight past her and upstairs without speaking. Her mother caught a glimpse of her face, white and pinched, with a stony look on it that hurt her more deeply than she could have put into words. She knew then beyond all doubt that the young Indian had kept his promise. She longed to go upstairs after Barbara to comfort her in her loneliness and grief. But she knew that it would be useless, tonight at all events.

Later she lay sleepless, tossing beside George, straining her ears for the sound of muffled sobbing from Barbara's room. Once she thought she heard it, and sat up in bed, wondering whether to go in to her. It was nearly dawn before she finally dozed off.

She went into Barbara's bedroom that morning, closing the door behind her in case Eddie should hear anything. It was plain that Barbara would not be able to attend school, because of her appearance, if for no other reason. Her blotched face and red, swollen eyes bore witness to the fact that she must have wept continually throughout the night. Helen had expected her to be upset, but she felt a pang of misgiving when she realised just how badly the girl was taking it.

'You'd better stay in bed, Babsy,' she said, trying to keep her voice steady. 'I'll bring you up a cup of tea as soon as I have a spare minute.'

She told George and Eddie that Barbara had a very heavy cold. After they had both gone out she took up some breakfast on a tray.

'I don't want anything.'

'Try to eat something,' said Helen coaxingly. 'Just a piece of toast, darling.' She wanted to let Barbara see that whatever she had done, however much she had deceived them, she was not going to reproach her about it.

She noticed the bangle on her arm, and she knew then that it had been a gift from the young man. That was why she had worn it so constantly. Helen felt that she would have to broach the subject somehow, and the sooner the better. Looking at her daughter, wan and heavy-eyed, she wondered afresh how this business had begun in the first place.

'I know it seems terribly hard on you now, but it's for the best, darling. You'll realise that when you're older. I'm not saying that he's a bad sort of boy—'

'Stop it!' cried Barbara. 'Don't say anything about Louis! I'm only going to do what you want for his sake—don't ever think anything else! I would go to the ends of the earth with him—I would go to hell with him—so don't stand there being patronising like that! And I'm not sorry about anything, you can be a disgusted as you like with me—'

She burst into wild sobbing, and Helen went out of the room and closed the door behind her. The passion in her daughter's voice and eyes made her feel physically sick. It was indecent; it was like looking on the naked face of love. Love, in its youth and violence, its terrible mocking beauty, and blind, trampling folly. And in the madness of her desire Barbara had lied shamelessly so that she could get out, and into her lover's arms, and she had come home and lied again, with her lips still moist from his kisses.

Helen stood for a moment, leaning against the door. Her head ached, and her eyes pricked with tiredness. There had been so many sleepless nights lately, and she wondered when they were going to end. Barbara was filled with resentment and defiance against her; on a sudden impulse she went back into the room.

'Listen, Babsy,' she said. 'Did Louis tell you to be like this towards your mother? No, I'm sure he didn't. You might try to see things from my point of view for a change. Do you think you're the only one who's upset by all this? All Daddy and I have ever thought about has been your happiness, yours and Eddie's. Do you think I want to see you unhappy like this? There are times when older people do know best—and don't tell me I don't understand what you two feel for each other. Don't tell me I don't know anything about love. I know a lot more about it that you do.'

251

Barbara felt her mother's arms around her then. They clung together, weeping, and for a few minutes they were close, as they had not been since Barbara's childhood. In that closeness, it seemed as if she had never left the womb.

Downstairs again, doing the routine chores, Helen wondered what she could do to help the girl. An idea had half formed in her mind the day before, but she had been too concerned as to whether the boy would keep his word or not to pursue it more fully. But now she turned it over in her mind. George having got his promotion at last, why not make a big push for him to put in for a vacancy in the south? If they could get out of Ruddersleigh altogether... give Barbara a chance to make a fresh start? A new life for her, new friends and new interests. The more Helen thought about it, the better plan it seemed. They could get Barbara's scholarship transferred; Eddie would just have to take his chance as to whether they could get him into a fee-paying school or not.

She had no idea how many people knew about this business of Barbara and the Indian boy, and if they stayed in Ruddersleigh it would always be on her mind. Even though it was all over now, she felt that there was danger as long as he and Barbara lived in the same city. There would be a row with George, of course, but another upset wouldn't make much difference. It had been nothing else but trouble lately. Anyway, if they moved south she would be nearer her mother, for her mother's health was another worry, constantly jangling at the back of her mind. She made coffee for herself and Barbara, and took it upstairs. Barbara was lying there listlessly, but her manner had changed.

'Do you want to get up today, Babsy?'

'No, I don't want to see anyone,' she answered in a low voice. 'I'm going to school tomorrow, though.'

Helen sat on the bed, and drank her coffee. 'I've been thinking, darling, how would you like it if we left Ruddersleigh and moved down south somewhere? It's a good chance, now Daddy's been promoted. He can put in for a vacancy now, and we can get you fixed up at a new school. What do you think?'

'I don't mind. I just don't mind either way.'

'I'll talk it over with Daddy then.'

The conversation dwindled and apathy claimed Barbara again.

Later, when Helen was busy in the kitchen, the telephone rang. To her surprise it was Miss Pickersgill. She asked why Barbara was not at school, and Helen explained that she had a cold, but would probably be back the following day.

'I'll tell you why I'm ringing, Mrs. Granger. I'm very pleased indeed with Barbara. I've just received word today that she's been awarded the Annitsford Essay Prize—isn't that splendid? It's books to the value of ten pounds, but it's not that which counts; it's the prestige for the school. She'll get the award on Speech Day next month; I hope you and Mr. Granger will both be there. I believe they had a number of very good entries, so more credit due to her. It was an essay on Trinidad if you remember. Yes, it seems a long time ago now, doesn't it? I think it's a marvellous effort on Barbara's part. Her work went down a bit last term—I was rather concerned about it—but I think it must have been just a passing phase. Give her my congratulations, won't you?'

After a few more words, Helen replaced the receiver. She remembered how keen Barbara had been to write that essay. It was a long time ago, though. The spring-cleaning had been in full swing, and she had been too busy herself to take much interest in the competition. An essay on Trinidad... Trinidad, yes that was where the Indian boy had come from. Somehow she was sure there was a link, but what it was she was equally sure she would never know. She would have to go upstairs and tell Barbara about it, though.

'That was Miss Pickersgill on the phone, Barbara. She's very pleased with you—you've won the Annitsford Essay Prize. Isn't that good news? I must congratulate you, and Miss Pickersgill says I must give you her congratulations, too.'

She stood at the bedroom door, trying to sound pleased and cheerful. She saw a strange look cross Barbara's face. It was quite unfathomable, and then the listless expression replaced it again. 'So they'll all be congratulating you tomorrow,' went on Helen. 'I know Daddy will be thrilled about this when he knows.'

There was so little response from the girl that she closed the door again. Barbara lay there, thinking about it. Of course, that was how it had all begun, writing that essay on Trinidad. It had seemed very important to beat Pringle in those days. Now, she could think of nothing less important. And yet, all this had happened to her because of that essay on Trinidad. Things had happened to other people, too.

To Louis... to Roger... to all her family, if they moved south as her mother was planning. How strange to think that a little, unimportant thing like an essay competition could affect the lives of people like that.

When Eddie arrived home from school that afternoon, Helen asked him what he thought about the idea of moving south.

'What for?' Who wants to go? I don't want to leave Ruddersleigh,' said Eddie, in genuine bewilderment. Helen had foreseen opposition from him; she knew that her son was well satisfied with the pleasant routine of his days. 'I thought Dad was putting in for that vacancy Mr. Chorley left,' he added.

'It doesn't mean he would get it, in any case. Anyway, I want to be nearer Grandma. She's far from well.'

'I don't want to leave Mousy—' began Eddie. Suddenly Helen felt like shaking him, although she knew he was a good-tempered, easy-going boy. He had always been more biddable than Barbara.

'Well, if Daddy asks you if you want to go, you can say you do,' she snapped. 'Because Babsy and I do.'

'Oh!' Eddie raised his eyebrows. 'Babsy wants to go, does she?'

'She doesn't mind—but I want us to go—I want to get her away from Ruddersleigh.' The anxiety on Helen's face communicated itself to Eddie.

'Why, what's wrong with Babsy?' he asked. A tiny little web of fear began to creep down the back of his head. He saw tears in his mother's eyes, and he knew that there was something dreadfully wrong.

'Eddie, don't make things harder for me,' she said. 'Say you want to go south if your father makes a fuss.'

'Is it... people you want to keep Barbara away from?' asked Eddie, going white beneath his freckles.

'What do you know about Barbara?' Helen spoke sharply. Oh, God, how many people had known about this affair? Surely Eddie hadn't known and kept it to himself?

'I don't know anything,' he said quickly, but Helen knew that he was lying.

'What have you heard? Tell me,' she demanded.

Eddie was thoroughly frightened by now. His mother

behaving like this, and Barbara still shut in her room—what had happened?

'It's only something Ian Bell said ages ago,' he muttered reluctantly. 'He said Barbara was going around with—' he paused, unable to get the words out. His mother looked so strange he felt petrified with fear; something nameless and horrible was threatening Barbara.

'Ian Bell!' exclaimed Helen in dismay. 'What did he say? That she was friendly with a foreigner?'

'Yes,' he said, with fervent relief. It sounded better put that way.

'Why didn't you come and tell me?' asked Helen. She burst into tears, reducing him to horrified embarrassment.

'Don't cry, Mum,' he implored, only too well aware that a lump was beginning to form in his own throat. 'I just didn't think it could be true. Ding-Dong's always saying daft things about people. Is it true?'

Helen nodded, trying to control herself. 'It's all over now, though. Eddie, promise me you won't breathe a word about it to Daddy—or ever mention it to Barbara.'

'Of course I won't,' promised Eddie. He would have promised anything to have taken that look off his mother's face. He loved her more than anyone in the world; the sight of her in tears moved him deeply. 'I'll say I want to go south. And I won't tease Babsy, or borrow her records or anything—is she all right?'

Eddie was just leaving the enchanted world of childhood behind him, and Barbara was a part of it. They had played together, and fought and loved and quarrelled within the close, secret bond of sister and brother. Of course, he knew that she could be rotten sometimes, but then all girls were rotten. If she was in a good mood, though, she would lend him records, and she still played darts with him sometimes in the garden shed. He and Mousy had once read a lurid paperback all about white slave traffickers, and he was filled with the most unspeakable fears. Mousy had an older brother who told him all sorts of things, and he passed on the information to Eddie. And Eddie knew that it was rotten having to be a girl, anyway. He wondered if his mother knew all the things that could happen to girls...

'Is she all right?' he repeated.

'Yes, she's all right. She's very upset about it, though. So be a good boy—I expect she'll be a bit irritable with us all for a while.'

'I don't mind that.' Eddie was so relieved to know that Barbara was all right that he felt he could put up with anything from her. By the time his father arrived home he was united with Helen in a desire to leave Ruddersleigh. Helen didn't broach the subject immediately though. Over their evening meal she told George that Barbara had won the Annitford Essay prize and he was delighted.

'I must go upstairs and congratulate her,' he said. 'We seem to be doing very well in this family lately, don't we?' He was in quite a jovial mood. Having recovered from the initial shock of being promoted, he was now enjoying sitting back and being congratulated. He regarded this promotion as his long overdue right.

'Babsy has a heavy cold. It's in her eyes,' warned Helen, although she knew he would still go upstairs to see her. She hoped he wouldn't stand there babbling about Trinidad. With some unease she heard his footsteps overhead. It seemed incredible that George was the one member of the household blissfully ignorant that anything unusual was going on. He was so happy, too; pleased about his promotion, and about Barbara's success at school. It was so rarely that nice things like this happened all at once, Helen reflected sadly. As it was, she was too worried and upset to be very interested in either the essay prize or her husband's promotion.

With a sudden rush of tenderness, George paused outside the door of Barbara's bedroom. He remembered how if she had been ill as a child, he had invariably gone upstairs to see her as soon as he came in the house. And always with some little toy, or a book he had bought her on the way home. The small figure lying in bed, unwontedly quiet, would suddenly become animated, and she would cry: 'Daddy, have you brought me something?'

He wished at that moment that he could put the clock back, and peep round the door to see a little girl in a winceyette night-gown. He tapped on the door, and waited until he heard Barbara's voice before opening it.

'How are you, darling? I hear you've got a nasty cold. Yes, I can see, it's all in your eyes. Isn't it great news about the essay? It's my turn to congratulate you, now. I hear Miss Pickersgill's very proud of you—well, so am I.'

'Thank you,' said Barbara, without even the vestige of a smile.

'I expect you feel rotten.' George spoke sympathetically. 'We'll talk about it tomorrow. What do you say if we have a joint celebration dinner somewhere when you're better?'

'It's a good idea,' she replied. George stood for a moment, a little baffled. She seemed really under the weather.

'Well, I'll see you tomorrow, then. We'll keep the old box low if we have it on. Goodnight.'

'Goodnight.'

He went downstairs again. 'She does seem peaky,' he remarked to Helen. 'Do you think we should ask Dr. Cresswell to call in tomorrow? It might be flu. There's some going around already.'

'No, she'll probably be back at school tomorrow. It's easy to throw a cold off at her age. I've been thinking, how about you putting in for a vacancy in the south, George?'

She said it so casually that for a moment he was too astonished to reply.

'In the south? Why, you know I'm hoping to get Chorley's job permanently—' He broke off, seeing the sudden hardening in her eyes. He knew then that the old, latent resentment against living in Ruddersleigh still smouldered inside her.

'Well, I want to go south,' she said. 'I'm not going to end my days in this cold, filthy place. I hate it—I hate it even more now than when we first came here. I've talked it over with Babsy and Eddie, and they're both agreeable—they both want to go. I don't mind where we go as long as it's a decent place, and in the south. I want to be nearer to Mother as well, and now is a golden opportunity to move. We can sell the house at a profit, and you know we'll get a good transfer grant—we'll be well in pocket. Barbara can easily get her scholarship transferred.'

'But what about Eddie?' asked George. 'What about his schooling?'

'He must take his chance of getting in another private school. There are plenty about; we shouldn't have any problems.'

'I'll go to a secondary modern,' chimed in Eddie, who could see an argument brewing about his education. He heartily wished it was all over and settled. 'I'm not a late developer, or anything like that. I'm just not going to develop at all, so you may as well save your money.'

It was rather a surprise to hear such a shrewdly practical remark from Eddie. While George looked at his son in amazement, Helen continued to press her point about going south.

'Just a minute,' said George. He could see that she had already got Barbara and Eddie on her side. After the initial surprise, his anger began to kindle. 'I see you've made your plans without troubling to consult me,' he said. 'You thought the only thing left was to tell me. Well, I don't see any reason why we should all uproot ourselves when the children are settled in good schools. Particularly as I'm practically certain to get Chorley's job now—and they're a decent bunch to work with now he's gone. It's just *your* whim, *you* want to go, and you've talked the children round. I'm not going to put in for a vacancy in the south. I had enough of it when I was stationed there for a time during the war, and I'm not going to live there.'

At this point Eddie stood up, not knowing whether to stay, or to rush off to Mousy Marfitt's until the storm was over.

All the strain that Helen had endured during the past three weeks seemed to explode inside her. George, unknowing, uncaring, sleeping away beside her night after night, while she tossed until it grew light. George trying to prevent them from going south and removing Barbara to safety, George taking the same attitude that he had taken years ago. By God, she would show him!

'Well *I'm* going!' she cried, her voice husky with anger. 'I'm going, and the children are coming with me. We can stay at Mother's—I'll soon get Babsy's scholarship transferred. And I'll get a job, and you can go to hell, because you've never had the slightest appreciation of anything I've done for you. You're selfish and thoughtless and pig-headed, and if you think you're going to stand there and dictate to me, you're very much mistaken. *You* can stay in Ruddersleigh if you like, but you can't make me stay.'

George was aghast. He hadn't seen Helen like this for years, not since the days when she had been young and passionate and quarrelsome. He wanted to call her bluff, and tell her to go. But suppose she did go? There were times when she got on his nerves, there were times when he wished her far away, but he was well aware that he couldn't really face the thought of life without her. He had told her that, many years ago. He had told her a lot of other things, too...

While he stood, trying to think of a suitable reply, fresh accusations and abuse came from Helen.

'I'm going to Mousy's, be back later,' muttered Eddie, dashing out in the midst of it. He couldn't bear to see his parents quarrelling like this, like two angry people, not caring that they were his mother and father. And in the heat of the scene that followed, he was scarcely missed. But Helen had the last word.

'I'm sick of being taken for granted! I'm absolutely sick of it, and I'm sick of you! You think I just exist for your convenience. Well, this is the end—you can think again!' She was breathless with anger.

The way she was looking at him—the things she was saying, as if she hated him, yes, hated him. Suddenly George quailed before her. She meant what she said. He had a chilling, fleeting vision of himself being left alone in Ruddersleigh. But surely she couldn't mean all those things she was saying about him?

He had always imagined he was a good husband, if he had ever thought about it at all. This was not so much because of the things he did, as because of the things he didn't do. He didn't drink very much, or bet, or anything like that. He didn't keep her short of money, or chase after other women, or use bad language in the home. Or treat her unkindly... but from what Helen was saying there were other things that he didn't do, and should. His, it seemed, was the sin of omission. Helen left nothing unsaid.

His anger faded. 'All right,' he said, uncertainly. 'No need to make all that fuss. I'll see about putting in for a posting south. I'm sure you needn't get so excited about things. But in any case, it could be ages before I got posted...'

He stood hesitating. Was anything wrong? Helen seemed absolutely distraught. She sat down, trying to control her nervous agitation. Was she so worried about her mother? She had never said much about it to him. He had an impulse to go to her, to put his arms round her, and ask her what was wrong. But he still remained awkwardly standing there, feeling hostility towards him emanating from every inch of her. She had withdrawn her support, that unspoken, unfailing, loyal support, without which he felt quite unable to cope with the day-to-day stresses and responsibilities of life.

'I'll see about putting in for the south, then,' he said again. She made no reply, and he walked into the hall. For a moment he stood there, still not sure what to do. Then he opened the door and went out, being careful not to bang it behind him.

He would have to tell Vi and his father, and his friends, and all the rest of his relatives about this going south business. But before he did anything, he would let things simmer down. He would wait—he wouldn't rush to get a posting south. He walked up Sycamore Avenue, thinking that he had looked forward to this promotion for years, and now that he had got it, it had just led to a flaming row, and harsh accusations from Helen. It should have been a happy night, with the news of Barbara's prize-winning essay coming straight after his own success. But then nothing ever turned out the way you thought it would.

* * *

Helen sat alone, busy with her thoughts. She knew that if she told George about Barbara, he would be eager to get her away from Ruddersleigh too. He would blame her for Barbara's misbehaviour, though, and she felt she couldn't endure being blamed for that, on top of everything else. Even if he didn't blame her outright, he would hint very strongly that she was guilty of some negligence. After all, Shirley didn't get herself mixed up with Indian bus conductors; neither did any of the other girls in Barbara's form at school. Only their daughter.

But it was not just the knowledge that he would hold her responsible that prevented Helen from telling her husband. She knew how he doted on his daughter. To tell him that Barbara had been having a disgusting, sordid little affair with that man, the sweepings of some tropical country—no, she just couldn't. It would be cruel to let him know how their beloved daughter had deceived them, making any excuse, using anybody's name to get out of the house and into her lover's arms. She intended to do everything she could to help Barbara, and by keeping quiet about it she was protecting both her husband and her daughter. Let George carry on in ignorance, his eyes following his lovely Barbara with immense pride and tenderness. Let him continue to think that she was set apart, when he viewed the goings-on of modern youth in shocked wonderment.

She sat thinking about the events of the past few days. She had vanquished Barbara's lover, and her daughter was back in the fold. She had exerted her influence over Eddie, and made him say he wanted to leave Ruddersleigh. She had crushed George with her anger and her threats. She had bent them all to her will, and she felt very tired.

She thought of the Indian boy, and how she had insulted him and blamed him. And he had taken the blame, and striven to protect Barbara. She remembered his sad eyes, his lamentable English, his heart-rending cry: 'Don't blame she!'

But Helen knew well enough that Barbara was every bit as much to blame. Somehow those two had met, a light had been kindled, a flame had sprung up. Things happened to people, incalculable things, chance meetings, a few words, a stray remark—things like that, and the whole course of a life could be changed. You never knew why, though.

Sitting there, Helen grieved for the lost innocence of her daughter's girlhood. Her own mother had always said that if you trusted a daughter she wouldn't betray your trust. She had trusted Helen, and Helen had not betrayed that trust, in spite of the many temptations and opportunities of her wartime girlhood. And she in her turn had trusted Barbara; a trust, which she now knew, had been entirely misplaced. There was no answer to bringing up children; there was no answer to a lot of things. But she would have liked someone to understand how she felt, someone to comfort her and make a fuss of her, just for a change.

* * *

Upstairs, Barbara still lay in bed. She had not troubled to draw the curtains, and the moonlight shone full into the room.

Love, passion, jealousy, joy, it all lay behind her now. It was as though a hurricane had swept through her life, leaving desolation and sadness in its wake. Desolation, and the raw grief of parting, mutilating as though a limb had been torn from her living body. She knew now why people gave up so much for love; why they made sacrifices that caused the outside world to look on in amazement.

She knew now why they relinquished glittering careers, exiled themselves from the mud-slinging herd, yes, even renounced thrones for this inexplicable, compelling passion. Nothing mattered but the human heart, and the strange power that pulled it towards another. It was nonsense when people talked of "giving things up" for love. Nothing you could give up could possibly be as cruel as the relinquishing of that other person. It was an act of renunciation which was one of the most deeply painful experiences possible for a human being to undergo, and those who said otherwise had simply never experienced it. It was like drowning in a cold, dark sea.

The beloved eyes and hands, the wilful hair, the boyish mouth... never, never could she forget him. She felt as if she had lived through a lifetime in the space of a few months; what came next she neither knew nor cared. She only knew, despite the anguish of her grief that she would not have changed an hour that she had spent in his arms. Not one hour.

Epilogue

The two women had arranged to meet outside the Pump Room. Barbara knew that she had arrived too early. She sat on a wooden seat within view of their rendezvous, and watched the summer tourists and the buskers. Yet somehow she wasn't really aware of the bustle around her. It all seemed a little unreal, almost dream-like.

Mentally she was back in Yorkshire, re-living that autumn morning so long ago, feeling desperately sick and ill. Her mother's uneasy suspicions were confirmed, and then there was the breaking of the news to her father. She remembered his first outraged disbelief, his anger, his grief, and his frenzied resentment against the man responsible for her condition. Naturally enough he took it for granted that the father lived in Dudley. When he learned the true facts he was so incensed that her mother was afraid.

She had finally given him the address he wanted, and he had gone to Dinningley to confront the man who had not only seduced his young daughter, but who had left upon her the proof of his virility. It was a frantic, fruitless journey.

After that came the great cover-up, masterminded by her mother. The banishment, the isolation, the story that she was having a nervous breakdown. The endless, wretched discomfort of that pregnancy. The hideous reality of that nightmare labour, culminating in the birth of a tiny daughter. Then came the handing over of Louise, and afterwards the long, slow fight back from the shadows, the piecing together of her own shattered young life. Eventually she had pleased her parents. Eventually they had been proud of her again, but not before she had done a long penance...

Suddenly she noticed a younger woman with a little boy, standing right in front of the Pump Room entrance. There was a queue to get in, but they were not part of it. They were both staring around. Barbara stood up and approached them hesitantly. She could not be sure, and yet, somehow she was sure.

The other woman spoke first 'I think we are looking for each other.' For a moment Barbara was unable to reply. Then she answered with a quick, forced little smile. 'You must be Louise. How are you?'

It was not so much the opening of old wounds as the probing of old scar tissue. And the child? The little boy staring around? There had been no mention of him in the letter.

'I'm all right, thank you. Come here, Louis. This is my son.' She took hold of the child's hand, and drew him closer.

Louis... yes, of course. She had named him after herself, nothing unusual about that. Her eyes were on Barbara, curious, searching. She tried hard not to stare back. How frail and vulnerable her daughter seemed. She looked younger than she was; pretty, with large blue English eyes in a slightly foreign face. Her eyes had stayed blue, then, and proved the genes experts wrong. They said that dark genes were always dominant. After a brief hesitation she dropped a swift kiss on her daughter's cheek. Louis seemed apprehensive, so she just gave him a reassuring smile.

'I think we'll sit in Parade Gardens,' she said. 'It will be nice for Louis there.' He was black-haired and pale, and his eyes were not blue. Great sad, dark, long-lashed eyes gazed up at her. They had skipped a generation, that was all...

A few minutes later they were sitting in slightly rickety deck chairs in Parade Gardens, with Louis eating ice cream and watching the Punch and Judy show with the other children gathered there. It crossed Barbara's mind that they must look like any mother and daughter enjoying the warm sunshine, with a young child nearby.

They weren't like any ordinary mother and daughter though. Between them lay a great gulf of years, of separate lives, of unshared memories.

'Louis' a very quiet child,' remarked Barbara.

'He's inclined to be shy, and the past year has been so traumatic that it's had an effect on him as well as on me.'

'Is he your only child?' Barbara felt she should show some interest without seeming to pry.

'Yes, I had to spend weeks in hospital to have him. I had a stillborn baby when I was just a kid. Then I had a lot of miscarriages, but it's all in the past. Louis' father was killed in a road accident in Australia a year ago.'

'I'm sorry to hear that.'

'I'm still in shock, I suppose. We went to Australia when Louis was just a baby. Tony, his father, left his wife and family for me. I didn't know he was so heavily in debt when he died, though.'

'So you're a widow?' Barbara spoke hesitantly.

'Yes. We were living together, and Tony had been divorced for a long time before we got married. We didn't marry until after Louis was born, I don't think we would have bothered otherwise. But I wanted him to be legitimate. It was the second time round for both of us. Things started to go wrong for me after my father died when I was fifteen. It was an awful blow; I was very attached to him. My mother and I were both devastated, and I thought it would just be the two of us, always. Yet before I was seventeen she remarried, and my stepfather had no time for me. My mother tried to make us like each other, but it was no use. I was at a good day school, a fee-paying school, and up to then I had been doing quite well. Then I started running around with a crowd they both hated. I stopped bothering about my schoolwork; I went out every night and came home all hours. There were awful rows, and one day I overheard my stepfather telling my mother that she couldn't expect decent behaviour from a girl with my sort of parentage. That made me worse. I dumped school and got a job as a shop assistant. I already knew Les. My mother hated him. He worked in a garage, and he hung around with a gang who'd been in trouble with the police. We got a bed-sitter and lived together, and when I got pregnant the Council gave us a flat. We got married when I was eighteen, and I had a stillborn girl. The marriage was a disaster, really, but we stuck it out for eight years. I didn't want to admit that I'd made a mess of things, and I kept trying for another baby, only to be disappointed again and again.'

Barbara listened while Louise talked about herself. 'I thought if I could start a family Les would mend his ways. He drank a lot, and he was frequently on the dole. I hated it. I went back to see my mother sometimes when my stepfather wasn't there. I wouldn't admit that I was unhappy, but she knew it, and she had been through the trauma of not being able to have a child.'

That poor woman, thought Barbara. Unable to bear children herself, she had given a loving home to a frail, tiny baby, whose very existence had brought her joy. Louise was well spoken and articulate, and although she was casually dressed in white trousers and a yellow T-shirt, she wore her clothes with style. It was plain that her adoptive parents had done their best for her; she had been brought up in a loving, stable home. Clearly she had been jealous of her stepfather, and too young to understand her mother's point of view. She had rejected her middle class background, and gone off with a teenage yob.

'When we finally split up, it was a relief. I'd had several dead-end sort of jobs, then I applied for and got a job as a hotel receptionist. It was one of a chain of hotels, and I moved around quite a bit over the next few years. I was free, and I had a good time. Of course, there were plenty of boyfriends. I had two quite serious live-in affairs, and then I met Tony. He was a chef at the hotel, and we were attracted right from the start. It didn't come to anything for a long time because he was married. Anyway, after Louis was born we decided to make a new life in Australia. Tony soon got a job, and then we branched out with a restaurant.'

'And were you happy?'

'Yes, we both liked Australia, and we had Louis. Tony hadn't much sense with money, though. He was in partnership with another man, a guy I never trusted, somehow. After Tony was killed he said there would be nothing for me, Tony owed him money. I won't go into all that, it was awful. I'm still on tranquillisers. I worry about Louis, too. He's become withdrawn a lot of the time. His father's death, and leaving Australia, it's a lot for a six year old to cope with. I couldn't stay in that country after what happened.'

'What made you want to get in touch with me?'

'I thought it might help me to sort my life out. My husband's death was such a blow; it has all been so awful. Just now I can't make sense of anything.'

'Well, you went in a roundabout way to find me. If I had been approached by the adoption agency, you wouldn't have been given my address without my consent.'

'I'm sorry about that. I thought if I wrote to you, you would agree to meet me. I would like to know certain things.'

'I can't really see that I can help you, Louise. We did our best for you when you were born.'

'Who did their best?'

'My parents... and I. I was very young.'

'You abandoned me. That's what it amounts to.'

For a moment Parade Gardens and the sunshine and the noise of the Punch and Judy show seemed to fade away. Barbara faced her daughter, the daughter she had not seen since she was a few days old, and saw judgement in her eyes.

'Why did you have me at all, if you didn't intend to keep me?'

'Abortions weren't legal in those days.'

'You should have gone on the Pill, then.'

'It was before the Pill. You don't understand how things were in those days—'

'I thought everything was supposed to be swinging in the Sixties.'

'Not in nineteen sixty-one. Not in Ruddersleigh. We were still living with Fifties standards, yes, people had standards in those days. It was before the Pill, before legal abortions, before the Beatles, before the mini-skirt and tights appeared. It was before everybody did their own thing. Schoolgirl mothers weren't treated like little heroines, far from it.'

'Why didn't you behave yourself, then?'

'Why didn't you? Isn't it a little late to query all these things? You were born, and we had you adopted by a dentist and his wife. They were delighted with you, and happy to keep the name I had chosen for you. I couldn't possibly have kept you, my parents made that plain from the start. Apart from anything else, they wanted me to continue with my education. I had always expected to go to university.'

'And did you?'

'In the event, no. The family moved away from Yorkshire, and eventually I got a place at a teachers' training college. I became a teacher. I'm doing Open University now, as a matter of fact. I'm still catching up with things.'

'I was told right from the start that I was adopted. When I got a bit older I was told that my father was Indian, and that was why I had a foreign look. It made me feel different, an outcast somehow. It's probably part of my problem.'

'I can't see why. You had a very good home background, that's what counts. Plenty of adopted children are mixed race.'

'Yes. Have you ever wondered why? I won't go into that,

though. I would like to know more about my natural father.'

'I'm sorry, but I don't wish to talk about him.'

'I suppose it was some casual affair that you've forgotten all about.'

'Look, I'll get a tray with some tea for us.' Barbara stood up, trying to hide the emotional turmoil she was feeling. How dare her daughter come like a wraith from a shadowy, unforgiven past, and condemn her for events long gone?

It was a relief to stand in the queue at the teashop in Parade Gardens. She bought tea and sticky buns, and crisps and lemonade for Louis. Carrying the tray carefully, she picked her way between the deckchairs back to where Louise was sitting.

One or two people idling away the afternoon watched her progress, moving their feet out of the way as she walked past. They saw a well-groomed, attractive middle-aged woman wearing an expensive looking summer two-piece in a soft shade of green. Coppery tones glinted in her carefully styled hair, and the whole effect was one of chic elegance. She and the younger woman she was sitting with were not alike physically. Louise had black, wavy shoulder length hair, and an olive skin. When she closed her eyes against the brightness of the sunlight, she suddenly had a very Indian appearance. Then Louis came running towards them, and they both smiled, the same smile, showing identical dimples. Louis was smiling, too. The Punch and Judy show was over, and he sat on the grass beside them, eating crisps and drinking lemonade through a straw.

'I like it here,' he announced. 'Are we going to stay here?' Barbara was amused to hear his slight Australian accent.

'No, we're just here for the afternoon,' his mother told him. A sudden breeze lifted up her hair, and she pushed it back from her forehead with a swift, graceful gesture that moved Barbara to the bone.

'We don't live in a very nice place; in fact it's a rented flat in a run-down part of Birmingham. We had a lovely house in Australia, not that we could afford it, but I didn't know that at the time. I left the money side of things to Tony, that was the way he wanted it, and a fine mess he made of it. I've become a statistic now, a single mother living on benefits.' Her voice was bitter.

'You are certainly going through a very bad patch just now,' agreed Barbara, trying to sound more cheerful than she felt after hearing about her daughter's circumstances. 'I'm sure things will improve for you though, they usually do eventually. We all have periods of despair, times when everything seems to be against us.'

Louise appeared to be pondering on this last remark. 'Things seem to have turned out well for you, anyway,' she said finally. 'A woman on the train started talking to me, and I asked her about the part of Bath where you live, and she said it was lovely.'

'Yes, I suppose it is.'

'I expect you have a good life-style and a happy marriage.'

'I have a very nice husband, and yes, I do have a good life-style.'

'You don't teach now, of course?'

'No, I gave it up years ago when the boys were born. I have two grown up sons. I knew their father when I was very young. We met up again years later.'

'So I have two half brothers.' Louise looked thoughtful.

'Yes, but you will never meet them. They know nothing about you.'

'Of course not. I'm the dark secret, and my father is an even darker one, I expect.'

'I agreed to meet you, Louise, but that doesn't mean that I am going to answer questions or talk about a part of my life which is personal and private. I'm very pleased to see you and very pleased to see Louis. He's enjoying himself this afternoon, and I don't suppose life has been much fun for him lately.' There was a slight note of reproof in Barbara's voice, and it was not lost on Louise.

'I don't cry in front of him now,' she said. 'I used to at first, but losing his daddy and seeing me weeping about the place was just too much for him. I know how I felt when my father died, but I was old enough to understand my mother's grief. I never lost touch with her; in fact we never stopped caring about each other. I wrote to her from Australia, and she wrote and told me my stepfather was very ill in hospital. I felt guilty about a lot of things then. I knew that it wasn't all his fault that things had gone so wrong when I was a teenager. I did everything I shouldn't have done, and I know now that he would have liked us to be friends. For a while he was in remission, and I wrote to him and said I was sorry for the worry I had given him in the past. I got a nice letter back, and he said he wished he had been more understanding at the time. He died not long afterwards. That was about two years ago.'

'And have you been to see her at all?'

'Yes. I was going to tell you about that. They went to live in Scarborough when my stepfather retired. I spent a few days there with her, with Louis, of course. I told her I wanted to trace my birth mother, and I asked if she would help me. She wasn't keen at first, but she gave me certain details on condition that I didn't disrupt anyone else's life. She was so thrilled to see me, and to see Louis—' Her eyes filled with tears. 'He loved it there. He cried when we had to leave and go back to Birmingham. In fact we all did.'

'Well, what made you settle in Birmingham when you came back from Australia? Have you connections there?'

'I'm there because of my husband. Tony's people live there. I thought his parents would want to see Louis, I thought we would be accepted into the family. I was wrong.'

It was obviously upsetting Louise to tell her mother this. Barbara listened sympathetically as her daughter explained the situation.

'When Tony's wife divorced him she kept their two boys away from him as much as possible. Before we went to Australia he had lost all contact with them, but he didn't mind so much when Louis was born. Anyway, his wife remarried, but Tony's parents see plenty of their grandchildren. Tony and his first wife produced two blonde boys; Tony was quite fair, but Louis hasn't inherited any fair genes. They just don't want to know about Louis; in fact they seem to think I'm responsible for their son's death. If he'd never met me, sort of thing, and what had he seen in me in the first place, the likes of me were two a penny in all the big cities. Tony's sister is just as bad. We're a couple of outcasts, and I'm not settled in Birmingham, in fact I'm very unsettled.'

She slumped forward in the deckchair, resting her elbows on her knees. There was a long silence, and Barbara was aware of the afternoon slipping away. 'Your adoptive mother,' she said at last. 'She's a lot older than I am. She was about twenty-eight when she adopted you.'

'Yes. She's getting on. I couldn't have had a kinder mother really. I must have disappointed her and worried her out of her mind with one thing and another. She knows how I am living now, and she wants me to go back and make my home with her. I'm not sure what to do for the best. I thought if I went to Birmingham Louis would have a family background, but things didn't work out like that. I was so keen to show my independence when I was a teenager, it would be like going back to where I started if I went to my mother now.'

'Not quite. It's pride, isn't it, Louise?'

'I suppose so.' She leaned out of the deckchair, and picked a daisy.

'Look at it this way. You have a child to bring up, and you are wanted and needed by her. Your in-laws don't want you or Louis. You would be giving as much as you would be taking if you went to live in Scarborough. You could get a job, and Louis would have a proper family life, and be in a nice environment.'

He suddenly came running back to them, and stood beside Barbara.

'Do you know the name of this flower?' he asked, handing her a tiny blue one.

'Yes. It's called a speedwell. I'll keep it,' said Barbara, putting it into her handbag.

Unable to resist touching him, she slipped her arm round him, and felt the tearing pain of holding him close. She showered him with desperate kisses, while he looked at her with dark, wondering eyes. She longed to love him and spoil him, and protect him from all the evils that lay ahead, yet she knew that he must take his chance in life, the same as everyone else. She was about to release him when he put his thin, little boy's arms round her neck and unexpectedly returned her kisses.

'You smell nice,' he said.

'We'll have to go to the station soon,' said his mother, glancing at her watch.

'I'll see you on the train, and then I can go and pick up the car. There's no point in walking to where I've got it parked and driving you to the station. It would take ages. It's so busy in Bath.'

It was the height of the season. The tourists were clicking their cameras everywhere; the Americans were taking photographs of the buskers as well as the Abbey.

'No, please don't see me on the train. I'd rather say goodbye here.'

'Very well, if you prefer it. Let me pay your travelling expenses, Louise.'

'No, it's all right, thank you. I don't want money. You didn't ask me to come looking for you. I didn't come for money, I just wanted to know certain things.'

'Will you take something for Louis, then? Please do.'

'Oh... all right.' There was a discreet rustle of notes changing hands.

'And I must ask you not to get in contact again. I know it's trendy for adopted children to trace their natural parents, but it's not always a good idea.'

'I won't try to see you again, don't worry. I'm glad we've met, though. And I'm glad you've seen Louis.'

'Yes. He's a dear little boy.'

They both stood up, and Louis looked from one to the other.

'Don't walk up the steps with me. Stay here and wave,' said Louise. 'I think I know the way to the station. If I keep left and walk straight on, I'll come to it.'

'Yes. Mind the traffic.' For a moment Barbara hesitated, then she took a bangle off her arm.

'I would like you to have this. It's very old. It was a gift from your father to me, a keepsake. Please keep it always, and by the way, there was nothing casual about our affair. We were very much in love.'

Strange to talk of love these days. People didn't seem to. They talked about sex a great deal, and of "relationships".

Louise took the bangle with a little cry of pleasure, and slipped it on her arm. The giving and accepting of that modest piece of jewellery devastated Barbara. The old scar tissue burst open and revealed the gaping wounds beneath. Uncaring that they were in a public place, she clasped her daughter in her arms, frightening her with her terrible tearless grief, with the hoarse, rasping sobs which shook her whole body. Without any words being spoken, Louise knew then that she had been conceived in great love and passion, and had been born in unspeakable sorrow and agony. Afterwards she had been given into another woman's keeping with a degree of emotional anguish and sacrifice that she could only dimly imagine.

Her mother had been nailed to the cross, and she had sought

her out after all these years, and made her re-live that crucifixion. She was abashed, awed, in the face of such suffering.

'Don't cry—please don't cry,' she begged, through her own tears. 'I'll treasure the bangle always.' Unknowingly she used the same words that had once been used by Barbara. 'I've been a rotten, ungrateful daughter to my adoptive mother, and now I've come upsetting you. I will get my life sorted out, though, I promise. I'll leave Birmingham and make a fresh start in Scarborough. It's time I made an effort, for Louis' sake.'

'Yes,' said Barbara, struggling to control her emotions. 'For Louis' sake.' She stooped and kissed him on the forehead, but it was not of the child that she was thinking. She watched them ascend the wide stone steps that led out of Parade Gardens. They waved from the balustrade as she stood on the grass below, and she waved back, smiling bravely. Then they were lost in the anonymity of the crowd, mingling with the shoppers and tourists of Bath.

Printed in the United Kingdom
by Lightning Source UK Ltd.
101345UKS00001B/7-30